"The best Peter Decker/Rina Lazarus mystery
yet . . . Faye Kellerman masterfully weaves family
and religion into a truly moving novel that is
as suspenseful as it is substantial."
Atlanta Journal-Constitution

"Compelling . . . a thriller with a heart . . .
Warning: Don't try to finish this book just before
going to bed at night. . . . [It] builds to a climax
that will leave your heart pounding,
and you wide awake."
Orlando Sentinel

"Gripping . . . This graphic, pungent novel shows
Kellerman at the gritty peak of her form."
Booklist

"She does for the American cop story what
P.D. James has done for the British mystery,
lifting it beyond genre."
Richmond Times-Dispatch

"Takes your breath away . . . An unusual kind
of thriller, one with a soul."
Bergen Record

"Shocking and fascinating . . . Kellerman blends
family and murder beautifully."
Ocala Star-Banner

"No one working in the crime genre is better."
Baltimore Sun

FAYE KELLERMAN

day of atonement

A DECKER/LAZARUS NOVEL

HARPER

An Imprint of HarperCollinsPublishers

HARPER

An Imprint of HarperCollins*Publishers*
195 Broadway
New York, NY 10007

First Harper premium printing: February 2011
First Harper mass market printing: January 2004

HarperCollins ® and Harper ® are registered trademarks of Harper-Collins Publishers.

Printed in the United States of America

Visit Harper paperbacks on the World Wide Web at
www.harpercollins.com

10   9

To my brothers—
Allan Marder and Stan Marder—
who teased me, but taught me

✨ Prologue

He wrote down the name Hank Stewart. Stared at it for a while and decided it was a good start.

A start.

But not there yet.

He wrote Dr. Hank Stewart. Then: Hank Stewart, M.D.

But hell, doctors were nothing *special*. Matter of fact, they were assholes, all puffed up and full of themselves.

So he wrote Hank Stewart, ESQ.

Crossed that off the list. Lawyers were bigger assholes than doctors.

How about Hank Stewart, Nuclear Physicist.

Or Hank Stewart, Nobel Prize Winner.

Give 'em a smile as they took his picture.

Hell with that. That kinda fame was too short-lived. A picture in a newspaper for about a day. Big effing deal.

Hank Stewart, CIA.

Stewart—Superspy.

Good ring to it.

Ah, that was stupid. Kid stuff.

1

Still, kid stuff was better than peddling fish.

I'll take one pound of snapper, please.

Yeah, lady. Right up your ass.

The old people always buying fish 'cause they didn't got no teeth to chew meat. They came up to the counter, moving their mouths over their dentures, whistling the word "snapper," their hands and head shakin', looking like they wasn't glued together very tight.

That was the worst part. Working behind the counter.

Now the gutting part was okay. Especially once you got the feel for it, didn't let the suckers slip out of your hands.

Fish were slimy little bastards, all the gook would get over your clothes and you never could get the smell out. Thing to do was just work in smelly clothes for a while, then chuck 'em in the garbage.

Or stuff 'em in the mailbox of that jerk who was giving you a real hard time.

Now if he was a real asshole, you'd stuff some fishheads in with the smelly clothes.

Good old fish. Flopping in the pail, looking up at you with glazed-over eyes sayin' "Put me out of my misery, man."

At first he used to do it just like the old man did. Cut the gills. But then he found a better way. He'd step on their heads.

Stomp!

All the brain squishing out.

That part was okay, too. But the best part was the

swim bladder. Bounce it with the tip of the knife. Careful, careful. It was delicate.

Bouncy, bouncy, bouncy.

Then if you were quick enough, you'd jam the tip all of a sudden and it'd pop.

But that was kid stuff, too. Old stuff. He'd moved on to better stuff than popping swim bladders. And things were going real good until he got caught.

Hell with that shit. No sense moaning about the past. Better to make something of the future.

After all, he was young.

He wrote Hank Stewart, Real Estate Developer.

Like that guy who owned all those casinos in Atlantic City. Man, he could have his pick of chicks 'cause he had *bread*.

Hank Stewart, millionaire.

Hank Stewart, billionaire.

Hank Stewart, trillionaire.

Ah, that was stupid, too. Money wasn't everything. It didn't show what you got in your pants.

Hank Stewart, *stud*.

Ah-hah!

Hank Stewart, rock star. Hair down to his ass, wearing nothing but a pair of tight jeans, sweat streaming down his hard, lean body. Girls coming after him, screaming their little heads off, waiting for him to *give* it to them.

Hank Stewart, King of Rock and Roll.

He paused a moment, then wrote: Hank Stewart, King.

King Stewart.

Emperor Stewart.

Lord Stewart.

God Stewart.

Or just plain God would do.

PART ONE

Tephila—Prayer

1

Brooklyn.

Not the honeymoon Decker had imagined.

Twelve grueling months before he'd rack up another two weeks' vacation time and here he was, alone in a tiny guest bedroom, his long legs cramped from having slept on too small a bed, his back sore from lying on a wafer-thin thing that somebody had mislabeled as a mattress. He'd bunked up in foxholes that had been bigger than this place. Most of the floor space was taken up by the pullout sofa bed. The rest of the furnishings were worn pieces old enough to be antiques, but not good enough to qualify. A scarred wooden nightstand was at his right, the digital clock upon it reading out ten-forty-two. The suitcases had been piled atop an old yellowed pine bureau adorned with teddy-bear appliqués. The sofa pillows had been stuffed into the room's only free corner. On the east wall, two wee windows framed a gray sky.

The honeymoon suite.

Très charmant.

Two days ago, he'd danced blisters on his feet,

whooping his voice raw, carrying his stepsons around on his shoulders. It had been a wild affair—the drinking and dancing lasting until midnight. Now his body was paying overtime for his exuberance.

Of course, the undersized sofa didn't help.

He chewed on the ends of his mustache, then pulled the sheet over his head.

They say Jews don't drink much, but they've never seen ultra-Orthodox rabbis at a wedding. The men downed schnapps like water. Decker had thought his father had a large capacity for booze, but Dad was a piker compared to Rav Schulman.

Dad and Mom. Sitting in the corner, wondering what the hell was flying. Cindy trying to coax Grandma to dance. Rina did get Mom to dance once. Even Mom couldn't turn down the bride. But that one time had been the only time.

Well, at least they came. A big surprise and a step in the right direction. They liked Rina, he sensed that immediately. Rina could charm anyone and she was truly a nice person. But his parents couldn't come out and *tell* him they liked her. Mom did admit that if he had to marry another *Jew*, Rina seemed like a decent woman. Very high praise. Then she added that Rina seemed sincere in her beliefs even though they were dead wrong.

Randy had liked Rina, too. Baby Bro liked all beautiful women, but he wasn't what you'd call a picky sort. Decker wished he could have spent some more time with Randy—shoot the bull about the job—but he and Rina just *had* to rush off. Had to make it to Brooklyn before the holiday of Rosh Ha-shanah started.

What was he doing, honeymooning in Boro Park of all places? He and Rina should have been in Hawaii, making love in the moonlight on the beach. Hell, he would have settled for staying back home on the ranch—just him and her. Send Sam and Jake off to visit Grandma and Grandpa in Brooklyn for the holidays.

But no, no, no. Rina had to visit her late husband's parents. His luck: to inherit not one but two sets of in-laws.

Decker stretched, his feet falling over the edge of the mattress.

At least her ex-in-laws were nice people.

So happy you joined us for the holidays, they had said. *Rosh Hashanah will be a wonderful New Year's with Rina and the boys and you as guests in our home. Thank you so much for allowing us the pleasure of being with you.*

But Decker hated looking into their eyes. He could tell what they were thinking.

Why couldn't you be our son, Yitzchak?

He ran his hands through damp ginger hair.

It had to be tough on them. Their only son gone, he the stepfather of their boy's children.

He wished he was back home. Too many ghosts here.

The clock glowed ten-forty-five. He hadn't heard Rina wake up, but he knew she wouldn't dare aban-don him. She was probably in the kitchen helping her ex-mother-in-law prepare for the big holiday meal.

His clothes weren't visible. They'd been thrown off in the heat of passion last night, both of them stifling laughter, hoping the flimsy bed could take all the weight.

Afterward, Decker wondered if Rina had made love with her late husband in this very bed. But he had kept his thoughts to himself.

Finding the energy to rise, he immediately tripped on his shoes, stubbed his toe, and cursed silently. He stripped off his pajamas, went over to the bureau and found that Rina had unpacked, his clothes neatly stowed in the first and second drawers. She'd put his Beretta under a pile of undershirts, the clips all the way in the back under his pants. God bless an efficient woman.

He attempted to open a door on the west wall. It came out about halfway before it hit the bed frame. He squeezed himself inside the cell and found a munchkin-size bathroom—sink, shower, and toilet. The water closet was done in old white tile and reeked of disinfectant, but someone had laid out clean towels. He took a quick lukewarm shower (others had gotten to the hot-water tank before him), his elbows hitting the walls as he soaped up. He had to duck a good foot to get his head under the shower tap.

He dried himself off and dressed, his skin prickly with goosebumps. There was no room to stand and dress with the bed unfolded. He straightened the sheets and pushed the mattress inward until it slid down into the sofa frame, then put the pillows on the couch.

A little more space, but he'd have to do his waltzing elsewhere.

He put on gray gabardine trousers, a white dress shirt, and a pair of black oxfords. People around here just didn't wear sweats. Strapping his belt around his waist, he felt lighter of weight without his shoulder harness and gun. And a little more vulnerable, too. He found a black yarmulke, bobby-pinned it onto his hair and quickly said *Shaachrit*—the morning prayers. Then he went downstairs to face what was in store for him.

He swore he'd be in a good mood. He swore he'd be friendly. But he felt grumpy, his leg muscles still bunched. His throat was tight, a sour taste had coated his mouth.

Relax.

No one was in the living room. It, too, was small, walls and moldings painted ivory and hung with dime-store landscape prints. The carpet was green shag, worn nearly flat. The couches were off-white velvet, the arms covered in plastic as were the lampshades. The room might have been described as old and musty had it not sparkled with crystal. On the coffee table, on the end tables, in a breakfront, in the connecting dining room. Decanters, vases, bowls, and goblets. Some of the glasswork had been intricately cut, catching the overcast light from outside and breaking it into thousands of colors. Other pieces were clear or etched—tinted deep iridescent shades.

All the crystal was smudge-and-dust-free. With the kids out of the house, this had to be mama lion's pride.

The dining-room table had been extended until the top practically abutted the living-room couch. Enough seating for forty people. The entire downstairs was filled with cooking smells—the aroma of roasted meats, spicy puddings, and fresh-baked bread and pastries. Decker realized his mouth was watering.

High-pitched magpie sounds emanated from the kitchen. With all their chatter, the women hadn't heard him come down. He stood at the kitchen doorframe waiting for someone to notice him. Rina's ex-mother-in-law, Sora Lazarus, saw him first. She was a small, compact woman with large brown eyes and thick lips. Her hair was pinned under a big kerchief and she had spots of flour on her face. She wore a white chef's apron and smiled at him, bursting into ooing sounds he interpreted as a welcome.

"Did you sleep well?" Sora Lazarus asked.

"Yes, thank you."

Rina emerged from the back, wiping her hands with her apron. She smiled at him and he immediately melted. She was exquisite even in a loose housedress. Sapphire eyes, inky-black hair, creamy complexion, full, red lips. Not to mention those curves. And now, she was officially Mrs. Decker. Two long, long years. But she was worth the wait.

She led him into the belly of the kitchen. The place was hot and misty. Most of Rina's hair was covered by a kerchief, but a few steam-limp strands had escaped and framed her lovely face. She slipped her arm into his and hugged his biceps.

"Akiva, I'd like you to meet my sisters-in-law, Esther and Shaynie."

Decker found it amusing that she had called him by his Hebrew name. Only in Boro Park. Back home, he was plain old Peter. He nodded hello to the women, but knew better than to try to shake their hands. Men and women in this culture didn't touch unless married, and even then public displays of affection were frowned upon. But Rina seemed to disregard this little bit of tradition and Decker was glad she did. He smiled at the sisters—women he'd spoken to many times on the phone. He said, "Nice to finally see the faces that go with the voices."

They both smiled back and immediately averted their gazes.

He put Shaynie at about his age—forty-one or -two. She was petite, with a long face, amber eyes, and warm smile. She wore no makeup, but her cheeks were rosy from the heat. She was married to Mendel, an accountant.

Esther was also small, but heavier than her sister. Her face was fuller, her arms thicker. She had the same amber eyes as her sister and also wore no makeup. But her face wasn't rosy, it was blood red. Her eyes rested on her feet.

And Decker knew why. Three months ago, her husband, Pessy, had been arrested in a massage-parlor raid in Manhattan. Through the police grapevine, Decker had found the proper connections and managed to spring the guy, expunging all the charges from the computer. He had mixed feelings about it. The guy was a first-class scumbag—had come on to Rina while she lived in New York. Clearing this little mishap meant he owed favors to some brothers in the NYPD. And he didn't like being in the red.

But the Lazarus family had been grateful, though no one had ever explicitly told him so. It was just *implied* that they were grateful because everyone was suddenly more respectful to him whenever he called Rina.

Another little piece of dirt neatly swept under the carpet.

Sora Lazarus said, "The men already went to the *mikvah*. You want me to take you there?"

"Let's let it go this time, Eema," Rina said.

It was customary for men to go to the ritual bathhouse before the high holidays. But the idea of bathing in communal water made Decker squeamish. He gave her an appreciative smile.

Sora Lazarus said, "Then maybe you'd like some breakfast? A cup of coffee?"

"A cup of coffee sounds great," Decker said.

"Then you sit at the table," the little woman said. "I'll get you some coffee and a little pastry—"

"Just coffee, please," Decker said. "Black."

"Black?" Sora Lazarus said. "No milk? No sugar?"

"Just black," Decker said. "Please."

"Rina," Sora Lazarus said, "sit with your husband. I'll bring you some coffee, too."

"I'll get it," Rina said.

"Don't be silly," chided Sora Lazarus. "Sit."

A moment later they were alone in the dining room, sipping coffee at a table fit for a mess hall.

"The Lazaruses are having a bit of company?" Decker asked.

"Thirty-six people. Not including the kids' table."

"A small intimate meal."

"It's tradition," Rina said. "My mother-in-law always has the Levine family over on the first night of Rosh Hashanah; we go over to the Levine house for lunch the next day."

"How many Levines are we talking about?"

"Rabbi and Mrs. Levine, their five children and who knows how many grandchildren. And Mrs. Levine's parents. They must be in their eighties by now."

"Is everyone going to talk in Yiddish?"

"The grandparents do, but the five kids are our age. The oldest must be a few years younger than you. Shimmy—nice guy, good-looking, too."

"You notice these things."

"I'm religious but not blind."

"Well, you'd have to be nearsighted to marry me."

"You're fishing for compliments, I'll give you one," Rina said. "I think you're gorgeous. Or as they say in Brooklyn, *gohjus.*"

Decker said, "Am I as gohjus as Shimmy?"

"*Better*," Rina said. "Shimmy—like you—has a good sense of humor. I think you'll like him."

"I can feel a friendship brewing."

"Oh, cut it out." She punched him in the shoulder. "Mrs. Levine's youngest son, Jonathan, is—believe it or not—a *Conservative* rabbi."

"A rebel in the midst."

"You make light, but his father's heartbroken."

Decker shook his head. "That kind of reactionary thinking is incredible to me."

"That's because you don't understand what it represents to Jonathan's father. Conservative Jews don't believe that oral law is as important as written law. So oral law—which is holy to us—can be changed by man. That's a major break, Peter. Even though Jonathan is pretty traditional in his own practices, his father feels that Jonathan has rejected him and everything he believes in."

"Is that what you think?"

"I don't agree with Jonathan, but I know he's sincere. And although I understand Rav Levine's feelings, I feel bad for Jonathan. His father makes this big show of not speaking to him—unless they're arguing Jewish law. Mrs. Levine ignores his hostility and invites Jonathan to every holiday meal. It's uncomfortable at first, the father addressing Jonathan in the third person. 'Can someone ask *Mister* Levine to pass the flanken?' Mr. Levine, mind you, never Rabbi Levine. It's become sort of a joke by now, but I know it makes Jonathan feel lousy."

"And here I thought this was going to be boring."

Rina smiled. "Jonathan's mother is more tolerant. You'll like her, Peter. She and Mama Lazarus are best friends. She's as feisty as they come. She was a legal secretary for the criminal court system in Queens for years, always worked, which was very unusual for Orthodox women her age. Being a cop, you two will probably have lots to talk about."

"Yes, we can talk about assholes"—Decker smiled—"excuse me—miscreants."

"You're going to have to watch that."

"No problem, honey," Decker said. "I don't intend to talk much."

"I know this is very hard for you," Rina said. "A lot of change in the last couple of years."

"True 'nough, woman, true 'nough."

Rina hesitated, then whispered, "Are you happy?"

"Ecstatic."

Rina looked at his deadpan expression. "I'm serious."

"So am I." Decker took her hand. "From the bottom of my heart, I couldn't be happier. I love being married to you."

"Good," Rina answered. But her expression was troubled. "Do you like being an observant Jew?"

Decker said, "I wouldn't have converted if I didn't like it."

"You didn't convert."

"You're talking semantics," Decker said.

"You're right," Rina said.

Technically, he hadn't converted. His biological mother had been Jewish, which made him Jewish according to Hebraic law. But having been adopted in infancy, he considered himself a product of his *real* parents—the ones who had raised him. And they had brought him up Baptist.

"You're a doll, Peter," Rina said. "A wonderful sport. I'll make it up to you."

Decker felt a tightening below his belt. "I'll keep you to your word."

She kissed the tip of his nose. "Want more coffee?"

"No, thanks," Decker said. "Maybe I'll take a walk. Want to join me?"

"Wish I could," Rina said. "But there's still a slew of work to do in the kitchen."

"Have fun."

"You, too. Bundle up. We're having a weird cold spell. *Enjoy*, Peter."

Yeah, Decker thought. He'd just have himself a ball.

2

He always hated this time of year.

The holidays.

It reminded him of fish.

Fish was real big this time of year, especially fish *heads*. Yum-yum, fish heads. And then there was ground-up fish—everyone wanting to make gefilte fish.

No carp, just white and pikefish.

Just whitefish.

Just carp.

Just carp and pikefish.

Can you put in some bread crumbs?

Can you put in an onion?

More onion.

Less onion.

No onion.

Fuuuuuuuccccckkkk you.

Carp were disgusting fish, smelling like garbage. They were bottom feeders so they ate a lot of shit. You are what you eat.

Open up carp and hold your nose. Finding all sorts of gunk inside them. Grit and sand and dirt and lots and lots of worms, especially if they'd been fished out of polluted waters. Sometimes he'd find pop tabs or bottle caps. Sometimes green bottleglass.

If he really hated the old lady, he'd grind the glass up with the fish.

A crunch delight.

Fuuuuuuccccck you.

Piss on the holidays.

They also reminded him of the family.

Piss on the family.

The *holidays*. They were supposed to inspire fear, but for him, all the prayers and shit were just simply . . . shit.

Last year on Yom Kippur, he woke up and ate a cheese sandwich.

Old God didn't strike him dead like they said He would.

Then he jacked off.

God didn't strike him dead.

Then he went out and drank a few beers, cussed with the guys, whistled at the chicks. Just hung out.

God didn't strike him dead.

Then he had a pepperoni pizza for lunch.

God didn't strike him dead.

Then he rented a porno video and whacked off again. Two times. Man, he was a *stud*.

God didn't strike him dead.

Why should God strike him dead?

He *was* God.

Or something close.

❧ 3

The streets of Boro Park vibrated with an air of urgency even though most of the local businesses were closed for the day. Black-clothed men marched along the avenues, middle-aged ladies toted sacks of groceries, picking up last-minute forgotten items. Young married women wrapped in winter coats were swept along with harried grace. Some wore woolen caps, but most wore wigs—the common look being locks of straight hair that fell to their shoulders, the ends curving inward, a modified pageboy. The pink-nosed women pushed loaded-down strollers along the walkways, their progeny bundled in layers of blankets to the point of near-invisibility. Decker didn't know if it was the unseasonable cold or what, but everyone was hauling down the streets as if fighting to make a curfew.

He stuck his hands in his overcoat pockets and told himself to slow down. *He* had nowhere to go, nothing to do. He tightened a tan cashmere scarf around his neck. It had been a gift from Rina—a waste of money since L.A. weather rarely necessitated scarves. But he knew she'd spent a lot of time picking it out so he wore it whenever he could. On his head was a skullcap instead of a hat. In most circles, the yarmulke would mark him as Jew. Here a *mere* yarmulke marked him as a "goy."

So be it. There was only so much changing he could do and he'd be damned if he became one of *them*.

He thought about Rina, about how much she had eased up. She'd become calmer when they were around other Orthodox people, had stopped making excuses for his mistakes of ritual ignorance. Instead, she'd shrug them off as if they were no big deal. Infinitely better than that nervous little laugh she used to let out every time he made a faux pas.

Lord, they were different. A year ago, they were having problems and Rina had to get away from him, had to *escape*. Out of all the places she could have run to, she chose Boro Park.

It amazed him.

It was a small community, easy to get a feel for. The numbered streets were residential—rows of small brick houses, each one with a modicum of individual trim, but collectively they were hard to tell apart. Landscaping was kept to a minimum—small patches of brown lawn, denuded trees, not one hint of color from flowers or shrubbery. Maybe that wasn't a fair assessment. Eastern foliage was deciduous, stripped by cold weather. He'd been judging it by L.A. standards, where the grass was green all year long. Rina had told him these homes could go for a million or more. Even with an Angeleno's jaundiced eye, he was astounded.

He took a deep breath, his nostrils tingling from cold and the smells leaking from steamy kitchen windows. Every now and then, shouts could be heard—a mother scolding her children, a spat between husband and wife, a slamming door. The town didn't seem to place a premium on privacy. Couldn't possibly survive if it did, the houses built on top of one another.

New York—crowded and crowding. Everyone hemmed in. Decker longed to elbow the city in the ribs.

Give me some room, Mama.

The avenues seemed to be the business districts, store-fronts gazing down narrow strips of bitten asphalt. The shops sold products that served the special needs of the community.

IZZY'S HATS; HOLIDAY SPECIAL FOR REBLOCKING. The place was nothing more than an aisle with racks of black hats.

ROCHEL'S SHAYTELS—this time the racks were full of wigs, as if some scalper had hit the mother lode.

CANNERY ROW—a store devoted to kosher dry and canned goods—all of the products certified by the Union of Orthodox Rabbis. This building was two-storied, the second floor occupied by Mendel the Scribe.

That's what the upstairs window sign said—
MENDEL THE SCRIBE: KETUBAHS AND GETS.

Wedding certificates, divorce certificates. Mendel was a man for all seasons.

Next to CANNERY ROW was GAN EDEN—the Garden of Eden. This outlet sold only fruits and vegetables.

Inside was one long gondola covered with a thick plastic tarp. A handmade sign stood atop the tarp like a flag on a ship, announcing a sale on fresh horseradish root.

Little storefronts, locked tight with metal accordion grating, the display windows frosted with age. No community standards when it came to the outdoor signs—some were neon, some were lit with old-fashioned blinking bulbs, some were hand-lettered jobs. Placards were hanging on the doors of the Jewish establishments; on them were written the Hebrew words: SHANA TOVA TIKATEVU.

Happy New Year. May you be written in the book of life.

Between the shops were *shtiebels*—tiny, no-frills synagogues, many without pulpit rabbis. All had signs wishing people a Happy New Year.

His mind flashed to the holiday caveat: *Only three things can avert the evil decree.* Ten days between the New Year and the Day of Atonement—the holiest day in the Jewish calendar. Ten days to right the spiritual and physical wrongs. Sins were expunged by immersing the soul in prayer, doing proper penitence, and giving charity. He thought: Ten days allowed for a lot of breathing space.

Down the road was GLUCK'S SEPHARIM: RELIGIOUS BOOKS AND ARTICLES. Decker peered through the steel gate, inside the window. The place looked dusty. Or maybe it just appeared dusty because it was chock-full of books; the shelves seemed to be double and triple stacked, piles of tomes that reached the ceiling. Did the proprietor even know what he had in stock?

Yeah, he probably did. If he was anything like Decker's father, he knew the store inside out. Ask Lyle Decker where *anything* in his hardware store was, he'd tell you.

Two-prong plug converter? Third aisle, left side . . . 'bout two thirds of the way down, third shelf, right next to the threeway light switches.

Randy telling him, *One of these days we should take inventory, Dad. Really organize the place.*

You do that and I won't be able to find a dern thing.

The air had turned biting, a bank of gunmetal clouds trying to block out the heat and light of the sun. But the mighty orb was fighting back, a burning white disk simmering in a sea of gray. The temperature was hovering in the low thirties. Decker blew hot breath onto his ungloved hands, turned up the collar on his overcoat, and moved on.

GITTEL'S BAKERY—HALAV YISROEL.

JERUSALEM GLATT KOSHER MEAT MARKET—CHICKENS FOR KAPPAROS.

The ritual of *Kapparos*—symbolically transferring sins to a chicken. A cock was used for a man, a hen for a woman. The chicken was swung in the air three times, special words were recited, then the bird was slaughtered and given to the poor as an act of charity. Some used money in lieu of chickens. The ritual was just custom, not law. In Decker's mind, it seemed like a very *primitive* custom. Yet these old rituals had become part and parcel of the religion.

Just a hundred years ago, thousands of Jews had poured into America, working ninety hours a week for a better life, for a chance to get *out* of the ghetto. But for some, so much freedom had seemed too frightening.

Solution: Why not bring the ghetto into America?

And Rina chose this voluntarily.

In all fairness, Decker knew that American affluence had brought on a host of trouble. Teenage children with adult problems—alcoholism, drug addiction, abortions, divorce. Confused adults running for cover.

Some of the assimilated Jews dealt with the pressure by going inward, seeking a God higher than a BMW. They joined the cults, est, environmental groups, or the society of animal activists and spray-painted fur coats in the name of Good. A handful went back to their roots and became traditional. The "Orthodox from birth" Jews seemed to go it one step farther, deliberately shutting out the modern world altogether.

Almost none of the ultra-Orthodox families owned TVs, few read *Time* or *Newsweek* because some of the pictures featured women in "prurient" attire. *U.S. News and World Report* was the big periodical around these parts. Movies were out, as was popular fiction. Too explicit, though Decker was sure there was a housewife or two with a Danielle Steel novel squirreled away.

He thought: It was good that he'd met Rina. His secular ways kept her from going over the edge. He'd also make damn sure that her boys could support themselves. Many of these children didn't bother with college—although their parents had. Instead, they opted to learn at a yeshiva, their parents or wives or in-laws supporting them.

No way he'd let the boys live on the dole.

He paused, then thought: Kids had a way of doing whatever they wanted. Just mind your own business, Deck, and let Rina worry about the boys. Besides, it was a ways off.

Decker had walked ten blocks before he realized that the neighborhood had started to change, the Jewish stalls replaced by video rental and liquor stores. He wondered whether any of the religious kids ever forayed into this neck of the woods. Did an invisible wall keep these Jews as insulated from the goyim as the Roman walls had three hundred years ago?

The Levine family flashed through his mind— the youngest son a Conservative rabbi.

And now Decker was Orthodox.

Win a few, lose a few.

He turned around and headed back to the Lazarus house, choosing to take another route, passing a kosher deli, then a little café. The café sign was written in both Hebrew and English and read: TEL AVIV—A DAIRY RESTAURANT—WE SERVE ESPRESSO AND CAPPUCCINO.

A modern reference in an ocean of Old World. He was heartened by the sight.

Decker entered the house through the front door, heard more female voices buzz-buzzing in the kitchen. The men had yet to return from the *mikvah* and he wondered where the boys were, wished they were around so he'd have someone to talk to.

For a moment he debated sneaking upstairs, locking the door, and reading until it was time for synagogue. But he knew that would set Rina off. Not that she minded his being by himself; she just wanted to *know* where he was and what he was doing.

After years of being single, he found this the hardest adjustment—having to explain your whereabouts to another person, scheduling your day with someone else in mind. Of course, *he* wanted to know where *she* was, but that was more for safety reasons.

Or so he told himself.

He slipped off his overcoat, draped it over his arm, and stood a few feet from the kitchen doorframe.

More women had showed up, the place as crowded as an ant farm. Through the bodies, he spied Rina's back. She was engrossed in conversation with an older woman. The lady looked around fifty-five, maybe sixty, with a long face with deep-set eyes and a wide mouth. Her skin was shiny and moist from the steam, and she kept brushing locks of brunette wig off her forehead. She was a tall woman, not slender, not fat, perfectly proportioned and dressed in business clothing as if she were attending a board meeting instead of a kaffeeklatsch.

There was something familiar about her, something very eerie. He fought down a weird sensation of having seen her before.

But that was ridiculous. He'd never met her before in his life.

Someone called out the name Frieda and the woman turned around.

And then it became painfully clear to him.

The stifling heat, the walls of the house, everything suddenly closed in upon him. Two invisible malevolent hands had reached out to strangle him.

Mrs. Lazarus noticing him. Her lips forming the word—Akiva.

Had to get out.

Out of the house.

Out of New York.

Decker bolted before she could get his name out, was halfway down the block before he heard someone racing behind him. He didn't turn around, couldn't. Something intangible kept his head from pivoting. With great effort, he managed to stop running, but his legs kept pumping him forward. Finally, someone caught up with him.

"Peter, stop!"

Rina's voice. She was out of breath.

Decker kept walking.

"Stop, for God's sake!" Rina said. "I . . . I have a cramp in my side."

But he kept going.

Gasping, Rina said, "What on earth has *happened* to you? You're white."

"I'm fine," Decker mumbled out. He sounded winded himself. Rina noticed his choppy breathing.

"You're not fine! Are you sick? Do you need a doctor?"

"It was hot in there," Decker said. "That's all." He willed his legs to stop but they wouldn't.

"Stop, will you!" Rina cried out.

Her voice—so desperate. He slowed his pace and said, "I just wanted to take a walk."

"You just came back from a walk."

"I wanted to take another one," Decker said. "What the hell is wrong with that!"

His voice sounded foreign—full of rage. Full of *fear*.

"I need to be alone."

"Peter, please . . ." She grabbed his arm. "I love you. Tell me what's wrong!"

Decker stopped abruptly, picked her hand off his arm, and kissed her fingers. "I've got to be by myself now. I'm sorry, Rina, but please leave me alone." He dropped her hand and ran off.

Six hours to kill with fifteen dollars and twenty-two cents spending cash. Decker had left the credit cards in the bedroom, so checking into a motel for the night was out of the question. Not that he'd do it, but he wished he had the option. He found a cab at Fourteenth and Fifty-eighth, slid onto the black bench seat and ran his hands over his face.

The cabbie was Indian or Pakistani—chocolate-brown skin with straight black hair and a name with a lot of double *o*'s and *ini*'s in it. After a minute of waiting, the driver said, "What can I do for you, sir?"

The "sir" came out like *serrrrr*. A rolling tongue gathers no moss. Decker felt mean and punch-drunk, realized he was probably scaring the poor guy.

"What's there to see around here?" he growled.

"See?"

"Yeah, see," Decker said. "Any interesting sights around here?"

"Around here?" the cabbie said. "Here is very, very Jewish area."

Very, very came out *veddy, veddy*.

The cabbie went on, "Not much to see except Jews, but you can see a lot of them."

Decker said, "There a public library around here?"

He needed someplace to think, someplace to figure out how to disappear for two days.

"There is Brooklyn Central Library," the driver said. "It is located in a very pretty park. Shall I take you there, sir?"

Decker told him to take him there. The cabbie was bent on giving a guided tour.

"I go by Flatbush Avenue. A very, very long time ago, I thought it was the longest street in Brooklyn but it is not. Bedford is."

The avenue at best was unremarkable, at worst it exemplified everything wrong with inner cities—old crumbling buildings, trash-strewn vacant lots, and gang-graffitied tenement housing. But the cabbie seemed oblivious to this, kept on talking about how Manhattan was for the rich, but Brooklyn was where the *real* people lived. Decker wasn't sure whether he was jacking up the fare by taking a longer route or was just one of those rare, friendly guys.

"Brooklyn Museum is in Prospect Park, sir. The same architect that designed Central Park in Manhattan designed Prospect Park. A very, very pretty park. You can go boating, but not now. It is tooooo cold."

Whatever the driver's reasons were for the tour, Decker wished he would shut up. He had to calm down and the sucker was making him veddy, veddy antsy.

He had to calm down.

Of all the people to meet.

Maybe it wasn't her. Just maybe it wasn't. There could be dozens of Frieda Levines. (Levine? He'd remembered it as Levy or Levin.)

Frieda Levine—a common Jewish name, it could be equivalent to Mary Smith. But even as he tried to convince himself otherwise, he knew it was no use.

The picture. That old, old picture.

It was definitely her. Decker had sharp eyes, had matched too many disguised faces to too many mug shots not to see it.

Just age the damn face.

The cabbie stopped the lecture for a moment.

"Where are you from?" he asked.

"Los Angeles," Decker said.

"Oh, L.A.," the driver said. "Very, very good. If you want I can show you Ebbets field where your Dodgers used to play."

"Just take me to the library."

"Not much to see," the cabbie went on, "a housing project now. But some people are very, very sentimental."

"I'm not."

"Are you interested in architecture, sir?" the driver said. "Or perhaps real estate? Two days ago I took a rich man to see the brownstones on Eastern Parkway. He was very, very impressed."

Decker tightened his fists and said, "Just the library."

"While you're here, you should see the Grand Army Plaza. It has a very, very big arch."

"I've seen loads of arches at McDonald's." Decker scowled.

"Oh, no," the cabbie answered. "This one is not like that. It is much bigger. And older too."

"I'm not interested in seeing any arch—"

"It is a very nice arch."

Decker enunciated each word. "Just take me to the library."

"We drive right past the arch to the library—"

"All right, show me the friggin arch!"

"Well, if you do not want to see the arch—"

"I want to see the arch," Decker said. "In fact, I want to see the arch so badly that if I don't see the arch, someone will *pay*."

Decker looked in the rearview mirror. The cabbie's mouth had frozen into an O. He steered the taxi by the arch, then took Decker to the library. Throughout the remaining portion of the trip, he didn't say another word.

❦ 4

This was the alibi: He'd suddenly remembered an important detail to a very important case and he had to use a pay phone because it would have been a breach of ethics to let anyone else overhear him and he had to get in touch with Marge at the station house because someone's life depended on it, well, not only someone's life but the whole California judicial system—

Then Decker thought: Even the most complicated phone call in the world wouldn't explain an absence of six hours. God's judgment day around the corner and his mind was full of half-baked lies.

The night held a bitter chill, dampness oozing through his clothes and into his bones. His toes and fingers were as cold and stiff as marble. Used to the temperate zone all his life, he had blood the consistency of rubbing alcohol.

He came to the street, then the house. Lights shining through the windows, smoke undulating from the chimney. And the smells. He dreaded the people but the structure looked so damned inviting. Approaching the door, he turned up his collar, tried to mask his face as best he could. Just in case *she* happened to be there.

As he stepped onto the porch, he pulled his scarf over his head.

So they'd think him psychotic. Who the hell cared?

Rina swung open the door before he knocked. Her face held an expression of complete bafflement.

"Anyone home?" Decker whispered.

"Everyone's gone to shul," Rina said.

Crossing the threshold, Decker took the scarf off his head and pulled down his collar. He headed up the stairs, heard Rina following him. He swung open the door to the tiny bedroom and immediately stubbed his toe on the fold-out bed. Swearing, he sank down into the mattress and ran his hands across his face. The room was illuminated by a single sixty-watt table lamp that rested on the floor. The night-stand clock read six-fifty-two.

Rina sat next to him.

"Peter, you're scaring the daylights out of me. What on earth is wrong? Did this massive dose of religion give you an anxiety attack or something?"

"Something."

"Please, Peter," Rina begged. "I deserve better than this—"

"What did you tell them?" Decker broke in.

"What?"

"What excuse did you make up for me when I stormed out of the house?"

"Something about your daughter . . . something you forgot to do for her."

"Cindy's a good excuse," Decker said. "Much better than the one I'd concocted."

Rina suddenly burst into tears. "We shouldn't have come out here. I should have told them no."

"Rina—"

"It's all my fault," she sobbed.

Decker put his arm around her and drew her near. "No, it's not."

"Yes, it—"

"It has nothing to do with religion," Decker said. "It's . . ." He stood, couldn't even pace in a room this small. He said, "How are we going to sleep if we can't turn the light off?"

"It's on a timer," Rina said.

Decker sat back down, stretched out on the bed, and buried his face in the blanket.

"You're not going to tell me, are you?" Rina said.

He picked up his head, then sat up straight. "You're right. You deserve better." He said, "This afternoon. You were talking to a woman in the kitchen . . ."

"Yes?"

"She's Frieda Levine, your mother-in-law's best friend?"

"Yes. So what?"

He sucked in his breath. "She's my mother."

It took Rina a moment to assimilate what he was saying. She could only respond with a breathy *what?* Then she added a whispered *oh my God.*

"You said it," Decker said.

"You're sure—"

"Positive," Decker said. "Faces are my business."

Rina was struggling to find something to say, but

all words had eluded her. All she could think of was that Peter didn't look a thing like Frieda Levine. And she knew that was the wrong thing to say, so she remained silent.

Decker couldn't sit any longer. He stood up and ran down the stairway, fully intending to run out the door. But he surprised himself and instead just paced the living-room carpet, further trampling the green-shag piling. The room was hot and bright, the crystal pieces giving off shards of color that splashed rainbows on the wall. As if that wasn't enough, an illuminated three-tiered chandelier made a glitter dome out of the dining room. He felt as if he'd stepped inside a heat-resistant ice palace. He longed to sweep his arm across the tables, smash what was whole and watch it crumble to dust. His sense of self, shattered. All of it a facade. He spied Rina sitting on a couch, she looking as sick as he felt, and he turned to her.

"What the hell am I going to do?"

"I . . ." Rina sighed. "I don't know."

Decker said, "Rina, I look just like my father—the image of the man down to the coloring. The woman is going to take one look at me, start doing a little mental arithmetic, and faint." He kept pacing. "Dear God, why did I ever come here? I knew she lived in New York. I knew she was an Orthodox Jew but I never ever considered the possibility of meeting up with her. Never! God, there are tens of thousands of Orthodox Jews in this city."

"There are," Rina said. "But we tend to live in concentrated areas. Peter, why didn't you tell me your mother was from Boro Park?"

"My mother is from Gainesville, Florida—"

"You know what I mean."

Decker forced himself to slow down. "Rina, I didn't *know* that this Frieda person lived in Boro Park. The adoption papers said she was fifteen, Jewish, born in New York and that was *it*. As I investigated a little further, I discovered she was still living in New York and was married with five kids. I didn't even know where she lived except that it was somewhere within the five boroughs because I tracked her using city records.

"Once I found out she was married with five kids, I stopped pursuing her. Instead, I put my name on this list of adoptees willing to meet their biological parents. I figured if she wanted to contact me, *I'd* be willing. I wasn't about to intrude on *her* life. Well, she never called me—and that was her decision, so fine. Fine. Just fine. I'll abide by that. It's obvious the woman wasn't interested and it's friggin fine with me to keep it that way."

Such hurt in his voice. Rina said, "I'm sorry, Peter."

"I'm not," Decker said. "I'm not the *least . . . bit . . . sorry*. I've done a damn fine job of living without her and she's done a damn fine job of living without me."

Rina didn't answer. Decker stopped pacing.

"I know I'm not making any sense."

"You're very agitated—"

"How would you feel?"

"Agitated . . . and hurt."

"I'm not hurt, okay!" Decker yelled. "Hurt is when you find out your wife is stepping out on you. No, that's not hurt. That's *fury*! But later after the fury wears off, it turns to hurt. That is *hurt*! Real *hurt*! *Got it?*"

Rina didn't answer.

"Okay, so I'm ranting—"

"You're understandably upset."

"I'm not upset . . . well, I am upset—"

"Peter, didn't you recognize her name when I first told it to you?"

"Somewhere in the back of my mind, I knew her married name was Levine or Levy or something like that. But *I* always thought of her as Frieda Boretsky—"

"That's her maiden name all right."

"You know her maiden name?"

"Remember I told you her elderly parents always have holiday dinner with my in-laws? Their names are Rabbi and Rebbitzen Boretsky—"

"Ain't that a hoot," Decker broke in. "I get to meet my grandparents."

"Peter, this must be awful for you—"

"Not as awful as it's going to be for Gramps and Grandma Boretsky. Much as they've tried, I'm sure they haven't forgotten old Benny Aranoff either."

"Benny Aranoff was your biological father?"

"Yep."

The room fell quiet. Exhausted, Decker plopped onto the sofa. "Rina, I can't face them. Any of them. Just say I'm sick—which is the truth—and can't come down for dinner. Then, after the holidays are over, I want to go home."

Rina closed her eyes and nodded.

"I'm sorry," Decker said.

"Don't apologize," Rina said. "I understand completely."

"I'll tell them I was called back to the station house on an emergency case."

"You don't have to say anything, Peter. I'll handle it for you. Least I can do, for dragging you into this mess."

Honey, the mess was created a long time ago, Decker thought. When a fifteen-year-old girl didn't say no to her boyfriend—with either the sex or the marriage. Decker was never too sure which came first. Only that they must have had some love for each other because they ran off and eloped. Then, the good Rabbi and Rebbitzen Boretsky found their daughter and annulled the marriage. To rid themselves of any remaining evidence of the attachment, they sent Frieda off to Florida to have a baby. . . .

Decker said, "It won't be so bad. I'll go back to work and take time off at a later date. Maybe we'll go to Hawaii—I know, we'll even take the boys. Hire a sitter. Make them happy. Hotels have sitters—"

"Peter, you're rambling again." Rina stood. "The family should be coming home any moment. Go upstairs, put on your pajamas, crawl into bed, and look sick." She regarded his face. "You don't even have to pretend, Peter. Go read and try to relax. I'll bring you up dinner. Can you eat?"

"Not at the moment," Decker said. "But by all rights, I should be starved."

Rina walked over to the living-room window and pulled the drapes back. Families were filling the streets—men and women dressed in their finest clothes. Jewelry glittered from fingers, ears, and necks. "Services must have ended at some of the shuls. People are starting to head home. Go."

Decker went upstairs. He stopped midway and shouted down, "Maybe this is all for the better."

Rina agreed that it probably was. Decker knew she was placating him, but even so, her response made him feel a little better.

A medley of voices said to Rina,

I'm so sorry.

Did you take his temperature?

Can he eat?

It must be jet lag.

His work is so stressful.

He should eat a little.

Those planes are so crowded, everyone coughing into one air filtration system.

Did you give him Tylenol?

These flus come on so all of a sudden.

Just a little soup.

Rina parried the questions like an expert fencer.

A minute later, Decker heard knocking on the door. Duo knocking. His stepsons, no doubt. But he asked who it was just to make sure. When they answered with their names, he told them to come in.

They patted his cheek, held his hand, smoothed out the covers for him, asked if they could get him anything.

He felt so damn guilty faking it. To make himself play the part with Strassbergian integrity, he thought about meeting Frieda Levine, meeting her *parents*, and his stomach legitimately churned.

Sammy asked him if he'd gotten sick because *he'd* been obnoxious on the plane ride over. Decker assured him that was not the case. But the boy remained unconvinced. Sam was the elder of the two, hypermature and, like his mother, willing to tote the world's problems on his back if he had a big enough knapsack. Decker kissed the boy's sweaty cheek; to make him feel better, he told him to bring him up some tea. To make Jake feel equally useful, he told him to bring up some lemon and sugar.

Jakey smiled: It was Rina's smile. The kid was Rina's clone. Sam had lighter hair, but was darker complexioned, looking like his dad. That must be hard on the Lazaruses, too.

In a grave voice, Sammy suggested honey in his tea instead of sugar. Honey was more soothing, and after all, it was Rosh Hashanah. Honey was traditional fare for the holiday, symbolizing a sweet New Year.

Decker said honey was a spiffy idea.

After the boys were gone, he locked the door behind them, not wanting any uninvited guests.

A moment later, the handle turned, a knock, and Rina said, "Peter, open the door."

"Yes, ma'am."

Rina came in. "Didn't mean to sound like an army sergeant."

"You've been fielding those questions like a pro."

"Thanks." She felt his forehead, then his cheeks, with the back of her hand.

"Rina, I'm not really sick," Decker said.

"Oh," Rina dropped her hand. "That's right. What am I doing? I don't know what I'm doing. You know, Peter, you actually feel a little warm."

"Life imitating art."

There was a knock on the door. The boys again, bringing up his tea.

Jacob said to Decker, "Everyone wishes you a speedy recovery—a *refuah shelema*."

"Thank you," Decker said.

"Want me to eat with you?" Sammy offered. "You look sort of lonely."

The truth of the matter was that Decker would have loved the company. But he said, "No problem, Sam, I'm just fine. I know there's a bunch of kids downstairs. Have a good time."

Sammy kissed his forehead. "You feel warm, Peter."

"I think your father has a *little* fever," Rina said.

"Rest," Jacob said, kissing his cheek. "I'll check on you later."

"So will I," added Sammy.

After the boys left, Rina said, "You want company?"

"I'm okay."

Rina said, "You do look lonely. Downright needy."

"No, I'm really fine."

"Friggin fine?"

Decker laughed. "No, I'm not fine at all. I want you to stay with me—"

"Then I will."

"No, I won't hear of it. Eat with your kinfolk . . ." He paused a moment, thinking: kinfolk. Except for her sons, Rina didn't have a single blood relative downstairs. But *he* did. "Go eat with them. But if it's no trouble, bring me up something to eat. My stomach's rumbling."

"Will do." She kissed his lips and left.

Decker locked the door behind her, then crawled back into bed. He thought about it for a moment. Kinfolk. A mother, grandparents, five half brothers and half sisters. God knew how many nieces and nephews. . . . He closed his eyes, felt any remaining energy drain from his body. He dozed until awakened by a hard rap on his door. It startled him and his heart raced inside his chest. Rina's voice announced her name.

Decker answered a groggy yeah and unlocked the door, then fell back into bed.

"I woke you up."

He didn't answer.

"Peter, you look so wan."

"I'm just tired," he said. Tired was the polite word. Fucked-up was the accurate description. But his olfactory nerve began to spark. He sat up and said, "What'd you bring me?"

"All sorts of goodies."

She set plates before him.

There was roasted rack of beef sitting on two bones, cooked crispy brown on the outside, juices sizzling and dripping. There was a separate dish of vegetables—browned potatoes with onions and green peppers, a carrot pudding topped with brown sugar and raisins, breaded cauliflower, steamed asparagus, zucchini in tomato sauce, a sweet noodle pudding topped with pineapple and macadamia nuts. And a traditional plate of sliced apples nesting in a pool of honey.

Food, food. Copious amounts of food.

"I think you'll need a tray or something," Rina said.

"Good idea unless you like gravy on your sheets."

She grinned. "Love the feel of a greasy bed. I'll get a tray for you and something to drink." She looked him over. "You need another pot of tea."

"While you're down there, how 'bout fetching some silverware and a couple of napkins?"

"Didn't I bring . . . ? I'm so absent-minded. Just snarf it down through your nose."

"Get out of here," Decker said.

She laughed and left. Decker couldn't wait for utensils. He ate a slice of apple and honey, then peeled a rib bone from the meat and took a big bite.

Words wouldn't do justice to the taste. He ate one bone and polished off the next. Picked up the breaded cauliflower and ate that, too. Then the asparagus spears, bending them in the middle and popping them whole into his mouth.

There was a knock at his door, then it was pushed open.

Decker looked up expecting to see Rina.

Instead what he saw was Mrs. Lazarus—and *her*.

Decker felt his eyes widen, his mouth open.

Too surprised to look down, too surprised to refrain from reacting.

She was *smiling*, her lips painted bright red, a spot of lipstick on her front tooth.

A toothy smile.

Not like his at all.

A stranger.

The two of them standing there, holding a silver tray of sweets—cakes, cookies, strudel, brownies . . .

He caught her eyes.

Smiling eyes.

But only for a moment.

Then came the confusion, the recognition, the shock, the plunge into despair.

With plates of food on his lap, there was nothing he could do, nowhere to run.

He turned his head away but he knew it was too late. He heard the gasp, the tray tumbling onto the floor. He looked up and saw her hand fly to her chest, her body staggering backward. Her eyes were fluttering, her pale lips were trembling.

Mrs. Lazarus yelling *Frieda!*

Rina screaming out *What are you doing here!*

Mrs. Lazarus shrieking *Call a doctor!*

Rina shoving her mother-in-law out the door, ordering her downstairs.

Frieda Levine hyperventilating.

Rina trying to catch her.

Mrs. Lazarus still shrieking to call a doctor.

And Decker sitting there—an army vet, a cop for twenty years, having served three different police departments, an expert with firearms, the perfect point man for any operation because he was always cool, calm, rational, stoic, so goddamn unemotional. Just sitting there, paralyzed by the sight of his mother falling.

❧5

The time has come.
The time is now.
Just go, go, go, I don't care how.
You can go by foot.
You can go by cow.
MARVIN K. MOONEY will you please go now!

Hank closed the dog-eared children's book and packed it inside his suitcase. Zeyde used to read it to him when he was just a little kid. Then they'd laugh together. . . .

Marvin K. Mooney was one stubborn sucker. Everyone in the book against him, telling him to get the hell out, but he don't care one single bit. He goes by his own time when *he* wants to go.

And no one was gonna tell him different.

He thought for a moment.

The time *had* come.

The time was *now*.

Do it, do it, I don't care how.

Go by foot, go by cow.

Just get the hell out, it don't matter how.

But you need someone to carry the bags.

Need someone to beat up the fags.

Need someone to wash your feet.

Need a wuss to take the heat.

Just look around, it's there for the takin'.

Your little boys willing to . . .

willing to . . .

willing to . . .

He stopped, unable to think up the rhyme.

What the hell. Poetry was for faggots anyway.

But there was truth to what he was sayin'. He had a faithful following of true believers. Little dummies just waiting to follow orders. Errand boys. And one of them would do.

The apartment was closing in on him.

Do it. Do it right away.

It was the time of year made him feel this way, all bent out of shape, all nervous inside. Everyone acting so damn godlike and then shittin' all over you as soon as the holidays was over.

Bunch of fanatical hypocrites. He'd love to buy himself an AK-fucking-forty-seven and take 'em all down in one moment of glory.

But that was too dangerous, too easy to get caught.

One glorious moment, but then it was the cooler for the rest of your life and having to knife off the shaved-headed *shvartzes* from reaming you in the butt and who needed that crap?

Anyway, he might hit a baby or something and even though the kid would grow up to be one of *them*, he couldn't see splattering the wall with baby brains.

Besides, no one had any respect for a baby killer.

Rip off a bank or something, now that got you respect. But killing a baby—even by accident—that was definitely out.

Besides, if you're gonna do anything like that, you don't do it yourself.

And then there was the principle of the thing.

You needed a gun, no doubt about that. Nothin' gets cooperation like the muzzle of a sawed-off resting between the eyes. But guns was only for last resorts, or people who couldn't do no better.

And he could do better.

The suitcase was full of them—knives for gutting, filleting, or butterflying. Cleavers for chopping off heads and tails, picks for piercing tough skin. And the portable hacksaws for the bigger bones.

A part of the old man that would be with him for life.

Best thing was, he knew how to *use* them, where to stick them to do the most damage with the least amount of blood.

The trick—whether it was a shank or an ice pick—was to keep 'em sharp. The sharper the blade, the cleaner the cut, the less blood.

And he'd packed his best stones.

None of that mass-manufactured sharpeners for him. Just good old-fashioned stones.

Had to have them—all of them. But shit, did they make the suitcase *one* heavy load.

He picked up a pencil and wrote on a piece of scrap paper:

Rule number one: Keep your hands cleen.

Rule number two: Find the rite dumshit to do the dirty work.

Excepchon to rule number two: First you gotta do the dirty work once to show the dumshit how to do it. Then you let the dumshit do the rest of the dirty work.

Rule number three:

Rule number three:

Rule number three:

He tapped the pencil against the paper, but couldn't think of anything else to write.

He threw the paper and the pencil in his suitcase, then rummaged through his other papers until he found the right one.

He consulted his hit list.

Three names held the number-one spot, each one just as dopey and stupid as the next.

Any one of the three would do.

Tomorrow morning he'd hang out, see which one came up first.

Then, like Marvin K., he'd be on his way.

❧6

Somehow Rina caught Frieda Levine before she hit the ground. Just as Peter predicted, she'd looked, she'd seen, she'd gone out cold. Through all the noise and confusion, Rina's first thought was: Get the woman alone for Peter's sake, for everyone's sake, before she blurted out something she'd regret.

She tried to shout over her mother-in-law's shrieking. She wanted Eema Sora out of the room and Mrs. Levine alone with her and Peter, but it was too late. A dozen adults swarmed around Frieda.

"Give her some air, for goodness' sake," Rina yelled.

Frieda's older daughter, Miriam, screamed out Mama, Mama. Shimon, her oldest son, grabbed his mother from Rina's arms, patted her face. The second son, Ezra, yelled to the younger daughter to fetch some water. The youngest son, Jonathan—the Conservative rabbi—suggested they call a doctor. His father said it was *yom tov* and if they needed a doctor he'd run down to Doctor Malinkov's house rather than violate the holiday. Jonathan answered that was ridiculous, that saving a life took precedence over the violation of a law and *he'd* call the paramedics if his father had difficulty with it. Rina interrupted the hysteria, yelling out that Frieda had just fainted, what she needed was air and a place to rest. Bring her into the other bedroom and give her a little breathing room.

Miraculously, they listened to her. Frieda's three sons carried their mother into the master bedroom, laying her on one of the twin beds. As soon as her head hit the pillow, Frieda opened her eyes and groaned. Rina sat down beside her, stroked her face. Miriam ordered her mother not to talk.

Frieda's husband said triumphantly, "See, there was no reason to break *yom tov*—"

Jonathan said, "Papa, she still could need a doctor—"

"She's up!" insisted the father. "She's up. She's up!"

Jonathan realized his father was trembling, that he was just spouting religion out of force of habit and was as shaken as the rest of them. He said, "Papa, sit down. You're pale." He turned to his sister and said, "Miriam, take Papa downstairs."

Miriam took her father's arm, but he pushed her away, then stumbled. Miriam caught him. Rabbi Levine announced he wasn't going anywhere and his children should stop ordering him around as he knew what was best.

The younger daughter, Faygie, returned with a sodden washcloth. Rina took the proffered cloth, dabbed Frieda's forehead, and gave a quick glance around the room—a wall of faces. Rabbi Levine's skin had taken on a grayish hue. Rina managed to catch Jonathan's eye.

"I don't think your father looks well," she said.

Jonathan threw his arm around his father. "Let's go downstairs, Papa. Mama will be fine."

The old man was too weak to argue.

Rina continued to bathe Frieda's face. The woman's eyes were still unfocused and Rina began to worry. Maybe something more serious had occurred. But a moment later, Frieda grabbed Rina's hands, and within seconds, her eyes became puddles of tears.

"What is it, Mama?" Faygie cried out.

"You overworked yourself," Miriam scolded. Her voice had panic in it. "You don't let me help you. You're getting too old to do all this cooking by yourself. Why don't you let me help you—"

"Miriam . . ." Shimon scolded.

She fell silent.

Frieda continued to cry. Rina brushed away her tears, told her everything was all right. But Frieda shook her head, violently.

"Talk, Mama," Shimon said.

"What is it?" asked another voice.

Rina felt her stomach turn over. Her sisters-in-law had come up. And their husbands. And some of the children. The room was so hot and stuffy it would make anyone a nervous wreck. With as much authority as Rina could muster she informed the group that Frieda needed quiet and not everyone fretting over her. It was just sudden exhaustion and would everyone please leave so the woman could breathe.

"I'll stay with her," Miriam said.

"I will," Faygie insisted.

"All of you out!" Rina ordered. "You're all much too excited to be of any use right now!"

Rina was surprised at how commanding her voice sounded. Shimon said that Rina was right and directed everyone out of the room.

"But she needs family," Miriam protested. "No offense to you, Rina, but she needs family."

"Why have you taken over?" Ezra asked Rina.

"Because I'm a bit calmer than all of you—"

"I'm calm," Miriam insisted. "I'm very, very calm!"

Rina said, "Miriam, you want to help out, go check on your grandparents. They must be worried sick."

Faygie said, "I'll do it."

Rina said, "Both of you do it. I'll call if she needs anything."

"Maybe Papa's right," Ezra said. "Maybe I should get Doctor Malinkov."

Rina said, "Give her a few minutes—"

"What do you know about nursing?" Ezra interrupted.

Frieda muttered something, eyes still flowing tears.

"What, Mama?" Miriam said.

The woman turned to her daughter, held Rina with one hand, and waved at the door with the other.

"*Nu?*" Rina said. "She wants you out."

"Are you okay, Mama?" Ezra said.

"Give her some room, please," Rina said.

Frieda nodded.

"Would you like me to stay with you?" Faygie asked.

Again, Frieda waved at the door.

Faygie said, "Don't be stubborn, Mama. I can stay with you."

"Go," Frieda whispered. "Go all of you. Rina will stay with me."

Faygie sighed, accepting her mother's words with reluctance.

Shimon placed his arm around Ezra, said to his sisters and brother, "Come." To Rina, he said, "Call us if she needs anything."

After everyone had left, Frieda turned her head on the pillow, away from Rina, but held her hand tightly. The woman seemed to be muttering to herself, but Rina could make out prayers through the sobs. She stroked Frieda's hand, tried to think of something to say, but she was as dumbstruck as she'd been with Peter.

Peter!

Dear God, what was *he* going through!

Rina's stomach was churning at full force. She took a deep breath, looked around the emptied room. She'd been inside this house hundreds of times but had never invaded the private sanctuary of her in-laws' bedroom. Twin beds, between them a large night table. Separate beds were required by Ortho-dox law, but she and Yitzchak had pushed their beds together, each of them sticking their feet in the crack at bedtime, playing with each other's toes. No such intimacy could be shared here. But despite the beds, there was something warm and loving in the room. Maybe it was the acres of family pictures that covered the bureau and the top of the chest of drawers. Pictures of her sisters-in-law, her nieces and nephews, her sons. Photos of her and Yitzchak before they'd been married, their wedding pictures, snapshots taken when her in-laws had visited them in Israel. Photographs that had showed Yitzchak as a robust young man. Not the skeleton that had died in her arms . . .

Frieda cried out to her and Rina was grateful for the distraction. Rina kissed her hand and smiled at the older woman. Frieda attempted a weak smile in return but failed.

"It's all right," Rina said.

Frieda shook her head no.

"Yes, it is," Rina said. "*Emes*, it's all right."

Frieda sobbed harder. Rina's voice had said it all. She looked at her and said, "You know."

Rina felt her eyes moisten. "I know."

"He knows, too," Frieda said.

Rina nodded.

"His eyes . . ." Frieda said. "He hates me."

"No, he doesn't—"

"I never stopped thinking about him," Frieda moaned. "Never. In my heart, I never stopped looking. Every time I saw someone his age, I wondered . . . I wondered . . ."

"I understand—"

"No," Frieda cried out. "No, you couldn't understand. Oh, such guilt, the *pain* . . . God is punishing me for my weakness. Rina, I was so young, so scared. My father was so frightening. I was weak—"

Rina hushed her.

Frieda was silent for a minute. When she finally spoke again, it was in a whisper. "Every time I gave birth to my babies, I thought of him. Of the baby I had and lost— No, of the baby I was forced to give up. I could never, ever not think of him. I *wanted* to keep him but my parents wouldn't let me. Dear God, forgive me . . ."

She started sobbing again.

Rina said, "Peter . . . Akiva has a daughter. He understands how you must have felt—"

"He hates me," Frieda said. "I saw it. I deserve it—"

Rina quieted her again.

"Your Akiva . . ." Frieda sobbed out. "My little baby boy. Oh, my God, after all these years . . . As much pain as if it happened yesterday. He wasn't sick at all, was he, Rina? He didn't want to see me."

"He didn't want to shock you."

"When you came to New York with him . . . he knew I'd be here?"

"Of course not."

"Then how did he know, Rinalah?" Frieda exclaimed. "How did he *know*?"

"I guess he found out your name a long time ago. But he knew you under your maiden name because that was on the birth certificate. I honestly don't know how he recognized you. Maybe he had a picture of you. Maybe his biological father sent—"

Again, Frieda broke into sobs. "He met *Benjamin*?"

"Once, I think." Rina's head was throbbing. "I'm not sure exactly what happened except that Peter got this big box of articles from his biological father after he died—"

"Benjamin is *dead*?" Frieda turned her face away. "Oh, my God! Too much has passed . . . *when*?"

"A long time ago, Mrs. Levine," Rina said. "Peter doesn't talk too much about anything, let alone something as . . . as . . . Peter keeps things inside. That's just the way he is."

"He's my Benny all over again," Frieda said. "I *loved* his father, Rinalah. Such love I've never known except with him. He worked for *my* father, did some carpentry . . . some bookshelves for him. I thought he was so handsome . . . I loved his hair, that beautiful thick red hair. . . ." Tears ran down her cheeks. "When my parents weren't looking, we'd talk. I loved him so, so much.

"When Papa found out . . . oooohh." She shuddered. "He *fired* him. *Hated* him. Benjamin had no family, no *yichus*, no head for learning. He was not a serious student, told too many jokes. Too frivolous for my father. When he found out we were still meeting behind his back, he slapped my face and forbade me to ever see him again. . . ."

There was a knock on the door, Miriam asking if everything was all right.

Frieda shouted, "We're fine. Go away."

"Mama, open up," Miriam said.

"I said go away." Frieda sighed. "Darling, I'm

resting. Take care of your father for me. Tell every-one I'm fine."

"If you're sure—"

"I'm sure," Frieda said. "Rina is taking good care of me."

No one spoke. A few seconds later, they could hear Miriam sigh, then the sound of receding foot-steps.

Rina said, "They're all terribly worried about you."

"I don't deserve it."

"Stop it," Rina said.

"Oh, my little Rina," Frieda said. "I have this empty hole in my heart since I gave him away. Noth-ing has ever filled it, nothing ever could. I wanted to find him. Yes, I wanted to do it. But I never had the courage."

"It's very frightening."

"He looked up his birth certificate," Frieda said. "He must have been curious. But he never contacted me."

"He said he put his name on this list—"

"Aaah," Frieda said. "I know about the list. So many times I reached for the phone . . . I was too ashamed, too afraid. Too embarrassed! But he knew who I was. He didn't come to me."

"He knew you were married with five other chil-dren. He didn't want to intrude on your privacy."

"He is a better person than I am."

Rina squeezed her hand. Frieda looked up at her, smiled. "He picked a beautiful bride. A young woman for *his* age." She knitted her brow. "He just turned forty-one. You must be . . . what, ten, twelve years younger than him?"

Rina nodded.

Frieda shook her head. "I talk stupidity. Tell him I love him. He will not believe me, but tell him anyway. Tell him I will leave it up to him what he wants to do. But I would like to talk to him, ask his forgiveness."

"There's no reason—"

"Yes, there is, Rina. There *is* reason."

"I'll tell him." Rina paused. "I don't think he wants to see your parents—"

"My parents!" Frieda blurted out. "They'll recognize him. Oh, dear God, my husband and children know nothing of my terrible shame."

"So we figured—"

"I feel like dying."

"Rest, Mrs. Levine," Rina said. "Let me talk to Peter. I'll find out what he wants to do."

"Tell him my parents go to my sister's house tomorrow for lunch," Frieda said. "It will be only my family . . ." She started to cry. After a minute she asked, "Does he have any family?"

"Of course!" Rina said. "Peter didn't grow up in an orphanage or anything like that. He had a very nice childhood. His mother and father live in Florida, where he grew up. They were taken aback by his conversion—"

"He doesn't have to convert," Frieda said.

"I know that," Rina said. "And you know that. But it was easier to tell everyone that he was a *ger* than to explain the circumstances. Besides, he feels like a convert. His mother is a religious Baptist. Peter speaks very fondly of his parents. And he's close to his brother."

"Just the one brother?"

"Yes, that's his only sibling," Rina said. "And of course, he adores his daughter, Cynthia."

Frieda clutched her heart. "A granddaughter I'll never know. Such a terrible fate to suffer. But I deserve such a fate, Rina. It's punishment from Hashem—"

"Shhhh," Rina quieted. "Everything will work out." But she didn't believe her own words.

There was another knock on the door. Shimon this time.

"I'll be out in a minute, darling," Frieda said. "I feel much better. It was just a little exhaustion."

"Rest, Mama," Shimon said. "I just wanted to know."

After he left, Frieda said, "You'd better go to him."

Rina stood. "I'll let you know what he wants to do."

"Tell him I love him, Rina," Frieda said. "I will not intrude on his privacy just as he didn't intrude on mine. I will honor whatever decision he makes. Please tell him that for me."

"I will."

Frieda said, "And if he doesn't want to see me, tell him I love him, I always have. And tell him I'm sorry . . . so very sorry."

❧7

The next day, Rosh Hashanah services lasted from eight in the morning to two-thirty in the afternoon. Never much of a churchgoer in childhood, Decker wasn't much of a synagogue goer either. But today he was grateful for every minute of delay. Less time to spend with people, specifically with *her.*

There was no purpose for flight now. His secret—so long buried, so seldom acknowledged even to himself—was violated. He knew and *she* knew. No one else knew of course, except Rina.

Rina, the go-between—a luckless role. She had played her part with aplomb and diplomacy.

She'll do whatever you want, Peter.

What does she want to do?

She wants to talk to you.

I don't want to talk to her.

That's fine.

Then she doesn't want to talk to me.

No, Peter, Rina had explained patiently. *She does want to talk to you, but she doesn't want to force you to do something you're not ready to do.*

I'm *not ready?* Decker had whispered incredulously. I'm *not ready? I was the one who'd put my friggin name on the list. I was the one who was willing to be contacted. Now she's saying I'm not ready?*

Rina sighed, gave him a "please don't kill the messenger" look. Maternally, she patted his hand and said, *Think about it, Peter.*

The upshot: He decided to eat lunch with *her*—and *her* family, knowing that the amount of contact *she* and he would have would be minimal.

Half of him wondered: *Why am I doing this?* His other half answered: *Because you're curious, jerk. That's why you started this whole thing rolling twenty-three years ago.*

He *was* curious. As they started back from shul, *her* sons at his side, he couldn't help but sneak sidelong glances at them. The detective in him—trying to find any signs of physical commonality.

The oldest was Shimon, the one Rina had called good-looking. He was a handsome man—solid, strong features. Decker put his age at around thirty-eight: There was a gray coursing through his trimmed black beard. Decker's own facial hair was full of rusty pigment, not a streak of white anywhere. For some reason that gave him an odd sense of superiority—as if his paternal genes were *better*. Although Shimon was dark, his pink cheeks—probably tinted from the cold—gave his face a splash of color. He stood about five eleven, had black hair and brown eyes, and was built with muscle—he and Decker had that much in common. In keeping with tradition, he was wearing his white holiday robe over his black suit. His *kittel* was a nice one—white embroidery on white silk.

The next in line was Ezra—same size as Shimon but thinner. Complexioned identically to his brother, Ezra was dark, his beard wide and wild. He wore glasses, and wrinkled his nose when he spoke. Decker was fixated on his ears—slightly pointed on top, exactly like his and Cindy's. Ezra had pulled his *kittel* tightly over his chest as he walked, stuck his hands in the robe pockets.

Jonathan was the baby of the family. The Conservative rabbi was tall—same size as Decker but slender. He was also dark-complexioned, but his eyes were lighter—hazel-green. He was clean-shaven and wore a Harris-tweed sportcoat over gray flannel pants. No *kittel*—either he wasn't married or the robe was too traditional for his taste. He was whistling *"Zip-a-Dee-Doo-Dah"* as they walked, eliciting dirty looks from Ezra. Maybe it was the modern clothes, but Decker found more of himself in this kid than in the two older brothers.

Kid? Jonathan must be Rina's age, maybe even a year or two older. A pause for thought.

All this mental game playing, it didn't amount to diddly squat. Unless he ever needed a transfusion or kidney transplant, it didn't matter what these jokers and he had in common. But he couldn't stop himself. He was trying to be unobtrusive about it, but more than a few times he managed to lock eyes with one of them, their expressions, in return, mirrors of confusion.

His furtive glances—like Jonathan's rendition of

"*Zip-a-Dee-Doo-Dah*"—had a slightly unnerving effect on Ezra. Shimon and Jonathan also seemed puzzled by Decker, but amused by him as well.

Rina was walking behind them with the women; her brothers-in-law were walking ahead with the older men. Children were all over the place. Somehow, Decker had been grouped with his half brothers. Did *she* notice it?

How could she *not* notice? He wondered what she was thinking at this moment, if the sight of all her sons together caused her untold pain or happiness. A moment later, Decker caught Jonathan grinning at him.

Jonathan said, "I want you to know, Akiva, that while Rina lived here, her phone never stopped ringing—"

"Half the calls were yours," Shimon interrupted.

"I was calling as a friend," Jonathan said.

"A very close friend," Shimon countered. His brown eyes were twinkling.

Jonathan looked at Decker. "She never even looked at another man."

Ezra adjusted his black hat, frowned, and said, "Is this *yom tov* talk?"

"I just wanted Akiva to know that Rina was loyal to him," Jonathan said.

"Look at the man," Shimon said, pointing to Decker. "Does he look as if he ever had any doubt? He has a magnetic effect on women. Look what he did with Mama."

Decker said, "Must have been my charm."

"I think it was the red hair," Jonathan said. He

took off his yarmulke, then repinned it onto his black hair. "Mama loves *gingies*. Stubborn woman that she is, she's always trying to set me up with redheads."

Decker felt his stomach tighten. He said, "You're not married."

"A sore point in the family," Shimon said. "One of many."

Jonathan said, "Know any nice Jewish women in Los Angeles? Preferably ones that look like your wife?"

Shimon said, "Religious women."

Jonathan said, "Not so religious."

Shimon said, "Another sore point."

Ezra turned red and said, "This is how you talk on Rosh Hashanah?"

"Take it easy, Ez," Jonathan said. "The Torah's not going to fall apart if someone cracks a smile on *yom tov*."

"What do you know from Torah?" Ezra said. "The way *you people* make up your own laws—"

"Ezra, not now," Shimon said.

"It would be better if you did nothing," Ezra's pointed ears were now crimson. "What you do now is *apikorsis*."

"That's your interpretation," Jonathan said. He held back a smile and began whistling again.

"It's a true Torah interpretation!" Ezra shouted. "And stop *whistling* that nonsense."

Jonathan said to Decker, "A point of fact. It was Ezra who took me to see *Song of the South* way back when before movies were considered unkosher—"

"Before you were *tref*," Ezra said, using the Hebrew word for unkosher.

"Low blow, Ez," Jonathan said.

"Both of you, enough," Shimon said. "Papa will hear you and get upset."

"Ach," Ezra said, waving his hand in the air. He picked up his pace and caught up with the older men and Rina's brothers-in-law.

Jonathan said, "The man has no sense of humor."

Shimon wagged a finger at him. "That is not nice."

"It's not a matter of being nice or not nice," Jonathan said. "It's a statement of fact, Shimmy." To Decker he said, "Ezra hasn't forgiven me for leaving the fold—"

"I haven't either," Shimon said.

"You?" Jonathan waved him off. "Who pays attention to you."

Shimon laughed. "Of all of us, Jonathan had the best head for learning. He's breaking my father's heart with his Conservationism—"

"Conservatism," Jonathan said.

"It's all the same foolishness." Shimon put a hand on Decker's shoulder. "He won't listen to us, but maybe he'll listen to you. Talk to him."

Decker smiled.

"*Gornisht mein helfun*," Jonathan said. "Give it up. I'm too far gone." He raised his eyebrows. "Unless you're willing to give up Rina—"

"Forget it," Decker said.

"Not even to save a soul?" Jonathan said.

"Your soul looks okay to me," Decker said.

Jonathan patted his brother's shoulder and said, "Hear that, Shimmy? An objective opinion."

"Then again, I'm pretty new at assessing souls," Decker said.

Jonathan smiled.

"Yonasan," Shimon said, "can you do us all one favor? Can you not bait Papa for one whole meal? His heart isn't what it used to be."

"So what do you want me to say when he starts in on me?" Jonathan said.

"Don't say anything."

"Papa loves to debate me—"

"He doesn't love it."

"It revitalizes him."

"Yonasan . . ."

"It does!"

Shimon spoke in a patient but parental voice. "Yonasan, Papa was shaken up by Mama's sudden attack yesterday. Do a mitzvah and go easy on Papa."

Jonathan threw up his hands. "Okay. I can always use another mitzvah at this time of year. I'll lay off Papa." He had a gleam in his eye. "But Ezra's fair game—"

"Yonasan . . ."

"He doesn't have a heart condition." To Decker, Jonathan said, "Everyone at today's table has a big mouth. Feel free to make a jerk out of yourself like we all do."

"Speak for yourself." Shimon turned serious. "I'm worried about Mama. She still looks a little shaky."

"She must have caught my bug," Decker said straight-faced.

"You felt shaky last night?" Shimon said.

"Very," Decker answered.

"You look okay now," Shimon said.

"I feel a little better," Decker said.

"How are you enjoying New York?" Jonathan asked.

"I'm not used to such close quarters," Decker said.

"It can be oppressive," Jonathan said. "Especially if you're used to a lot of space. Rina says you have a ranch with horses."

"A small ranch," Decker said. "A few acres."

"Do you police your area on horseback?" Shimon asked.

Decker stared at him. Shimon had asked the question sincerely. He cleared his throat and said, "We don't live on the wild frontier. We have regular houses, regular streets—"

"But no sidewalks," Jonathan said. "Rina said there are no sidewalks."

"The major streets have sidewalks," Decker said. "How *well* do you know Rina, Jonathan?"

"You have streets without *sidewalks*?" Shimon said.

"Some of the streets don't have sidewalks," Decker said. To Jonathan, he said, "You and Rina do a lot of talking?"

Shimon said, "Where do you walk if you don't have sidewalks? On people's lawns?"

"There are these dirt curbs—"

"How quaint," Jonathan said.

"Quaint is cobblestone streets," Decker said. "Our area isn't at all quaint."

Jonathan said, "Rina says you have a lot of Hell's Angels living near you."

"Not right near us—"

"Hell's Angels, gang shootings, highway shootings, and all those crazies on drugs . . ." Shimon shook his head, adjusted his hat. "And they say New York is bad? I bet I'm safer here than where you live. Because here I have neighbors that know me."

Jonathan said, "Rina says in Los Angeles no one knows their neighbors."

"That's not really true," Decker said. He realized he was sounding defensive. "Well, it's sort of true. What else has Rina told you, Jonathan?"

Jonathan didn't answer right away. Then he said, "Did Rina tell you I was her late husband's best friend? Yitz and I grew up together."

"Yitz and Yonasan used to learn together," Shimon explained. "Every single night until Yitz and Rina moved to Israel. The two of them were amazing. Whenever they learned in the *Bais Midrash*, people gathered around them just to hear their fertile minds click—"

"A real dog and pony show," Jonathan said.

"You loved to learn back then, Yonie," Shimon said. "I remember the fire in your eye whenever you proved a point."

"That was a glazed look from lack of sleep."

"You loved it." Shimmy became grave. "Yitz was a good influence on you. Now he's gone and you've become an *apikoros*. We lost both of you in one year."

Jonathan looked pained. "Not quite the same thing."

Shimon put his arm around his brother and said, "You're right. It's not the same thing at all. I'm just saying you lost your love for learning when Yitz—"

"I pay an analyst for this, Shim," Jonathan said.

"Ach," Shimon said. "Analyst, shmanalyst. I have faith. *I* haven't given up on you."

Jonathan started to say something but changed his mind. They walked the next few steps without talking. Turning to Decker, Jonathan said, "I used to razz Yitz the same way I'm razzing you." He rolled his tongue inside his cheeks. "He was a good guy."

There was another moment of silence. Jonathan managed to put on a cheerful smile, then punched Decker lightly on the shoulder. "As far as Rina goes, I tried. God *knows* I tried . . . and tried . . . and tried and tried."

Decker let out a small laugh.

Jonathan shrugged and said, "The better man won out—both times."

Decker didn't know if that was true. But he certainly wasn't going to argue the point.

The house that Rabbi Levine built was nearly identical to the Lazarus abode. Crystal, Decker decided, must be symbolic of something. Frieda Levine, like Rina's ex-mother-in-law, Sora Lazarus, seemed to be inordinately fond of the glistening glass. The dining area was lit with a mammoth-sized chandelier—a four-tiered job with scores of icy stalactites dangling from the frame. It completely overpowered the room.

And as had been the case at Sora Lazarus's, the

adjoining living room–dining room had taken on the appearance of a mess hall. One long rectangular table and four folding card tables crammed every available inch of floor space. There were enough chairs to fill an auditorium.

Rina took Decker's hand and explained that Frieda had invited a few families—ones that hadn't lived in the community for so long.

"Nice that the woman is hospitable," Decker said.

"Peter . . ."

"Okay, okay."

"How was your walk over here?" Rina asked.

"You know, you might have walked with me," Decker said. "Especially after all that happened."

"You're not going to like this, Peter, but I felt Frieda Levine needed me more than you did."

Decker stared at her. "Feel the need to mother her, do you?"

"I think that's a rhetorical question," Rina said. "I'm not going to answer it."

Decker jammed his hands in his pockets. "Did you happen to notice who I was walking with?"

"Yes, I did," Rina said. "So did Mrs. Levine."

"Did she say anything to you?"

"No, but she did have this real . . . wistful look in her eyes."

"*Wistful?*"

"Maybe that's not the right word."

Decker bounced on his feet, unable to pace because they were in public and there was no room to pace even if he wanted to. He said, "Is there assigned seating at this shindig?"

"I don't know."

"Do I have to sit separate from you?"

"I don't know that, either."

"Can I put my elbows on the table?"

"Peter—"

"Forget it." Decker dug into his hip pocket and pulled out a pack of cigarettes. "Anywhere I can get a light?"

"You need to smoke?"

"Very badly."

Rina sighed. "Give it to me. There's probably a fire under one of the kitchen burners."

Decker handed her a cigarette. A moment later, she came back with his lighted smoke and suggested they take it outside. Decker said that was a wonderful idea. On the front lawn, they met Jonathan puffing away.

He said, "Great minds think alike."

Rina took Decker's arm and said, "Would you two like a formal introduction?"

"Not necessary," Jonathan said.

"Jonathan grew up with Yitzchak," Rina said.

"He's had his history lesson for the day," Jonathan said.

"Excuse *me*," Rina said.

Jonathan laughed. "Sorry. I'm in a bad mood. I hate these things. Every year I swear I'm going to beg off coming, and every year my mother pleads and I give in. Mama can be very persistent. It's *religion* to her. The family's got to be together on holidays!"

Rina felt Decker's arm tense.

Jonathan said, "I've got to marry a woman who doesn't get along with my family and use her as an excuse." He said to Decker, "How 'bout yourself, pal? You look really excited."

"I'm thrilled."

"Can read it all over your face."

Decker laughed.

Rina said, "I think her hospitality is nice."

"*You're* nice." Jonathan said to Decker, "Rina says I'm too sarcastic. Do you think I'm sarcastic?"

"Don't get me involved in your squabbles," Decker said.

"You're way too sarcastic, Yonie," Rina said. "That's why you're having trouble finding a nice woman."

"*His* sarcasm doesn't put you off," Jonathan said, pointing to Decker.

"Akiva is not sarcastic," Rina said.

"I'm not?" Decker said.

"No," Rina said. "You're cynical. There's a big difference."

The men laughed. Decker crushed out his cigarette, feeling a bit more relaxed. Jonathan followed suit a moment later.

"What the heck," he said. "It's a bad vice."

A woman stormed out of the house. She was short and thin and had she been in a better mood might have been considered attractive, but her expression was chiseled out of anger, her blue eyes flashing sparks like a hot wire in water. She was wearing a navy knit suit, the skirt falling three inches below her knee, and a pair of matching leather boots.

Covering her hair was a blue headdress pinned with a rhinestone brooch. She marched down the walkway, tented her eyes with her hands, then scanned the sidewalk.

"Lose something, Breina?" Jonathan said.

The woman turned to him and wrinkled her nose in disgust. "Have you seen Noam?"

"Which one is he?" Jonathan said. "I get them all mixed up."

"That's *not* funny, Yonasan," Breina said.

"No, I haven't seen him," Jonathan said.

Breina took one more look down the block. Muttering to herself, she stomped back into the house.

"Ezra's wife," Jonathan explained. "She adores me."

"I can tell," Decker said.

Jonathan said, "Noam's the second of five. A weird kid. Always smiling but he never looks happy."

Rina said, "Jonathan . . ."

"It's true," Jonathan said. "She blames it on me. Anything remotely bad is blamed on my secular influence. God, I wish I had the power they attribute to me."

He paused a moment.

"I feel bad for Noam. He's a lost soul."

"You're projecting," Rina said.

Jonathan said, "I'm a lost soul. I admit it freely."

"Aren't we all?" Decker said.

"Yeah, but it takes on greater significance in this community," Jonathan said. "The object in Boro Park is to conform."

"That's not true," Rina said.

"It is true," Jonathan said. "Noam's an obnoxious kid, but I feel for him. You know, about six months ago, he came to me to mooch twenty bucks. I was a little put out, but I gave him the money anyway. Before he left, he started asking me some pretty soul-searching questions."

"What kind of questions?" Rina asked.

"Why did I leave Boro Park? Why did I become a Conservative rabbi? Did that mean that I really didn't believe in God?" Jonathan sighed. "According to the Orthodox, I really don't believe in the same God as they do because I think oral law is not as holy as the written law."

Rina squirmed. Jonathan picked up on it. He said, "See, she thinks I'm an *apikoros*, too."

"Cut it out, Jonathan," Rina said.

"For your information," Jonathan said, "I was very careful not to explain my decision to Noam because I didn't want to subvert my brother." To Decker, he said, "Ezra and I have a very sticky relationship and I didn't want to add any more hostile fuel to the fire."

"So what did you tell Noam?" Decker asked.

"I told him he should ask his father."

"Smart man," Rina said.

Jonathan shook his head in disgust. "It was a cop-out, Rina. Noam still has those doubts. Who's he going to discuss them with? And don't say the *rabbaim*. They'll just do to him what they did to you—"

"Jonathan, you have no sense!" Rina snapped.

"No, wait a minute." Decker held out his palms.

"Wait a minute." He turned to Rina. "What did they do to you?"

Jonathan said, "I thought you told him."

"You are really, really . . ." Rina clenched her fist and faced Peter. "They didn't do anything."

"I'm supposed to believe that?" Decker said.

"They tried to talk her out of marrying you," Jonathan said. "Subtly, of course. They'd visit in pairs—one of them the guy who's trying to be your pal. Almost like a good cop, bad cop kind of thing." He looked at Decker. "You guys really do that, don't you?"

Decker said they did.

Jonathan said, "I guess good psychology is good psychology. You really have to be aware of what's going on, or else you'll fall for it."

"I think you've said enough, Jonathan," Rina said.

"Let him finish," Decker insisted.

Jonathan went on, "They came over late at night when she was zonked, turned the lights real low, talked in very soft voices. . . . 'Rinalah. You're a young woman. You shouldn't be closing yourself off to one man. You're a woman of valor, you should have a Torah scholar like Yitzchak *alav hashalom*. I know such a boy. And he wants to meet you—'"

"Stop it!" Rina whispered. She looked at Peter. His face was flushed with anger.

Jonathan turned to Decker. "She'd call me afterward. See, they pulled the same shtick on me when I decided to quit the yeshiva. We commiserated. You don't have to be angry at them, Akiva. In their own minds, they were just doing what they thought was right. Besides, Rina seemed angry enough for both of you. Her mind was made up a long time ago. She only had eyes for you."

No one spoke for a moment. Finally, Decker let go with a laugh, put his arm around Rina.

He said, "At least I know you're loyal."

"It's called *love*," Rina said. She looked at Jonathan. He was very troubled. She said, "It's okay. I'm not mad."

"I'm glad, but that's not what's bothering me," Jonathan said. "I'm thinking of Noam. Who does he talk to, Rina? Maybe I should try to approach him. Take the plunge and incur my brother's wrath."

Ezra Levine came out of the house, repeating the exact dance his wife had performed minutes ago. He noticed Jonathan and said, "You've seen Noam, Yonasan?"

"No, I haven't, Ez."

"You didn't see him or talk to him today?"

Jonathan noticed a hint of concern in his brother's voice. "No, I didn't."

Ezra looked down the sidewalks again. Lots of people walking home from synagogue. But nowhere was his son.

"Want me to look for him, Ez?" Jonathan said. To Decker he said, "Noam wanders off all the time. Maybe now's a good time to reestablish some contact."

Ezra took off his hat, adjusted the black yarmulke underneath, then returned the hat to his head. He rocked on his feet for a moment, then said, "Do you mind, Yonie?"

"No problem," Jonathan said.

"I'll come with you," Decker blurted.

Rina gave Decker a look of surprise. "Anything to get out of lunch."

Decker tossed her a smile laced with emotion. Immediately, Rina felt his sadness. What that smile had told her.

Jonathan.

His brother.

Talk about establishing contact.

Decker caught himself. "I'm not trying to get out of anything. I just thought Jonathan might want to avail himself of my trained eye."

Everyone burst into laughter that held more relief than mirth.

8

It was taking too long, everyone making desperate excuses for the delay.

"They got lost," Breina said. "Go look for them, Ezra."

"That's ridiculous," Ezra countered. "Yonie grew up here."

"Yonie's been away," Breina fired back.

Shimon said, "Yonie didn't get lost, Breina. Calm down. They'll be back soon. Yonie probably started talking to someone and forgot there are forty people waiting for him to come back. You know how he is."

"He's the absentminded professor, Breina," Miriam said. "Don't worry."

"He's impossible when it comes to time," Faygie added.

"Always late," Rina's sister-in-law, Esther, chimed in.

Rina didn't buy it. Even if Jonathan was irresponsible, Peter certainly wasn't. But she didn't say anything.

Everyone was quiet for a minute. Ezra broke the silence.

"I thought you were watching him," he scolded his wife.

"I had the girls," Breina said. "The boys are your responsibility."

"Noam's a year past bar mitzvah," Ezra said. "I should watch him like an infant?"

"I'm not saying you should watch him like an infant," Breina said. "But you can keep your eyes open. You know how Noam is. Lost in his own world. Just like Yonasan—"

"So if you know how he is," Ezra interrupted, "you can't keep your eyes open?"

Breina repeated, "He's just like Yonasan—"

Frieda Levine broke in. "Stop bickering, both of you. You're making all of us nervous." But Frieda's sense of dread had started long before this happened.

This was not something that would right itself. *This* was *Yad Elokeem*—the hand of God—punishing her, condemning her for not being strong enough. It had taken Him forty-one years, but she'd known that the time would come eventually. And now He had chosen the weakest of her sons, her most vulnerable grandchild, knowing how much it would hurt.

Her lost child—had he come as part of God's vengeance? Or had he been sent for some other reason? Perhaps the Almighty in His infinite wisdom was also testing her. Perhaps she could earn redemption if she showed herself worthy—worthy of His mercy, worthy of Akiva's mercy.

Whatever was expected of her, whatever she must do, she would do. She would be strong. To her husband, Frieda said, "Make kiddush. Akiva and

Yonasan will make their own kiddush when they come back."

Alter Levine was sitting at one of the folding tables, a volume of Talmud in front of him. He looked up when he heard his wife speak, but returned his attention to the Talmud when no one else moved.

Ezra gathered his other children and asked, "Who was the last one to see Noam?"

Aaron, the eldest, said, "He walked to shul with us, Abba. I davened after that. I didn't pay attention to him."

"He probably went to a friend's, Ezra," Miriam said. "He shows up at my house unannounced all the time."

"He does?" Ezra said. "What does he want?"

"I don't think he wants anything, Ezra."

"What does he do then?"

"I don't know. I give him a snack."

"He can't come home for a snack?" Breina said.

"It's part of being a teenager, Breina. Sometimes a snack at your aunt's house is better than a snack at home. Maybe he went to a friend's house for a snack."

"On *Rosh Hashanah*?" Breina said.

"Maybe he went to your brother's," Ezra said. "If he went to one relative, maybe he went to another?"

"Enough!" Frieda said. She turned to her husband and again instructed him to make kiddush.

"No one is sitting," Alter said.

"Everyone sit down," Shimmy said.

"Where should we sit, Frieda?" asked Sora Lazarus.

The next few minutes were spent trying to get everyone seated. Rina instructed the boys to sit at the same table as their cousins. She asked them if they had seen Noam. Both shook their heads no.

Sammy whispered in his mother's ear, "I didn't see him in shul today."

Rina said, "You probably just missed him, Shmuel. Aaron said he walked to shul with them."

"He wasn't in shul," Sammy insisted.

"How do you know?" Rina said.

"Because anytime I'm in town, Noam'll hunt me out just to bug me. And he didn't bug me today."

Rina said, "Maybe he's bored with bugging you."

"No way, José. He bugged me yesterday, first thing. He's a real jerk, Eema."

Rina sighed. The kid did have problems. And she knew why Sammy was hostile toward him. Behind Sammy's back, Noam had dubbed Peter and her with crude epithets. Naturally, Sammy had found out about it. There had been a fight, and Noam, being older and bigger, had given Sammy a black eye. At the time, Rina had been outraged, about to make a huge stink. But Sammy implored her not to say anything to Breina and Ezra. She backed off, knowing that her son had been fighting for her honor and her interference might somehow emasculate him. The whole incident eventually blew over, but not without psychological ramifications. She was cool to Breina after that, aware that Noam's thoughts didn't originate out of nowhere.

"Any idea where he might have gone?" Rina said.

"I don't know and I don't care," Sammy said. "Noam's always getting into trouble. He's a mental case."

"Shmuli, try to be charitable."

Sammy gave her an impish smile. "Is Mrs. Levine serving us kid food or do we get to eat the good stuff like you guys?"

Rina was about to launch into a speech, but Sammy preempted her. "Forget it, Eema." He kissed her hand. "Go sit down."

Rina wanted to squeeze him and would have if they'd been alone. But alas, her boys were at *that* age—embarrassed by her hugs and kisses. So she just smiled at her sons, then found her place at the table. Her seat was sandwiched between her sisters-in-law.

Alter Levine made the ritual blessing over the wine. Following kiddush came the ceremony of the washing of the hands, then the breaking of bread. With all the people and one sink, the washing and blessings took over ten minutes. Finally the meal was about to be served and six women jumped up to help Frieda Levine. Frieda instructed the guests to sit, her daughters and daughters-in-law would help her and there was no room in the kitchen for anyone else.

Esther patted Rina on the shoulder and whispered, "You look pale."

"It's been a tiring trip," Rina said. "And this incident isn't helping."

Rina's other sister-in-law, Shayna, agreed. "Poor Breina. Noam has been giving her such a rough time lately. Not a bad boy. Just doesn't have any sense. No *sechel*."

Esther said, "Remember that fight that he and Sammy—"

"Yes," Rina said. "He's a very impressionable kid."

"A lonely boy, if you ask me," Esther said. "This thing must be bad news. Why else would Ezra ask Akiva to look for him?"

"Jonathan volunteered to look for him," Rina said. "Not Akiva. Akiva just went along to keep him company. Akiva doesn't even know what the boy looks like."

"Poor Breina," Shayna repeated. "It's tough to raise teenage boys."

Rina said, "Shhh, she's coming."

The appetizer was served. Rina was on her second sweet and sour meatball when there was a loud knock on the door. Shimon and Ezra leaped up at the same time. Ezra got to the door first.

Rina studied the men as they came into the room. Jonathan seemed anxious. Peter, on the other hand, was calm, expressionless—his eyes unreadable. His professional demeanor. That was really worrisome. For a moment, she flashed to those young faces plastered on milk cartons. The images were too gruesome to dwell upon.

Ezra said, "You didn't find him."

The women came out from the kitchen. Breina's lip started to quiver. Frieda began to stagger backward. Esther stood up and offered Frieda her chair. Ezra told everyone to just calm down. But he was anything but tranquil.

"He's probably at a friend's," Jonathan said. "I didn't know all his friends—"

"He wouldn't go without asking me," Breina said. Her voice was shrill. "They wouldn't let him come without asking me. Not on *Rosh Hashanah*."

Ezra said, "Did you check the house? Maybe he went home?"

"Twice," Jonathan said. "If he's home, he's not answering."

"I'll go check," Ezra said to Breina. "I'll check his friends, your brother's house—"

"I already checked Shlomi's house," Jonathan said. "He's not there." He whispered a damn under his breath.

Decker said to Ezra, "How about if I come with you—"

"No," Ezra snapped. He hugged himself and exhaled slowly. "No, that isn't necessary."

"Let Akiva come with you, Ez," Jonathan said.

"Why?" Ezra said. "Do you think I need a policeman to look for my son?" He turned to Decker, his face a mask of pure fear. "Do *you* think I need the police, is that it?"

"No," Decker said.

"Then why do you want to come?" Ezra shouted.

Decker shrugged and said, "Up to you, Ezra. You want some company, I'll be happy to tag along."

"I don't care who goes," Breina shrieked. "Just *go*." She burst into tears.

"Why don't the two of you split up," Shimon suggested. "It will go twice as fast."

Decker answered, "I don't know who his friends are or where they live."

"I can take you to them," Aaron, Noam's eldest brother, volunteered.

"I don't *need* anyone with me!" Ezra protested.

"Then go already," Breina said.

Frieda spoke up, "Ezra, take Akiva with you."

"Mama, there's no reason for a policeman—"

"Take him!" Frieda ordered. "You shouldn't be alone right now."

Decker caught Frieda's eye. Outwardly, she seemed in control. Her voice was firm, no tears to be seen. Her hands weren't shaking but they were clenched into balls, her knuckles almost white. What he saw was a frightened grandmother, trying very hard to keep a tight rein on her emotions. An expression he'd witnessed countless times as a detective in Ju-vey Division. Time to put the past aside. He gave her a shrug that said the situation was no big deal. She shrugged back.

Their first real communication: a series of non-committal shrugs.

Ezra, on the other hand, was losing ground to his anxiety. He continued to bite his nails. His posture was stiff, his feet frozen in place as if he couldn't quite figure out how to move.

Not that Decker thought he was overreacting. Although the kid had been gone for only a few hours, the circumstances were unusual. The cop in him didn't like it. He was experienced enough to know that most of the time, the panic did turn out to be much ado about nothing. But he couldn't help think-ing about the flip side—those ice-cold, barely pubes-cent bodies lying on steel slabs in the morgue. . . .

He needed to prod them into action. He put his arm around Ezra and gently propelled him to the door. "Let me come with you, Ezra. I can use the exercise. How many houses are we talking about?"

"Where should I go, Breina?" Ezra asked of his wife. His voice cracked.

Breina rattled off a list of ten names.

"Piece of cake," Decker said. "You know all of the houses?"

Ezra nodded.

"Okay," Decker said. "Let's get it over with." He patted Ezra on the back. "You lead."

He noticed Breina Levine had her hand to her chest. She seemed to be breathing rapidly. As he crossed the threshold of the door, Decker whispered to Jonathan to keep an eye on his sister-in-law.

The food was served and the groups broke down into two categories: those who ate because they were nervous and those whose stomachs were shut down by anxiety. The wait seemed interminable. In fact, it took only an hour for Decker and Ezra to return. Breina Levine took one look at her husband's face and collapsed into a chair. Frieda rushed into the kitchen to get a glass of water for her.

Decker said to Jonathan and Shimon, "Send everyone except family home." He paused, thinking about that.

He was friggin family.

"You think it's bad?" Jonathan asked.

It wasn't good, Decker thought. But there was no point in offering a worried uncle his professional opinion.

"We don't know where the boy is. That's all we know right now. We don't know where he is. One step at a time. First, you clear the place. Send the guests home. Have the kids—the brothers, sisters, and cousins—wait in the back room. I'll talk to them in a moment."

It took fifteen minutes for everyone to find coats and jackets. People patted hands, reassured the distraught parents and grandparents. Nobody believed a word they were saying.

When everyone was gone, Decker sat down at the dining-room table and tried to clear his mind of morbid thoughts. Perversely, all he could think about were the tragedies. The overwhelming grief on the parents' faces as he broke the bad news. It made his stomach churn.

The table was still piled with food. But the salad had wilted under the weight of the dressing, the cooked vegetables had wrinkled, the edges of the roast beef had begun to curl. It was past four and Decker hadn't eaten all day. He needed nutrition if he was going to think clearly. He picked up a chicken leg and bit into it.

"Sorry, but I've got to get something in my stomach," he said.

Shimon gave him a clean plate. "Of course. Of course. You need to eat. Can I get you anything else?"

"No, this is just fine," Decker said.

Absently, Ezra said, "*Mincha*'s in twenty minutes."

No one said anything.

"*Tephila!*" Ezra said. "I need to pray." His eyes flooded with tears. "*Tephila! Tzedakah! Tshuvah!*" He buried his head in his hands and held back tears.

"It's my fault. . . . I don't learn with him anymore. . . . I'm not patient enough—"

"Ezra, stop it," Shimon said. "You're a fine father."

With moist eyes, Ezra looked at Decker. "I'm sorry."

"Don't apologize," Decker said. "It's tough. But there's still a lot we can do. Ezra, did you specifically ask your children if they knew where he might be?"

"Yes. Yes, I did."

"And they don't know?" Decker said.

Ezra shook his head.

"Has Noam ever run away before?"

"Not like this," Ezra said.

"But he's run away?" Decker asked.

"No!" Ezra said. "He wanders off sometimes but he always comes back. And he wouldn't wander off on Rosh Hashanah. There's no place for him to go."

No place in Boro Park, Decker thought. He turned to Jonathan and said, "Whose Ford Matador is parked out front?"

"It's mine," Jonathan said.

"Give me the keys," Decker said. "A car can cover ground we can't do on foot. I'll start as soon as I finish with the kids."

No one said the obvious. Decker's willingness to drive on Rosh Hashanah—violating the holiday—indicated a serious situation. Decker broke the moment of silence and asked Ezra for a picture of his son. Ezra said he didn't carry one with him, but his mother must have a couple of recent pictures somewhere. He'd dig some up.

After Ezra left, Decker said, "The best thing to do in situations like these is a door-to-door search. You people know most of your neighbors, which is a big plus. Ask if anyone's seen Noam today, and if so, when was the last time they saw him. Ask the teenage *boys*—see if any of them look nervous and scared—"

Decker stopped himself, regarded his two half brothers. Scared witless, shaken to the core. They stared at him as if he were speaking gibberish.

Shimon said, "Maybe we should phone the police?"

Decker made a conscious effort to slow himself down. He explained that if NYPD was anything like LAPD, they wouldn't do anything for children over ten or eleven. It would be at least a twenty-four-hour wait before a missing-persons report would be filed.

"But he's only a boy," Shimon protested.

"He's fourteen, considered a runaway rather than a kidnap victim—"

"*Chas vachalelah*," Shimon blurted out. "My God, I can't believe this is happening."

How many times had Decker heard those words. *The sense of unreality.* But it was real and they needed a game plan. Decker told himself to speak simply. "Look. Maybe he'll show in an hour, or maybe he'll show up tonight—"

"But maybe not," Jonathan said.

"Don't say that!" Shimon scolded him.

"Jonathan's right," Decker said. "It's possible that Noam won't show up tonight." *Or ever.* But he knew his negative thinking was an occupational hazard—an igniter to drive him to action. "Time is important, people. I know you two aren't used to this like I am. But you can do a whole lot more with your neighbors than I can."

"We go door to door," Jonathan said. "We ask if anyone has seen Noam. That's all?"

Decker said, "Use your eyes. If anyone suddenly turns red, buries his face, stutters, shakes, looks like he's hiding something—remember it and report back to me. There were a couple of kids that looked hinky to me when Ezra and I were out the first time. I'll go back and question them. But first I want to comb the area by car."

"Want me to come with you?" Jonathan asked. "I'll drive so you can look."

"You must think it's very serious to break *yom tov*," Shimon said to Decker.

Decker didn't answer. Instead, he told Jonathan that he could look around by himself. He instructed the two brothers to go together. One should do the talking, the other should study the faces.

"And look at the adults, too," Decker said. "Hate to say this but you can't rule out molestation—"

"Not here," Shimon said.

"It's everywhere," Decker said.

"No, you don't know Boro Park," Shimon insisted.

Decker put his big hand on Shimon's shoulder. "Okay. Have it your way. And I hope you're right. Just do me the favor and take a look at the adults."

"I'll keep my eyes open," Jonathan said.

"Do it that way," Decker said. "Shimon, you do the talking—you're more a part of the community. Jonathan, you observe." He paused to catch his breath. "Also, I'm very concerned about your mother, brother, and sister-in-law. Shimon, have your wife and sisters stay with Breina. Best thing to do with Ezra might be to send him to shul—keep his mind off of what's going on and make him feel like he's doing something—"

"*Tephila is* doing something," Shimon interrupted. "Praying to Hashem is the single most important thing he could do right now!"

No one spoke for a moment.

"You know what he means—Shimmy," Jonathan said.

Shimon let out a deep breath. He said, "Yes, I know, I know . . . I'm sorry. Go on."

Decker threw his arm around his shoulder. "That's it. Hey, things like this do happen all the time. Kids stay away for a day, drive their parents completely nuts. Then they come sneaking in at two in the morning and wonder why everyone's so upset. Your brother and sister-in-law are the ones who'll need support until this thing is resolved."

"These kind of things get resolved?" Jonathan asked.

"All the time," Decker said.

"*Eem yirtzah Hashem*," Shimon said.

"God willing," Jonathan repeated.

Eyes swollen and red, Ezra came back clutching a photo, then handed it reluctantly to Decker, as if parting with it was tantamount to the loss of his son. As he did with all missing-persons photographs, Decker studied it as if it were text.

Noam Levine was a mature-looking boy, posed with a very cocky smile. He had a lean face, square chin made nappy by peach fuzz, strong cheekbones, a petulant mouth with thick lips. He had his father's dark complexion, his mother's bright blue eyes. There was something off about his expression. Decker stared at the photo until it hit him. Noam's mouth was smiling, but his eyes were troubled.

"How tall is he?" Decker asked Ezra.

"Big for his age," Ezra said. "Five seven or eight. Part of the problem. He always thinks he knows more than anyone else—" He stopped himself. "What am I saying?"

Decker weighed the possibilities, leaning toward the theory that Noam's disappearance was a voluntary decision. Big, burly boys usually don't get snatched—too strong, too much struggle. A child molester is an opportunistic beast. Steal the ones that go the quietest. The plus was that runaways were easier to find than kidnapped children. And there was the teenager's arrogant smirk. Boy seemed like a survivor.

But he was still a child—a sheltered one at that. The streets of New York City could easily turn an impulsive adventure trip into a horror story.

Decker pocketed the picture. To Ezra, he said, "I want to talk to your children first."

"Why?" Ezra said. "I told you they don't know anything."

"I'm sure you're right," Decker said. "It's just the way I was trained—"

"If they say they don't know anything, they don't know anything."

"Ezra," Shimon said, "let him talk to the kids. What could it hurt?"

"And I'd also like to look at Noam's room," Decker said.

"Look at his room?" Ezra said. His voice was full of suspicion. "Why? What do you think you're going to find?"

"Ezra," Shimon said, "just let him do it." To Decker, he said, "Aaron, my oldest nephew, has a key. He'll take you to the house."

"I can take him to the house," Ezra protested.

Jonathan put his arm around his brother. "Let's go to shul, Ezra. We'll walk you there. Afterward, we can learn a little."

"Learn with *you*?" Ezra said.

"Learn with me," Jonathan said. "What are you doing now? *Masechet Sukkot?* It's a *masechet* I know pretty well."

"We'll all learn together," Shimon said. "Come, Ezra." He put his arm around Ezra's waist. "Come."

Decker watched as Shimon and Jonathan gently guided Ezra out the door.

Three of the same blood.

Three brothers.

9

The children had segregated themselves—the boys in one room, the girls in another. Eleven boys, eight girls—the Levines were a fecund bunch.

Decker started with the girls. Ranging in age from three to fourteen, they sat in little groups, whispering and giggling. Because the preschoolers were so young and shy, many having just a rudimentary grasp of English, he decided to concentrate on the older ones—three cousins aged seven, eight, and fourteen, and Noam's eleven-year-old sister, Tamar. They were still dressed in their holiday clothing, full of lace and velvet and ornamented with jewelry—pearl earrings, gold chains, thin bracelets or watches. The oldest, Shimon's daughter, wore a string of pearls. She also had on heeled shoes and a touch of lipstick.

They knew what was going on—their cousin or brother was missing. It was their job to help Decker find him. They seemed nervous and excited, but not unduly scared. It was as if Noam's disappearance was viewed as a tricky math problem waiting to be solved.

As they talked further, Decker realized that to them, Noam was an enigma—a loner, a strange boy with creepy eyes. Even Noam's sister viewed him with trepidation. A very strange reaction. Most sisters might view a brother as an object of hatred or jealousy. But a brother was not usually feared.

It was clear that the girls had kept their distance from Noam. But that didn't stop them from throwing out suggestions as to where he might be. Most of the proposals were exotic and off the wall—akin to Noam's running off and joining the circus.

Their offerings might have been wonderful projective tests, but Decker didn't feel they gave a clue to the boy's location. He thanked the young ladies for their time.

The boys were holed up in a guest bedroom that was hot and stuffy from sweat and hormones. The younger kids were running around, crashing into the twin beds and the walls. Five older ones had taken out a Talmud and were learning in the corner. All wore black hats and had their hair cut Marine short, which drew Decker's attention to their ears. Some were big, some flat, some had banjo lobes, some stuck out like Alfred E. Newman's. As he approached the group, one of the older boys put down the volume of Talmud and looked up. He had blue eyes, soft skin, also with a hint of peach fuzz. His features were those of Noam Levine, but softer, more rounded. He appeared to be around fifteen.

"Hi," Decker said. "Aaron Levine?"

The teenager nodded.

"Your uncle Jonathan said you have a key to your

house," Decker said. "I want to look through Noam's room."

Again, Aaron nodded.

"Does he have his own room?" Decker asked.

"He shares with me and Boruch."

Aaron's eyes fell upon his younger brother. Boruch was around twelve. There was a definite family look—smooth skin, blue eyes, good jawline, dark hair. All of them resembling Breina. But Noam, at least from the photograph, projected a huskier build.

Decker told the brothers to hang on a moment and questioned the cousins first. The boys were polite and cooperative, anxious to help. The oldest one was Shimon's son. He was Aaron's age—almost sixteen—and didn't have much to do with Noam. The other two also kept their distance. They all explained that their cousin was prone to wandering off by himself, but they seemed genuinely puzzled by his disappearance on Rosh Hashanah. That was not like him. After five minutes more of questioning, Decker felt they really didn't know anything and let them go.

Then he concentrated on Noam's brothers. Both Aaron and Boruch seemed nervous.

Decker said, "Any ideas where your brother might be?"

The boys shrugged ignorance.

"You must have some thoughts about it," Decker pressed.

"Noam keeps to himself. He's . . ." Aaron squirmed. "*Lashon harah.*"

Lashon harah—gossip. Disreputable in any society

but a grave sin in Jewish Law. Decker said, "Aaron, *if* Noam is missing, I need to know everything about him. Including the incidents that make him look bad."

"It's nothing like that," Aaron said. His voice cracked. A faint blush rose in his cheeks. "It's just . . . Noam has a hard time fitting in. And he can be pretty obnoxious about it sometimes. It's like he's either off by himself or bothering me or my friends." The teenager adjusted his hat. "Then . . . out of the blue, he'll be the nicest person in the world for about a week. Do all your chores for you, straighten up your clothes, just be real . . . nice. But it never lasts long. I can't figure him out. Honestly, I've given up trying."

Boruch was nodding in agreement.

Decker said, "That sound about right to you?"

"Yes, sir," Boruch said. "Noam's always the one who remembers the birthdays, more than Abba and Eema do. But most of the time, he either ignores me or beats me up." He paused, clearly upset. "Is he in trouble?"

Decker said, "I don't know, Boruch." He smiled reassuringly. It was the best he could offer the boy. "Does Noam have any hobbies—baseball-card collecting, stamp collecting? Is he into cars or hot rods?"

The boys shook their heads.

"Does he spend a lot of time riding his bike, playing sports, skateboarding—"

The boys laughed.

"Skateboarding not too big around here?"

"No," they said in unison.

"Does he play a lot of sports?"

"Not that I know of," Aaron said.

"Then if he doesn't play or learn a lot," Decker said, "if he doesn't have any hobbies, what does he do with his time?"

Boruch said, "He spends lots of time with the computer."

"Games?" Decker asked.

Boruch said, "We don't own any computer games. We use it for school, for our reports. We have a *Gemara* program that asks us questions. It's really neat."

"Noam use that program?" Decker asked.

Both shook their heads no. No latency of response.

"Could you play games on the computer if you wanted to?" Decker asked.

Aaron said, "No. It doesn't have a graphics card. Unless Noam's put one in there. I don't think he knows enough about computers to do that. You have to know where to put it. Then you have to reset the dipswitches. Noam can't program. I can't see him tinkering with the hardware."

Boruch added, "He has trouble just using canned software."

"Then what does he do with the computer?" Decker asked.

Aaron said, "I think he writes stuff. I once tried to look at what he was doing, but he hid the monitor with his arms."

"Yeah, he does that to me, too."

"Is Noam a good student?" Decker asked.

"Not really," Aaron said. "He's sort of . . . well, lazy."

"You boys have no idea where he wanders off to?"

Again, they shook their heads.

Aaron said, "He has a few friends. They might know better than us."

Decker said, "I'll ask them a little later. First, how about we take a walk over to your house?"

The boys said sure.

Nice kids, Decker thought. Breina and Ezra must be doing something right.

Up until yesterday, the pain had only surfaced on his birthday. Now it was an open wound festering inside Frieda Levine's shattered heart. None of this would ever resolve until she made peace with the one she had abandoned.

God was giving her a test, using His most precious gifts to her. Though all her grandchildren were special, Noam was her most cherished because he had always been so troubled. In the many hours they had spent together, Noam seldom talked. But oh, how he'd been captivated by her tales, entranced by the criminal cases that had passed over her desk in the years she had worked at the court.

Hours of talking her throat dry, with him staring with those mystical eyes, drinking in her every word. Communicating without speaking, saying to her: *So this is what the goyishe world is like.*

Noam never asked questions, even when they were begging to be asked. Frieda felt he wasn't very bright. But unlike Ezra, who also wasn't bright, Noam never had the determination to overcompensate.

She and Noam hadn't talked like that in four or five years, yet she remembered those conversations as if they had taken place yesterday.

Then he had stopped coming to her.

She thought nothing of it. There is that aching point in every grandmother's life when the grandchildren cease to look at her as fun and simply view her as an old lady. It was normal.

But it hurt a little more with Noam—his rejection had been so sudden, so complete. As the others grew, they still made periodic stabs at being interested in her, inquiring about her health, pinching her cheek, complimenting her baking skills.

Your cookies are the best, Bubbe.

But Noam had withdrawn without looking back.

Still, she couldn't take it personally. Noam was retreating from everyone. She should have seen it for what it was, a sign of deep-seated trouble. But having been accustomed to burying grief, she had looked the other way.

Now she was encountering both of her mistakes head-on. As she lay in her darkened bedroom, shades tightly drawn, tears skiing down her cheeks, she realized that she could no longer be an ostrich. She must right what had been wronged years ago.

But first she must wait until Noam was found.

If he was ever found.

The thought gave her chills.

He would do it. Her firstborn—brought to her by

God. If it was meant, if it was *basheert*, it would be *he* who would save Noam. God had deemed it so. She felt this as surely as she had felt his little feet kicking in her womb. As surely as she had seen his face emerge from her body, a head full of bright orange hair, cheeks sunburn red, his head misshapen and bruised from a long and painful labor.

The doctors had considered taking him out by cesarean. But her father had remained steadfast that she deliver normally. A cesarean would have left a scar, a telltale sign to her future husband that he had not been the first.

At the last minute, *he* had saved her, had come out on his own. His downy soft body molded with muscle even at birth—long limbs, big barrel chest. Nine pounds, twenty-three inches. But what she had remembered most was his temperament. He never cried—only let out small whimpers to remind everyone that he was a healthy newborn. The doctor even remarked upon it.

Big guy seems pretty happy.

Frieda heard deep soft sobs. She thought it might be Breina in the next room and she should go and comfort her daughter-in-law. Then she realized that the sounds were coming from her own throat.

Ezra's three sons shared a room that was cramped but meticulously neat. The beds were made, the closet was organized; even the computer and work area were free from clutter. Decker asked the boys' secret to keeping a clean desk.

Boruch let out a breathy *Eeee*ma.

But there was a note of affection in his voice.

All three headboards touched the same wall, lined up like a hospital ward. Sheets tucked in, the pillows plumped and rolled under the top cover like the stuffings of an omelet. Above the headboards were three rows of bookshelves. Most of the space was devoted to Hebrew and religious books, but there were about a dozen textbooks of secular study. No posters or art work adorned the wall, the sole exception being a framed picture of a small elderly bearded man in a big black hat. He had a round face, scores of wrinkles, and crinkly eyes that exuded a physical warmth.

"Rav Moshe Feinstein, *alav hashalom*," Aaron said.

Decker nodded, recognizing the name. Rabbi Feinstein had been the leading Torah scholar of his day, a man noted for his exceptional kindness as well as his genius mind.

He turned away from the picture. The boys were sitting on their beds. He said, "I'll try to put everything back the way I found it, but I'm going to have to go through all the belongings."

The brothers nodded understandingly.

Decker said, "In the meantime, I want one of you to turn on the computer and bring up any files that might be Noam's."

The boys didn't move. Aaron said, "Did you discuss this with my father?"

Decker sighed. "Look, I know you're not allowed to use computers on *yom tov*, but this is an emergency. If you don't want to do it, at least tell me how to do it."

"No, no," Aaron said. "I'd be making you do an *aveyrah*. Boruch, you do it. You haven't been bar mitzvahed yet."

"It's okay?" Boruch asked Decker.

"It's more than okay; it's very important."

"Then I'll do it," Boruch said.

Decker began with the desk. Because it was so organized, the search would be a snap. Starting on the right, he opened the top drawer. It contained notebooks of math work; the second was full of lessons in other secular subjects. The bottom drawer contained sheaves of papers written in Hebrew. The left side was a carbon copy of the first. Inside the top middle drawer were office supplies—pens, pencils, rulers, a stapler, a box of rubber bands, a box of paper clips.

So much for the desk.

Boruch announced that there weren't any files of Noam's on the first disk. He'd try the others. Decker told him he was doing a great job, and went on to the closet.

It was as organized as the desk. Decker thought a moment. For a room housing three teenaged boys to be this compulsively tidy, Breina must be one stern taskmaster. He remarked upon that and gauged the reaction of the boys. They smiled, didn't appear to be resentful.

The left side was open shelves containing piles of laundered and starched white shirts. Must have been around twenty of them. The hanging rack held pressed black pants, lint-free black suit jackets. Above the rack was a shelf full of black hats. The right side was more open shelving. Underwear, undershirts, socks, and a couple of dozen *talitim k'tanim*—small prayer shawls worn on top of the undershirt but under the dress shirt. A belt and tie rack bisected the inside of the door. Above the rack was a small square mirror.

"What size is Noam?" Decker asked.

"Shirt or pants?" Aaron asked.

"Both."

"We wear the same shirt size," Aaron said. "Men's fifteen. Pants, I wear a thirty. I think Noam's closer to a thirty-one or -two."

"He's heavier than you?"

Aaron said, "Heavier and taller."

Boruch looked up from the computer screen. "I tried all of the disks here, brought up the files. I don't see anything that looks like his stuff. Either Noam has his own disk or he erased everything he ever wrote."

"Thanks, Boruch," Decker said. "It was worth a try."

Boruch turned off the screen.

Decker said, "You wouldn't notice if any of his clothes were missing, would you?"

The boys peered into the closet.

Aaron said, "It looks about as full as it always does. But he could take a shirt and pair of pants and I wouldn't notice."

On the floor of the closet were the boys' knapsacks. Decker opened Noam's first. Just books and school supplies. His papers contained no doodling, no names of girls. Decker asked the boys if he could look inside their knapsacks. Both of them said sure. Their cooperation showed him that the boys had nothing to hide. He took a quick peek, then moved on.

He stripped the beds. Finding nothing, he removed the mattresses, checked all three out individually. Still nothing. Then he removed the box spring. Underneath Noam's bed was a sales slip— slightly faded pink, dated ten months ago. Someone had purchased a Guns 'n' Roses T-shirt for fifteen fifty. He asked the boys if Noam ever wore the T-shirt when the folks weren't home.

"I never saw him wearing any T-shirt with a gun or a rose on it," Aaron said.

Decker said, "Guns 'n' Roses is a rock group."

Aaron shrugged ignorance.

"How about you?" he asked Boruch. Sometimes kids confide more easily in younger siblings than in older ones.

Boruch said, "I never saw him wear any T-shirt except as undershirts for our *tzitzit*." He thought a moment. "You know we have this old transistor radio. I think Noam listens to it late at night when he thinks we're asleep."

"I never heard anything," Aaron said.

"I think he uses the earphone," Boruch said. "We can listen to the radio as long as we've finished our studies and it's news or sports. Abba and I are Knicks fans. Rock music is out of course. But some of the kids at school listen to it anyway. They even watch MTV—go down to the electronic stores and watch the television on display. It's a hard thing to do because most of the stores are owned by *frum yiddin* and the kids don't want anything getting back to their parents, you know."

"You'd like a TV?" Decker asked.

"Nah," Boruch said. "Turns your brain to rot."

Decker smiled. The way the kid said it—just a line he'd picked up somewhere.

"Maybe that's what he does when he wanders off," Aaron said. "Walks around Prospect Park listening to rock music."

Decker thought: Noam sneaking off, maybe wearing his Guns 'n' Roses T-shirt under his traditional garb. When he was alone, like Clark Kent turning into Superman, he'd pull off his regular shirt, untuck his T-shirt, and blast his pathetic little radio.

Trying to hang out, trying to fit in.

But always looking over his shoulder, making sure no one would see him.

Decker put back the box springs and mattresses. He re-made the beds, then checked the pillows. He unzipped a slipcover and felt a hard flat surface about the size of a playing card. He thought it was probably a calculator, but it turned out to be a miniature Nintendo game—Octopus. Sammy had the same game. The idea was to score as many points as you could before a tentacle squeezed you to death. He showed it to the brothers.

Boruch said, "Some of the kids at school have them. Hey, wait. Doesn't Shmuli have this game?"

Decker nodded.

"He's lucky." Boruch looked at Decker with longing. "Abba won't let me buy one, even with my own money. Says it's a waste . . . which I guess it is."

For the first time, resentment had crept into the boy's voice.

"But if a friend brings them over," Boruch went on, "like when Shmuli brings it over? Abba'll let me play with it. As long as I've finished my schoolwork."

Decker said, "So your abba doesn't know that Noam has this."

"Definitely not," Aaron said. "Abba's pretty strict on what we can have. But it's not like he doesn't like us to have fun. If we have free time, he likes us to get exercise. We have basketballs, baseballs, footballs. He even plays with us sometimes. Especially basketball."

Slightly defensive tone. Decker said, "Well, with all you boys you must have quite a team. Noam join along?"

"Sometimes," Boruch said.

"You know, Noam's a little taller than me and all," Aaron said. "But he's not real coordinated. He's slow."

"He also has trouble keeping his mind on the game," Boruch said. "I'd pass him the ball and it's like he'd be on Mars. The basketball would bounce off his chest. Lucky he's so big; otherwise he'd be knocked down all the time. He doesn't play with us too much anymore. Guess it isn't fun for him."

"Guess not," Decker said, thinking of his own youth. Always a head taller than anyone else, he was a natural choice for center. But like Noam, he also had *weight*. Lumbering across the court, it was especially embarrassing because everyone *expected* him to be so good. Agility was never his forte. He gave up basketball in his freshman year of high school, moved on to football. Made State All Star six months later. All he had to do was mow over the opposition—a piece of cake. At the age of sixteen, he'd been six two, one eighty-five.

He pocketed the Nintendo game. If Noam had run away, why had he taken his T-shirt but not this portable video game? Surely he didn't forget it.

Decker thought about it for a moment.

Maybe the kid was subconsciously leaving behind clues.

Even if that wasn't the reason, the game served the same purpose as if it had been left behind intentionally. Now Decker knew that Noam liked rock and roll and played arcade games. The shirt and the game indicated places to search.

Decker said, "I can walk you guys back to your bubbe's now."

Boruch stood, but Aaron didn't move. Decker asked him what was wrong.

"I'm worried," Aaron said. "I'm not worried like somebody kidnapped Noam. But I'm worried that he did something stupid and now he's in some kind of trouble. He wouldn't just not show up, unless he was in trouble."

Decker didn't answer.

"The way I talked about Noam," Aaron said. "It sounds like I don't care. But I do."

"Of course you do." Decker put his hand on Aaron's shoulder. "I know you love him. Both of you do."

Aaron sighed. "He's still my brother. . . ."

"You gonna find him?" Boruch asked.

"I'm going to do my best," Decker said. But there was a queasy feeling in his gut as he spit out the words.

He walked both of the boys back, then stopped by the Lazarus house to pick up his piece.

The sun was setting. Though he didn't know Brooklyn, he knew it contained some mean areas. He had no intention of searching for Noam in a ghetto, but there was always the possibility of getting lost. Along with his Beretta, he'd taken four clips, sixteen rounds apiece. That should hold him nicely.

❧ 10

Number-one item on the agenda: Get a good street map.

Though the sidewalks of Boro Park were populated with Jews walking home from synagogue, the streets were nearly empty—few cars, all businesses shut down for the holidays. Decker took off his yarmulke, put the photograph of Noam Levine on the seat next to him, and took off, searching for an open service station.

He found one about a half mile down, filled the tank with gas—Jonathan had left the car bone dry—and paid two seventy-five for a map of Brooklyn. He asked the gas station attendant or maybe it was the owner—the man was about fifty with a pot belly and white hair—exactly where he was. The older man scrunched watery blue eyes and answered,

"What do you mean where are you?"

It came out: *Whaddeyeh mean wheh arh youse?*

"You're in Brooklyn—Boro Park."

Boro Park was *Burrow Park.*

"This is still Boro Park?" Decker asked.

The attendant said, "You lost or something? Give me the numbers, I'll tell you how to get there."

Decker said, "So Boro Park isn't all Jewish?"

"Well, most of it is Jewish. You lookin' for the Jewish part?"

"No, I just came from the Jewish part," Decker said.

The attendant said, "Funny, you don't look Jewish." He spasmed with laughter at his joke.

Decker waited for the man to finish, then asked, "If this isn't Jewish Boro Park, what part is this?"

"Here you got your basic working Eyetalians, a few Puerto Ricans and Asians." The man hooked a thumb over his shoulder. "You go that way—that's east—you got Bay Ridge, your basic Eyetalians also. You go south, that's Bensonhurst. What you got there is rich Eyetalians. You got relatives in Bensonhurst, *no one's* gonna mess with you, hear what I'm sayin'?"

Decker said yes.

The attendant said, "You go west, you got Flatbush. Keep goin' west, well, you don't wanna go there, that ain't good for nuttin'. You go north you eventually gonna hit Williamsburg. That's them religious Jews again and lots of Puerto Ricans. We got every type of person, place, or thing here. Lots of *things*, let me tell you. What are you lookin' for?"

Decker handed him the picture of Noam Levine. The attendant gave the photo a cursory glance, then handed it back to Decker.

"Never seen the kid," he said. "Not that I'd know him if he was staring me straight in the eye. All those boys look alike to me with their Shirley Temple curls. Why would they want to do that to their boys, take the chance of turnin' them into fags or something."

Decker gave a noncommittal shrug. He remembered the talkative taxi driver saying that Flatbush was the main thoroughfare through Brooklyn. He asked for directions to Flatbush Avenue. He had addresses of a few arcades and movie theaters. But before he checked them out, he wanted to get a cursory feel for the city. Riding at night, alone . . . it helped him think.

Dusk had just about turned to night, Flatbush Avenue darkening, fading into sinister loneliness. Neons and shadows characterized the street. Every mile or so, Decker spotted groups of ski-hatted youths, convening in cloistered areas, bouncing on their feet, rubbing fingerless weight-lifting gloves together. Like cockroaches they sank deeper into their crevices whenever too many headlights illuminated the spot. Off the side streets were pods of homeless camped out in corners, warming their hands over trash-can fires.

As he'd done so many times before, Decker tried to place himself inside the mind and body of his quarry. This one was a fourteen-year-old boy with an ultra-religious background. If Noam was a runaway, Decker supposed part of the kid's motivation was excitement. In a routinized world such as Boro Park, earthly sins were mighty tempting dishes.

But there was more to it than that. The interviews had painted a picture of an angry, lost boy. By running away, Noam was trying to find himself, emphasizing his schism with the community by leaving on Rosh Hashanah. An act of defiance, an act of hostility.

Noam was big physically, maybe considered a

tough one in Boro Park, but he wasn't streetwise. He would eventually fold on foreign sod. That meant, if he stayed away long enough he'd probably do something stupid—commit a minor crime such as shoplifting and get caught. The act had a two-fold purpose. It was protective—sitting in a police station was safer than being mugged in a back alley— and getting arrested would get his parents' attention.

Running away on Rosh Hashanah. Talk about spitting in your parents' faces. The only other day that would have elicited greater outrage would have been the Day of Atonement—Yom Kippur. All sins against God and Man were washed away on Judaism's most holy of days. The soul cleansed of all its contaminants—but only if there was *true* repentance.

Maybe Noam hoped to be back home by Yom Kippur so he could repent. The trick was to find him before he self-destructed or before someone destroyed him.

As Decker headed north, the neighborhood deteriorated even further, not the kind of place where a white teenager would take refuge.

He pulled to the curb and spread the map over the seat of the car, planning his route of attack. A moment later, he heard a heavy thump on his car door. Jerking his head up, he saw three dark-skinned youths, one of them mouthing the words "Need help?" through the locked window. Decker pulled out his Beretta and laid it on his lap. He smiled, winked, and mouthed back a "No, thank you." The young man gave him a palms out "no-problem, man" gesture; then the three backed away, doing a fade-out into blackness.

Decker sat a moment, lit a cigarette. Doing crap like this on his honeymoon, the whole situation drawing him deeper into the Levine family—a friggin mess! He jammed his unloaded Beretta into his waistband, started the car, and headed south.

Through a series of turns, he found himself in friendlier territory. Not that the area was beautiful—this would be considered a down-scale neighborhood by L.A. standards—but at least the buildings weren't gutted.

Working-class white.

Probably your basic Eyetalians.

Time to get down to specifics.

Along Ocean Parkway, he found his first stop on the list: SID'S ARCADE—MINORS WELCOME. As good a place to start as any. He parked Jonathan's Matador, stretched, then walked over. On the door was a hand-printed sign stating no smoking, food, or drink allowed on the premises.

He went inside.

The arcade was dark and it took a few moments for Decker's eyes to adjust. But the assault on his ears was immediate. Bings, bangs, bongs, whistles, screeches, low-pitched wails—a cacophony created by bits and bytes. His pupils finally dilated and he was immersed in flashing lights in Day-Glo colors. The place was twenty by sixty, the walls lined with arcade machines and bisected by two rows standing back to back. At the rear were the cashier's kiosk and a half-dozen enclosed booths containing simulated consoles of spacecraft, race cars, and submarines. There were also a couple of air-hockey boards.

Decker could hear the steady chock, chock, chock of the puck caroming off the walls. Fantasyland—where a lonely kid could be something for a couple of hours.

He soon saw that two categories of adolescents populated the arcade. The Dungeons and Dragons set featuring wispy mustaches, unwashed hair, pencils in shirt pockets, and glasses with taped nosepieces. Then there were the super-coolers with slicked-back hair—also unwashed—clad in leather and denim adorned by metal chains. The D&D'ers played the machines with class, expending energy and sweat only when the heat was on. The wiseguys, on the other hand, banged on their buttons at frenetic speed, muttering constant obscenities regardless of the outcome of the game:

"I was fuckin *robbed*, man."

Or

"I was fuckin *hot*, man."

He glanced to his right. A monitor exploded into a thousand pinpoints of light. An electronic rendition of the *Star Wars* theme tooted out. That was drowned out by the chuck, chuck, pops of Centipede, the pops turning to rapid machine-gun fire as the target worm parts were blasted to oblivion.

Onward and upward.

Decker showed the picture around—first to the brainiacs, next to the leather set. The results were the same. Nobody had ever seen Noam Levine. Decker realized the snapshot was probably misleading. If Noam had fled to the outside world, the first thing he'd do was change his appearance. But he tried anyway, asking people to make allowances for the ethnic dress, saying Noam might be wearing a Guns 'n' Roses T-shirt.

Still no luck.

After meeting with rejection, he tapped a D&D'er on the shoulder and asked if he could speak with him for a few minutes. The boy he'd chosen was a lanky pimply-faced teen with glasses and very straight teeth—an ortho job that had taken four thousand buckeroos out of Dad's paycheck. The lanky kid looked at Decker suspiciously.

"What do you want?" he asked.

"I want to ask your opinion about something."

The boy's eyes went to Decker, then to his friends, then back to Decker. A slow smile spread over his lips. He said, "My opinion will cost you."

Decker said, "I'm a cop."

"Just kidding," the kid announced.

"Thought so," Decker said.

The lanky boy said, "How can I help you, Officer? As I stated before, I don't know the boy in the picture. But I'll be happy to assist you in any way."

Playful mockery in the kid's eyes—an Eddie Haskell gleam.

A low-pitched trombone slide culminated in a foghorn blare. That was followed by a human voice uttering a staccato "Shit."

Decker started to speak, then he smiled and asked, "First, where exactly am I?"

Another boy broke into the conversation. He was around fifteen, not exactly fat but soft around the middle, with a double chin. He said, "You mean in metaphysical terms or simple physical location?"

Decker said, "I know I'm in Brooklyn south. What do you call this part of town?"

The lanky kid said, "If you're a cop, how come you don't know where you are?"

"I'm with the Los Angeles Police Department," Decker said.

"That kid you're looking for is from Los Angeles?" the lanky kid said.

"No," Decker said. "He's from Boro Park. Am I in Boro Park?"

"Sheepshead Bay," said the soft kid.

"You don't look like a Boro Parker," said the lanky kid. "You don't even look Jewish."

"Are you Jewish?" Decker asked the lanky boy.

"We go to temple once a year on Yom Kippur for half a day," the boy answered. "Does that qualify me to be an MOT?"

MOT—member of the tribe.

"Fine by me, kiddo," Decker said.

A loud snap of a handclap.

"All right," a voice shouted out. "All right! All right! All right!"

"That's Marc," the soft kid said. "He must've finally rescued Zelda."

"Way to go Marc," Decker said. "Let me ask you guys something. Suppose you wanted to run away from home. Where would you crash for the night?"

"Depends whether you're a meaner or a beaner," the lanky boy said.

"You want to run the lexicon by me?" Decker said.

"A meaner is one of them," the first boy said, pointing to the wiseguys. "A beaner is one of us."

"A beaner not meaning a spic," the soft boy explained. "It comes from the word *bean*—meaning head, as in cerebrum."

The first boy explained, "Now, in answer to your question, because the outcome is totally dependent upon the input, you have to decide which of the characteristics best exemplifies your missing kid."

The soft boy said, "We get the Chasids in the arcades."

"You do?" Decker said.

"Not a lot," the lanky kid said. "But some. They break down into two types—those who are just like us only they're wearing black and have the side curls, and those I'd categorize as beaners wishing to be meaners. See, *we* have no desire to mix with those other species. But a few of the real religious kids would like to rebel. They *want* to be like tough guys."

"But they're too scared," the soft boy said.

"So they hang around us," the lanky boy said. "And they're real pains in the asses, because they give us a hard time—say stupid things that they think are put-downs."

The soft boy said, "Which category does your kid fall under?"

Decker said, "Probably the latter."

The lanky boy took out a tissue and blew his nose. "I'll bet he's at one of the arcades now, trying to mix with the meaners. These places are pretty safe. Good ones like this have bouncers; they don't like trouble."

"Or," the soft boy said, "there're a bunch of all-night movie houses. If the kid could pass for seventeen, he could be sleeping in the balcony of the Cresta right now."

Decker took out his sheet of paper and showed the kids the addresses. "Any of these places look like possibilities?"

The lanky boy studied the street numbers. "You used an old phone book, didn't you?"

Decker didn't answer. Instead, he opened his wallet and waved two five-dollar bills in front of their faces. He said, "Think you can get me some current addresses of safe late-night establishments the kid might go to?"

The boys looked at each other. They smiled, then each of them pulled out a wad of bills as thick as a sodden sponge. The soft boy said, "Could always use a few more bucks. You got the pencil and paper, I got the addresses."

Decker took the bills from one of the boys, snapped them between his fingers—not just ones, they were tens and twenties. "Where does a kid like you get so much money?"

The lanky boy laughed. "Teaching meaners remedial math for *Papa e Mama*, so that sonny boya would finisha uppa de high school."

"A truly lost cause," the soft boy said.

"But I'll tell you something," the lanky boy said. "They can be taught. But you have to change your terminology."

"Phrase everything in terms of getting laid," the soft boy said. "If Tony got laid six times in a day and Ernie got laid fifty percent more times than Tony, how many times did Ernie get laid?"

"The answer?" The lanky boy held his crotch and said, "'Six fuckin' times a day? Dafuck is Tony's *secret?*'"

The two boys cracked up.

"The addresses, boys?" Decker said.

"Sure," the lanky kid said. "I love to help a man with a mission."

After five hours of searching the streets, combing movie houses, discos, arcades, and finally the shelters, Decker was left with a giant goose egg. He called it quits at half past midnight and checked in with Jonathan and Shimon. Their door-to-door hadn't yielded anything of significance. Jonathan reported that some of the boys Noam's age had seemed uncomfortable as Shimon talked to the parents. Not trusting his memory, Jonathan wrote down the names and addresses—again infracting the religious law. But this was clearly a case of *pekuah nefesh*—the saving of life taking precedence over almost everything.

The Levines were all up and beside themselves with worry. Decker and Frieda Levine exchanged quick glances. Her eyes were red, her hands made raw by her own kneading fingers. The look in her eye had been nothing more than a fleeting moment, but, ah—what her expression had told him.

Please, help us, help *me*.

Where was *her* help when he needed her forty-one years ago?

But his heart couldn't hold any anger—not at this time. He turned to the rest of the family and suggested they try to bed down as best they could. In the morning, Decker would talk to the kids. The next step right now would be to talk to the police and file the missing-persons report. The family wanted to come down with him, but Decker said no, it was better handled cop to cop. All he needed was a good clear picture of Noam, his physical stats, and what he'd been wearing when he disappeared.

Before he left for the police, he pulled Rina aside.

"You want me to walk you back to the Lazaruses' house?"

"No," she said. "I'll wait here for you." She brushed strands of limp red hair off his forehead. "You look exhausted."

Decker smiled. "I'd be lying if I said I was spunky."

"You're a godsend. That's what Mrs. Levine said. You were sent here by Hashem."

"She said that, huh?"

Rina nodded.

"Everything is in the hands of God," Decker said. "That's a neat, compact way of dealing with your guilt."

"Oh, Peter—"

"That was stupid." He exhaled forcefully. "I really do feel sorry for her. For her, for the parents. It's hell, no doubt about it."

"I know you care," she answered. "I know that's why you're doing what you're doing. And don't think the family isn't grateful. That's all they talk about— how fortunate they are to have someone like you at a time like this—"

"Rina—"

"They *are* fortunate." She kissed him lightly on the lips. "Everyone has confidence in you—"

"Yeah, we've got a slight problem with that," Decker said. "I'm in an uncomfortable position here. Depending on how this thing resolves, I'll either be a savior or a bum, and neither of those hats wears well with me. If we don't get anywhere by tomorrow, I'm going to recommend that Ezra and Breina hire a professional—"

"You're a professional."

"I've got a very demanding day job. I'm not interested in doing unpaid moonlighting."

Rina didn't say anything.

"I didn't mean it like that," Decker said. "I don't care about the money—"

"I know you don't."

"I don't want the responsibility, Rina," Decker said. "The whole situation is just too damn close to home. If it were my kid, I'd hire out. A good PI agency has networks all over the country, honey. They've got the interdepartmental contacts, the best skip tracers, and the *manpower*. They can cover more in a day than I could in a month."

Rina said, "Ezra's not a rich man. The only thing of value he owns is the house. How much do these agencies cost?"

That gave Decker a moment of pause. "If they find the kid quickly, it's not that bad. And the good ones usually find them fast."

"And if they don't?" Rina said.

Decker sighed. "I'll do what I can until the holiday is over. Then I want out. I'll find the family the best PI available. One that *knows* the city of New York. Hey, if it was L.A., maybe I'd take another day or two. But I'm a foreigner here, Rina."

"Whatever you want, Peter."

Her voice was glum. Decker said, "You think I should do more?"

Rina sighed. "No . . . No, of course not. It's just that . . . well . . ."

"What?" Decker said. "What? *What?*"

"I just know that . . ." Rina sighed again. "If it were Sammy or Jakey, I'd want you to handle it."

"But *I* wouldn't handle it if it were Sammy or Jakey. That's what I'm *telling* you. I'm just one person and that's a big problem. Plus, you don't take on cases where there's personal involvement."

He realized he was shouting and dropped his voice to a whisper.

"This is what I call a swell honeymoon. First, I come out here, sentenced to be a weak substitute for your late husband—"

"That's not—"

"Yeah, right. It's not true. They love me for my hair color."

"Peter—"

"I'm not saying anything against the Lazarus clan. Your former in-laws happen to be nice people. But look at it from my perspective, my background, then tell me I should feel right at home."

Rina lowered her eyes. "I know it's hard."

"Damn right it's hard. But I can handle it. And if I may say so myself, I was doing a fine job of adjusting until I got my long lost *mother* slapped in my face. I'm still reeling from *that* blow and *this* nightmare pops up. And now I'm supposed to be the objective, third-party professional. *For chrissakes*, Rina, the kid is my blood-nephew. I have a tangle of emotions inside me that's going to take years to unravel. What do you *want* from me?"

"Oh, Peter!" Rina hugged him as tightly as she could. "I'm sorry!" She burst into tears. "I'm sorry!"

"Forget it," Decker said, hugging her back. "I'm sorry, too. Part of me wants to walk away from this mess. And the other part is yelling at me to do more. And I'm not getting anywhere, which makes me feel like a failure. I've got plenty invested in this. I'm a juvey cop; I've located hundreds of missing kids. *I*, of all people, should be able to get somewhere." He paused a moment. "Fuck this noise." Then he said, "Pardon my Hebrew."

Rina smiled, kept him locked in her embrace.

After a minute, Decker pulled away. "I'm going to talk to the police. File the report, see what I can come up with."

"Want me to come with you? It's only a ten-minute walk from here."

"No."

"I can just walk with you to the building—"

"No, I've got my map. I'll be back in about an hour. Sure you don't want to go home?"

"I'll wait for you."

"You don't have to do that."

"I want to," Rina said.

Decker smiled. "I won't object."

❧ 11

Boro Park was under the auspices of the 66th Precinct, which local cops called the Six-Six. The building was tucked into the corner of Sixteenth and Fifty-ninth, a two-story brick rectangle attached to a taller towerlike edifice also made of bricks. It was a fortress that would have protected the Three Little Pigs from any wolf for many years to come. Atop the lower portion of the structure was an American flag waving in the breeze.

Outside the station were a black Ford LTD unmarked and three bright-blue-and-white cruisers perpendicularly parked on the sidewalk. Decker hopped up three concrete stairs, opened a rust-scarred door, and stepped into a sally port. The entrance was done in faded mustard tiles held together by black grout. On the floor were blocks of lackluster green marble surrounding a dim square of teal-blue marble. The ceiling plaster was buckling, ready to shower gypsum. Against the walls were a pay phone, a beverage-vending machine, a candy-bar machine, and a uniformed patrol officer. The cop was dark and short, had a thick black mustache, and needed a shave. His name tag read Melino. He wore a light-blue shirt, navy tie, navy pants, and rubber-soled black oxfords. He sized Decker up and didn't like what he saw.

Decker was used to that. His height made many men wary. Then he realized that Melino was staring at the bulge under his jacket. Decker said, "I'm a cop from L.A. I'm packing and I've got a license to carry in the state of New York." He raised his arms in the air. "Check it out."

The patrol officer strolled over, frisked him, and pulled the Beretta from Decker's waistband. He stared at it, turned it over, then stared at it again.

He said, "Nice. Standard issue?"

Decker lowered his arms. "One of our options."

"Nice," repeated Melino.

"You want to check my carry license?" Decker asked.

The cop shrugged. "Yeah, sure."

Decker pulled it out of his wallet. Melino gave it a quick glance, then returned his eyes to the Beretta. "You don't have a clip."

"I know that," Decker said.

"This for show or what?" the cop asked.

"No, it's my piece," Decker said. "I just didn't think it was a good idea to come in here with a loaded semi-automatic."

Melino handed the gun back to Decker. "What can I do you for?"

"I need to file a missing-persons report," Decker said. "A local boy—fourteen."

"Local? One of the Hasids?" the cop said.

Decker smiled. The cop pronounced *Chasid* with a soft *h*, just like he did.

"Yeah, kid's a black-hatter."

"Is he a mental problem?" Melino said.

"Not that I know of."

"How long's he been gone?"

"About fifteen hours."

"And you're just filing a report now?" the cop asked. "Usually we get kids missing, we get a hysterical parent in here in two to three hours."

"You get a lot of missing kids in this area?"

"Nah," Melino said. "I can think of only a few in ten years. So many damn kids in this precinct it's hard for a parent to keep track of them. This precinct's one of the few in New York with a Community Patrol Officers Program—beat cops. When we get a missing kid, we assign a C-POP officer to go out and find the boy—they're usually boys. We almost always find the kid at a friend's house and he forgot to tell his mother where he went."

"Yeah, I thought that might be the case," Decker said. "Reason I didn't file earlier is because I wanted to do a door-to-door and a street search—"

"You already done those things, there's nothing more we can do except file the report," Melino said.

"Yeah, I know."

"You a family friend or what?"

"A family friend."

The cop said, "Go inside. Desk sergeant named Weiczorek will help you out."

Decker passed through the entry cubicle and into the main precinct.

And he'd thought his station house was in need of repairs.

The room looked like an unfinished basement. There were exposed pipes and electrical wires vining down the walls, fluorescent tubing running across the ceiling. Immediately to his right was a wall lined with rusted file cabinets that probably contained old cases—all out in the open. The main reception area was about twenty by forty feet, bisected by a corridor floored with the same washed-out-green marble he'd seen in the sally port. The corridor led to a wall made up of the same mustard tiles and several closed doors—no doubt the offices of the higher-ups. In the back corner was a table that held two computers with keyboards, a typewriter, a pea-green phone, a paper cup with lipstick marks, and a stack of papers defying gravity. Above the table were more exposed wires, a junction box, a wall-mounted cabinet of keys, a small map of the precinct, and a framed RAPID MOBILIZATION PLAN hung too high to be effectively read—even for a man his size.

Flanking the corridor on the right was a long cubicle enclosed by a one-way mirror—probably the dispatch area. In front of the mirror were royal-blue plastic chairs bolted to the floor and a seven-foot locker decorated with a poster of a group of police officers, the caption saying that New York was looking for "THE FINEST." On the left side of the walk-way was the reception desk, fronted by a four-foot-high wooden barrier that spanned the length of the room. The front desk was filled by a computer, a log-in sheet, and loose papers. Behind the desk was a cork bulletin board covered with memos, business cards, wanted posters, and two Polaroids— a snapshot of a missing old man and a picture of a pit bull. Under the dog someone had written, *"He goes for the nuts."*

The place smelled old and tired. Decker thought about a policeman's lot in life, then felt something nuzzle his leg—the mangiest golden retriever he'd ever seen. He thought of his own dog, an Irish setter. On her worst days, Ginger never looked so disheveled. The dog's breath was noticeable even though Decker's nose was a good six feet above the animal.

"Our mascot," said a male voice. "Gertrude."

The man was sitting behind the reception desk, doing some paperwork, eyes focused downward. He had a broad face made wider by a crushed nose, and a square jawline. His eyes were deep-set, his brows heavy and continuous. His lips were full, and a cigarette was dangling from his mouth.

Decker said, "That dog's the ugliest thing I've ever seen."

"Ugly doesn't bother me," the man said. He looped his hand over his shoulder and scratched his back. "It's the fleas that are the real killers." He looked up from his desk. "You waiting for someone or what?"

"I need to file a missing-persons report," Decker said. "You Sergeant Weiczorek?"

"I was last time I checked my birth certificate," Weiczorek said. "Which precinct are you from?"

"I'm not with NYPD," Decker said. "It's a local kid. I'm doing a favor for the family."

"But you're definitely a cop," Weiczorek said. "You got the look."

"Los Angeles," Decker said.

"Can spot 'em a mile away," Weiczorek said. He stubbed out his cigarette. "Hop over the fence. Tell me about the kid."

Decker stepped over the wooden barrier. The precinct was having a quiet night—a few uniforms wandering in and out, muffled voices dispatching calls from behind the one-way mirrored cubicle, not a perp in sight. He gave Weiczorek Noam's vitals, then showed him the picture. Weiczorek punched the data into the computer.

The desk sergeant said, "Sometimes another precinct will pick the kid up without ID. Computer will spit out anything that seems like a match. Takes a few minutes."

Decker nodded, stared over Weiczorek's shoulders, hypnotized by a flashing *waiting* that blinked on the computer screen.

Weiczorek seemed hypnotized too. Without looking up, he said, "You do a door-to-door?"

"Yes. Nothing."

"Street search?"

"Five hours."

A sudden scream echoed through the walls.

I know de law, man! I wan' my fuckin' phone call!

Weiczorek looked up and called, "Melino, take care of Mr. Torrentes."

Melino disappeared behind the mirrored cubicle.

"You've got your holding cells pretty close to the desk," Decker said.

"That's cell in the singular," Weiczorek said. "And yes, it is close to the front desk cause we ain't got no room anywhere else. If we run outta room in the cell, we chain 'em to the pipes. Once, a perp took offense to this and gave himself a shower with thirty-degree water. Goddamn place oughta be condemned."

Weiczorek scratched his head and said, "Here we go . . . The Seven Two has a kid. That's Crown Heights—another pocket of black-suiters. Boy like yours would certainly blend in there."

He picked up the phone and dialed the precinct. Decker held his breath as Weiczorek asked about the pickup.

Weiczorek said, "Yeah, I'll wait." He turned to Decker and said, "They're checking it out for me."

Melino returned, announcing that Mr. Torrentes had apologized for using bad language.

"Didn't he get his phone call?" Weiczorek asked.

"First thing, Sarge," Melino said. "But he was too stoned to remember it."

"Did you log it?" Weiczorek said.

"You bet," Melino said. "Made it at ten-oh-seven."

Weiczorek waved his hand in the air. "Idiot don't remember a damn thing." He picked up Noam Levine's picture and said, "You know, this one looks familiar."

"Where do you think you know him from?" Decker asked.

"I think he's one of the wilder boys around here,"

Weiczorek said. "Every so often, the boys in this area go nuts, start breaking things. These teenage boys sit all day in school, studying till dark. No physical activity, hormones running wild, no contact with the females. Just awhile back a group of 'em smashed up a parked bus that runs through the area on Saturday. It was a pile of junk by the time we got there and the little suckers ran off before we could catch any of them. Think the rabbis helped us out?"

"No?"

"Couldn't squeeze a drop of piss out of them as far as who the perps were. But they assured us that they'd take care of the boys who did it. This kid . . ." Weiczorek hit the photograph with the back of his hand. "I think he was one of them."

Decker nodded, not surprised at all. "You get into a lot of conflicts—"

Weiczorek interrupted him with a palm-up sign. "Yeah, I'm still here. No, that's not him. Thanks." He hung up. "Unless your boy's got nappy hair and a dark suntan, we ain't talking about the same kid."

Damn, Decker thought.

Weiczorek said, "You was saying before I interrupted you?"

Decker thought a moment. "I just wondered if there was a lot of tension between the locals and the law."

"Not much," Weiczorek said. "They're pretty easy once you know what to expect. You don't muscle these people around. They get mad—not violent but stubborn as a constipated mule. Give you an example. About three years ago one of the officers who hadn't worked long in this district gave a jay-walking ticket to one of the rabbis. Well, it was on a Saturday and the rabbi wouldn't sign the ticket cause it was against their law to write on Saturday."

Decker nodded.

"The young buck . . ." Weiczorek smiled. "He thought the old man was bullshitting him and was determined to show him who was boss. He hauled the old man into a cruiser. Next thing he knows he's got about a hundred rabbis and associated black-suiters laying down in the street. The officer and his car ain't going nowhere." Weiczorek laughed. "A week later the guy transferred out of here. Know where they sent him?"

"Where?" Decker asked.

"Williamsburg." Weiczorek burst into laughter. "He thought *these* guys were bad, those blackies in Williamsburg don't take no shit. Mean, rotten tempers. They got this cattle call—*chaptzum*. It means grab him. Someone calls out *chaptzum* and every person on the block comes pouring out and pounces on the poor schmuck who made the mistake of mugging the wrong person."

Weiczorek laughed again.

"About a week ago, the Nine-Oh found three Puerto Ricans beat up pretty bad and stuffed into an empty trash bin. Nobody died and the PRs ain't talking, so we really don't know what happened. At first, we thought it was some sort of turf thing with the gangs—who cares about them beatin' each other up, right?"

Decker nodded.

Weiczorek went on, "Except one of the cops duly noted that the PRs had been shitcanned in the Jewish section of Williamsburg right next to one of their all-boys high schools. Course no one will say nuttin'—you question the rabbis and all of a sudden they only speak Yiddish. Been living in this country for all of their lives, and they only speak Yiddish."

"Weird," Decker said.

"Glad to hear you say that," Weiczorek said. "I think it's weird, but what do I know? You hear them in their schools, teaching the first-graders '*Das es ein A. Das es ein B.*'" He shook his head. "Wanna know my opinion, I think those Puerto Rican scumbags were up to no good and the Jew boys *chaptzummed* 'em."

Weiczorek ruminated on his theory for a moment. "I say more power to them. They want a safe neighborhood, they're not afraid to fight for it."

"They take care of their own," Decker said.

"*Exactly*," Weiczorek said. "Gotta take care of your own. That's the trouble with America today. Everybody's only looking out for themselves." He scratched his head again. "Sorry we couldn't give you good news. I've got the family's number; I'll personally keep my eyes open. Maybe something'll turn up. Usually, the kid comes home after a few days. Course, that doesn't make the waiting any easier."

Decker felt sick. The prospect of facing the family was wearing him down like sand in a motor. And he knew that there was going to be a big scene at the suggestion of putting some new blood on the case.

Stubborn as a constipated mule.

Not the type of people to let go easily.

"Let me ask you this," Decker said. "Think he might have holed up in Prospect Park?"

"Not likely," Weiczorek said. "Being a native, he'd know better. Besides, it's cold outside."

"Well, maybe I'll take a look anyway."

"Up to you," Weiczorek said. "Just keep the door locked and the engine running."

Decker said, "'Preciate your help." He pulled out an identification card and gave it to the desk sergeant. "You ever need a favor from our boys in blue, give me a call."

Weiczorek studied the card, nodded. "Detective Sergeant First Grade—you must be a hot dog."

Decker said, "No, not a hot dog. I'm like your pit bull posted on the board. I go for the nuts."

Weiczorek laughed. "I'll pass the word along, tell the cruisers to pay special attention to this one. New York, Los Angeles, it don't matter. We cops take care of our own."

❧12

Waiting, waiting, waiting.

He'd had enough of waiting.

Sitting in school waiting for the bell to ring, sitting at home on Saturday waiting for the sun to go down, sitting at the dinner table waiting to be excused. Waiting around for the old man to clean and clear the fish cases.

The old man. It took him a long time to do that, each fish counted and put into the freezer or cooler. Then he had to drain all the ice. Old man used to buy him a soda to drink while he waited. But the soda didn't last long enough and he was forced to wait, wait, wait.

Once, while the old man was packing fish, he went out back to the trash barrels––the ones with the entrails. It was cold outside; he could still remember shivering, the wind whipping through his flannel shirt, pricking him on the neck. The back lot was wet and damp, reeking with stink. But something drew him to that damn barrel.

He popped open the lid, the sickening sweet smell filling up his head. It gave him a rush. He dipped his finger inside, swirled it around. The guts were still pliable but were coated with thin slivers of ice. Shaking, he rolled up the sleeves of his shirt, the air causing goosebumps on his naked arms. With one sudden motion, he plunged his arms into the barrel and squeezed his fists, feeling the frosted blood and guts ooze through his fingers. It felt so neat . . . so, you know . . . whatever. He kept doing it and doing it, knowing he had to stop. For one thing, his fingers were nearly frozen, the smell was making him dizzy. But he continued until the innards were nothing more than a bloody slush.

Then the old man caught him at the barrel, asked him what he was doing.

He was paralyzed with fear, couldn't answer him. How could he explain how good it felt without making himself look like a freak?

But the old man seemed to understand. All he said was wash up, we're going home.

Now the *dickhead* woulda never acted so cool. The dickhead woulda said something nasty and made him feel low.

Well, fuck him 'cause he's gone with the wind and that was fine with him.

He lay on his pillow thinking about the wad of bills in his wallet, the cash stolen from the old lady's private reserve along with a bunch of her jewelry, most of it looking like junk.

But the pearl necklace looked pretty good. It might get him a few bucks if he found a decent fence.

If the fucking sun would ever come up.

Three-oh-six.

More waiting, waiting, waiting.

Him, stuck in this dump that stunk of piss and pesticide, this crap hole that was nothing more than four paper walls and a floor so sticky it made him nervous to go barefoot.

Who knew what kind of shit was tossed on it?

The only ones who didn't seem to mind were the cock-a-roaches. He played his usual game, saw how many he could squish, then stopped counting after twenty-two.

Who really wanted to squish cock-a-roaches anyway? No body to them, nothing that you could really *feel*. Like the fish heads, now them you could feel underfoot. The *only* fun thing about the cock-a-roaches was squishing them in the corners, seeing the white junk pop out of their bodies.

He closed his eyes, trying to ignore the outside noises seeping through the closed window. The middle of the night, and the streets below were full of honks, beeps, shouts, and drunks throwing up.

Fuck it. Tomorrow, he'd be flying to Paradise— where the sun shines bright and the babes are bitchin' all year long.

But in the meantime, it was waiting, waiting, waiting.

He remembered someone saying that all good things come to those who wait.

He thought about that for a moment.

Then he decided whoever said that was a fucking idiot.

🕊13

"Ezra, my pearls are gone," Breina Levine announced.

Groggy and nauseated, functioning on only three hours of sleep, Ezra Levine rubbed his eyes. "You're worried about your pearls at a time like this?"

Breina pushed around the trinkets in her jewelry box. "My pearls, my gold necklace, my gold hoops—"

"We were robbed last night?" Ezra said.

"I don't know," Breina said. "I'll check the silver."

Ezra sat on the edge of his bed. His eyes were puffy and raw, his skin ultrasensitive, prickling when hit by the slightest draft. His temples ached from clenched jaws.

Hashem was testing him. That could be the only reason for such bad fate. Hashem was testing him, just like Job.

Where was Noam now? Ezra wondered. At this very moment, where was his son? He prayed that the boy was unharmed. Salty rills ran down his cheeks, feeling like liquid fire. He didn't think he had any more tears left, but here they were again.

Breina came back in the bedroom. "The sterling's still in the breakfront."

Ezra brushed his cheeks, whispered, "In all the confusion, you probably left the pearls at Eema's house."

"No," Breina said. "I didn't wear them yesterday—"

"Breina, I don't care about your necklace right now."

"Do you think *I* do?" Breina shouted. "Do you think *I* care about it?"

"So why are you going on and on about it—"

"I'm not going on and on—"

"Just drop it!" Ezra said.

"Okay!" Breina said. "Okay! It's dropped! Happy?"

Ezra buried his face in his hands, lifted his head a moment later. "Let's not fight."

Breina's lower lip trembled. She leaned against the wall and exploded into deep sobs. Ezra sighed, rose from the bed, and walked over to his wife. He put his hand on her shoulder; she turned and fell against his chest. He held her for a minute, patting her back as she cried against his undershirt, letting her wring out her grief. When she seemed to have quieted, he pulled away, saying he had to get ready for shul. Breina nodded, said she might as well dress also.

She thought about her second son, always a difficult child. A premature baby, he was colicky and a poor sleeper. As he grew, he became willful and restless.

There were times she felt immense sadness for

him, his loneliness was so palpable. She'd reach out and hug him, wrap him in the cocoon of a mother's arms. Noam would respond, embrace her back with such ferocity she could hear her bones crunch. But then he'd pull away, retreat into his shell or lash out and act like a wild animal.

She would try to talk to him, get him to tell her what was on his mind. Again he'd act silly, ask her childish questions.

How do we know Hashem is all around if we can't see Him?

Questions like these she expected out of the mouth of a four-year-old, not from a teenager. He seemed to be making fun of her. But she took him seriously and told him to ask his rebbe. Of course, he never did.

So unlike Aaron—the model child.

How could two brothers be so different?

Then she thought of Cain and Abel, Jacob and Esau.

She went inside the walk-in closet, closed the door, took off her robe, and slipped on her dress. Quickly, she zipped it up and fitted her wig atop her head. When she reopened the closet door, Ezra was sitting on the bed, putting on his socks.

"Ez?"

"What?"

"Do you think Noam took the pearls?"

Ezra looked up. "Why would Noam take your pearls?" A look of horror crossed over his face. "What? You think he's a *faygala*?"

"No, no," Breina said. "I was thinking that maybe

Noam took them for money—" She stopped herself.
"My emergency money!"

She moved toward the door, but Ezra held her
back. It was still *yom tov*; he would not allow her to
touch the money and violate the law for something
as trivial as this. If Noam took the money, so be it.
If he didn't, the money would still be there when
yom tov was over. Breina agreed not to count the bills
but wanted to see whether they were there or not.
At least, if the money was gone, she'd know that
Noam instead of a burglar had taken her pearls. No
burglar could have found her secret cache without
turning the house upside down. To know that they
weren't robbed last night would be a small, comfort-
ing thought. Ezra hesitated, then told her she could
look at the money, but she shouldn't touch it at all.
Breina stated she had no intention of touching it
and dashed out of the room. A moment later, she
returned.

"It's gone." She sank down into the bed. "Noam
took it. He must have taken my jewelry, too. I can't
believe that even he would do such a thing."

Ezra said, "Not that it matters, but how much did
you have?"

"Two hundred and thirty-five dollars," Breina
said. "I've been putting away pennies for ten years
to save up that much. How could he *do* that to me?"

Silence was her answer.

"I'm going to check on the girls," Breina whispered. "Do you want some tea, Ez?"

"Nothing, thank you."

Ezra felt his wife's hand on his shoulder. He patted it gently. A moment later, he heard soft receding footsteps, then the bedroom door close.

Alone, Ezra thought of the four sons mentioned in the Passover story. The wise one, the simple one, the one who doesn't even know how to ask a question. And the *rasha*, the wicked son.

No, that was terrible. How dare he think such a thing. Noam was not a *rasha*, just a confused boy, needing a little more guidance than the others. More attention.

At least that was what the rabbis at the school had told him. They had called Breina and him into conference one day, sat them down on two folding chairs, stared at them with grave eyes. The oldest— Rav Leider—was the only one who spoke. The others nodded in agreement with what he had said.

He's a troubled boy. He can learn but doesn't seem to want to. Furthermore, he's distracting the other boys from learning. It is clear to us that he needs more attention.

Ezra could still feel Rav Leider's eyes boring into him.

More fatherly *attention. You must learn with him.*

Ezra had tried. He and Noam had agreed to try *Sanhedrin*—a very difficult tractate of Talmud. He had his doubts but Noam had been insistent, claiming he had an interest in learning how capital crimes were punished by the rabbinical high court. But after the third session, Noam had begun to act up. Started asking questions that had no answers.

If Hashem created everything, who created Hashem?

Hashem didn't have a creator, Ezra had explained. *Hashem always was, always will be.*

That doesn't make any sense.

That's the way it is, Noam.

But it still doesn't make any sense.

What was the sense of arguing? So he stopped debating Noam. Another mistake. Noam started asking stupider questions. Like how much did Moses Malone make a year? He'd made learning such a miserable experience that, in desperation, Ezra had lost his temper. Yet Noam hadn't seemed the least bit upset. In fact, he'd seemed happy.

They had stopped learning together, a big mistake. He must ask Hashem to forgive him for his failure as a father.

Without thinking, he found his lips moving in silent prayer—*tehillim*—the psalms of David. It was so natural, the Hebrew words just spouting from his subconscious. He had said *tehillim* for Breina's mother two days before she succumbed to cancer. He had said *tehillim* the day his father underwent a double bypass, when his best friend was hit by a car, when his niece was born with a hole in her lung.

So many times he had said *tehillim*, he knew all the psalms by heart.

Decker listened as Ezra told him about the stolen money and jewelry, noticing that Ezra chose his words carefully. He emphasized that the money wasn't important to *him*—as a matter of fact, he was grateful his son had something in his pockets. But the theft might mean something to Decker as a policeman, and since he'd been kind enough to help out with this dreadful business, he should know everything.

When Ezra finished the story, he thanked Decker, then immediately followed it with grateful prayer to Hashem for sending a Jewish policeman. Decker being here was Divine Intervention—*basheert*—fated.

To Decker's ears, Ezra's thinking was childlike. But he'd seen people act irrationally under stress. All logic breaks down. . . .

Ezra asked what the next step was.

"Well . . ." Decker stifled a yawn. "The whole community knows that Noam is missing. That's good, Ezra. You have hundreds of eyes working for you. Maybe someone will remember something."

"*Eem yirtzah Hashem,*" Ezra said.

If God wills it . . .

"I want to have a personal talk with some of Noam's friends," Decker said. "We'll wait until after shul—"

"We can go now," Ezra said.

Decker shook his head. "Some may already be in shul, some may still be sleeping, some may be getting dressed. If we catch them after services, they should all be indoors, eating lunch."

"A good point," Ezra conceded. "We'll go to shul first, then I'll take you to their houses afterward."

Decker said that sounded fine.

Ezra brushed the floor with the tip of his shoe. "And what do I say if people ask me questions?"

"That's up to you," Decker said. "You don't have to say anything if you don't want."

"They'll think I'm hiding something."

"Ezra, at a time like this, you don't have to worry about what people think. Besides, your neighbors seem like fine people. Rina has already had a dozen offers from women willing to help—"

"What did she tell them?"

"Nothing. She said everything was under control."

"But it's not, is it?" Ezra began to pace. "He's still missing."

"At least we have a plan."

"And the police are looking for him?" Ezra asked.

"As much as they can. He's not top priority, but they'll keep their eyes open." Decker paused, then said, "You don't have any idea where Noam might have gone?"

"I've been racking my brain all night," Ezra said. "He's never, *never* disappeared from Boro Park before. Sure, he goes places and forgets to tell his mother, but never like this. As far as I know, he's never even been out of Brooklyn."

Part of the problem, Decker told himself. The boy is overly sheltered. Then he thought: Stop being so *damn* judgmental. This kind of thing could happen in *any* family. His thoughts shifted to Cindy, how he'd been blessed to have a daughter as terrific as she was. He was a good father, but not a great one. He kept long hours at work when she was growing up, wasn't home a lot. But he had tried to be there whenever she needed him, whenever she had performed in a school pageant. He had even addressed her class on Parents' Careers Day. All her schoolmates thinking it was cool when he had taken them for a ride in his cruiser. He remembered her face—her eyes had actually sent out beams.

He returned his thoughts to the present and said, "I talked to a lot of local Brooklyn boys last night. Noam seems unknown outside of Boro Park."

"Just like I said," Ezra said. "I just pray and hope that you're right about him being a runaway. If it's the other . . ."

"I can't guarantee it," Decker said, "but big strapping fourteen-year-olds are unusual kidnap victims unless it's a kidnap for ransom—"

"I'm not a rich man," Ezra said. "I'm a bookkeeper for a sporting goods store and Breina teaches a little at the local girls' school. We get by but have nothing other than the house. Who would kidnap for a house?"

"How about your parents? Your brothers or sisters?"

"No one on either side is rich. My brother Shimmy is comfortable, but he's not exactly a millionaire. In this community, there are richer people to grab from." Ezra sighed. "It's bad, *nu?*"

Decker said, "It's only been one night, Ezra. It's way too early for gloom and doom." He was about to bring up the notion of a private investigator, but the look in Ezra's eyes held him off. And those self-deprecating words: *I'm not a rich man*.

Ezra said, "You are very reassuring, Akiva. Not full of false promises . . . but calm . . . reassuring." He took a deep breath and blurted out, "I was a loud-mouth yesterday—"

"Please—"

"No," Ezra went on. "Yom Kippur is in ten days. I ask you to forgive me."

Such a plaintive note in his voice. Decker thought: Put the goddamn PI on hold. Now was not the time. It was useless to tell Ezra there was no need for forgiveness. To him, forgiveness was the first step in the process of cleansing the soul.

"Of course I forgive you," Decker said. "And forgive me if I did anything to offend you."

"You didn't," Ezra said. "But it just shows me once again, how wrong it is to go on first impressions."

Mine was that bad? Decker thought.

Ezra said, "Now I can see why Rina married you."

Decker wasn't sure, but he thought that was a compliment.

Decker told Ezra to meet him at Frieda Levine's house after shul, then immediately wondered just why in hell he had designated *her* house as a rendezvous spot. Yes, there was some logic to it—it had been the center of activity yesterday—but he could easily have told Ezra to meet him at the Lazarus house.

Why did he do that?

Why?

Oh, the hell with analyzing. He'd figure it all out when he was back in L.A. When he was safe.

At the appointed hour, Decker arrived at the Levine house, opening the door and stepping inside without bothering to knock. The whole family was waiting, greeting him with muted nods, with somber eyes, with unspoken pleas for help.

He felt twice his age, shackled by a not-so-subconscious motivation to prove himself to these people. Yes, he wanted out. But he also wanted them to like him even if he left them hanging. He nodded back at the clan and told Ezra he was ready to begin his interviews with Noam's friends.

Just as he and Ezra were about to leave, Ezra lurched forward. Shimon looped his arms around him as Jonathan grabbed a chair. Together, they eased their brother into a sitting position. His mother and sisters served him water, fanned his face. After he caught his breath, Ezra told everyone that it was simply a bad case of nerves, suddenly his knees had buckled. Decker told him he'd been under an extraordinary amount of stress, adding that he'd been holding up very well.

"Maybe it would be better if I went with Akiva," Shimon said to Ezra.

"I'll go," Jonathan said.

"Why don't you both go?" Frieda Levine said.

Decker forced himself to look at her. "Too many people."

"Of course," Frieda said. "You know best."

Those eyes! They begged his forgiveness, pleaded with him for help. Goddamn her eyes. They drew him under like a riptide.

Decker focused in on his watch. "I'll take Shimon along. No offense to you, Jonathan, but Shimon is better trusted in the community."

Jonathan clasped his hands together. "Whatever you say, boss."

The way he said it, Decker had to smile.

When he and Shimon were out of the house,

Shimon asked what his function would be other than to introduce him. Decker explained that he wanted to talk to the kids in private. Shimon was to reassure the families while he interviewed their children. Since he was a stranger, parents might feel skittish allowing him to be alone with their progeny. Shimon's job was to tell everyone what a great guy he was.

"And if the parents want to come with you?" Shimon asked.

"That's what I'm trying to avoid," Decker said. "I can get kids to tell me things they won't dare admit in front of their parents."

"My kids tell you our deep dark secrets?" Shimon asked.

He had tried to keep his voice light, but Decker knew there was something behind it. Shimon was worried about what his children had told him yesterday, what kind of impression they had made. The truth was, they had been very nice and well-behaved.

Decker said, "Your oldest told me you do funny things with a whip and a chain."

Shimon said, "He forgot the handcuffs."

Decker laughed.

The day was cool, but the sun was out. Wedges of bright light shone upon the rows of townhouses, turning the red brick into metallic copper. They had waited a good hour after services were over, wanting to be sure most people had settled down for the big holiday afternoon meal. At three o'clock, they were the only ones on the street, their shoes echoing against the blinding white sidewalk.

Decker stuck his hands in his pockets and said, "Your kids are great."

Shimon tried to stifle a smile, but couldn't. "Thanks. I like them."

"The boys don't seem to be close to their cousin."

"To Noam?" Shimon said. "No, they're not. They get along well with Ezra's other boys, and my second son and Ezra's oldest learn together. But Noam? He's a strange boy."

"In what way?" Decker asked.

Shimon threw up his hands. "It's terrible I should be telling you this right before Yom Kippur, but maybe it's important."

"Tell me."

"He's a sneak," Shimon said. "My wife doesn't like having him over because he skulks around the house, rummages through drawers. It seems harmless enough, but most children—relatives or not—just don't behave that way."

"Did he ever steal from you?" Decker asked.

Shimon turned red.

"What did he steal?" Decker inquired.

"Nothing big," Shimon explained. "Nothing valuable." He collected his thoughts. "My daughter Shuli was going through a kind of rebellious stage. She'd just turned fourteen. You have a teenage daughter, you know how they can be."

"Moody," Decker said.

"Very moody," Shimon said. "Very cranky. Easily bored. Not a lot of energy. My wife tells me it's normal. So . . ." He shrugged. "Anyway, I made a deal with Shuli. She—of all my children—seems the most preoccupied by the craziness of the outside world. She likes makeup, she likes clothes, she thinks she's a movie star . . . I don't know. Anyway, I told her if she did more housework and got along better with her mother and brothers and sisters, I'd buy her *People* magazine for a year. To you, this may sound stupid—"

"I understand, Shimon."

"The people around here just don't read that sort of thing—"

"I understand," Decker repeated.

"Anyway, it worked," Shimon said. "Shuli is like a different child and doesn't seem to be harmed by the exposure. I'm happy, she's happy.

"Well, about six months ago, my wife went in to clean Shuli's room and caught Noam there. The boy, according to her, scampered out like a little mouse. My wife didn't think too much of it—she was annoyed—but that was typical behavior for Noam. When Shuli came home later in the day, she was all up in arms, mad at me, burst into tears. 'What? What?' I asked her. She was upset because it was *People* magazine day and we forgot to buy her the precious magazine. My wife insisted she had purchased the magazine, but suddenly she remembered that Noam had stuffed something in his jacket when she walked in. We figured he must have stolen the magazine."

Decker waited for more.

"That's the whole story," Shimon said.

"And that's the only thing he has taken from you as far as you know."

"As far as we know, yes, and that was awhile ago."

Shimon paused. "You know, I almost suggested to Ezra that he buy Noam the magazine. But Ezra's a little more strict than I am. And, I'm ashamed to admit it, I didn't want Ezra to know that I buy the magazine for Shuli. Around here, we pay way too much attention to what others think."

Decker patted him on the back. "Don't we all, Shim."

"Really?" Shimon shrugged. "I've lived here all my life, Akiva. Every day I carpool with men I grew up with. We go over the bridge together, I go to work, then we go home together. I have a silver business. I sell wholesale to major retailers. Most of my work is selling over the phone. I rarely see my buyers face-to-face after I've made my initial contacts. I don't have a good idea what others do, what others think."

"And that doesn't bother you?" Decker asked.

"Not when I see what kind of world they've created for themselves—girls pregnant and on drugs at ten years old. Young boys murdering each other with the crazy gangs—they even murder their *teachers*." He shook his head. "I don't want any part of that world."

Decker didn't answer.

"Of course," Shimon said, "I'm sure all of the world isn't like that."

"You're talking to a cop," Decker said. "I don't see a very accurate picture of the world, either."

"And that's why you became religious, *nu?*" Shimon said.

Decker gave him a shrug.

Shimon smiled. "Maybe Rina had a little to do with it?"

"A little," Decker said.

Shimon pointed to a small brick townhouse. The front porch was filled with toys and enclosed by storm glass. "That's our first stop. You said you wanted to speak with Ephraim and Moshe Greitzman. I know the father very well. I'll do the talking."

"Great."

Shimon opened the porch door and knocked on a locked screen. The front door was wide open, pouring out heat and loud conversation. The little girl who came to the threshold was five or six, had a round face and ketchup stains on her chin and on her new dress. Her hair was braided tightly, which made her cheeks look even chubbier.

"Malkie, is your abba home?" Shimon asked her.

The little girl shouted the word "Abba." A man around forty unlocked the screen and stepped outside. He had a thick middle and a thick heavy beard.

"Shim," he said and shook his hand.

"Danny," Shimon said. "This is Rina Lazarus's— uh—Rina's new *chassan*, Akiva."

"*Shana tova umitukah. Mazel tov.*" Danny stuck out his hand. "We met yesterday. You were here with Yonasan."

Decker nodded.

"So what?" Danny asked Shimon. "Anything?"

Shimon shook his head.

"Ach," Danny said. "A rotten thing. Tell Ezra we prayed for him today."

"I will," Shimon said. "Danny . . . Akiva is a policeman—a detective. He's been wonderful to us, to the family."

There was an awkward pause.

Shimon said, "He wants to talk to Ephraim and Moshe about this thing."

Danny's eyes went from Shimon's to Decker's and back to Shimon's.

"He needs to talk to them in private," Shimon said.

"My sons had nothing to do with this terrible thing," Danny said.

Shimon threw his arm around Danny. "Of course not. We're just going through the motions. I'm doing it for Ezra. Please, the boy is my nephew. Ezra and Breina are worried sick. My mother and father are not well. Let him do whatever he needs to do."

Danny exhaled, looked confused. "Why in private?"

"Just standard procedure," Decker said. "That's the way I'm used to talking to kids."

"What are you going to ask them?" Danny said.

Decker said, "It'll probably take only a few minutes."

Shimon said, "Danny, we have four other houses to go to and as the time passes, things look worse. Please."

Again, Danny exhaled. "Where do you want to talk to them?"

"Their rooms are fine," Decker said. "Or I'll just walk around the block with them if you want it out in the open—"

"No, no, no," Danny said. "Go upstairs in the

boys' room. I don't want the neighbors to see you interrogating my sons."

"Believe me," Decker said, "it's not an interrogation. Very simple. In and out."

"Help us out," Shimon said.

"Of course." Danny stepped aside, let them cross the threshold.

The household was full of guests, full of kids. Danny took his wife aside and told her what they wanted. She didn't seem pleased by the request, but Danny had made up his mind and that was that. He told his wife to lead Decker and the boys upstairs. As Decker was climbing the steps, he noticed how easily Shimon had integrated himself into the table conversation. Smiling, talking—he seemed to know everyone. The man was so at home, Decker half expected him to take his shoes off.

Outgoing. So unlike himself. Would he have ended up this friendly had he lived here all his life?

Probably not, because he, like Jonathan, wouldn't have lasted in this insular environment. He was a big man—demanded open spaces, unspoiled land. The first thing he'd done after his divorce was buy ranch land out in Tujunga.

They reached the top of the stairs. Danny's wife was petite and blond, her head stopping at the middle of Decker's biceps. The boys were small as well, but had some of their father's bulk. They looked alike, both with sandy-colored hair, fair cheeks, full lips, and cleft chins. But one had light eyes, the other, irises as dark as coal. They reminded Decker of Chip and Dale.

The wife said, "Can I wait outside the doorway?"

"It's better if you wait downstairs," Decker said. He put on his professional smile. "Your guests might need you."

"Yes, you're right," the woman said. She hurried downstairs.

Decker gently ushered the boys inside their room and closed the door behind him.

In this community, pinups of bikinied models and rock stars were taboo. But the local mores hadn't banned professional sports. The walls were plastered with posters of the Mets, the Yankees, the Knicks, and the Giants. Larger-than-life figures leaping into the air for impossible catches, soaring through the sky to make a slam dunk, ramming through piles of meat to make a touchdown. The room was small and, with the posters as an audience, the floor space seemed like a tiny stage. The beds abutted one another, the desk was a pyramid of papers. A computer had been stuffed into a closet, resting on cinder blocks. Clothes were all over the place. A square grated window was open, airing out a stale, unwashed smell.

Decker motioned the boys to sit on their beds. He leaned against the wall, sandwiched between Don Mattingly and Steve Sax. He pointed to Sax and said, "He was one of ours."

The boys smiled.

"We were sorry to see him go," Decker said.

The light-eyed boy said, "We were sorry to let the Dodgers go."

Decker smiled. "You guys didn't deserve the Dodgers. You treated them like bums."

"From their stats," the dark-eyed boy said, "they played like bums."

"They've earned their keep in L.A.," Decker said.

The dark-eyed boy said, "That's for sure."

It came out: *Datsfohshua*.

Decker said, "Which one's Moshe?"

The light-eyed boy raised his hand. He looked to be around fourteen. The dark-eyed one, Ephraim, was maybe a year or two younger. Decker said, "You know who I am?"

"Sure," Moshe said. "You're Shmuli and Yonkie's stepdad. The cop."

Decker smiled.

"Mrs. Lazarus's husband," Ephraim said. He looked at Decker. "I guess she isn't Mrs. Lazarus anymore."

Decker laughed.

"She's very nice," Moshe said.

"Thank you."

"Yes, she's very nice," Ephraim agreed.

There was a pregnant pause, the obvious not being said.

She's very pretty.

He wondered how many boys had a crush on her?

Moshe said, "Shmuli's in my *shiur*."

Sammy was twelve; how could he be in this kid's class? Then Decker remembered that the *shiurim*—lessons in Jewish studies—weren't based on age but on ability.

Decker said, "Is Noam in your *shiur* too?"

The boys laughed nervously. Moshe said, "Noam sits with us, but in learning he's behind Yonkie."

"He's real dumb," Ephraim said.

"He's not dumb," Moshe said.

"He's dumb," Ephraim repeated.

"He's not dumb," Moshe insisted. "He's just a cut-up. When he had to learn his bar mitzvah *parashá*, he put it off until the last minute. Then he memorized the whole thing in three months. He pulled it off and did *Musaf*, too. And he did a decent job. He's not dumb."

"Well, he acts dumb," Ephraim said.

"*That* is true," Moshe said. He turned to Decker and said, "You haven't found him, huh?"

Decker shook his head. "You two good friends?"

"Good friends?" Moshe said. "A long time ago. Now we just kinda know each other. The older we get, the less I have to do with him. Noam keeps to himself, doesn't talk too much. Our interests are different. As you might have noticed, I like sports, I like cars, I like . . ."

Moshe blushed.

"You like girls," Decker filled in the blank.

"We don't see the girls too much," Moshe said. "Our school hours are long and we're in separate buildings."

"Noam like sports and cars?" Decker said.

Moshe shook his head. "Couldn't care less."

"How about computers?"

"Noam likes computers?" Moshe said. "That's news to me."

"I mean computer games."

"Oh." Moshe thought a moment. "He had this little pocket game—Octopus. Used to play that all the time. I find those things boring but a lot of kids are into it. Mostly the younger ones."

"Do you know if Noam ever hangs around the arcades?" Decker asked. "Maybe he has a friend with a Nintendo game system?"

Moshe shook his head. "We don't have a TV so we don't have any game systems. No one around here does."

"Does he have any other pocket games besides Octopus?"

"Not that I know of."

"How about girls?" Decker said. "Does Noam ever talk about girls?"

Moshe's blush returned to his cheeks. "Yeah, he likes girls."

"Talks about them?"

"Yeah."

"A lot?"

Moshe said, "Depends on what you think a lot is?"

Decker said, "When he talks about the girls, is he crude, graphic in how he likes them?"

"Yeah," Moshe said. "That kinda bothers me. We weren't brought up to talk like that."

Refreshing, Decker thought.

"I think Noam's a pervert," Ephraim said.

"He's not a pervert," Moshe said.

"He's a pervert," Ephraim said. He turned to Decker. "He hangs around the younger kids a lot."

Decker raised his eyebrows. Moshe came to Noam's rescue.

"It's not like you think. It's all out in the open. He just plays with them."

"How young are we talking about?" Decker asked.

"First of all," Moshe said. "He doesn't hang around them. Sometimes he plays tag or mouse-in-the-middle with the younger kids at shul. They're maybe six or seven. He's real nice to them. They like him, too. So he'll make a good camp counselor. What's wrong with that?"

"Do you think it's strange?" Decker said.

Moshe was uncomfortable. "Yeah, it's a little weird."

Ephraim said, "It's very weird."

"Shut up, Ephraim," Moshe said.

Decker said, "Does Noam have a girlfriend? Maybe a secret girlfriend?"

Moshe shook his head. "Not that I know of. Most of the girls I know think he's a little off. My sisters won't go near him."

"Noam ever brag about things he's done with girls?" Decker asked. "Maybe things he's done with girls that weren't even Jewish?"

Moshe paused a long time. Decker knew the teenager was in conflict. He said, "Moshe, if he has a non-Jewish girlfriend, maybe that's where he's hiding out."

"I don't think he actually *has* a non-Jewish girl-friend," Moshe said. "Or any girlfriend. He used to talk a lot about the Italian girls, about things they'd do . . . I don't know where he learned all this stuff from. Noam likes to play hotshot. I think all his hotshot talk is made up on the spot."

"Wishful thinking?"

"Exactly."

"You ever notice him hanging around the Italian boys?" Decker asked.

"No," Moshe said. "But I don't hang around them, so I don't really know if he was or wasn't."

"Did Noam ever try to sell you drugs?"

Moshe shook his head.

"Did he ever sneak drugs or alcohol inside school? Try to get some of his friends interested in getting stoned?"

"Not that I know of," Moshe said. "Once in a while, he'd smoke in the bathroom. Lot of kids do it. Smoking isn't allowed in school, but a lot of the rabbis smoke right in front of us." He suddenly reddened, started to speak but changed his mind.

"What is it?" Decker said.

Moshe focused his eyes on his lap. "It's really no big . . . well, it is a big deal if my parents and teachers ever found out. I don't want you to think I'm a pervert or gross or anything. I just happened to be there when Noam passed around the magazine."

"A dirty magazine?" Decker said.

Moshe nodded.

Smiling, Ephraim said, "This is interesting."

"Shut up," Moshe said to his brother.

From *People* to porno. Decker said, "Know where he got hold of it?"

"No."

"How many times did he show it to you?"

This time, the boy was red. "Maybe . . . a couple of times."

"A couple is two times, Moshe," Decker said. "I'm not asking you these questions to get you into trouble or embarrass you. I'm asking them because they help me find out what kind of a boy Noam is and it's always easier to find someone you understand than a mystery person. See what I'm saying?"

Moshe nodded.

Decker said, "How many times did he show you the magazine?"

"Maybe five times."

"*Very* interesting," Ephraim said.

Moshe lit into him. "You tell Abba and you're dead."

"I wouldn't do that, Moshe," Ephraim said. "Even I have a code of honor."

The kid seemed sincere. Decker felt better. He asked, "Was it always the same magazine?"

"Two different ones," Moshe said.

"Were they *Playboys*—just naked women—more explicit?"

"No . . . they were . . . more . . . explicit," Moshe said.

"Where'd he get them?"

"That I don't know . . . honest."

"I believe you," Decker said.

"He used to bring them to school," Moshe said. "Once I almost got caught. That was it. I told him not to show them to me . . . at least not at school. It just wasn't worth what would happen if we got caught."

"Did he show them to anyone else?"

"I don't think I should get anyone else in trouble."

"Moshe, New York is a dangerous place for an adult, let alone a kid your age. He's easy prey for all types of perverts and felons. No one's going to get in trouble, I personally promise you that."

Moshe sighed. "There was a group of us. Chaim Belser, David Ramy, Yossie Weinstein, and Menachem Takinoff. Noam had a few of the magazines; once Yossie Weinstein brought in one, too. David, Chaim, Menachem, and I . . . we just looked."

All the boys' names were on Jonathan's list. Man had good instincts. Would have made a good detective . . .

"You've been great," Decker said.

"I just hope I don't regret this," Moshe said.

Decker smiled, patted the kid's fuzzy cheeks. "Your parents ask you what we talked about, say mostly sports, a little about Noam, okay?"

The boys nodded.

"You boys ever make it out to L.A.," Decker said, "and if it's okay with your parents, I'll take you and my boys out to Disneyland."

"*Really?*" they said in unison.

"That's a promise," Decker said. He smiled at them. Their eyes were gleaming. He left, heartened to see that there were still some children allowed to remain children.

✒14

Shimon asked how did the interviewing go. Decker said it went fine. Their next stop was Yossie Weinstein's house. Shimon said they were closer to the Belsers, but Decker said he wanted to talk to Yossie before he talked to any of the others.

"Why Yossie?" Shimon asked.

"Because he seemed to be the closest to Noam," Decker said. "By the way, just do what you did at the Greitzman house. You handled the parents perfectly. Made my job a snap."

"We're a good team, huh?" Shimon said.

Decker stopped walking for a moment, feeling his throat tighten. He suddenly longed to reach out to Shimon, to embrace him. Caught in a cruel practical joke. He swallowed back an emotional swelling, held himself in check. He resumed his pace and said softly, "Yeah, we're a great team."

"You work with a partner?" Shimon asked.

"I'm not assigned a partner, per se," Decker said. "But if I do team up, it's usually with a woman named Marge Dunn. Man, I sure wish she were here now.

We bounce a lot of ideas off each other. You need someone like that."

"You work with a woman?" Shimon said.

"Sure."

"And Rina doesn't mind?"

Decker smiled. "No, Rina doesn't mind."

They walked a few moments in silence.

"Your partner—or sort of partner," Shimon said. "She's young?"

"Marge is thirty-one. She's five ten, one hundred sixty pounds."

"A big woman."

"A big woman," Decker said. "You wouldn't want to confront her when she was mad. She and Rina seem to get along."

"They're friends?"

"Well, not friends exactly. They just know each other through me."

Shimon said, "My wife chose my secretary. She's sixty years old, ninety pounds, and wears too much perfume. Not lovely to look at, but very efficient."

"I'll take efficiency over looks any day of the week," Decker said.

"Marge is ugly?"

"No, Marge isn't ugly at all. She's actually quite attractive if you like big Nordic women."

"She's blond?"

"Blond with dark eyes," Decker said. "She's got great eyes; they inspire trust. Kids love her; our rape survivors confide in her. That's the kind of partner you want. Someone you can depend on, someone who's *good*."

"That makes sense," Shimon said.

They took a few more steps without speaking.

Shimon said, "She's single, this Marge?"

"Yeah."

"You're not distracted by her?"

"Distracted by Marge?" Decker laughed. "She keeps my mind *on* work, not off of it. She's a great cop."

"You like her," Shimon said.

"She's a good friend," Decker said.

Shimon put his hands in his coat pockets and shrugged.

To him, Decker realized, the idea of women friends was as alien as pork. In this community, working closely with a woman could only lead to trouble. But his half brother happened to be a nice guy and was trying hard not to be judgmental. Decker felt that was worth some points.

They stopped walking and Shimon pointed to another small brick townhouse.

"Here's where the Weinsteins live," he said. "Tell me, Akiva, am I as good a partner as your great cop and friend, Marge?"

"Shimon, my man, you're the only one in town who could pull off this assignment. And that's no lie."

"*Eem yirtzah Hashem*, all my talents won't go to waste." Shimon turned serious. "Do you think we'll find him, Akiva?"

"I don't know," Decker answered. "But we'll do whatever we can."

"Ultimately, it's up to God," Shimon said.

That was true. Decker thought. But just in case the Old Man was overbooked at this time of year, he was going to do his damnedest to take the case off His hands.

Unlike the Greitzman boys, Yossie Weinstein seemed scared. He was a tall, slender boy, very pale with hazel eyes and ash-colored kinky hair. His features were long; two weals of pimples dotted his cheeks. He slept in a converted closet off his older brother's room. He sat on his bed; Decker sat next to him. The boy's breath smelled of garlic and onions. A protoplasmic grease stain decorated his shirt. Decker asked him if he knew who he was and Yossie identified him as Shmuli and Yonkie's stepdad, the cop.

That seemed to be the official title—Shmuli and Yonkie's stepdad, the cop.

That was fine with him.

He spoke to the boy about sports, about cars. Yossie was shy and Decker had a rough time establishing rapport. After ten minutes of discussing the Mets, specifically whether or not the Mets could beat the Dodgers should both teams be in the play-offs, the kid seemed to settle down. Decker eased into questions about Noam, taking guidance from his last conversation with the Greitzman boys. When he asked about dirty magazines, he thought Yossie would faint.

Decker said, "Did Noam ever show you dirty magazines, Yossie?"

The kid's nod was barely perceptible.

"How many times did he show you the magazine?"

"Coupleoftimes."

*Mumble, mumble. We don't want to talk about this
at all.*

Decker repeated, "A couple of times. You ever *buy*
one from him, Yossie?"

The boy buried his head in his hands. Decker put
an arm around his shoulder.

"Yossie, I'm not going to tell your parents anything. I *promise* you. They ask you what we talked
about, you say a little about Noam, and a lot about
sports. Tell them Shmuli and Yonkie's stepdad—the
cop—is a big Dodger fan, okay?"

Yossie nodded.

"I'm not here to get you into trouble," Decker
said. "I'm here to find Noam before he gets hurt.
Please. Now, did you ever buy a dirty magazine off
him?"

The boy shook his head.

"Then where did you get it?" Decker asked.

"Fromaguy."

Hallelujah! Calmly, Decker asked, "Which guy?"

"Just this guy," Yossie said.

"Does this guy have a name?"

"Hersh," Yossie said.

"Hersh," Decker repeated. "And does Hersh have
a last name?"

"I don't know it."

"Hersh," Decker said. "You know where Hersh
lives?"

Yossie shook his head.

"No," Decker said. "Then where did you meet Hersh?"

Yossie mumbled something. Decker asked him to repeat what he said.

"I met him at this liquor store," Yossie said. "I thought I was going with Noam to buy a bottle of wine for his family. Then Noam introduces me to this Hersh guy. I didn't even want the magazine, but I didn't want to look like a dip and not buy it. So I bought it. Cost me ten bucks, too." He looked down. "Boy, was I a jerk."

"We all get talked into doing things," Decker said. "Every single one of us, so don't feel bad about it. What you should feel *good* about is helping me out. It's a mitzvah. You're doing great. Can you tell me *which* liquor store?"

"I don't remember the name of it," Yossie said. "It was in the black section of Crown Heights on the other side of Empire."

"Hersh is from Crown Heights?"

"I don't know."

"Hersh is a Jewish name," Decker said. "So am I correct in assuming Hersh is Jewish and not black?"

"Definitely," Yossie said. "He might have even once been *frum*—religious—because he seemed to know Yiddish. But if he was *frum* at one time, he *isn't* now. I was really angry at Noam for taking me there. I have relatives in Crown Heights. If they had seen me in that store with this Hersh guy, it would have been all over for me."

"What does Hersh look like?" Decker said.

"He's about twenty . . . twenty-one." The boy scrunched his eyes. "He's dark, not real tall."

"Let's start at the beginning," Decker said. "Stand up."

The boy obeyed.

"Okay," Decker stood straight. "How far would he come up to me?"

Yossie thought for a moment, then put his hand at Decker's shoulder.

About five eight or nine.

"Okay," Decker said. "Clean-shaven?"

Yossie nodded.

"Good," Decker said. "By dark, you mean dark eyes, dark skin, dark hair—"

"Dark hair and eyes," Yossie said. "He's not dark like an Iranian or something. He's just like normal white."

"Fantastic. Okay, he's clean-shaven with dark hair and eyes. Does he have any acne, any moles, any warts . . ."

"I don't think so."

"Let's try something," Decker said. "I use this method all the time with my witnesses. You mind being my star witness in this case?"

"Sure," Yossie said. "I mean, sure, I don't mind."

Decker held back a smile. "Close your eyes, Yossie, and picture Hersh's face." He waited a moment. "Describe the forehead to me—see a lot of it, a little of it . . ."

"High forehead."

"The eyebrows?"

The boy knitted his eyes in concentration.

"Don't force it, Yossie," Decker said. "Just relax. Let it flow. If you don't remember, that's okay."

"I don't remember his eyebrows," Yossie said.

"Fine," Decker answered. "His nose—"

"Big."

"Long, wide, bulbous—"

"Long and big."

"Good. The cheeks."

"Just cheeks."

"Fleshy? Lean? Rosy-colored?"

"Just plain cheeks."

"Okay," Decker said. "Doing great, kid. Let's go to the mouth."

"Big mouth," Yossie said. "And a weird smile. Lopsided."

"Lopsided? In what way?"

"I don't know . . . just kinda lopsided and weird."

"Can you show me?" Decker asked.

Yossie curled the right side of his mouth upward, leaving the other side flat. "And he'd like . . . scrunch up his eyes when he smiled, too." He grimaced again, then started to laugh. Decker laughed too, happy that the boy was loosening up. Relaxed people have better memories.

"That's great, Yossie," Decker said. "Now tell me this. When Hersh talked, was his mouth also crooked?"

"Uh-uh," Yossie said. "Only when he smiled." He looked up at Decker. "It was a real weird smile, made me nervous. That's why I bought the magazine."

"Did he threaten you?"

"No."

"Okay," Decker said. "Back to the smile. Could you see his teeth when he grinned?"

"On the one side. They were just teeth."

"Big? Yellow? Did you notice any dental work?"

Yossie shook his head.

"Okay," Decker said. "A weird, crooked smile. Let's go on to his chin. Long? Square? Dimpled?"

"Just a chin."

"That's fine. Now I want you to move your eyes down from his face to the body. Can you picture his body?"

Yossie nodded, his eyes still closed.

"Good," Decker said. "Take a nice long look at the body. When you're done looking, tell me if he's fat or thin or regular."

"Thinnish."

"Okay. How 'bout his shoulders? Are they wide—"

"He's thin but he has muscles." Yossie opened his eyes. "I remember now. He was wearing this sleeveless shirt—a muscle shirt I think they're called—and I could see his arms. He looked like he'd been lifting barbells."

"Terrific," Decker said. "Just terrific. Can you tell me anything else about his body? Was it hairy?"

Yossie shook his head.

"Wasn't hairy or you don't know?"

"I don't know."

Decker said, "Did he walk with a limp?"

"No."

"His voice. Was it high or low?"

"Medium."

"All right. Did he talk with a stutter or a lisp?"

"No."

"Did he have a Brooklyn accent?"

"What do you mean?"

"Let me rephrase that," Decker said. "Did he sound like he was a native Brooklyn boy? Did he sound like he was from around here?"

"Yeah, I think so. He didn't talk like a Californian or a Southerner."

Decker recapped to Yossie the man he had just described. "Does that sound right?"

"Yeah," Yossie said. "That's about it."

"You did fine," Decker said. "Now this Hersh guy was maybe from Crown Heights?"

"Maybe."

"But you think he was a local?"

"I guess so."

"You met him at a liquor store in Crown Heights?"

"Yes."

"In the black area of Crown Heights?"

"Yeah. It was right past Empire." He thought a moment. "You know, it might have been on Empire Boulevard."

"Hey, that's great," Decker said. "You've got a terrific memory, Yossie. You can be my witness anytime."

The boy smiled.

"Now you only met Hersh the one time."

Yossie nodded.

"Did he and Noam seem like good buddies?"

"No," Yossie said. "Not like good buddies. More like Hersh was a big shot and Noam kinda worshiped him like he was something hot. Frankly, I thought Hersh was a jerk, even jerkier than Noam."

"Did you get the impression that Hersh and Noam had met more than once or twice?"

"Definitely."

Decker clapped his hands. "You did a great job. If you knew how important your information was to me, you'd really feel good about yourself. We want to find Noam, Yossie, before he gets into big trouble. You may have helped him more than anyone else."

The boy lowered his head, holding back a grin. Very slowly, he reached into a hidden cubbyhole in his closet-room and pulled out a magazine.

"Here." He gave it to Decker. "I should have thrown it away a long time ago, but I was too nervous someone would see me throwing it out. Every time my mother comes in here, I get nervous that she'll find it. Can you get rid of it for me?"

Decker flipped through the well-used rag. The kids sure knew the difference between *Playboy* and the real thing. He stuffed it in his jacket. "No problem."

The kid let out a sigh of relief. "Boy, do I feel better. Thank you very much."

"You're very welcome," Decker said.

"Is Noam in big trouble?" Yossie asked.

"Honestly, I don't know."

"He gets into trouble a lot. I just hope he's not over his head. He's kind of a jerk, but he isn't evil or anything like that. I'd feel real bad if something happened to him."

"I understand." Decker stood and helped the teenager up. "You're a good friend, Yossie. Thanks for the help."

Yossie nodded gravely. Decker put his hand on the boy's shoulder and extended the same offer he gave the Greitzman boys. Yossie's spirits seemed to perk up immediately.

Good ole Disneyland—the ultimate kid picker-upper.

15

Another sundown, this one signifying the end of the Jewish New Year. Decker dropped off Shimon Levine, then headed for the Lazarus house, thinking how the first two days of his honeymoon had been spent in emotional upheaval.

Dusk was blanketing the neighborhood. A thick gray fog had settled upon the rooftops, obscuring chimneys and rain gutters as if the houses had been set in badly cropped photographs. Decker turned up his collar. Black-garbed shadows whooshed past him on their way to evening prayer, their shoes making clopping noises against the sidewalk. He took a deep breath, then exhaled, blowing out a stream of warm air. Just how *far* did he intend to take the case?

It was hard to come up with rational decisions because he was tired and hungry. He hadn't eaten breakfast because he'd overslept. With an empty stomach and puffy eyes, he had rushed off to morning services. Afterward, he'd bolted down a small lunch because he knew a full stomach would make him sleepy. He had wanted to be in top form for the interviews. The most insignificant thing might prove to be important; a kid's life could depend on how alert he was.

The interviewing had gone well. Good old Yossie Weinstein had provided a crack in the vacuum.

Decker thought about the kids who lived here. The ones he'd spoken with seemed remarkably well adjusted. Even those who had strayed a bit from "the path" knew the difference between curiosity and trouble. The boys he'd interviewed had thought of Noam as an oddball at best, a bad apple at worst. But all agreed he seemed lonely.

A lonely, naïve boy somewhere in the city. Frightening. He looked at Noam's picture again. There was something cocky about his expression.

His mind flashed to Jonathan's first assessment of his nephew.

Kid smiles a lot but never looks happy.

And what Yossie had said about Hersh.

He has a weird smile—lopsided.

Mentally, Decker rummaged through his past case files: thousands of problem kids. Some were actually redeemable. But then there had been the others—the real badasses destined to do hard time if they lasted that long. They had many common attributes, but the one that was sticking in Decker's mind was their *affect*—always out of sync with what was happening to them. No matter how much trouble they were in, they just sat there with these eerie smiles plastered on their faces, grinning as if you'd just told them a dirty secret.

He stifled a yawn, his only wish—to pump something bulky and nontoxic into his stomach and close his eyes.

Rina was waiting for him at the front door of the townhouse. She came out and gave him a bear hug.

"All right!" Decker threw his arms around her. "To what do I owe this burst of affection?"

"I love you. I realized it's been a long time since I've told you that."

"Love you too, kiddo," Decker said. "I'm beat."

Rina said, "We've got a full house inside—"

"Christ—"

"No one expects you to make chitchat. Everybody knows how hard you're working. Just say hello, then go upstairs. I'll bring you some dinner."

"Will you eat with me?"

Rina smiled. He looked like a puppy begging for table scraps. She pinched his cheeks. "Of course I'll eat with you." She slid her arm around his waist and led him inside, gently pushing him through the throng of women—all of them wishing him their best. They would have asked him more—Decker saw curiosity etched into their faces—but Rina was a skillful guide. She whisked him into their room upstairs, then helped him off with his jacket. She pointed to the folded-down bed and said, "Sit down and I'll take off your shoes. And I'll even rub your feet."

Decker eyed her. "Are you doing this to keep me on this case?"

Rina said, "Are you assigning ulterior motives to my wifely behavior?"

"Your behavior isn't wifely," Decker said. "It's . . . geisha-esque."

"That's not a word, Peter," she said. "Would you like me to take off your pants?"

"Hell, yeah."

Rina laughed. "No argument about that one."

"In fact—"

"The boys will be home any second."

"I'll be quick and I'll be quiet."

Rina looked upset, regarded her watch.

Decker said, "I was just kidding, darlin'."

"You don't mind waiting until tonight?"

"Honey, it's a necessity unless you're into necro-philia."

Rina smiled, then stared at her feet. Decker knew what questions were coming. Might as well preempt them, get it over with.

"The interviews went well," he said. "If the kids take me up on my offer, we're going to have to rent a bus."

"What?"

"To show my appreciation for their cooperation I promised them all trips to Disneyland if they come out to California. And Pete Decker does not break his promises."

"Did you find out anything substantial?"

"Nothing to make me do a handstand," Decker said. "But I got a new lead. I'm going to follow it up tonight."

"What kind of a lead?"

"A liquor store and the name of a kid—a twenty-year-old, rather. His name is Hersh." Decker described him. "He sound familiar?"

Rina thought awhile, then shook her head.

Decker said, "He didn't sound familiar to Shimon, either. The kid I interviewed said Hersh might be from Crown Heights. I'll check out Empire Boulevard. If I don't get anywhere, I'll canvass Crown Heights tomorrow."

"I thought you wanted out," Rina said. "I had this whole elaborate speech prepared to defend your decision."

Decker collected his thoughts. "I *do* want out. And if I could find an *Orthodox* investigator, I'd gladly bid the whole clan adieu. But I have a feeling religious PIs are hard to come by and I can't send average PI Joe into Crown Heights. I may not be ready to be ordained, but at least I have inklings as to what makes these people tick. An ordinary PI ain't gonna know zilch."

Rina gave him an uh-huh.

"And," Decker went on, "I suppose, as a cop, I can communicate to the local police better than a PI could." He glanced up at Rina. She was grinning. "Rina, I'm not being noble, just practical."

"Of course," she said. "And also being practical, I think I should help you canvass Crown Heights."

Decker gave her a dubious look.

Rina said, "Peter, I can talk to the women better than you can."

"Forget it."

"What are you going to tell me, Peter? It's too

dangerous? Some irate Lubavicher Chasid might curse me to death?"

"I don't work with my wife."

Rina stared at him. "That is so ridiculous. I'm not going to respond to it."

Decker smiled. "Your prerogative, darlin'."

"We both want to find Noam," Rina said. "It's also *my* honeymoon that's being affected. I don't see you a lot. You work long hours. At least let me ride with you so I can remember what you look like."

Decker said, "Now she's trying guilt."

"I'm in the room, Peter. You don't have to talk about me in the third person."

"Okay, okay." Decker paused a long time. "All right, you can ride with me. Truth be told, I'd love to have your company. But if things start getting hairy, promise me you'll back off."

"I've been through horrible situations before," Rina said. "I think I've survived quite well."

"This has nothing to do with your ability to survive, hon," Decker said. "Let's just say I'm being selfish. My home—our home—is my refuge, a place where I can leave my work behind. If you're in the field with me, Rina, I can't do that. You understand what I'm saying?"

"Yes, I do," Rina said. "And I know how you feel about discussing your cases with me. If you don't want to talk to me about work—if you're afraid of burdening me or defiling the sanctity of our household, I understand. And that's fine. Thank God you have Marge for catharsis.

"But this is a special situation. I know the family.

I'm personally involved. But more important, there's something else going on. This whole Frieda Levine situation: It *has* to be affecting you. And except for me there's *no one* else for you to confide in. I just want to be near you in case you need someone to lean on."

Decker gave her a weak smile, then averted his eyes. Goddamn, the woman was perceptive. Those walks with Ezra and Shimon, the talks with Jonathan: They had opened a Pandora's box he'd never realized he'd owned. Whenever he seriously thought about it, he became dizzy, sick. Then he'd chastise himself for feeling that way. He had *parents*, he had a *brother*—what the hell did he care what these strangers thought of him? Yet the feelings of kinship had pierced his skin as subtly as a pinprick.

He reached out to Rina like a poor man begging for alms. She was his heartbeat, the steady rhythmic pulse that gave him life. In her embrace, he found a place he would forever call home.

Even accounting for getting-lost time, Decker figured Crown Heights to be no more than a twenty-minute car ride from Boro Park. It took him a half hour to realize he'd been assuming "L.A. Driving Time" instead of "New York Driving Time." The streets were narrow and potholed, crowded by rows of double-parked cars and pedestrians who didn't believe in red lights. At least Jonathan's car had ample stretching room because Jonathan—like him—had stilts for legs. Kid had been kind enough to let Decker borrow the car again.

A full hour later, after battling several traffic jam-
ups, taking three trips around Prospect Park, and
overshooting himself to Eastern Parkway, Decker
managed to find the elusive Empire Boulevard. It
didn't appear to be a thoroughfare by L.A. standards, but it stretched about two miles. It was also
a line of transition. The street gave occupancy to
several Jewish storefronts but many more secular
establishments—a doughnut luncheonette, a pizza
parlor, a small mart called the L.A. Special which
didn't typify L.A. or seem special. But it did sell
candy and cold beer and soda and felt these items
were noteworthy enough to advertise. Empire Boulevard also had several video sales and repair centers—
places not meant for the Crown Heights Jews because
they—like the Boro Parkers—didn't own TV sets.
And as in Boro Park, many of these discount setups
were run by ultra-Orthodox Jews.

At nine P.M., with most of the commercial stores
closed, the sidewalks didn't harbor a large population. The pedestrians he did see were black. After
cruising the street twice, he wrote down the names
and addresses of the liquor stores—three—and the
places that served alcohol—eighteen, counting all
the restaurants and bars. Though Decker was sure
that Yossie Weinstein hadn't met Hersh in a bar, it
was possible that Hersh had frequented saloons alone
or with others.

Decker consulted his list.

The first candidate was the Empire Liquor House,
a small storefront no more than six hundred feet
square. There was a Doberman guarding the door,

the dog's head as big as a toaster oven. It appeared to be sleeping, but Decker noticed its ears perk up when he crossed the threshold.

The store was a little larger than a cubicle, the area on his immediate right crammed with gondolas full of cheap wine and whiskey. On the left was a counter manned by a black in his mid-forties. He was as thin as a drinking straw, had a face sprinkled with salt-and-pepper stubble, and had a circle of shiny mocha skin on the crown of his head. Behind the counter were the expensive potables. If someone wanted to steal some class he'd have to jump the barrier to get to it. Tucked into a corner was the cash register.

The thin man said, "What do you want?"

His voice was high. The question had not been posed as a true inquiry. Rather, it asked: *Why the hell are you hassling me?*

"I'm not with the NYPD," Decker said.

Thin Man didn't answer.

Decker said, "Did you ever sell some hooch to a boy named Hersh—"

"Don't know no Hersh."

"Let me describe him—"

"Don't know no Hersh."

Decker smoothed his mustache, then pulled out his wallet. He flipped a ten onto the counter. The thin man eyed the money, then Decker, but didn't say a word. Decker described Hersh. This time Thin listened. He shook his head.

"I get a million baby Rambos walkin' in and out of this place—Eyetalians thinkin' they're tough meat. I told you before, I don't know no Hersh."

"Hersh is Jewish, not Italian," Decker said.

"Jews, Eyetalians—all the white boys look alike to me."

Decker pulled out another ten, then the photograph of Noam Levine. "Ever seen *him*?"

Thin said, "If you're looking for *that* kind of Hymie, you're on the *wrong* side of Empire."

"You never get Jews crossing over to your side?"

Thin became mute again. Decker pulled out a third ten. Thin broke into a wicked smile. He had wide spaces between his teeth. He said, "I get a few that come in here."

"Why?"

Thin shrugged, feigned innocence.

Decker said, "Look, buddy, the kid in this photograph is missing and I've just spent two days beating my meat for nothing. I'm tired, I've laid out a few bucks for you, so do something for me before I get pissed off and take it out on you."

Thin said, "You ain't with NYPD, but you're some kinda fuzz. You talk like fuzz and you're packing."

"You're very astute. Wanna answer my question?"

"Yeah, a few hymies come in here."

"Why?"

"They ain't gettin' enough at home, they think I can help them out." Thin broke into a smile. "Course they're wrong."

"Of course." Decker threw a fin on the counter. "What do you tell them?"

"All I do is give them directions," Thin said.

"To where?"

"Willyburg Bridge," Thin said. "It's all out in the open. The sisters service their needs before they go home to the old ladies. You oughtta see them, those little curls bouncin' while the ladies are outta sight doin' a righteous hoover on their pipes."

Decker groaned inwardly, but kept his expression flat. Men were men in any culture, but the thought of rabbis getting blow jobs from hookers . . . it was like imagining your parents having sex.

"Look," Decker said, "I'm going to write down my local phone number. Keep the photograph. This kid or someone named Hersh comes into view, you give me a call." He put his wallet in his coat pocket. "There's a sawbuck or two in it for you, if your information pans out."

Thin nodded. Decker walked out of the store. At least he hadn't promised the man a trip to Disneyland.

Rina was waiting up for him.

She must be interested in another round. Decker felt a pull below his belt. Another round? Why sure, ma'am, Detective Sergeant Decker is here to protect and *serve*. Goddamn, did she look edible in that peignoir. She patted the empty bed next to her and he was stretched out within seconds, having stripped nude in record time.

"You want the lights on or off?" Rina said.

Decker raised his brows. He still wasn't used to a woman who liked making love with the lights on. But this time his eyes were tired and the harsh incandescent glare was giving him a headache.

"Turn them off," he said. "There's a full moon out tonight."

Rina laughed, flipped the switch, and climbed on top of him. She took off her nightie, caressing his face with a swatch of pink diaphanous material. He bit the hemline, she tugged it out of his mouth.

Man oh man, this was what life was all about.

His stomach rumbled. He was hungry but no matter. Skip dinner and go directly to dessert.

16

Decker was ready by nine in the morning and waiting for Rina in the car. When she finally emerged from the house, she was wearing a down-filled jacket over a long denim skirt and a pair of thick black boots that looked suitable for trout fishing. The outfit was incongruous with her hair, which was jet black and fell to her shoulders in a nest of curls. She climbed into the passenger side of the car, kissed his cheek, and put on her seat belt. She wore no makeup other than lip gloss and mascara, her cheeks pink with a natural blush.

"Did you get an overnight perm or something?" Decker said.

"It's a wig—a *shaytel*." Rina fluffed up the curls. "I wouldn't go out with my hair uncovered. Do you like it?"

Decker said, "When did you get it?"

"I bought it in Los Angeles for Rosh Hashanah. Only so much had happened, I didn't feel right wearing it."

"Oh, that's what that furry thing in the suitcase was."

"Do you *like* it, Peter?"

"It's sexy. It doesn't match your boots."

"My feet got so cold in this weather."

"You don't have to come with me."

Rina said, "Maybe I'll bring you better luck than you had last night."

Last night, Decker thought. A few of the men he'd spoken to on Empire thought they might have met a kid like Hersh, but no one was sure of anything. Noam's picture was met with empty stares, shakes of heads.

"What do I do?" Rina asked.

Decker started the motor. Jonathan and his Matador had gone back to Manhattan, so Rina's mother-in-law had immediately volunteered her car for his use—a Plymouth Volare. It had a bench seat and even though he'd pushed it all the way back, his knees were still slightly bent. Here he was, three thousand miles from L.A., doing police work driving Volares and Matadors—typical unmarkeds. He might as well be home getting paid for it. Rina repeated her question.

"What do you do?" Decker said. "You sit in the car and keep me company. I'll holler if I need you."

"Okay."

Decker floored the pedal and peeled off. He flipped on the radio, couldn't find a station he liked, then, without thinking, pushed a waiting tape inside the tape deck. The speakers projected a gravelly male voice emoting in Yiddish. Decker pushed the eject button.

"What *is* this?" he said, pulling out the tape.

Rina took it from him and read the label. "Oh."

"What's oh?"

"It's number five in a series of lectures given by Rav Pearlman on *Midos*—manners."

Decker said, "That's what these people listen to when driving?"

"I wish you wouldn't refer to them as 'these people.'"

Decker smiled. "Music isn't allowed?"

"Of course *music* is allowed." Rina flipped open the glove compartment. "She has a ton of tapes in here."

"Such as?"

Rina started reading the labels. "For your listening enjoyment, we have Rav Chaverstein singing cantorial classics—"

"Put a bullet in that one."

"We have the Lubavich Boys Choir singing *Shabbos Zmirot* and other favorites."

"The Lubavich Boys Choir," Decker said. "Anything like the Castrati Choir in Italy?"

"No, Peter," Rina said. "These boys grow into men."

"Notta gooda for business," Decker said. "Too mucha turnover."

"Do you know how to get to Crown Heights?" Rina said.

"I got there last night, didn't I?"

"You seem to be taking the long route," Rina said. "At this rate, it will take us an hour to get there."

Decker didn't respond right away. Finally, he said, "You want to drive, Hotshot?"

Rina smiled. "You're doing fine, darling."

"Jesus, how'd you talk me into letting you come?"

"Because you need another set of eyes and someone who can shoot."

Decker whipped his head around. "*What?*"

Rina gasped, Decker slammed on the brakes. He almost rear-ended the car in front of him.

"You okay?" Decker said.

"Maybe I should drive, Peter."

"I'm a fine driver," Decker said. "What did you mean by someone who can shoot? I thought you gave up guns."

Rina didn't answer.

"Rina . . ."

Slowly she unbuttoned her jacket. She was wearing her Colt .38 snub-nose detective special inside her waistband.

Decker said, "I don't believe it—"

"It's not loaded—"

"Why are you so *obsessed* with guns? Last time you had a chance to fire it, you froze—"

"I didn't freeze," Rina shot back.

"Oh?"

"Yeah, oh!" Rina closed her jacket and crossed her arms. "I didn't shoot your weirdo friend because I had this sixth sense that he wasn't going to hurt me—"

"Oh, that's worth a lot!"

"He didn't, did he?"

"You didn't know that!"

"Yes, I knew it—"

"How'd you know it—"

"I just knew—"

"You just knew—"

"Yeah, I just knew."

Decker held up his hands and flopped them back on the steering wheel. His "weirdo friend" had been an old war buddy waiting for someone to push his self-destruct button. He'd tried to get Rina to detonate him by advancing upon her as she held a loaded gun. When she'd refused to pull the trigger, he'd taken the gun from her, aimed it at *her* head. But a moment later, he gave it back to her and simply walked away. Decker had known immediately what the bastard had been after. He had wanted retribution for his love murdered in the war. He blamed Decker and maybe that was justified. Decker had never told Rina about the incident. He wouldn't ever tell her. Some things were just too painful to admit to anyone, even your wife.

He slammed on the brakes again. Rina didn't say anything. Her silence was more potent than words.

"Rina, let me ask you something."

"Sure."

"Why on earth are you carrying a gun—the very one that you *supposedly* sold? First of all, you *know* I've got my piece, so *what* do you need yours for? Second, why are you carrying a weapon into an area like Crown Heights?"

"I told you it's unloaded."

"Then why bother bringing it? What is it with you? You have a strong desire to be Bonnie and Clyde?"

"Just Bonnie."

"That's not funny," Decker said. "I find your preoccupation with guns extremely disturbing. It almost got your head blown off."

"You're sounding very parental."

"Stop it, Rina."

She sighed. "Okay. You asked me a reasonable question, I'll answer you honestly. I brought my gun with me because I wanted you to know that I own it."

"You *told* me you sold it."

"I was going to sell it—"

"You *lied* to me."

"You were harping, Peter," Rina said. "I just wanted to—" She stopped in midsentence.

Decker said, "You wanted to shut me up, so you lied to me. Nothing like honesty in a marriage."

"Well, I'm admitting it now," Rina said. "And I've felt very guilty about it. I'm sorry. Will you forgive me?"

"If you sell the gun."

"Peter, it should be *my* decision, not yours."

"You're my *wife*! According to Jewish law, I *bought* you."

Rina glared at him. "I hate when you use religion to prove a point."

Decker said, "This conversation is pointless."

"So drop it!"

They rode in angry silence for the next few moments. Decker broke it.

"After two years, I finally see that no matter what I say . . . what I do . . . you're going to carry that stupid gun."

"You're right."

Decker drummed his fingers on the wheel. "I hope to God you know what you're doing."

"Peter, you have no trust in my judgment. A marriage should be based on mutual trust."

"Now who's sounding preachy?"

"What do I have to do to earn your trust?" Rina said. "Outshoot you?"

Decker broke into laughter.

"Yeah, laugh," Rina said. "Want to know what I think? I think you're threatened."

"And I think you're a bit overwrought," Decker answered.

Rina crossed her arms over her chest, again too steamed up to answer. It was his tone of voice. So condescending.

Decker said, "You don't want to talk, I'll shut up."

Rina thought that was a very good idea. They drove awhile without speaking. But when they hit Eastern Parkway, Rina took his hand. She hated it when they fought. Life was too short. He looked over her way and broke into a smile. He thought he was angry, but he took one gander at those eyes and he melted. He adored her, couldn't stay angry at her. And hey, what the hell was wrong with that?

Crown Heights was another small island of ultra-Orthodox. Today not being a holiday, it was business as usual. Metal accordion grates had been pushed to one side, the doors were wide open. A few proprietors were hosing down the sidewalks at the entrances of their shops. An elderly lady wearing a bandana was on a ladder checking out a gash sliced into the store's front awning.

EISENSTAT'S DRY GOODS had piled the sidewalks with boxes of marked-down items. ETTI'S WHOLESALE OUTLET had run a metal bar across the front of its stall. Hanging from the bar were dozens of jackets and coats, not a moment's thought given to sorting the merchandise according to size or sex. Next to the overcoats were makeshift shelves filled with assorted shoes. Another wholesale outlet was selling linens. Stacks of towels and sheets loaded down several folding tables placed in front of the store window. A bakery had set up tables and chairs on the front sidewalk. Two black-hatted men occupied one table. They were drinking from Styrofoam cups, eating onion rolls. Out of a double-parked van, a bearded Chasid was selling fruits and vegetables to a bevy of housewives. Another bearded man was crossing the street, shoving a steaming pushcart over a pothole.

The block seemed more like an open-air market than a business district. Decker half expected to hear hawking cries from the vendors as his car rolled by.

The metered street parking was already taken and cars had begun to double-park. By Los Angeles standards, an area this size could be easily canvassed in a day. But here the population was dense. In terms of questioning people, it was as if he had to cover an area four times the actual square footage.

He hunted for a parking space, frustrated by the narrow streets and the hordes of people who thought nothing of jaywalking.

"Why don't you double-park?" Rina said. "I'll sit in the car while you ask around."

Decker looked at her as if she'd said something profound. "That's a good idea."

"Thank you. Oh—and Peter?"

"What?"

"I've been thinking . . . not that I want to tell you your business—"

"What?"

"Well, rather than ask about your Hersh in specific, maybe it would be better to just ask about Hershes in general."

"Come again?"

"Ask the people if they know any Hershes who are about twenty-one. Hersh is a common name and your Hersh could be living a double life."

Decker didn't answer.

Rina said, "Forget it. It was just a thought—"

"It's a good thought. I'll take it into consideration."

"And maybe you should also ask about people named Zvi. Hersh and Zvi are used interchangeably in the community."

"Hersh and Zvi?"

"Hersh is Yiddish, Zvi is Hebrew. Both mean 'deer' . . . as in 'hart.'"

"Oh." Decker was aware that only an insider could have known something like that. He was glad Rina had come along. "You've got good horse sense, kiddo."

"Thanks."

She lowered her head, but Decker saw that she

was smiling. He reached over and kissed her cheek. Then he got out of the car.

The sun was shining, the temperature a crisp forty degrees. The streets seemed to dance with their own energy. People conversing, horns honking, the smell of yeast dough and onion and grease wafting through the air. Decker took out the picture of Noam and started his task at the beginning of the block, questioning people in each store as well as approaching random passersby. After two hours of inquiries, he came back to the car. Rina was reading a book—a biography of Menachem Begin. At her side was this morning's crumpled newspaper, the crossword puzzle completed in ink.

He got into the driver's seat. She looked up.

"No luck?"

"No one I spoke to recognized Noam. I've got a list of two Zvis and five Hershes or Hershels still in their twenties, with approximate addresses. You know how people are. 'Oh, there's a Hersh Goldblum who lives down that way.' Well, 'that way' could be any one of five streets or forty houses. I'm going to drop by the local police station, which I found out is the 72nd Precinct. They've got all the backward directories at their fingertips. I can phone telephone security and DMV from there."

Rina said, "Do you want some lunch first?"

"Nah, I'll wait until I get this over with. You go get yourself something."

"If you don't need that picture of Noam, maybe I could try my hand at canvassing the houses, talking to the women. I could pick you up at the station house in about an hour."

"You really want to do that?"

"Yes," Rina said.

"Okay, lady, you've got a deal." He handed her a bunch of photographs of Noam. "It would help me out."

Rina said, "We make a good team, huh?"

Decker laughed.

"What's so funny?"

She sounded hurt.

"We make a great team," Decker said. "It's just that Shimon said the same thing to me yesterday."

"Everybody wants to pair up with a winner," Rina said.

"I wish," Decker said.

An hour later, Decker returned to the car and they exchanged their findings. The Hersh/Zvi list had been pared down to three possibilities since two Hershes and the two Zvis had moved out of town. He'd spoken with Hersh One's wife and found out her husband owned a fish store in Williamsburg. He was a bearded man of six one, approximately two hundred pounds and thirty years old. Decker scratched him off the list. The other Hersh learned in a *kollel* all day and spent evenings at home with his wife and newborn son. He was about the right size, but was bearded and didn't seem to have any muscles to speak about. The third—a *Hershel*—was a jeweler and worked in Manhattan. Decker had talked to his wife and found out that he had blond hair and blue eyes and was twenty-eight.

Rina had struck out as well. Noam was a cipher to all of the housewives she'd talked to.

"We're back to square one," Rina said.

"Not just yet," Decker said. "And for what's next, I think I'll need your help."

"Whatever you want."

Her voice was full of excitement and he hoped he hadn't started her on something.

Decker said, "I want to talk to the teenage boys in this community. Maybe they—like Noam and Yossie—have met with Houdini Hersh. The easiest place to find them is at their schools. Now, the rabbis aren't going to be cooperative with me. I just look and act too goyish. But you know Yiddish and you're beautiful."

"I don't think my looks are an asset in this case."

"That's what you think. Men are men, and if these guys have eyes, they'll be sneaking looks at you. If you act modest and sincere and move your hips a little, I think you could talk your way in for us."

"How do I move my hips and act modest at the same time?"

"Nobody ever said detective work is easy." Decker winked at her. "I have the names of three local high school yeshivas. You want to break for lunch or do you want to work straight through?"

"Who can eat at a time like this?"

Decker said, "Then let's do it."

* * *

The first academy on the list was the Ner Tamid Yeshiva of Crown Heights. Its address was on Eastern Parkway—a wide boulevard graced by immaculately kept townhouses, structures erected long ago when labor was cheap and architects could afford to pay attention to detail. Doric columns flanked stately entrances; the spans above the doorways were crowned with intricately cast keystones. Front bay windows were framed with fluted moldings. Old-fashioned streetlights sat at the foot of each stone walkway; well-planted patches of front lawn were fenced by wrought-iron railings. The district held the elegance of a bygone era.

The yeshiva was a four-story building, the first floor fronted by limestone blocks, the remaining three stories masoned in brick. Zigzagging across a center column of windows were the metal rungs of a fire-escape ladder. The entrance doors were large and darkened by smoked glass. Three Chasidic boys were conversing outside. They wore black suits, black slouch hats, buttoned-to-the-neck white shirts, and no ties.

Decker parked the car at the front curb and hopped out. But Rina began searching through her purse. She pulled out a tattered scarf, folded it in half along the bias, placed it on top of her wig and tied the ends under her chin.

He looked at her. "But your head's covered. You're wearing a wig."

"I don't think *this* wig is appropriate."

Decker frowned. "Now your head matches your boots. Please may I have a pound of halibut, Molly Malone?"

"At least you said please." She punched him in the arm. "Don't worry. I've thought about this on the ride over. I have it all worked out."

"Great."

They went inside. The front hallway was lit by a gleaming bronze chandelier hanging from a plaster-cracked roof. That was as good as it got. The rest of the room was in the process of renovation—raw drywall, the baseboard around the floor full of nails from recently pulled-up wall-to-wall carpet. Off to the side, manning the reception area, was a fifty-year-old woman with a pencil behind her ear and bosoms that could feed India. She was wearing a brown suit and a Buster Brown wig. She sat at a card table, stacks of papers to one side, a phone and Rolodex on the other. Her eyes fell first on him, then on Rina.

"Can I help you?"

Rina smiled pathetically. She had a worried look on her face as she pulled out a picture of Noam. She spoke in a pitifully small voice, explaining that this boy was missing and she was a close friend of the family. That was as much as Decker could understand. As Rina laid it on thicker, she began to speak in Yiddish.

Decker stood there, trying to look like something more than an ornament. Stupid of him to think he could have pulled this off without an insider. But he conceded himself one pat on the back: An ordinary

PI would have really flubbed it. He was hog-tied, forced to stay on this case, until it resolved or at least moved out of the religious Jewish community.

As Rina spoke, the woman responded with grave nods of her head. Rina finished her plea and the woman said something in Yiddish, stood up and walked away.

"*Voos?*" Decker asked. *Voos* meant "what" and it was the only Yiddish word he knew.

"She's calling in the big boys," Rina said.

"What'd you tell her?"

"The truth," Rina said. "Which is sad enough. When I stop and think about it, I start to feel sick all over. Poor Breina. She must be dying inside."

"Well, you're doing your bit to help out."

"How are you doing?"

"What do you mean?"

"I mean . . . you know. Do you think about Mrs. Levine much?"

Decker gave her a sour look. "Not unless someone brings it up."

"Sorry."

He put his arm around her, remembered where they were, and quickly removed it. "Sorry I snapped at you. This whole family thing makes me very anxious. Someday I'll figure it all out. But now's not the right time."

Rina gave his hand a quick squeeze. He liked that.

Buster Brown came back with two rabbis. One looked to be in his early fifties and had a black beard streaked with gray. The other was younger—around

Decker's age. His face was baby smooth; a wispy line of red fuzz floated above his upper lip. Buster introduced them to Rina as Rav Seder and Rav Miller, respectively. Rina pulled out the photograph and went into her Yiddish spiel.

After a moment, the younger Rav Miller eyed Decker and said, "You're a policeman?"

"A detective," Rina answered. "A detective sergeant."

"You don't work in a uniform?" Rav Seder asked.

"No, detectives don't wear uniforms," Decker answered.

"How do you manage with Shabbos?" Rav Miller asked.

"It's probably like doctors," Rav Seder said. "You have someone taking your calls on Shabbos?"

"Usually," Decker said.

"What do you want with our boys—our *bochrim*?" Rav Seder said.

"Just to ask them a few questions," Decker said.

"And you think it will help?" Rav Seder said.

"It might," Decker said.

"If you can do it quick, by me, it's all right," Rav Seder said.

"Thank you," Decker said.

Rina smiled.

"Rav Miller will show you to the study hall," Rav Seder said. "The boys are learning there."

"What *Masechet*?" Decker asked. A *Masechet* was a tractate of Talmud. He had to throw that in. Just to show them he knew the terminology. Rav Seder seemed more annoyed than impressed.

"What *Masechet* is *shiur beis*?" he asked Rav Miller. "*Bava Metziah, Bava Basra?*"

Rav Miller shrugged ignorance.

Rav Seder waved them on.

The study hall was located in the basement—twelve hundred square feet packed with adolescent boys who hadn't mastered the art of using deodorant. The walls had been paneled in bad rosewood veneer and supported twenty unmatched bookcases. The floor was covered with industrial gray carpeting. The holy ark stood against the east wall and was dressed by an elaborately embroidered orange velvet curtain. The boys sat at desks facing one another, shouting questions or answers to their learning partners, gesticulating wildly with their hands. A few teenagers studied alone, rocking back and forth as they analyzed the religious text. A middle-aged rabbi wearing a wide-brimmed Stetson sat in the corner, an oversized tome in front of him. He appeared to be explaining something to two teenage boys who had yet to develop any bulk. The noise level was deafening, the lighting was bright and harsh. Even though communal learning was not a foreign concept to Decker, he still found the tumult unnerving. Rina, who had taught in a yeshiva for years, seemed completely at home.

Rav Miller held up his hand, telling him to stay put. He approached the rabbi wearing the Stetson, leaned over and said something in his ear. Two minutes later the Stetson rabbi banged on his lectern and the noise immediately died down to a few moribund whispers.

The Stetson rabbi said, *"Sheket . . ."* His voice was deep and raspy—a smoker's voice. "A policeman is going to talk to you." He looked up at Decker.

Not much by way of introduction. Decker explained that he was trying to find out the identity of a man who might be responsible for abducting a boy their age. He planned to speak with all of the boys individually. In the meantime, everyone was to go about their own business.

The boys looked at Decker, wide-eyed with excitement, and Decker wished he had something more awe-inspiring to present.

He decided to begin at the east end, with those closest to the holy ark. Rav Miller, seeing he was no longer needed, excused himself. Rina stood just outside the doorway, per Decker's orders. His presence was enough of a distraction, *her* presence—fishmonger look notwithstanding—would completely addle the boys' minds.

Twenty minutes later, Decker felt he had his first break—a kid who knew something. He read it on the boy's face before he opened his mouth.

The kid was handsome, his smooth skin unravaged by hormones, with strong cheekbones and firm chin. He had dark eyes rimmed with a circle of bright green; his brows were thick and gave him an adult look. But in those eyes was fear.

Decker started out slowly, asked the kid his name. He was Eli Greenspan, and he lived a few blocks down on Eastern Parkway. Eli had a hard time making eye contact. Decker showed him the picture of Noam, and predictably, the boy denied knowing him.

Decker asked him about Hersh.

He denied knowing him, too.

Decker asked him to think a little longer—just to make sure.

Eli said he was positive, then bit his lip. But Decker knew he was lying. To confront him in the presence of his friends, in front of his teacher, was out of the question. But he'd get back to him later. The rest of the interviewing took around an hour, the other boys having nothing of interest to report. But Decker was optimistic.

He and Rina left the yeshiva and headed for the car. He opened the door for her, slipped into the driver's seat, and started the motor. He waited until traffic had cleared both ways, then made an illegal U-turn and parked on the other side of the block. Rina asked him what was up.

"Ever been fishing?" Decker asked.

"No."

"This is called 'waiting for the bite.'"

"You've got something?"

"Maybe."

Rina looked at him. "Do you really need to be this oblique?"

Decker laughed and explained his plan. Eli Greenspan lived only a few blocks away, catch him on his way home from school. He asked Rina if she had any idea when the place let out and she said maybe four or five—three to four hours from now. A few minutes passed.

Rina said, "Is this what you call a stakeout?"

Decker said uh-huh and fell quiet.

"Then where's the thermos of coffee?" Rina asked.

Decker smiled but kept his eyes on the school's entrance.

"Can we talk during these things?" Rina said. "Or do you do your staking out in silence."

"We can talk," he said.

But neither did.

Five minutes later a group of students came out of the building and milled about on the front steps. Then two boys broke away and started down the street.

Decker suddenly sat up. "That's the kid." He started the motor. "Where the hell are they going?"

Rina looked at her watch. Two-thirty. "They're not supposed to be going anywhere. Kids that age don't get off-campus privileges."

"Then something's cooking," Decker said. "Keep your eyes on our boys."

He pulled the Volare into traffic. Eli hadn't lied about one thing. He and his companion had been walking only a few minutes before they turned into a walkway just a couple of blocks from the school. Decker made another illegal U-turn, parked in front, and leaped out of the car. He stuck his two forefingers inside his mouth and let out a whistle that could be heard a block away. The boys turned around. Decker jogged up the walkway.

The companion was heavier and shorter than Eli. His face was even-featured, but his cheeks and forehead were mosaics of tiny red bumps. He hadn't been in the study hall when Decker had done the interviewing—maybe the boy was in a higher grade or lower grade. He looked at Decker and nervously asked what he wanted.

Decker said, "Why don't you explain to your buddy who I am, Eli?"

The friend turned to Eli, who was staring at his feet.

No one spoke for a moment.

"What's going on, Eli?" the friend said.

Eli remained mute.

Decker said, "What is it, son? You need your lawyer present before you speak?"

"I can't talk to you here," Eli mumbled.

"Then where?"

"Come back tomorrow—"

"No way," Decker said.

"You don't . . ." Eli shook his head. "I can't think right now. I'm in a hurry."

"I'll be quick." Decker pointed to the Volare. "You want to talk in the car?"

"Eli, who is this man?" the friend said. Boldly, he looked up at Decker and said, "He isn't going anywhere with you."

Chalk up one for the kid's nerve, Decker thought. He was scared, shaking, but did exactly what you're supposed to do when someone you don't know confronts you. You speak up.

"Shai, he's a cop," Eli said.

"You want to talk out here for the whole world to see," Decker said, "that's up to you."

"I only have ten minutes left on my break," Eli pleaded. "If I'm late again, I'll get sent to the office."

"How about after school?" Decker said.

"My sisters will be home," Eli said. "Please. I'll meet you early tomorrow morning—"

"Can't wait that long," Decker said. "Tell me what you know about Hersh."

Shai involuntarily gasped. Decker turned to him.

"Name's familiar to you, too?"

"*Vey is mir,*" Shai said. "We can't talk here. Too many people. Let's go inside."

Eli seemed paralyzed. Shai pushed him forward to a unit on the first floor. Eli took out the key and opened the door.

The living room was spotless, the sofa and matching love seat done in white velvet upholstery. The dining room was to the right. Decker suggested they talk around the table.

When everyone was seated, he said, "You know this man named Hersh, boys. So don't try to tell me you don't. Okay?"

Eli looked at Shai, Shai looked at Eli. They both nodded.

Decker said, "What's Hersh's last name?"

His question was met with silence. Finally Eli said, "I don't know—"

"Don't *lie* to me, son," Decker broke in.

"I swear I don't know it exactly." Eli's face had become flushed. "I think it's Schwartz or Shartz or Shatz. Something like that."

Though Decker remained expressionless, he rejoiced inwardly. He said, "Where'd you meet him?"

Eli said, "He just sort of hangs around the school—"

"You're lying again," Decker interrupted. He took

off his yarmulke and repinned it. "That *really* makes me mad. He isn't known by the other boys in your class so he doesn't hang around the school." He bored in on Eli. "Now, I'll ask you again. Where'd you meet Hersh?"

Eli averted his eyes, then buried his face in his hands.

The lightbulb went on in Decker's head. The kid didn't have dark eyes—he had green eyes that were dilated. Had it been in any other context, Decker would have spotted a "head" in a minute. But he didn't expect to find one in this community. Eli had probably sneaked off school grounds to take a quick toke. Or afraid of all the questions, he'd come home to destroy evidence.

Flatly, Decker said, "I know Hersh is your dealer, Eli. Now that we've got that over with, you want to tell me where you met him—or meet him? I'm assuming you're still in contact with your dealer."

Head still buried, Eli mumbled something. Decker yanked the kid's elbows off the table, causing his head to fall forward. Decker raised the boy's face by his chin and said, "You're lucky. You're lucky you're talking to me instead of a narc. You're lucky you're talking to me and not your parents. You're also damn lucky you're not Noam Levine because who the hell *knows* what happened to him. A kid's life could depend on you, so cut the hysteria and answer my questions. Where do you meet Hersh?"

Eli looked up, the dilated eyes moist with tears. Shakily, he said, "We meet all sorts of places, mostly on the other side of Empire Boulevard."

"Know where Hersh lives?"

"No!" Eli cried out. "I swear I—"

Shai broke in, "He once mentioned to me that he was originally from Flatbush—"

"You wouldn't be conning me, would you, son?" Decker said.

"No sir, I'm not," Shai said.

Decker regarded Shai. For whatever it was worth, the boy seemed lucid. He said, "So Hersh is named Schwartz or Shatz or something like that. And he's from Flatbush originally."

Both of the boys nodded. Kewpie dolls with coiled necks.

"Okay," Decker said. "Where in Flatbush did he say he was from?"

"He never said," Shai said.

"Never mentioned any street, any road, any house, any landmark?"

"No, sir," Shai said. "Not to me."

"Me, either," whispered Eli.

"Hersh ever mention any family?"

Both boys shook their heads.

"So," Decker said, "if he didn't work out of his house, where'd you guys score from him?"

"He hangs around liquor stores on Empire," Shai said.

"Which ones?" Decker said.

"All of them," Shai said. "He hangs out with a group of Italians. I thought he *was* Italian until he told me his real name was Hersh."

"What name did he use?" Decker said.

"Tony," Eli whispered.

"Tony?" Decker repeated.

"Yeah, Tony," Shai said. "He called himself Tony."

Decker said, "I'm not from around here. What kind of area is Flatbush?"

"Flatbush is mixed," Shai said. "There're very religious areas, there're black areas, there're Italian areas. That's why I thought he was Italian. He hung out with the Italians, he looked Italian, he even talked a little Italian. But then there was this one time. He was ticked off at his so-called friends. He showed his true colors. He pulled us aside and said he wasn't a wop—his words, not mine—and his name was really Hersh. He even spoke to us in a *bissel* Yiddish, remember, Eli?"

There was no response.

Decker looked at Eli. He'd buried his head in his hands again. Decker said, "Go drink a quart of water right now, then make yourself a cup of strong black coffee."

Eli dutifully got up and went into the kitchen. Decker shouted, "Bring the water here. I don't want you out of my sight."

Shai said, "I don't take drugs—"

"Save your breath, son. This isn't confession."

"I *swear* I don't. Drugs are dangerous."

Decker studied the boy. "You're right about that."

"But Eli . . . I've known him since we were little kids. I try to look after him. See, he's under a lot of pressure because his father runs a small Lubavicher shul in North Carolina and lives more there than here. His mother refuses to move 'cause she hates North Carolina. So they're always fighting about it when he gets home. Now Eli's mom's got a full-time job and all the household stuff is falling on Eli's shoulders 'cause he's the oldest."

Eli walked back into the room. He held a pitcher of water—no cup—and his hands were shaking. Decker stood, told the boy to sit. He fetched a glass from the kitchen, poured the water, and made sure the boy drank at least half the pitcher.

A minute later, Eli announced that he had to go to the bathroom. Decker told him that was the idea. After Eli left for a second time, Decker said to Shai, "If you're his keeper, get him off drugs."

"I've tried and Eli's tried," Shai said. "It's hard. See, when Eli isn't stoned, he gets real, real nervous and his ulcer starts to act up. One time it acted up so bad, he was in the hospital for a week." Shai pounded his forehead several times with his fists. "I don't know what to do. Eli seems to be smoking more and more every month. I'm afraid he's gonna try something stronger. Then I *really* won't know what to do."

Decker said, "He only uses pot?"

"Yeah."

"You're sure?"

Shai paused, then nodded. "That's what Tony . . . Hersh sells. Never seen him sell anything stronger and he would if he had it."

Eli returned. Decker made him finish the rest of the water. Then he pulled out the photograph and said, "You boys ever see this kid with Hersh?"

Both boys looked at the picture, Eli for the second time, Shai for the first. It was Shai who first spoke up.

"I've seen him with Ton—Hersh. I was real surprised, because you could tell he was one of us."

"By one of us," Decker said, "you mean religious—*frum*?"

Shai nodded.

Decker turned to Eli. "You've seen him with Hersh?"

"Once or twice," Eli said.

Shai said, "I think he called himself Nolan, but it was obvious that that wasn't his real name."

"It's Noam Levine," Decker said.

Both boys shrugged.

"Did they seem like good friends?" Decker asked.

"This Nolan seemed more like Tony's servant than like a friend," Shai said. "Ton—Hersh would show up with these kids—kids our age. He knew a bunch of them. Most of them were like these skinny, wimpy-type kids. But this Nolan or Noam . . . First off, he was big. Second, you could tell right away that he was raised *frum*. For some reason I think Tony liked Nolan *because* he was *frum*. Also 'cause Nolan was bigger and a bully. He wasn't a bully to us, Eli's bigger than him. But you had the feeling, Nolan liked to boss around little kids. Also, he wasn't put off by Hersh's knives—"

"Knives?" Decker said.

"Hersh loves knives," Shai said. "He's always showing them off. He has lots of them."

Swell, Decker thought. Noam's possibly involved with a psycho. Maybe Noam *was* a psycho. He said, "Did Hersh ever threaten you with his knives?"

"Not me," Eli said. "But once . . . this was real

weird . . ." He knitted his brow. "He asked me what my father did for a living. I told him he was a rabbi and a mohel—"

"Oh, yeah," Shai interrupted. "He started asking all these questions on the kind of knife used for circumcisions. Then he offered to trade Eli . . ." The boy sighed. "He offered to trade stuff for his father's *bris milah* knife. He liked the fact that it was sharp on both sides."

"Did you do it?" Decker asked.

Eli shook his head vehemently. "I don't steal."

One point in his favor. Decker said, "So Hersh liked knives. What about Noam?"

"No idea," Shai said. "I only saw Nolan once or twice."

"And from what you saw, Noam and Hersh didn't relate as equals," Decker said.

"Not at all," Shai said. "Hersh used to boss Nolan—or Noam—around. 'Move here, go there, get that, take that.' Nolan just took it."

"Did he threaten Noam with the knife when he was ordering him around?"

Shai thought a long time. "I don't think so. I would have remembered if he did. But I do remember him waving this big long knife around. Just showing it off. It was very scary."

Decker kept his face impassive and turned to Eli. The boy shrugged, said he didn't remember if Hersh ever threatened anyone. While Decker had Eli's attention, he said, "Your friend Shai tells me he's clean, he's not a user. You smoke solo."

Eli nodded.

"Okay," Decker said. "Then this little speech is for your ears, Eli. Before I leave, you're going to get me your stash. Then, as far as you and I are concerned, it's almost Yom Kippur, you get a clean slate. If you want to hang out with losers, that's up to you. But think about this for just a moment. Life may seem terrible, but prison is *worse*. You've got to talk to your parents, Eli. Tell them what's on your mind."

"They don't understand," Eli said.

"They may understand more than you think."

"You don't know my parents." Eli shook his head vigorously. "You just don't *know* my parents."

"How about this?" Decker said. "I'll get you the name of someone you can talk to."

Eli's eyes filled with tears. "I don't have any money. I don't have a car. So who's gonna talk to me who lives close? Who's gonna talk to me for free? Who's gonna talk to me and not tell my parents? Who can I talk to who will understand the kind of life I have to live?"

Without missing a beat, Decker said, "*I'll* find someone for you."

"*Who?*" Eli said.

"Hey, that's my end of the bargain," Decker said. "Now what you've got to do is stay off drugs until I find someone."

No one spoke for a minute. Finally Eli said, "How long will that take?"

"Three days," Decker said, picking a number out of the air. "Lay off drugs for three days and I'll find someone for you to talk to. We've got a deal?"

Eli lowered his head. He mumbled, "You gonna tell my parents?"

"You're off drugs, right?" Decker said, "I really don't have anything to tell your parents, do I?"

Eli didn't respond.

Decker said, "Son, if you mess up, eventually your parents will find out. So try and save yourself some heartache. Give me a chance to find someone for you."

Eli's eyes overflowed, tears drawing tracks down his smooth cheeks. Slowly he nodded consent.

"Great." Decker stood, laid a hand on Eli's shoulder. "Now let's get you back to school."

Eli nodded, then said thanks in a cracked voice.

Decker wondered who the hell he was going to find for the boy. No matter. If he had to scour all of New York, he was determined to find someone. He told Eli to fetch him his stash and was surprised when the kid returned with a coffee can full of primo stuff. Made Decker wonder if the kid wasn't a dealer himself. Or maybe he was just an economy shopper.

Decker took the coffee can, emptied the contents into the toilet and flushed several times. Gonna be lots of mellow rats in Brooklyn for the next few hours. He walked back to the living room and motioned the boys to the door with his thumb. The interview was over.

After he dropped off the teenagers at the yeshiva, he filled Rina in on the details and asked her if she knew any religious shrinks.

"No," Rina said. "Shrinks aren't big in this community."

"I bet," Decker said. "I've got to find someone."

"Couldn't you have promised him a trip to Disneyland instead?" Rina said.

Decker gave her a dirty look.

"Some people have no sense of humor." Rina was quiet for a moment. "I bet Jonathan might know of a good therapist. As a matter of fact, I think Jonathan has some sort of counselor's license."

"Wonderful," Decker said. "I'll call him as soon as I get back to your in-laws' house."

"You know what, Peter?" Rina said. "You try to hide it, but you really are a good guy."

"Aw shucks."

She pinched his cheek. "So, what's next?"

Decker said, "First, I'm going back to the liquor stores on Empire Boulevard. I asked the owners about a guy named Hersh. Now I'm going to go back and ask about a guy named Tony. If I'm extremely lucky, one of the men may even know Tony's assumed last name. I don't want to be looking for Hersh Schwartz when he's going by the name Tony Palumbo.

"Then, we'll hit Flatbush. See if we can find Tony/ Hersh's apartment. I'm going to check in with the local precinct there. I want to see if Hersh aka Tony has a record—maybe a drug bust. Or maybe he's been involved in a local incident. You start talking to these guys, they start to remember all sorts of things. That's how these cases go forward—legwork and mouthwork. Talk and walk. I just hope this Hersh holds the key to Noam's disappearance. If not, we're back to square one."

He smiled at Rina; she returned his smile. For

the first time, he noticed she'd become a little pale.

"Have you eaten lunch yet?" Decker asked.

Rina shook her head.

"Let's go grab a couple of big sandwiches at a local deli," Decker said. "You need some protein."

"You know," Rina said, "there's a wonderful kosher dairy Italian place in Flatbush on Coney Island Avenue. Red-checkered tablecloths, sawdust on the floor. There are even wine bottles hanging from the doorway. And they make a mean eggplant parmesan."

Decker shook his head. "Don't want to waste the time. I need to cover as much ground as possible before it gets dark."

"Of course," Rina said. "I mean, we're here to find Noam, not eat."

Decker patted her hands and gave her a warm smile. She was disappointed but trying not to show it. The glamour of detective work was fading fast.

That was good.

🌾17

Decker took off his yarmulke, then walked into the Empire Liquor House. The same thin black man was at the register. He was reading a magazine and looked up when he heard the Doberman grumble.

"I was hopin' for someone like you. I could use some more pocket change."

"Then it's your lucky day." Decker flipped out a twenty, held it between his first and second fingers. "You don't know any kid named Hersh, how about a kid named Tony?"

Thin smiled. "They's all named Tony."

"Do these Tonys have a last name?"

"I don't pay attention," Thin said.

Decker leaned over the counter until he was almost nose to nose with Thin. "Well, maybe you should pay attention, buddy, because some of these Tonys are dealing. Now it may seem like nothing to you to pass a little weed back and forth, but man, if these rabbis find out you're polluting their kids—"

"Who said I was pollutin'—"

"Let alone having minors hang around your store—"

"*What!*"

"These *hymies* have tempers," Decker said. "But hell, with a dump like this, a smashed window isn't going to make much of a difference—"

"You tryin' to muscle me, man?"

"God forbid," Decker said. "I'm just trying to jog your memory." He smiled. "Now where were we? Oh, yes, you were going to tell me all your Tonys' last names."

Thin just glared.

Decker threw up his hands. "Don't say I didn't warn you." He headed for the door, then turned around. "Does the word *chaptzum* mean anything to you?"

Thin screwed up his face. "I know what you're sayin'."

"Then why don't you give yourself a break?"

"Hmmmmm." Thin pondered a moment. "Maybe I can come up with a name or two."

Decker walked back to the counter and waited.

"They's a Tony Madiglioni," Thin said. "He's 'bout twenty-six or -seven—"

"Too old. I'm looking for a Tony who sells weed and brings along thirteen-year-old boys for gofers."

Thin thought a moment. "Yeah, that'd be a Tony. 'Bout twenty, maybe twenty-one. Never said his last name—"

"Cut the shit—"

"I'm tellin' it *straight*, Mr. Heat. But for your twenty . . ." Thin snapped the bill away from Decker. "I will tell you something of in-te-rest. This Tony—no last name—once crashed with a kid named

Ernie Benedetto in Flatbush. Now I haven't seen Ernie in a long time. Could be the kid got busted, could be the kid took a hike. But the two of them—they used to live together."

Decker asked, "Did Tony and Ernie do more than room together?"

Thin shook his head. "Don't think so. Tony, he sure knew a lot of teenage boys, I always suspected that kids was his thing. But I don't *know* that he did something with them. Ernie liked girls—least he used to talk like he liked girls." He looked at the twenty in his hand. "I think I've given you more than your money's worth."

Decker said, "We'll see about that." But he dropped another ten on the counter anyway. Informants in foreign cities were hard to come by.

"Ernest Benedetto," the desk sergeant said. His name was Mahoney, a man in his forties with a florid complexion and pecan-colored hair that had been combed straight back. "No, Ernest Benedetto don't ring no bell to me. But that don't mean nuttin'. All it means is that there's so many assholes, I can't keep track of 'em all."

It was four in the afternoon. Decker had wanted to drop Rina off, but she was determined to stick it out with him. Besides, she said, she was reading a good book. So she waited in the car while he talked shop with the boys at the Six-Seven. One thing about NYPD, they were accommodating to the brothers.

Decker said, "Can you punch Benedetto into the computer, find out if he has a yellow sheet?"

"No problem," Mahoney said, typing in the name. "Let's hear it for electronic wizardry." He waited a moment, then said, "Oh my, oh my, Ernie's been a busy boy."

Decker studied the monitor. Benedetto had been busted for possession—six months' jail sentence. Served his time as a trusty until one day he'd walked off the premises and forgotten to return. A warrant had been issued for his arrest.

Mahoney regarded Decker. "Is he involved in your kidnapping?"

"I don't know," Decker said. "Can you punch up his last known address?"

Mahoney said, "Man, with these computers, I could tell you the last time he took a dump."

Mahoney fed the computer, gave Decker the information a few moments later.

Decker said, "Now can you cross-reference that address with any other names?"

"I can cross-reference it," Mahoney said, "but the computer's only gonna spit out names of record holders. To get names of Joe Civilian, youse gonna have to use the backwards directories or call the phone company."

Decker said, "Try it anyway."

"Sure."

There were no other names.

"Okay," Decker said. "Can you try this? Can you see if you can get hold of Benedetto's former addresses."

"We can try," Mahoney said. Three other sets of

numbers appeared on the monitor. "Now you want me to cross-reference those with other names?"

"You bet," Decker said. He held his breath.

Nothing.

Which meant either Tony/Hersh didn't have a record or the list of addresses was incomplete.

"I'll have someone bring you out the last five years' worth of backwards directories," Mahoney said. "You can look up the addresses; they'll tell you name and phone numbers of the people they used to belong to."

"That would be super," Decker said. "In the meantime, can you punch in the name Hersh Schwartz, Shartz, or Shatz and see if anyone with those names has a record?"

"You got it," Mahoney said.

Five minutes later, Decker saw a woman officer teetering under the weight of five large phone books. It wasn't until he took the books away that he noticed she was gravid, ready to drop any moment. She smiled as he stared, saying that the exercise was good for the baby.

Decker parked himself at an empty table, out of the way of foot traffic.

He opened the first book.

Nothing.

Mahoney called out that their computer had no record of any Hersh Schwartz, Shartz, or Shatz.

A half hour later, Decker hit the mother lode with book number four. A Benedetto address was cross-referenced to a man named Tony Sacaretti.

He walked over to Mahoney and asked him to feed
the computer the name.

"Tony Sacaretti?" Mahoney said, punching in the
letters. "Never heard of him."

It came out *nehvahoidovem*.

Decker waited, jaw clenched. All he needed was
for Hersh to fuck up just one time. For a scumbag
like him, that wasn't too much to ask for.

His faith in the depravity of human nature was
rewarded.

Bingo!

Tony Sacaretti alias Hersh Schaltz. Arrested for
misdemeanor possession three years ago, nineteen
at the time. Sentenced to two years' probation. Hersh
was now a free man. The computer hadn't mentioned
the name the first time around because the address
had been an old one—before Hersh had been entered into the computer.

Mahoney said, "That your man?"

"Bet your ass," Decker said.

"Okay," Mahoney said. "Now if you just hang on
a sec." He typed rapidly onto the keyboard, then
waited. A few seconds later, there was another read-
out. "Movin' right along, this is Schaltz's last known
address according to Probation."

"There a phone number with the address?" Decker
asked.

"Yep." Mahoney pushed another button. In a matter of seconds, the information on the monitor was
printed on paper. He tore off the sheet.

Decker regarded the printout. This address, this
lone address. He hoped it was the place where Noam

Levine was hiding out. But if Hersh Schaltz had nothing to do with Noam's disappearance, Decker had *nothing*. He asked Mahoney if he could use the phone. Mahoney said it was right behind him, press the third button.

Decker called the number listed. It rang and rang and rang.

At least it wasn't disconnected.

Then he called the phone company. Using Mahoney's badge number, he asked for a name to match up with the number in question.

A deep-voiced woman told him the number was billed to a Hersh Schaltz.

"And the number is still operable?"

"Yes."

"When was the last time the bill was paid?"

The woman told him to hold on a moment. She came back and announced that the bill was, in fact, a month overdue. If he was intending to talk to Mr. Schaltz, she'd appreciate it if he informed Mr. Schaltz of that fact.

Decker thanked her and hung up.

"I am out of here," he announced to Mahoney. "If you ever get out my way, you've got a free trip to Disneyland for you, the wife, and the kids."

Mahoney smiled broadly. "No shit? Hey, that's real nice of you."

"M'pleasure," Decker said, thinking: Tickets to Disneyland were twenty-one fifty per adult, not much cheaper for kids. At this rate, he'd spend a week's worth of salary making good on his promises.

* * *

Hersh Schaltz lived in a ten-story tenement house off Flatbush Avenue. It was a square brick thing, tattooed with graffiti, its front walkway overrun with papers, broken glass, and beer cans.

Decker parked in front. He turned to Rina and said, "I don't want you to come in with me, but I don't want to leave you alone outside. Maybe I should take you home."

"I don't want you going inside by yourself," Rina said. "I'll be your backup."

"With an unloaded gun?"

"Give me some bullets."

"I don't have any thirty-eight shells. All I have are clips."

"Well, nobody's going to know if the gun's loaded or not," Rina said. "It's all in the appearances."

Decker stared at her. She'd removed the old kerchief and looked about as threatening as a Playboy Bunny. "You don't strike a mean pose, Rina."

"Well, I'm not going to wait out here by myself. And you'll waste a lot of time if you go back and forth. Let me come with you."

Against his better judgment, Decker agreed.

When they got to the front door, they found out it was a security building. Directly to the left was a long column of numbered buttons with no names to identify the people living inside. Decker peered through the glass doors. A dimly lit hallway, old linoleum on the floor, paper peeling from the walls. A bank of mailboxes was visible to the right.

"Your eyes are better than mine," he said. "Look at

the mailboxes and see if you can find me the building manager's number."

Rina squinted. "I can't make out anything."

"Damn," Decker said.

Rina pressed a random button.

"What are you doing?" Decker asked.

A speaker-slurred voice said a muffled "Who's there?" through the intercom.

"Waterworks," Rina said. "Which unit is the super's?"

"One-oh-four," the voice answered back.

"Thank you," Rina said. She looked at Decker and smiled.

"Clever," Decker said.

"You can take it from here," Rina said.

Decker smiled sarcastically and pressed 104. He identified himself, and a second later they were buzzed in.

The super met them in the hallway wearing a torn sweatshirt and a pair of sweatpants a size too small. He was a rotund man with coarse black hair and matching mustache. He said his name—something Slavic and unpronounceable.

The super knew it and said, "You can call me Jerz." He eyed Rina. "What can I do for the police?"

His voice was a foghorn, thickly accented.

"I'm looking for a tenant named Hersh Schaltz."

"Hersh Schaltz?" Jerz thought a moment, then shook his head.

"How about Tony Sacaretti?"

Again, Jerz said no.

Decker showed Jerz the printout. "Who lives in unit six-eighteen?"

"Six-eighteen?" Jerz scratched his head. "That is the German . . . Heinrich Stremmer."

"Heinrich Stremmer?" Rina said.

Jerz nodded. "Kid 'bout twenty-one, skinny body but big shoulder muscles. Dark hair. He don't look German."

"I think he's the one," Decker said. "Can you open his place for us?"

"Why don't you knock on door?"

"I don't think he's in," Decker said.

"I don't know," Jerz said. "Two people snooping around."

Decker said, "You do us this small favor, and I'll mail you back bus fare plus free passes to Disneyland for you and the family."

Jerz's eyes lit up. "You not joking?"

"I'm not joking."

"For me, my wife, and my son?"

Thank God, he only had one kid.

"For all three of you," Decker said.

Jerz shrugged. "I do it for you. But you don't make no mess."

"No mess," Rina said.

"I believe you, young lady," Jerz said. "Follow me."

They climbed the stairs. Jerz was winded and wheezing when they reached the sixth-floor landing. Heinrich Stremmer lived in a flat in the middle of a dark, musty hallway redolent of urine. Muted sounds could be heard from the other units, greasy smells leaked under doorways. The passageway was cold and Rina let out a small shiver. Jerz first knocked on the door. When that didn't produce a response, he pulled out a ring of keys.

Decker said, "Do you know if Mr. Stemmer—"

"Stremmer, Str—emmer."

"Mr. Stremmer," Decker corrected himself, "was behind on his rent?"

"I don't know," Jerz said. He sorted through his keys. "You have to ask owners."

"Who owns the building?" Decker said.

"Corporation with letters," Jerz said. "ICMB, IBMC, BCIM—ah, here's key."

Jerz inserted the key in the lock, the door opened.

Rina said, "Uh-oh."

Mentally, Decker echoed the sentiment. But the first words out of his mouth were, "Don't touch anything!" Jerz started to enter the flat, but Decker gently held him back.

"Wait," he said.

Then he did what he always did when about to enter a crime scene. He used his eyes as cameras.

The place was as stripped as a motel room past checkout time. The living room held a scarred coffee table scored with deep gouges, and two mismatched end tables also pocked with knife wounds. Both were void of any newspapers or magazines. The sofa was lumpy, the carpet spotted with grease. The shades were yellowed, pulled down, swallowing the incoming light. Only a beam sneaked through where one shade had been neatly slashed down the center.

The kitchenette, done in high-gloss ivory enamel

paint, was more of a closet than a room. It was right off the front door and hadn't been cleaned for a while. The linoleum floor was missing a few tiles and dotted with dozens of dead roaches. The burned Formica counter top was filthy, a trail of ants swarming around a large fishhead, marching in and out of the eye sockets and gaping mouth. The drawers and cupboards had been opened and left naked. Inside the sink was a paper garbage bag stuffed with used paper plates.

The place stank of fish. But Decker was happy with what his nose told him. No *decay*. He told the others to wait by the doorway, he was going to investigate. Something about his tone of voice was commanding. Jerz didn't put up a squawk.

Decker took a closer look at the trash—paper plates, dried pieces of fried fish—homemade, not your typical takeout stuff. Its odor was mixed with the acrid vinegar smell of leftover coleslaw and tartar sauce—both items prepackaged. Used plastic cutlery. He pulled his jacket sleeve over his hand and poked the plates out of the way, trying to avoid scampering roaches. He found a half dozen crumpled bits of paper and unfolded the first.

Times, dates—an airline schedule. Or maybe a bus schedule.

He unfolded the second one.

More time schedules. The word UNITED printed in bold black letters.

Airline schedule.

Times of departure—8:10, 9:20, 10:30 . . .

To where?

He read the next wrinkled note, penned in the same crude, bold print.

HANK STEWART.

DR. HANK STEWART

HANK STEWART, ESQ.

HANK STEWART, NUCLEAR PHYSICIST.

Decker skimmed down the list. A psycho with delusions of grandeur. The last two entries scared him.

GOD STEWART.

Then just plain GOD.

He pocketed the note, unfolded another one.

More times, dates—yesterday's date circled in red.

Decker cursed to himself.

Missed the fucker by one day.

He heard Rina call his name.

"I'm still here," he said.

"What do you have?"

"Some paper." He walked back over to her and Jerz. "Was this apartment rented furnished?"

"Don't know," Jerz said. "You have to call corporation with letters. You think Stremmer left without paying?"

"I think Stremmer has just changed his name to Hank Stewart." He showed Rina the letter.

"Any sign that Noam has been here?" she asked.

"Not so far." He unraveled another note—more flight times—then took a look at the last note.

A list of items, penned in a different script— cursive instead of printing. But lacking the assurance of an adult's handwriting.

He said, "This note seems to be written by a

different person. We'll bring this back to Breina and Ezra. Find out if this is Noam's handwriting."

"What is it?" Rina asked.

"A checklist," Decker said. "Toothbrush, hairbrush, flashlight, suntan lotion, two shirts, two pairs of pants, socks, underwear . . . like the kid was going off to camp."

"Any idea where they went?" Rina asked.

"I haven't seen anything written down," Decker said. "But I'll bet money we should check United's flights to Fort Lauderdale, Miami, Los Angeles, or Hawaii. Wintertime is around the corner and someone's packing suntan lotion."

"You're going to call up the airlines?" Rina asked.

"Eventually," Decker said. "First I'm going to check the bedroom."

It was the same story—dresser drawers pulled out and empty, the tiny closet as bare as Mother Hubbard's cupboard. The bed was unmade and smelled as if it had been awhile since the off-white linens had been changed. Decker bent down, looked under the bed. He spied a crumpled piece of white cloth, stretched his arm all the way, and pulled it out.

When he unfolded it, Rina gasped.

Tzitzit—the fringed prayer shawls Orthodox males wore under their shirts. It was sized a men's small. He turned to Jerz. "I'm going to take this with me."

"What is it?" asked Jerz.

"A religious garment," Decker said. "I think it belongs to the kid I'm looking for."

"You're looking for a kid?"

The time was right. Decker told the super what

was going on. Jerz listened, then said he wasn't surprised, Stremmer always seemed strange. And was always with young boys. Once, when Jerz asked him about it, Stremmer claimed he was a Big Brother.

Jerz said, "But I always think he don't tell truth."

Decker showed him the picture of Noam. "Ever seen this teenager before?" He described his stature to Jerz.

The super studied the photo. "No." He shook his head. "If boy come up here, he don't look like that."

"The face isn't familiar?"

"No, sorry."

Decker handed him his card. "You hear of anything from either of them, call me at this local number right away."

Jerz nodded. "Do I still get trip to Disneyland?"

"I'm a man of my word," Decker said.

It was easier to work straight through than to return to the family and let them know what was going on. So Decker took the coward's way out and made the phone calls from the Six-Seven. Rina sat by him, checking off flights as he called them out.

He inquired about tickets issued yesterday to Florida or California, reservations made under the name of Hersh Schaltz, Tony Sacaretti, Heinrich Stremmer, Hank Stewart, or any male with the initials HS. With the exception of the Italian name, Hersh was choosing aliases close to home.

There was nothing on any United Flight or on American Airlines or TWA. But Continental had booked a reservation for a Hank and Nolan Stewart on Flight 710. It had left yesterday at 10:30, had arrived in Los Angeles at 2:00 P.M. PDT.

Were Mr. Hank Stewart and Mr. Nolan Stewart on the plane?

I don't know, sir, but the tickets were cashed.

One friggin day off.

"What are you going to do?" Rina asked.

Decker said, "Looks like I'm going to hop a plane back home."

"Now's your chance to back out," Rina said. "They aren't in the religious Jewish community any longer."

"But now I've lost my convenient excuse—a New York PI knows his way around better than me." Decker shook his head. "Unfortunately, the suckers had the audacity to invade *my* turf. So for better or worse, I'm going to get them."

PART TWO

Tzedakah—Charity

🌱 18

Hank thought:

Flyin' out three thousand miles to trade one pigsty for another. Dafuck's goin' on, already? The room smelled like a sewer, the sheets felt like sandpaper and if that wasn't bad enough, it was *raining*.

Rain. He coulda stayed back home for that shit. Only reason it was California instead of Florida was that the kid wanted to see *Movie Stars*. If it was up to him, he woulda chose Florida 'cause it was a lot closer and the fare was cheaper. Both had the ocean and both had Disneyland. Or Disney World. Whatever the hell they called it, was the same thing. Stupid rides and midgets who don't talk dressed up like Mickey Mouse or Clarabelle Cow.

But noooooo! Nick-O had to see *stars* on Hollywood Boulevard.

Fine. Make the kid happy and go to California, all the same to him.

He burped. Sprawled out on the bed, he had stripped down to a sleeveless undershirt and a pair of jockeys. He'd sent Nick-O out to do the laundry two hours ago and now wondered if that was a mistake.

The kid seemed all hepped-up at first, but now he was all quiet and mopey. What Hank *didn't* need was someone draggin' down his spirits. Enough talk. There was work to be done. The kid better snap out of it or there was gonna be some serious problems. There musta been at least three boys back home who worshiped him and he'd only hooked up with Nick-O 'cause he was the biggest and the first one he saw standin' outside shul. Nick-O was all pissed off at havin' to wear a suit. When he offered to take him away, he thought the kid was gonna kiss his ass. First thing the kid did was throw away the suit and wear that dumbass T-shirt with the faggy-lookin' rock group on it.

Now Hank was wonderin' if Nick-O was the right one for the job. The kid seemed pretty together at first. Didn't get all squirrely when Hank played with his knives. Nick-O didn't flip over them though, and that showed a definite lack of taste. Thinking about it, that wasn't good.

No, not good at all.

It was real smart to only give him enough money for laundry. Not that he was *really* worried that the kid was gonna flake out and call his parents, but there was always that possibility.

Nick-O had begged to come along, callin' them brothers in spirit. Tellin' him that his buddy Hank was the only one he could really talk to. Yeah, he understood it all 'cause he'd been there. But enough of the yap, yap, yap. It was time to get past all that religion crap and move on. Nick-O was real good about talkin' about movin' on, but he weren't so good at the real movin' on.

Hank didn't like the way the kid was acting. He'd warned him what he'd do if the kid tried anything dumb. He thought he made the message pretty damn clear.

Nick-O, you call home, go to the police or do anything stupid, you're dead meat.

Hey, can't get any clearer than that.

Hank scratched his crotch and picked up a Styrofoam container half full of chow mein. He sniffed it, then found a plastic fork somewhere within the rolled up bedcover.

He took the fork to the bathroom, washed it off with soap and water, then plopped down on the bed. The stuff wasn't bad cold, although all the sauce had congealed to a brown goop that looked like somethin' found in the crapper.

How the hell did he wind up in this dump? He shoulda knowed the area was for shit when he saw all the XXX on the hotel signs, but he was thrown off-track by the name.

Englewood, New Jersey, was a classy place. How the hell was he supposed to figure out that Inglewood, California, was a dump with the names soundin' practically the same?

Well, Inglewood was history as far as he was concerned! Tomorrow, they were splittin', rain or no rain.

Hank scratched himself again, turned on the TV. Same old junk—this time the girl was gettin' porked by an old guy who had to be at least forty, and a shvartze. The shvartze was a gorilla, *his* boobs bigger than the chick's. He also had a gorilla-sized dick, but he couldn't keep it hard.

All those inches and he couldn't keep a boner.

He shut off the TV, bored, not even horny.

It was a long time since he'd had any action. He was sick of doin' it himself, but at least he was clean. He had sent Nick-O to buy skins yesterday—hoping to phone up a service girl tonight. But instead, Nick-O came back all whiny, sayin' that he couldn't do it without lookin' suspicious.

Then Hank told him: You ain't gonna do my shit, what the hell did I need you for?

That made the kid stop and think a minute.

Then Nick-O said in that same whiny voice that the druggist wouldn't sell it to him even if he asked 'cause he just looked too young.

Hank smiled, remembering how like patient he was as he told him what to do.

Since when did I say you have to buy it, Nick-O?

Maybe that's what was taking the kid so long.

He finished the Chink food and tossed the Styrofoam cup in the garbage.

Place was a sty, but in a weird way, he was at home in sties. After the divorce, the old lady fell apart. Everything just fell to shit.

Twenty-five moves in three years. He'd counted every goddamn one of them. The old dickhead always givin' them money to move into the places, but never enough money to pay monthly *rent*. Always kicked out 'cause no one wanted freeloaders. Three, four months later, she'd call up the dickhead again, tellin' him the same story over and over. She couldn't find a job without skills and she couldn't go to school because she couldn't drive and it was too hard to take the bus.

The dickhead would remind her that she used to teach in the yeshivas.

But that was before the headaches started. And it hurt her eyes to type on computers and strained her voice to do telephone sales. And the world was a scary place when you're alone and blah, blah, blah, blah, blah.

Then the dickhead would forward another check—made out to *him*, not the old lady.

They were always made out to him, but like a jerk, he always gave them to the old lady 'cause at the time, he didn't know better.

A week later, they'd stuff their belongings into trash bags and move again.

Then the dickhead had the nerve to ask him if he wanted to *live* with him and his broad. God, did the old man have rocks for brains or what?

Not that the old lady wasn't without her problems before the breakup, but it was the broad that drove her over the edge.

The old lady was nuts, but the dickhead was worse. Pretendin' he was so fuckin' holy, then runnin' out on both of them when pussy was flashed in his face.

The turning point. When Hank decided that pussy would *never, ever* have that kind of *power* over him. Better to buy the broads for an evening than to get involved with a chick. Besides, he was always more interested in lost kids—like himself. He'd teach them how to be a *man*, how to *survive*.

There had always been a good supply of lost kids. They came to him like bees to honey 'cause he was the one who gave them attention when their parents didn't have the time. Man, *he* did a better job with kids than the dickhead ever did for him.

The old lady just couldn't handle the breakup. She'd curl up in the corner, forgetting to bathe, forgetting to *eat*, for crissakes! Him, having to spoon-feed her, undress her, and dunk her in the tub. Man, she screamed every time she took a bath. It got so bad that he just gave up.

But then he had to deal with the smell.

And the old dickhead, saying he wasn't without sympathy.

Wasn't without sympathy.

Didn't you just love that little diddy?

Hersh, I'm not without sympathy, but there's nothing I can do for her anymore. I've got my own life to live and Mama isn't a part of it.

That's when the dickhead made his offer. Live with him.

Oh, yeah, right!

The broad hated him almost as much as he hated the broad.

Well, they got theirs.

Ha-ha, the joke was on you, asshole.

The old lady. God-only-knew what the hey she was doing. He couldn't be bothered thinkin' about her. He had his own life to live.

Hey, you know how it is.

Like father, like son.

Noam wiped the tears away from his eyes and hoisted the plastic lawn and leaf bag full of laundry over his shoulder. Of all the stupid things he'd ever done, this was the stupidest. Everything they ever told him turned out to be true. He was nothing but a loser.

How was he gonna get out of this mess? He thought of running away, hitchhiking back. But he was afraid of the weirdos that might pick him up, what they might do to him. Hersh was scary but he never touched him in that way. *Boruch Hashem* for small blessings.

He prayed: Please, please get me out of this mess. Get me back home safely. I'll do everything my parents ask, I'll never fight with my brothers and sisters, I'll study real hard, I'll do anything You want, just please, *please* get me out of this mess.

Vey is mir, he was stupid!

At first, it seemed like such a right thing to do. Hersh . . . like he knew everything that was on his mind. He understood all of his doubts, all of his questions. He could *talk* to Hersh. Hersh *listened* to him. It was like Hersh had been there before and that made sense. Hersh had told him he came from the same type of family—all of them a bunch of hypocrites.

Not that his family was all bad, just . . . they just didn't understand, didn't *listen*! All they ever did was criticize, criticize, criticize. He'd given up on his parents a long time ago. But he expected more out of aunts and uncles. Aunt Miriam was nice but all she ever did was feed him. Aunt Faygie was a scatterbrain. Uncle Shimmy was never around, Uncle Jonathan had brushed him off like dirt.

Bubbe was okay but she was old. Zeyde? He was old, too.

But Hersh. He *listened*!

Noam knew it was too good to be true. Hersh had played him for the stupid kid he was. And now he was acting real weird, showing him those stupid knives all the time. When Noam mentioned that maybe he might go back home, Hersh had a fit, scared the wits out of him. Screaming, swearing— well Hersh always swore—but this time the words were directed at him.

And then he threatened to . . . it was too scary to think about it.

The thing about Hersh was, you never knew what to expect. One minute he'd be pretty cool, even nice. But then he'd *turn* on you like an untrained dog.

Noam knew he'd taken too long and he was frightened. The knives were starting to get to him. It was those knives. Hersh loved those knives. Even when nothing needed to be cut, he was playing with them—sharpening them, spinning them.

And then there were the fish. Hersh just loved to gut fish. Noam should have known something was wrong with him a long time ago. First time they went to his flat in Flatbush, Hersh gutted a fish. That was *weird.* But still, Hersh *listened* to him when he talked. That seemed so important.

He felt his heart beat in his chest as he walked up to the door. His head felt dizzy, his stomach about to chuck up the *tref* food he'd been eating. At first, it seemed so neat. You could eat anything you wanted and no one was here to make you feel guilty. Now it all seemed so silly, so stupid.

Stupid, stupid, stupid.

He put down the bag of laundry and inserted the key into the door lock. A sour taste rose from his throat. He opened the door.

Hersh looked up, then turned his eyes back to the TV. Noam thought—watching *those* kind of movies again. He came inside and closed the door. Waited for instructions. He had to go to the toilet but was too nervous to leave the room until Hersh talked to him.

Hersh just kept watching TV. Then he pointed to a spot on the floor and told Noam to leave the laundry there. Noam swallowed, got up enough nerve to ask if he could go to the bathroom.

Hersh said, "Why you askin' me? You got a plumbin' problem or somethin'?"

"No," Noam whispered. He rushed off to the bathroom and threw up. Tried to be as quiet about it as possible. But Hersh was staring at him when he came back in.

"You sick or somethin'?"

"I guess the food didn't go down real good," Noam said.

"Yeah, it's pretty shitty," Hersh said. "We'll buy better stuff next time, 'kay?"

Noam nodded. That was the real killer—you never knew how he was going to take things. Now he was acting all nice. He thought maybe now was a good time to bring up going home, but something warned him off.

Don't push it.

Noam said, "I can fold the laundry if you want. I'm real good at that. My . . . my mother—"

"I don't want to hear about your fuckin' mother, Nick-O. She's a bitch, right? Ain't that what you told me?"

That wasn't what he'd told him. Noam had told him that his eema was mean and critical and never had a minute to listen to him. But he had never, never called her a bitch. He could never do that. But he nodded anyway.

How could he have been so stupid!

Noam dumped out the clothes and started folding them.

"Hersh?"

"Hank," Hersh said, eyes still on the TV. "How many fuckin' times do I have to tell you it's Hank?"

Yeah, it was Hank this time, Noam thought. Hersh had gone through at least a half-dozen names in the past six months. There was Tony and Frankie. Then it was Heinrich and Hart. Hart, Hersh said, was the name of a movie star. When Noam told him the name sounded sort of like a *faygala*, Hersh flew into a rage. From then on it was Hank. Remember! Hank! Hank! Hank!

"Hank?" Noam tried.

"What?"

"I got 'em," Noam announced.

Hersh pointed the remote at the TV screen and flicked it off. Noam saw him turn slowly, regard his face. Then he flashed that crooked smile of his. Sometimes the smile meant he was happy, sometimes it meant he was mad. But it was always a weird smile, scary. Hersh was nodding now.

"You got 'em?"

"I got 'em," Noam said.

"Hey, hey, hey." Hersh leaped off the bed and pinned Noam in a headlock. He punched him gently in the cranium. "Ya got somethin' in there. I told you you could do it."

Noam smiled but inside he felt like dying. What if the pharmacist had seen him? What if he was reporting him to the police right now? What if they threw him in jail and let him rot?

What if? What if? What if?

The whole thing started out like an exciting adventure story. It had turned into a nightmare.

Hersh said, "Where are they, Nick-O?"

Nick-O? That's right. He wasn't Nolan anymore. He was Nick-O. Noam liked Nolan better—like Nolan Ryan. But Hersh insisted on calling him Nick-O cause that sounded more tough.

"In my pocket," Noam answered.

Hersh reached in and pulled out the condoms. "Did you get the extra large?"

Noam turned red. "I . . . I didn't know they were sized—"

Hersh let go with a wicked peal of laughter. "You are so fuckin' stupid. You really don't know shit. But you still did good, Nick-O. You did good."

Noam studied Hersh's smile. He was genuinely happy. *Boruch Hashem.*

"You did good," Hersh repeated. "Real good. Like a pro!"

Noam shrugged, embarrassed by the compliment. No one at home ever, *ever* complimented him. Criticizing him all the time. Still, all he could think about now was how to get home. How he could manage to call them. But if Hersh found out . . . His throat tightened, he began to feel weak inside as if the first bout of vomiting hadn't emptied his stomach.

He felt a sharp rap on his head. Hersh had him in another headlock.

"You still up in there?" Hersh said, knocking on Noam's brain.

Noam struggled until he was free from Hersh's grip. "I had to wait a long time before the cashier left the checkstand."

"That's what took you so *long*?"

Noam nodded.

"You wouldn't be thinkin' about callin' anyone, would you, Nick-O?"

Noam's eyes widened. "Oh, no way, Hank. No way. Who would I call?"

"Liar," Hersh said. But his voice was light. He grabbed Nick-O by the neck again. "You did good."

"I didn't call anyone," Noam said. "I swear I didn't."

"I believe you," Hank said. "Now shut up about it."

Noam clamped his lips together.

Hank said, "You only took two packs. Why'd you only take two packs?"

"I just took what I saw—"

"You know, Nick-O, you do somethin', you do it all the way." Hersh slapped his cheek gently. "What you did is like robbin' a bank for five bucks, know what I'm sayin'? But what the hey. You got time to learn, *capich*?"

Noam hated it when Hersh spoke Italian.

"Besides," Hersh went on, "this is only the beginning. I was just checkin' you out, seein' what kind of balls you have. And they're not too bad."

Noam felt his stomach lurch. "What do you mean?"

"You think I sent you to the store just to swipe some skins?"

That was exactly what Noam thought.

"I got bigger things in mind," Hersh said.

Noam paused, waited for Hersh to explain. But he didn't.

"What things?" Noam asked.

And there it was. The weird, lopsided smile. Only it didn't really look happy now. It looked scary and mean.

Hersh plopped back down on the bed. "Fold the laundry and start packin'. We're movin' on, Nick-O."

Noam stared at him. "Where we going?"

"Does it matter?"

"No—"

"So what you askin' me all these questions?"

"I'm just curious—"

Hersh sprang up, drew his neck in another head-lock. But this one hurt.

"You shouldn't be curious, Nick-O. It's a very dangerous thing to do."

"I just meant—"

"Shut up," Hersh said, squeezing.

"Ouch, you're hurting me—"

Hersh let go with a push. Noam fell against the bed.

"You bug me with your questions, know that, Nick-O?"

Noam felt the tears come back. He forced himself to blink them gone.

"Just pack and don't ask questions," Hersh said.

Noam didn't answer. The tears kept coming so he buried his head in his hands. Then he felt an arm pat his shoulder.

That was the thing with Hersh. You never knew.

"Don't ask me no questions," Hersh said, softly. "I don't like it."

Noam nodded.

"Now pack," Hersh said.

"Okay." Noam's voice was barely audible. He sat down in the corner and began to fold the laundry.

"We're movin' to someplace better," Hersh said.

Noam nodded.

"I mean, you don't want to stay in a dump like this, do you?"

Noam shook his head no.

"So we'll go someplace better."

"Okay."

"I mean I got plans, Nick-O. You gonna be able to handle my plans?"

Noam forced out, "I can handle your plans."

"Good," Hersh said. "I was hopin' you'd say that."

"I can handle them," Noam said. Trying to say it with more confidence.

"So then I'll tell you part of the plans."

Noam waited and folded a shirt.

"Plan number one," Hersh said, "I get laid tonight, Nick-O. I'm gonna order up a broad. Now if you want a piece of her ass, hey, it's on me. You don't, you wait in the bathroom. Understand?"

Noam nodded.

"Think you might want some action?" Hersh said.

Noam shook his head.

"Hey, it'll put hair on your face," Hersh said.

Again, Noam shook his head.

"Fine," Hersh sulked. "Suit yourself."

Noam didn't answer. He resumed folding the laundry.

"Hey, aren't you gonna ask what the rest of my plans are?" Hersh said.

Noam closed his eyes. Just a minute ago, Hersh had almost bitten off his head for asking too many questions. Now he was all mad at him for not asking enough questions.

"What are the rest of your plans?" Noam whispered.

Hersh said, "My dickhead old man's inheritance should be cleared any day now. I'm gonna give the insurance company a call this afternoon. I got it all planned out."

Noam nodded.

"But we need to do somethin' for money in the meantime, know what I'm sayin'?"

Noam stopped folding laundry. His stomach . . . boiling acid. He swallowed the bilious taste down.

Hersh went on. "Look. We're almost busted. I mean your old lady's cash didn't exactly go too far. And the jewelry?" He shrugged. "I don't got a good fence yet. What we need is ready bread, know what I'm sayin'?"

Noam looked at him—at that scary lopsided smile. Hersh got off the bed and went over to the suitcase. He rummaged through the contents, then pulled out something metallic. He explained that it was the same kind of weapon used by the LAPD—a Beretta semiautomatic. He'd bought this one from a buddy of his back in Hackensack, New Jersey—an ex-con who dealt in firearms.

"Cons can't own guns legally, you know," Hersh said. "But that's all shit. You can get anything you want if you have enough money and know who to ask."

He petted the gun gingerly.

"You think I had you rip off some skins, just to get some skins? Huh? *Huh?*"

"I don't know," Noam whispered.

"I was just givin' you a trial run," Hersh said. "Figurin' out if you could handle bigger assignments. Testing you for the next time around, know what I'm sayin'?"

Noam felt nauseated.

"Now, I'm not sayin' we're gonna take anybody

out," Hersh said. "But sometimes . . . you know me, I love knives. But knives don't always do it. People just don't take knives seriously and that can be messy. I mean, you do something, you want it clean, not messy, right?"

Noam didn't answer. Hersh went on.

"Knives are great for a surprise attack. Some joker wants to fight you off, you just get in there and stick 'im. Right between the ribs. You go up on it and move it around—well, never mind. See, I love knives but guns get attention."

Noam remained silent. *Vey is mir. What did Hersh have in mind now?*

Hersh said, "You did good on the skins. See, I was testin' you. Well, congratulations, Nick-O." He shoved the gun into Noam's hands. "You aced the test."

❧ 19

From the airplane window, disks of white cloud looked like lily pads floating in a pond. Decker leaned his seat all the way back and stretched his legs. He wore a kelly-green knit shirt, faded jeans, and a new pair of Reeboks—first time all week he'd dressed in casual clothing. Rina had upgraded their tickets to business class—an absolute necessity for anyone six-four. For just a moment, he let himself relax.

Rina pushed her seat back until it was level with his, then slipped her arm around his neck and started massaging the tightened musculature. Though dressed as simply as he, Rina still personified regal beauty. Decker felt a swell of pride every time he thought of her as *his* wife.

"Feels nice," Decker said.

"Am I hitting the right spot?"

Decker smiled. "You don't *really* want me to answer that."

She laughed. Decker took her hand away and kissed her fingers. "It was nice of you to come out with me."

"I wouldn't think of *not* coming out with you, Peter."

"Well, thanks anyway."

"You're welcome anyway." She chucked his chin. "The color has returned to your cheeks."

"It's the western climate," he said. "I just think of all that L.A. sun and I get a burn."

"You're happy to be going home, no doubt about that."

"I'm not *really* going home," Decker said. "Not with the boys still in New York and this case hanging over my head."

"At least you'll see Cindy before she goes off to college."

"True," Decker said. "A wonderful side benefit."

Rina sighed. "I'm sorry about all this."

"You didn't make the kid run away," Decker said. He smiled at her. "Now that I'm a little distanced from all the people . . ." The *family*, he thought. "I can approach the whole thing more professionally. It's okay, Rina. I'm in control."

"It's good to hear you so full of confidence."

Decker paused. "Any reason why I shouldn't be confident?"

"None at all."

"This is my business, Rina," Decker said. "I've been a cop for twenty years."

"You're the best—"

"I'm not the best, but I'm good."

"You're very good."

"Damn good."

"Damn good," Rina repeated.

Decker broke up. "I'm still wired, I guess."

Rina said, "Would you like to talk about the case?"

"You know I don't like to talk about my cases."

"I just thought it might help you get some of the tension off your chest."

"I'm fine, Rina. Tension and I have become good buddies over the years."

Rina said, "You know yourself better than I do."

"Of course, if *you're* curious . . ."

Rina smiled to herself. He was dying to talk to someone, but didn't want to burden her. She took his hand and said, "Maybe I am a little curious . . ."

Without a moment's hesitation, Decker gave her the low-down.

Hersh Mendel Schaltz—currently twenty-one— was the only child of Peretz and Bracha Schaltz. He grew up in Kew Gardens, Queens, living in the same apartment house until he was eleven years old. The family then moved to Williamsburg, Brooklyn. A year later, the parents were divorced, Hersh staying with his mother, the father leaving the community. After that, it was almost impossible to trace Hersh's life. He and his mother seemed to have moved dozens of times, often living in apartments for only a few months at a time. Then, the big news. Peretz Schaltz remarried—a Gentile woman.

"My own interpretation about her religion," Decker said. "The second wife's name was Christine McClellan."

"Obviously Hersh's father wasn't Orthodox," Rina said.

"Apparently at one time he was," Decker said. "A former neighbor told me he'd been a Satmar Chasid, one of the reasons the family moved to Williamsburg."

"Then why did he live in Kew Gardens all those years?" Rina asked.

"Beats me," Decker said. "Hersh was well remembered by his teachers because he stood out. He spoke more Yiddish than English when he first came to school. He dressed differently. Apparently he went to a religious day school, but it was considered modern Orthodox."

"I grew up modern Orthodox," Rina said. "We were indistinguishable from the rest of the neighborhood kids except that we kept kosher and observed Shabbos. Most of us had American names, grew up on cartoons, TV sitcoms. We rode bikes and skateboards and went to the movies and rock concerts. Our mothers didn't cover their hair."

She paused a moment.

"I remember thinking my parents were just a little hypocritical. Keeping kosher in the home, but eating fish in non-kosher restaurants. We wouldn't turn on the TV, but it was on a time clock so Papa didn't miss *Sanford and Son*. One of the things I liked about Yitz was his consistency." She smiled. "I felt very righteous back then. Now I'm much more tolerant."

"So I've noticed."

Rina regarded the gleam in her husband's eye. She kissed his cheek. "Don't worry. You're a keeper."

"Aw shucks. Anyway, from what you described,

Hersh wasn't modern Orthodox. His grammar-school teachers remember him dressed like a little rabbi, always wearing long sleeves, black coat and hat, even in the summertime. Plus he had the ear-locks. One teacher described them as long sausage curls."

"He must have had to put up with a lot of teasing."

"Think you're right," Decker said. "Seems Hersh was always scrapping with someone, a real trouble-maker. But the teachers I talked to felt sorry for him. He didn't have any real friends and wasn't real swift in his English studies. His parents spoke to him only in Yiddish. Oftentimes, his parents weren't even around. His sixth-grade teacher said whenever she had a problem, she dealt with the grandfather, who also spoke more Yiddish than English. She said Hersh seemed very attached to him. It was very traumatic for Hersh when he died. He didn't return to school for almost a month."

"Where'd you get all this information?"

"Once you know the person's full name, all the rest is easy," Decker said. "You go backward. Get the name, get the birth certificate, then the parents' names, then their addresses. You canvass the old neighborhood, talk to old teachers, shopkeepers, friends. The family didn't have any close friends as far as I know. Neighbors describe the Schaltzes as people who kept to themselves. Hersh never played with the kids on the block—probably one of the reasons why his English was so bad when he started school. Had he been sociable, he would have picked up English even if his parents spoke only Yiddish."

"Sad."

"Yeah, it's sad. If you're lucky, that kind of loneliness can spawn creativity. But in most of us, it does strange things to our heads. Anyway, I figured it was worth spending an extra day in New York discovering what makes this guy tick. Besides, Marge volunteered to do a lot of preliminary footwork in L.A."

"Nice of Marge."

"We'll owe her a good dinner," Decker said.

"Anytime," Rina said. "So what makes Hersh tick?"

Decker shrugged. "His religion made him an outsider. I don't think there's any love lost between him and Judaism."

"That's a shame," Rina said. "There must have been some sort of conflict for them to live in Kew Gardens when they were Satmar Chasids. Maybe the mother wasn't as religious as the father. Maybe she insisted they live there. Even among the Orthodox, there can be splits within families."

"Just like with Eli Greenspan," Decker said. "His father working in North Carolina, his mother insisting the family stay in New York."

"Exactly," Rina said. "How's Eli doing, by the way?"

"Jonathan found him somebody to talk to, God bless the dear rabbi." Decker paused. There were aspects of Jonathan that reminded him of his own baby brother. Jonathan and Randy were almost the same age, both of them sensitive beneath a facade of misanthropism. Decker wondered if they'd get along, then, realizing the stupidity of the fantasy, he turned his attention back to Rina. "The counselor Jonathan found isn't *frum*, but he's Jewish and works only a few blocks from Greenspan's house. Eli did show up for his first appointment. Beyond that, I don't know."

Rina said, "You know, as naïve as it sounds, I always thought we were immune to worldly problems. Silly, huh?"

"No community is *immune*," Decker said. "But I'll tell you this, darlin'. Most of the kids I met in Boro Park seem very well adjusted. Well-mannered, respectful of their parents, nice to their friends. The religious schools don't have truancy problems, big drug or alcohol problems. Almost all the families are intact. Hey, if you don't mind living in a big insulated box, it's probably a great place to bring up your kids. It's just that when there *is* a problem, you people don't want to admit it."

"Here you go again with 'you people.'"

Decker smiled. "Okay, we don't want to admit it."

"Much better," Rina said.

Decker said, "Seems to me that Hersh was that kind of a problem child."

"The family must have had its own problems," Rina said. "First to divorce. Then for the father to marry a shiksa. He couldn't have been that committed a Jew."

"You're being judgmental."

"When it comes to intermarriage, I'm judgmental."

"There were a lot of people who were judgmental when you started dating me."

Rina bristled. "You were willing to convert, Peter. Besides, you were Jewish."

"But you didn't know that at first."

"Are you going to start a fight?" Rina asked.

"Not intentionally," Decker said. "And who knows? Maybe Christine McClellan converted."

Rina said, "I imagine a swift detective such as yourself could find that out."

"Not so easy a task, Holmes," Decker said. "And unless we find Hersh, we never will know. Seems Dad and new wife have met their maker. Apparently they were chemists, working for the Darrick-Bothhell lab in Connecticut, and died in a freak accident about a year ago. Their laboratory blew up."

Rina stared at him. "*That* gives me shivers."

Decker said, "Their field of expertise was stabilizing volatile cleaning solutions. Accidents *can* happen. I've gone through all the reports. There were stacks of them. No indication of arson or foul play."

"But?"

"How do you know there's a but?"

"Your tone of voice," Rina said. "Am I right?"

"Yep," Decker admitted. "During the day the lab was very well populated. When it blew, Dad and Christine were working alone at night."

"Did the father have a life-insurance policy?"

"You're thinking like a pro," Decker said. "You bet he did. Christine was the primary beneficiary, but old Hersh was Number Two on the list. Insurance has been dragging its feet because we're talking about a policy of two hundred and fifty thousand dollars owed to a young man with a police record. Insurance has managed to stall Hersh, but it can't last much longer. Pretty soon, Hersh/Tony/Heinrich/Hank is going to be a rich kid."

"And Hersh was cleared of wrongdoing?"

"Well, he wasn't anywhere near the place when it blew," Decker said. "That was checked out first. Whether he hired a firestarter or not, who knows? Hersh dealt a little, knew disreputable people. He could have hooked up with a bomber or an arsonist. The company tailed him for a while, never came up with anything incriminating. And Hersh hasn't pushed for the money. He keeps in contact with them, asking when are they going to deliver. But he hasn't hired any legal mouthpiece to pour on the heat."

Rina was silent.

"Maybe it *was* an accident," Decker said. "Or maybe the motive was revenge rather than money. Hersh's life seemed to fall apart after the father left. People who knew the family said after the divorce Hersh and Mom were the proverbial wandering Jews."

"Is Mom still alive?"

"I think so," Decker said. "Jonathan went poking around Williamsburg for me yesterday—"

"You enlisted Jonathan in this thing?"

"It's his nephew, Rina." Decker smiled. "And I needed somebody who could speak Yiddish. Jonathan was happy to help out."

"You two seem to be building quite a relationship," Rina said.

Decker tossed her a look that told her to drop the subject. Quickly Rina asked, "So what did Jonathan come up with?"

Decker said, "A few former neighbors have reported seeing Mrs. Schaltz in Williamsburg from time to time. Apparently, she's become a bag lady."

"That's awful," Rina said. "I'm beginning to see where the present Hersh came from."

"Yep," Decker said. "Although sometimes rotten kids come from nice homes and loving parents."

"Look at it from Hersh's point of view," Rina said. "His mother's a bag lady, his religious father deserted the family to marry a Gentile. I talked about the hypocrisy I felt in my home—it wasn't really hypocrisy, just little inconsistencies. I can just imagine how Hersh might have felt."

Decker nodded.

"Still," Rina said, "a normal person doesn't blow up his father just because he's a hypocrite."

"Who said Hersh blew them up?" Decker said.

"What do you think?" Rina said.

"I think . . ." Decker paused. "I think it's not a good idea to make Hersh mad."

❧20

In the past year, Mike Hollander had gone up another pants size. But the increase in girth did not
stop him from stuffing a doughnut into his mouth.
Crumbs fell onto his shirt and lap, another wad became trapped in the bristles of his walrus mustache.
Between chomps, he said to Decker, "Couldn't keep
away from us or did Rina turn out to be a typical
pain-in-the-ass wife?"

Decker stared at him, resisting the urge to brush
off his tie. "Batting oh for two, Mike." He glanced
around the squad room, what had always seemed like
a crowded, archaic place to work. Wood-scarred or
metal desks, tables and chairs of the cheapest industrial grade. Never enough room to walk freely. The
floors were dingy, the walls needed a paint job. A
few computers, but most of the communications
were done with rotary phones. The place was hot in
the summer, cold in the winter—the interior temperature made tolerable by portable fans or heaters.
Yet, compared to the Six-Six in New York, the room
seemed state-of-the-art.

He pulled out his chair, put his feet up on his

desk. For the first time in umpteen years, the top was clear of paperwork.

Paul MacPherson was snickering. The black detective was on robbery detail this rotation and Decker knew he had better things to do than sit around with a smirk on his face. But damned if he was going to let it bother him. Coolly, Decker said, "Something on your mind, Paul?"

"It's not nice to leave your wife on your honeymoon, Rabbi," MacPherson said. "Or do they do that in your religion?"

Decker wondered if he deserved an answer, decided he wasn't going to let Paul get away with it. "Fact is Rina came out with me. Guess she can't stand the thought of us being apart."

"Touching," MacPherson said.

"I think the man looks pretty content," Hollander said.

"I think you're being charitable," MacPherson said.

"Hey, Rina came out with him," Hollander said. "He didn't say he brought the kids."

"You bring the kids?" MacPherson said.

"No," Decker answered.

"See," Hollander said. "He has big plans when he gets home."

"The rabbi's makin' plans," echoed Ed Fordebrand. He was a big, beefy dick from Homicide, always in need of mouthwash. He claimed his halitosis was a weapon used against the perps. Decker felt it came from Ed's love of strong cheese. "Let's hear it for a man with plans."

MacPherson said, "Yeah, well, if he's got such big plans, why's he here in the first place?"

Decker turned to Hollander. "You didn't tell him?"

"I told him," Hollander said. "He didn't believe me."

MacPherson said, "You expect me to believe you canceled a honeymoon with that delectable wife of yours to look for a runaway?"

Putting it that way, it really did sound absurd. "God's honest truth," Decker said.

"You're an asshole," MacPherson said.

Decker laughed.

"Kid related to Rina?" Fordebrand asked.

"No," Decker said. "Just doing a favor for one of her friends."

"Hell of a favor," Fordebrand said.

"You know how it is," Decker said. "Starts out as an 'I'll look into it' and turns out to be a mess."

"All runaways are messy," Hollander said.

Ain't that the truth, Decker thought. He should have removed himself from the case when he had a chance. Should have packed up the crew and gone to Florida—to his *real* family. *Why* didn't he back out?

Then he told himself, You know why, schmuck. Something to do with a grandmother's eyes.

"Well, I'm off to court," Fordebrand said. "This case gets any more continuances, the foreman of the jury's gonna keel over. Think the guy's ninety-two or something."

"Why do they pick them that old?" MacPherson asked.

"The victim was old," Fordebrand said. "That juror was one for the prosecutor's side." He started singing: "I owe, I owe, so it's off to work I go . . ."

The off-key song was accompanied by off-key whistling. After he left, MacPherson said, "There goes Dopey."

"Dopey couldn't talk, Paul," Decker said. "Maybe you should try to emulate him."

MacPherson sighed. "Can anyone do something about the man's breath?"

His request was met with silence.

Hollander said, "Marge should be in momentarily, Pete. She has a pile of papers for you, but I don't know where she put them."

"I'll wait for her," Decker said. "I don't think she'd appreciate me ravaging her files."

"As long as you're here," Hollander said, "you remember that sexual assault you picked up before you left—"

"Don't want to hear about it—"

"It's turned into a real mess," Hollander said. "The girl has a psychiatric history and they want to subpoena your notes."

"Christ."

"I told them you were out of town—"

"Consider me not here—"

"PD's throwing a shit fit," Hollander said. "Claims his man put the injuries on her, but it was part of a game—"

"So what?" Decker stated. "She claims she told him to stop when it got too rough and after seeing her wounds, I believe her. She was beaten to a pulp."

"Sexual games gone wild."

"PD doesn't have a good defense. That's why he's angry."

"Just keeping you up to date," Hollander said.

"Well, I don't want to hear it until I'm officially on duty," Decker said. "I've got enough crap to worry about—"

"Yeah, speaking of that, a Terry Vadich called yesterday . . . day before yesterday, something like that. Sounds like another loonybird. Says she's got something of importance to tell, but she'll only talk to you. I left her number on your desk."

Decker slouched in his chair and closed his eyes. "I'm out of commission for the next ten days."

"I suppose you don't want to hear about—"

"You suppose right, Mike," Decker said.

"I don't blame you," Hollander said. "I'm out of here day after tomorrow. Mary's niece is getting married."

"Who's going to cover for you?" Decker asked.

"Beats me," Hollander said. "Somebody's gonna be in the shop. Let him . . . or her take it up with the Watch Commander."

Decker knew "her" was Marge. He felt bad, but not bad enough to cut short his so-called vacation. Besides, Noam needed him more than Marge did.

A moment later, a pair of strong hands pushed his legs off the desk.

"I work and he sleeps? What a deal!"

"I've been thinking about you." Decker smiled.

"How long have you had those nightmares, Rabbi?"

"I've missed your lilting tones, Detective Dunn."

"You missed someone kicking your butt," Marge said.

"Rina kicks my butt," Decker said.

"But I pack a bigger wallop."

"True." Decker opened his eyes. A looming mass of female flesh was staring down at him. But the eyes—soft and brown—they sparkled. Her cheeks were pink from the cold, her wispy blond hair stuffed into her coat collar. Her face was even-featured. She was a good-looking gal, especially when she bothered to put on makeup. Decker usually didn't think of Marge in sexual terms. But Shimon's questions about her made him aware of her femininity.

"What do you have for me?" Marge asked.

Decker sat up. "You don't have to do overtime, Marjorie."

Marge smiled, held herself back from tousling his hair. She didn't bother to remind him of the extra hours he'd spent with her at the academy shooting range. All those long nights over coffee, Pete bolstering her ego, keeping her spirits up after an asshole blunted her forehead with an iron. If it hadn't been for Pete, she would have folded, probably been reassigned to some ass-spreading desk job meant to baby-sit those lost to combat fatigue.

"I don't mind," she said. "Come over to my place, honey, and I'll give you what I got."

"Best invitation I've had all day." Decker stood and pulled some snapshots out of his desk drawer. "Our boy, Hersh Schaltz, captured on film."

Marge took the pictures. Class photos from the

seventh grade in a Williamsburg school. A group picture—all the boys dressed in black coats, slouch hats, white shirts, and ties. None had any visible hair but all of them had those funny long earlocks. Hersh seemed grim but nothing unusual in the sea of serious faces. What was noticeable were his sunken cheeks—not a molecule of fat on the gaunt face.

She turned her attention to the next photograph. Tenth-grade high school shot. Public school. Gone was the somber dress. Hersh was wearing a Def Leppard T-shirt, the short sleeves tight around his developed arms. His face was still lean, but it seemed like an affected look of hunger rather than one created by lack of food. An expression designed to connote toughness.

She asked, "Did Hersh graduate from high school?"

"I haven't found any record of it," Decker said.

Marge studied the photograph again. Hersh's expression. Very scary. Especially the eerie smile. Then she focused in on the mug shots. Same lean face, same crazy smile. Wise-guy leer.

"A real sweetheart," she said. "You have some of Noam as well?"

Decker gave her Noam's school photograph. She said, "He looks kind of cocky, too."

"Yep," Decker said.

"But it's more adolescent cockiness," Marge said. "A kid trying to be tough."

She sat down at her desk, unlocked her files, and pulled out a folder. "I started at the beginning. The rental cars at the airport. No one named Schaltz or

Stewart or Stremmer, et cetera, rented any vehicles from the airport at least."

"He could have changed his name again."

"Could be," Marge said. "Clerks I talked to see thousands of people. No one recalled seeing him—or him and a teenaged kid. If they were there, they got lost in the shuffle. I also talked to the various bus lines and as many cabbies as I could find. Also zip. Just too many people."

Decker nodded.

Marge pulled out a piece of paper, turned it over. "Called Hollywood PD, put them on notice. Last night, I checked out the cheapy motels on the strip, also the shelters. Nothing."

Starting from square one again, Decker thought. This time, no friends for leads. But at least he knew Los Angeles, knew the cracks that hide the untouchables.

"Did you have a chance to check out Westwood Village at night?" Decker said. "Tons of kids hanging out there now."

"Didn't get to it," Marge said.

"I'll do it," Decker said.

"Hey, I'm free," Marge said. "Keep you company if you want." She thought of Rina. "You know what, Pete, I can do it myself—"

"No way, Charlie."

"You stay with Rina."

Decker shook his head. "She won't mind. She got me into this mess."

A lie, but a convenient one.

"I'll get you home early," Marge said.

"What a peach," Decker said.

"I'll pick you up around eight," Marge said. "What are your plans now?"

"I have a few ideas," Decker said. "Could be they settled around Disneyland. You know, kids on an adventure. Disneyland might be a big draw for both of them."

"Sounds okay," Marge said.

"I'll head out for Anaheim now," Decker said. "Pick up Rina, she can keep me company on the long ride over."

"Any excuse to see the Magic Kingdom, eh?" Marge said.

"Any excuse to be with Rina," Decker countered. "Another thing that occurred to me. Both Hersh/ Hank and Noam/Nolan are or were religious Jews. Noam especially could get homesick and run to what is familiar. Rina knows the Jewish areas in Los Angeles. We can check that one out together as well."

"Got yourself another partner, eh?" Marge said.

Decker hesitated a moment. Marge was smiling when she said it, but her tone of voice wasn't light. He joked, "Just trying to conserve your energy for the big ones, Detective."

Marge's smile widened. It seemed genuine and Decker felt relieved. Jesus, for Marge to feel displaced by his *wife* . . .

Women!

"I'd love to come with you to Disneyland," Rina said.

"If it's no bother."

"It's no bother."

Decker was sprawled out on his bed, enjoying the feeling of a mattress big enough to handle his entire frame. Curled against him was Ginger, the Irish setter given to him by his daughter for his thirty-fifth birthday. Exhaustion was creeping under his eyes and he would have loved to close them and drift away. But there was no time to lose.

"Boy, is she happy to see you," Rina said.

"Feeling's mutual," Decker said. "Guy come to feed the horses today?"

Rina nodded and scratched Ginger's scruff. "You want to take her with us?"

"They don't allow dogs in Disneyland. Besides, we won't be gone all that long. I want to make it back by eight. Marge and I are going to check out Westwood."

Rina looked at the clock. Two-fifteen. The ride was two solid hours, maybe three in traffic. "That's cutting it close. Maybe you should hold off until tomorrow."

Decker was suddenly irked. "Look, I have a job to do. You don't want to come, fine with me—"

"It's not that I don't want to come—"

"Rina, these kids had to park themselves someplace. The sooner we find out where, the better it is for everyone."

"I don't doubt that," Rina said. "I'm just wondering how well you can cover Disneyland and Anaheim and make it back to Westwood by eight."

"So we'll make it back by nine."

"I've been thinking," Rina said.

Decker said, "*What?*"

"You don't have to snap at me."

"I'm not snapping at you."

"Yes, you are."

"What's your brilliant idea?" Decker said.

"I didn't say it was a brilliant idea."

"Well, *what* is it?"

Rina sighed, feeling guilty. It was her fault he'd been brought into this mess. "It may be stupid, but I was just thinking. Since Hersh didn't seem to rent a car or take a bus from the airport—"

"He could have taken a bus," Decker said. "Hundreds of people take the bus. Unfortunately, no one remembered him."

"Yes, you're right," Rina said. "Forget it. It's probably just a waste of time."

Decker slowed himself down. "You're right. I did snap at you and I apologize. I'm not used to getting ideas from my wife. Tell me, honey. What's your idea?"

"Well," Rina started out, "maybe they didn't take the bus out of Inglewood right away. Being tired and not knowing where they were, maybe the two of them checked into one of those cheap motels near the airport. Those places have closed-circuit TV, the type of junk that might interest Hersh. . . ."

Bingo!

He said, "How do you know about closed-circuit TV, Rina?"

"They advertise on the marquee, Peter."

Decker said, "The ones that say XXX, nudes—

topless, bottomless, adult entertainment in each room."

"Yes, those."

"Never look at them." Decker got off the bed, walked over to Rina, and gave her a kiss on the cheek. "You've got a good mind, darlin'. Better than your old man's. Let's go."

Rina tried to hide a smile by rummaging through her purse.

Decker said, "Hey, you think if I muscle the desk clerk hard enough, he'll comp us a room for an hour?"

"I'm not doing anything on those sheets," Rina said. "You don't know where they've been!"

❧21

Rina could never figure out why men became unglued behind the wheel of a car. She said nothing as Peter weaved in and out of traffic, swore, banged the dashboard of the unmarked, and talked not only to himself but also to drivers who couldn't hear him. A psychiatrist witnessing the situation out of context would have declared her husband psychotic.

At least his mood didn't dampen the day. It was already ugly. The sky was overcast with clouds and smog, the air smelled of chemical emissions, and the temperature had fallen to a dank sixty degrees. Nothing like New York freeze, but cold for Los Angeles in early October. The trip from the east valley to Inglewood under the best of circumstances took over an hour. In stop-and-go traffic, it was going to take a lot longer. The extra time allowed Rina to observe landmarks such as the Fox Hills shopping mall, the complex just a stone's throw away from the Doric columns of Al Jolson's cemetery edifice. Ten minutes later the oil derricks came into view, pumping oil from the surrounding mountainside, looking like skeletal dinosaurs bobbing for apples.

She heard Peter mutter a "fuck" and turned toward him. He offered no apology—just a "Did you see that asshole?" When Rina didn't respond, he jerked the car into the far right lane, slamming on the brakes to prevent rear-ending the Honda in front of him. She breathed a sigh of relief when he exited on Century Boulevard.

Decker glanced at his watch, then started groping his seat cushion.

"What are you looking for?" Rina asked.

Decker swung left, then a right onto Century. "My list. I put it next to my—"

"It's in my purse," Rina said. "It was just lying there and I didn't want it to get lost—"

Decker said, "Can you *tell* me next time you take my stuff?"

Rina handed him the list and folded her arms across her chest. Decker consulted the addresses and drove at the same time, his eyes darting back and forth between the scrap of paper and the road. Rina was tempted to say something, but thought better of it and kept quiet.

Decker stuffed the list into his shirt pocket.

The strip leading into the airport was filled with high-rise office buildings, business hotels, and freight warehouses. Once the road had been littered with dozens of seedy, X-rated motels, but it looked as if time had forced the boulevard to clean up its act. Land values were too expensive to waste on "adult" motor inns, and porn films were found in most of the established hotels. Why would Joe Jr. Exec bother with something so downscale when he could get his rocks off in a clean place complete with room service?

Decker drove all the way to the airport, turned around and worked backward, figuring that to have been the route taken by Hersh and Noam.

Still some leftover fuck motels. Big marquees framed with pink and orange blinking lights, the black lettering advertising all the naughty pleasures found within. Decker turned left into a large parking lot. The place was a one-story job faced with dingy plaster and high, narrow windows. The lobby was fronted with a big picture window, next to it two vending machines—one for soda pop, the other for ice. Both machines looked like they hadn't been used in a long time. He parked and turned to Rina.

"Maybe you'd better come in with me," he said. "This is not a great spot for you to be left alone."

"Sure."

"I snapped at you before," Decker said. "Sorry."

Rina said, "Don't worry about it."

"Well, you're awfully patient."

"One of us has to be."

The clerk behind the desk held the photographs at arm's length. His name was Clint Willy. He appeared to be in his early thirties, had thin blond hair and milky blue eyes. His skin looked tissue-thin and was pitted with acne scars. His eyes widened as he stared at the snapshots.

"I'm farsighted," he said. "Forgot my glasses." His voice was deep. "That's the problem with being farsighted. You can drive without glasses, but you can't *see* close up. Man, I can't even read a newspaper with my Coke bottles. Now, if I was nearsighted, I couldn't drive without my glasses, see? So I'd never forget them."

Decker noticed that ole Clint could see Rina just fine. His mouth had dropped open the moment they walked through the door. His leers had lessened to sidelong glances after Decker had presented his shield. But Clint's eyes still managed to wander in Rina's direction.

The lobby was small and smelled of insect repellant. One wall was taken up by the registration desk; any leftover room was filled by a worn plaid couch accented with peeling Naugahyde strips and a coffee table graced with out-of-date airline in-flight magazines. In the corner was a pay phone. Rina was huddled between the phone and the front window.

Decker said, "I've got a magnifying glass in the car."

"Nah," Willy said. "S'kay. I can't make out any detail—like I couldn't tell you if this dude was blue-eyed or brown-eyed. Course the picture is in black-and-white, but I mean I couldn't tell you if the pupil was light or dark." He handed Decker back the photos. "But I can make out enough to tell you that these two dudes were here. Checked out yesterday morning, paid their bill. No problems."

Home run first time at bat. Decker reminded himself to give Rina a big kiss. He said, "Did they say where they were going?"

"Nah," the clerk said. "They never do. If I'm lucky, they'll just pay the bill and leave. These dudes were no problem. Paid in cash."

"How did they leave?"

"Through the door." Willy had a proud smile on his face.

Decker said, "Were they driving a car or did they take the bus?"

Willy thought for a moment. "Think they just walked out. Whether they caught a taxi or hopped the bus?" He shrugged.

"Were they loaded down with suitcases?"

"Each one had a suitcase—medium size. Nothing they couldn't carry a few blocks."

"You happen to notice the age of the younger one?"

Willy shrugged his bony shoulders. "His ID said eighteen—"

"C'mon, Clint," Decker said. "Your eyesight couldn't be that poor."

"So maybe I thought the kid looked more like sixteen—"

"Try fourteen."

"No!" Willy gasped. "No way he looked fourteen. Kid was bigger than fourteen."

Decker said, "Next time ask for proper ID and you won't have charges brought against you."

"Charges?" Willy turned red. "What are you talking about? They said they was brothers. They looked alike. Both of them dark and talking with New York accents."

"They weren't brothers, Clint," Decker said.

"Well, I didn't know that," the clerk said. "And if there was any indication that they was gay, I would have booted their butts out of here. Me and my brother don't put up with that shit. Start getting the gays in here, it scares away the straight perverts. John Doe starts having homosexual panic." He broke into laughter.

Decker said, "I'm talking child molestation—"

"I told you," Willy said. "The kid looked to be about sixteen, seventeen. We get single guys in here all the time—ex-cons trying to wipe the slate clean by moving to another state. Sometimes they come in twos—buddies renting a cheap room. Never for a moment did I think that something hinky was going on between them." He paused. "Was something hinky going on between them?"

Ignoring the question, Decker asked, "How did they register?"

The clerk grinned. "It wasn't under Mr. and Mrs. Smith."

Decker waited.

Willy cleared his throat and opened the registration book. "They registered under the names of Mr. Hank Stephens and Mr. Nicholas Stephens." He showed Decker the book. "Like I said before, the older dude said he and the younger dude was brothers. So I gave them separate beds and everything. They didn't look like they was pulling anything."

"What did they look like?" Decker said.

Willy cracked his knuckles. "They looked a little shopworn. And maybe they looked like they were out to hustle. Especially the older one. He had that

look in his eye, the know-it-all grin. He was definitely up to no good. But hell, everyone who comes
through those doors—present company excepted—
looks like they're up to no good. Who comes to a
dump like this? People hiding from their past, people
hiding from their wives, their husbands, from their
parents. We get a lot of losers who bring their
broads here 'cause they're still living at home."

He cracked his knuckles again. "I checked their
ID and then I registered them. After that, I minded
my own business."

Decker said, "It would be very bad for business to
have the police raiding this place for contributing
to the delinquency of a minor—"

"Come on, Sergeant," Willy whined. "I told you
the kid's ID said eighteen. I'm not required to ask
for a birth certificate—"

"Close you down for a couple of months, not to
mention all the fines—"

"I'm just trying to make a living," the clerk said.
"What do you want from me?"

"For starts, why don't you show me their bill,"
Decker said.

"I'm not required to do that," Willy said. "But to
show you how anxious I am to cooperate with the
law, I'll be happy to show you their bill."

The clerk sifted through a file, then pulled out
a computerized slip of paper. On it was a record of
phone calls. Decker pulled out a pen and his notebook and started to copy down the numbers.

Willy said, "Don't bother. I can tell you what

all these calls are. These nine-seven-six numbers are porno lines. They made five calls to them. This number . . . it's an outcall service. I think this one belongs to Embassy Girls. This is Joe Bittelli's number. He owns Wong Lee Mandarin-Style Cuisine. Guess the boys ordered some Chinese takeout."

Decker copied down the number of Embassy Girls. He said, "The girls come here?"

Willy shrugged and said, "Guy wants a massage in his room, I can't stop him."

Decker tossed him a dirty look.

Willy said, "People come here to be unwholesome. I don't help them do it."

"Right," Decker said. "And you're just trying to earn an honest buck."

"I don't get any kickback from the girls," the clerk said. "These guys want to call up a young lady, I don't make a dime off of them."

Decker shook his head. "What can you tell me about the young lady who was sent up?"

"No one passed through the lobby. However, a couple of months ago I did happen to notice a blonde walking around the back . . . musta been around six. Hard to miss. She was wearing white hot pants and a halter top. My first reaction was that she must be freezing her ass off." He looked at Rina and apologized. "But then I saw she was well-endowed in certain places and thought maybe all those extra pounds were keeping her warm."

"You noticed all this in the dark?"

"I got some lighting in the back," Willy said.

"Security purposes. I could see her well enough. Like I said, I'm farsighted. But I'll be honest. I wasn't looking at the face."

Decker looked at the motel bill again. "What are these charges for?"

"Using the in-house adult TV channel," Willy said. "The boys watched three movies. Three's about an average day's worth of viewing. Seen one, seen them all."

Decker asked if there were any more charges made to their room. Willy answered none that he knew of.

"Did they ever leave the room, go somewhere?" Decker asked.

"I didn't pay attention to their comings and goings," Willy said. "The day they checked in, the younger kid brought out this big bag and asked me where he could do the laundry. I directed him to a spot a block and a half down the road."

"I want to take a look at the room," Decker said.

"You can, but it's been cleaned," Willy said. "You know, my maid usually doesn't mention the state of the rooms after the people leave." He looked at Rina and lowered his voice. "I mean, she's used to all sorts of smells, if you know what I'm talking about."

"I know what you're talking about."

"But she did mention to me that their room had a very fishy smell in it." His voice dropped to a whisper. "Dirty sex can be very fishy-smelling but she said the odor was out of the ordinary."

Decker thought back to the apartment in Flatbush.

The bits of home-cooked fish in the garbage. "Did she find any remnants of fish lying around?"

"She didn't say," Willy said. "And believe me, she don't check the trash. The woman cleans with thick gloves. But I thought I'd pass that bit of info on to you. Just to show you that I'm cooperative."

"If you wanted to be Mr. Joe Citizen, you should have called the cops the moment you saw those two walk through the door."

"On what basis?" Willy said. "Yeah, maybe the kid looked a little scared, maybe he even looked stoned. So what? How many scared or stoned kids you see in this town, Sergeant? How many are you gonna stop and ask what's wrong?"

"I don't see a lot of kids checking into a dump like this," Decker said.

"That's 'cause you don't work here," Willy said, suddenly assertive. "Know what I see? I see exactly what you see, Sergeant. The leftovers."

Embassy Girls was nothing more than a name. All its calls were routed through a tiny little shack discreetly labeled Ace Messenger Service. The service, sandwiched between a dry cleaner and a printer that advertised FAX MACHINES AVAILABLE, was located on Aviation Boulevard, a half mile south of the airport. Looking at the place, Rina would never have suspected it was a front for outcall services although all the blinds were drawn tight. She sat in the unmarked, listening to the cars on the 405 freeway whizzing by, waiting for Peter to finish up.

She wished she had brought Ginger for company.

Ten minutes later, Peter appeared with a smile on his face. If Rina hadn't known better, she would have been jealous. He opened the driver's door and slid in.

"Did you find the massage girl?" Rina asked.

"I found her." He turned the ignition key and the motor charged up. "Caught her just before she was about to go out."

"Was she well-endowed?" Rina asked.

"Clint didn't lie," Decker said.

"One of your more enjoyable interrogations?"

"Rina, this isn't my idea of a good time. I'd gladly trade looking at a pair of large breasts for a little peace and quiet."

Rina patted his hand. "What did she say?"

"Well, she identified Hersh immediately," Decker said. "Noam she was less sure of. Apparently, he was in the bathroom the whole time. Out of choice. She said Hersh offered to pay for her to . . . well, 'to do the kid' was the way she put it. But Noam refused."

"*Boruch Hashem* for that!" Rina shook her head. "Peter, he must be so *scared*."

"I'm sure he is," Decker said. "According to the girl, Hersh—or rather *Hank*—loves his knives. And he loves fish."

"What do you mean?"

Decker said, "Hersh had the hooker bring up a whole monkfish. Then he butterflied it while she performed oral sex."

Rina buried her head in her hands. "That's *disgusting*!"

"It's out of the ordinary," Decker said.

"It's perverted," Rina said.

"Yeah, I guess it's pretty weird."

"*Pretty* weird?"

At least he didn't hurt anyone, Decker thought. Except the fish. But he was assuming the fish was dead. But maybe not. If Hersh dissected a live fish while getting a blow job—now that would be really disgusting.

Rina was looking out the window.

"How about you staying home tomorrow and resting?" Decker said.

"Sounds good to me."

Decker couldn't get his mind off the fish. What had Hersh done with it after he had butterflied it? He thought of the fried fish found in Hersh's New York apartment. Could he and Noam have eaten it? Hersh and fish. The connection was eluding him.

It was almost six-thirty. By the time he took Rina back home, he'd have just enough time to shower and eat and be ready for Marge by eight.

"I feel like doing something productive," Rina said. "Maybe I'll bake a cake while you're gone. A cake can be very life-affirming."

"I can think of other activities that are life-affirming," Decker said.

"You have time?" Rina said.

"For you? Always!"

"I can't do it," Noam insisted. "I won't do it."

"Will you keep your trap shut?"

"I can't do it—"

"Shut the fuck up and listen to me," Hank told him.

Jesus M. Christ, the kid was having another shit fit. Just what he needed. Here he was in another sleazy hotel room with the kid having a shit fit. What did it take to get something done around here?

He took a deep breath. The heater was bad, but it wasn't that cold outside. He could live with a faulty heater. What pissed him off were all the bums downstairs. Who wants to look out the window and see bums pissin' on the sidewalk? Even the first dump didn't have bums.

But the room was cheap and they were within walking distance to the place. He'd staked it out and it was perfect. Queer businessmen meeting after hours at a secret fag bar. Great targets 'cause they were all in the closet. Churchgoing men. Married with kiddies, some of them even grandfathers.

Rocky John had told him about the spot. Hank remembered him grinning when he explained the deal.

Think they'd ever admit they were rolled by a hustler?

Last Hank heard, Rocky had been busted for multiple B and Es. Hank had learned a shitload from him. He wondered if he'd ever see Rocky again.

A Wall Street fag bar, Rocky had called it. Hank had sneaked out last night when Nick-O was asleep. But he had taken all of Nicky's clothing just in case. He had found several marks that looked good. The one he had in mind had an office right near the bar.

Perfect setup—*if* the mark would show up tonight. If not, well, he'd just find someone else and wing it.

"Listen to me, Nick-O," Hank said, softly. "I'm not sayin' you have to do somethin' with it. Just wave it in front of the mark's face and I'll do all the hard part."

"I can't—"

"Listen, for chrissakes," Hank said. "*I'm* the one that's doin' all the hard stuff. I'm the one that's gonna bait him, bring him to the spot. Man, all you hafta do is wave the gun. You can even wear a mask, Nick-O. I wouldn't make you do anything dangerous."

"I just can't do it," Noam said.

"Stop saying that!" Hank shouted. "You're making me pissed off!"

Noam stopped protesting. He felt his limbs shake. And the tears come back. "I can't take this anymore, Hank. I wanna go home—"

"You *what*?" It came out a whisper.

"I want to go home," Noam said. "Just let me go, I won't say anything about you—"

"I didn't hear you right, did I?" Hank said.

Noam didn't answer.

"'Cause if you said you want to go home, 'cause if you said that, know what I have to say to you?"

Noam remained silent.

"I'm gonna say I'm pissed off. And you know what I do when I'm pissed off?"

"Stop threatening me," Noam managed to say.

"What'd you say?" Hank asked, incredulously.

"I said stop threatening me," Noam repeated.

Hank bit his lip. "Fine. You want to go . . . go."

Noam didn't move.

"Go on, hotshot . . . Go." He pushed Noam by his shoulder. "Go . . . go, go, go on. Dafuck outta here before I cut your balls off."

Noam didn't move.

Hank said, "See how fuckin' far you'll get without me. What'll you do for food, hotshot? Where ya gonna sleep tonight? You think you can just call *home* and all your piddlyshit problems will be solved?"

He shoved Noam.

"That what you think?"

Another shove. Harder. It hurt his chest.

"Huh?" Hank yelled out. *"Huh?"*

Hank slammed him against the wall. Noam slid down, holding his head, crumbling into a pile of loose bones.

Hank pinned him down to the floor. "Whaddaya think your mama's gonna say to you, huh? Welcome back, sonny boy? That what you think she's gonna say? Whaddaya think the *rabbaim* are gonna say? Know what they're gonna do? They are gonna lay this . . . this biggest guilt trip on your head. They're gonna tell you what a rotten kid you are and how you fucked up for life for doing such a terrible thing to your parents. Then everybody in the whole community is gonna stare at you like you're some freak. The girls are gonna laugh at you. *'There goes weirdobrain No-am. What a jerk! What a freak!'* And the boys— they ain't gonna be no better. They'll be laughin' just as hard. No one will talk to you. Everyone'll treat you like you got boils on your face. Like you're nothin' but a disease. You're gonna be one big *embarrassment* to your whole family."

He jerked Noam up by the arms and pushed him to the door. "So go, if that's what you want. Go ahead, hotshot! Go! GO!"

Noam burst into tears, letting out huge gulps of sorrow. Hank pulled the teenager into his arms and rocked him.

"Hey, guy," Hank said. "It's okay. It's *okay*."

Noam sobbed on Hank's shoulder.

Hank said, "I know how you feel. And maybe I don't got enough patience all the time. But let me tell you this, Nick-O. You're my buddy. You can trust me. Hey, everything you're feelin' . . . they crapped on me too, man. My parents. The rabbis givin' me nothin' but grief. I know the scene 'cause I've been there. Shit, all of them loonies. Only one who was ever nice was my zeyde."

Noam stopped crying and wiped his eyes on his sleeve.

"My bubbe's nice," Noam said.

"Yeah, but she's probably an old lady by now," Hank said. "How long you think she's gonna last? Then she croaks and you're all alone again. Believe me, I know."

Noam didn't know. Bubbe didn't seem sickly, but she was old. He used to talk to her all the time. But then his brothers teased him about talking to her so he stopped. And when he stopped talking, so did she.

"You think I brought you out here to jump fags?" Hank said. "Hey, this is only temporary. Insurance is still dickin' around with my money. But I'll get it.

And then you and me can live in style. But we need some bread now, man. You gotta help me. We're in this together, you know."

Noam nodded.

"Hey, that's what I like to see," Hank said. "We're like brothers, know what I mean?"

Again, Noam nodded. But deep inside he knew something wasn't right. He shouldn't be talking to Hersh, he should be talking to his mother or uncle or aunt. Or Bubbe. But they never listened to him. Hersh . . . at least, he would listen. Or seemed to be listening. *Vey is mir*, he was so confused. His head hurt from the bang on the wall. His hands were shaking. All he wanted to do was curl up and die.

"Lookit," Hank said. "You wear a ski mask over your head, no one will know who you are, all right?"

Noam paused a long time. Finally he agreed.

"Good guy, man, good guy." Hank picked up the gun. "You gotta get comfortable with it, Nick-O. You gotta hold it. Touch it. It's like girls, Nick-O. You gotta start sometime. At first, it's gonna feel weird, but after a few times . . ." He snapped his fingers. "You get the hang of it. Hey, after we pull this thing off, I'll get us another girl—"

"No," Noam shook his head. "Not for me." His stomach started to churn. He remembered hearing all those grunts, those slurping noises. The smell of raw fish oozing under the bathroom door.

"You gotta start sometime."

"Not yet," Noam insisted, his voice cracking.

"Okay, buddy," Hank said. He offered him the gun. "But this. You gotta get comfortable with it."

Noam took a deep breath, then clasped his fingers around the gun.

"Ain't so bad," Hank said.

No, Noam thought. No it wasn't so bad. All it was was a piece of metal. A piece of metal . . .

"Is it loaded?"

"No," Hank said.

"Will it be loaded when we . . ." Noam's voice trailed off. He looked up at the lopsided smile.

"Up to you," Hank said. "You can convince the mark it's loaded, I don't care if it is or isn't. But if it isn't, you'd better not fuck up." He paused a moment. "Course, I'll have my gutting knife for a backup."

"Then I don't have to do it with a loaded gun?" Noam said.

"Can you pull it off?"

"Yes," Noam said. "Yes, definitely. No problem."

"Then it won't be loaded."

Noam broke into a big smile. "I'll do it, Hank. I can do it for you."

"Hey, buddy," Hank said. "That's what I like to hear."

✤ 22

"Why am I obsessing on the fish?" Decker said to Marge.

"Someone gets head while cleaning a fish . . ." Marge rubbed her arms. "Somehow that has to be significant."

She wore a white cotton blouse, a pair of Levi's, and a yellow windbreaker. But the zipper on the jacket was broken and every time the wind kicked up, she felt tiny electric shocks prick her skin.

"You want my jacket?" Decker asked.

"You're not cold?"

"No." Decker handed her his denim jacket. It would have swallowed up any ordinary woman. Marge filled it nicely.

"It goes beyond the sexual perversity," Decker said. "There's a connection and I can't bring it up."

"Don't fight it. It'll come to you." Marge scanned the crowds. "Besides, if you're concentrating on fish, you're going to miss what's around you. And that's why we came to Westwood."

She was right. There were just too many people

cluttering the street. He needed all his energy for observation.

They were walking north on Westwood heading toward the skyline of UCLA. The queues for the eight o'clock movies were around the block. Most of the boutiques were open—a western boot store, sports paraphernalia, a cubbyhole that specialized in humorous greeting cards. All the eateries were open as well. Most sold portable grub—ice cream, chocolate-chip cookies, muffins. Decker was munching on a buttermilk doughnut bought from a pushcart, sorting out the faces.

There were groups of college kids, that was to be expected. But there were also groups of children too young to go unsupervised. Boys and girls junior high school age. Plump little girls barely pubescent, sporting five earrings in each lobe, dyed green tufts of hair sticking out at odd angles. They wore miniskirts even though it was cold. The boys were dressed in baggy pants or combat fatigues, using cigarettes to look grown-up because their facial hair and muscle layer hadn't come in yet. They made a lot of noise but for the most part, they were innocuous.

Not the case with the homeboys. Black teenaged boys, in oversized clothing—convenient duds if you're hiding a gun. They checked out the scene, on the prowl for enemy color. Confrontive eyes, short haircuts covered by baseball caps worn backward. The Crips' rivalry with the Bloods was so fierce, they wouldn't even pronounce words that began with B— saying cecause for because.

Rap music boomed from ghetto blasters. Sometimes two rival groups would pass each other, eyes filled with malice, the music a cacophonous mix sounding like competing marching bands. The jaunty walks would slow just a tad. Cold glances exchanged, more threatening than words.

Westwood was well patrolled. It showcased L.A.'s first-run movies and held some upperclass restaurants. But with this many people cruising the sidewalks, so many cars clogging the streets, it would be easy for bystanders to catch a stray bullet if the gangbangers went to war.

Lots of people. But so far, no Hersh or Noam.

They had canvassed almost all the shops, all the ticket booths at the movie theaters. Now they were down to using their eyes.

Marge said, "I don't think they've been here yet."

Decker agreed.

"It's almost ten-thirty," she said. "Want to call it a night?"

"Might as well," Decker said. "If they show up, most of the store owners have our business cards."

"Yeah, it was worth coming down just to pass out the pictures," Marge said. "They might not be here tonight, but to quote Scarlett: Tomorrow's another day."

"I like Rhett's line better," Decker said.

"You don't give a damn?"

"Not right now."

Marge smiled and yawned.

"I keep forgetting you have to work tomorrow," Decker said. "Let's go."

"You're still thinking about Hersh and the fish," Marge said.

He shrugged.

Marge said, "Look at that guy." An emaciated six-foot man on roller skates was weaving through the crowds. He wore a black veil over his head. "Is there a point I'm missing?"

"Got me."

Marge said, "You know, Pete, I never did get a chance to tell you how much fun I had at your wedding."

Decker broke into a broad smile. "It was a great wedding, wasn't it?"

"Like nothing I'd ever seen before," Marge said. "You always hear about Jewish weddings. But it's different when you're there."

"Especially if you're the groom."

"Know what I liked best? Cindy dancing with Rina. It was really touching."

Decker smiled.

Marge shook her head. "And now you're reduced to doing this on your honeymoon?"

"Call it collecting points with Rina." He stopped a moment and finished off his doughnut. "I have this delusion that what I really want is vacation and rest. But here I am working . . . I'm not unhappy."

"Gets in the blood, doesn't it?" Marge said. "I act like I'm doing you a favor by cruising with you. What would I be doing otherwise? Harry's always on call. We meet for bed." She paused. "Not a bad arrangement."

"Not bad at all—" Decker snapped his fingers. "Goddamn, *that's* what it is!"

"What?"

Decker smiled. "This is so stupid . . . Hersh. One of the Hershes I inquired about in Crown Heights was a fish vendor."

"And you think that's the Hersh you're looking for?"

"No," Decker said. "That Hersh was bearded and weighed over two hundred pounds. His last name was different. I think it was Hersh Berger or Bergman. But it is a little weird, isn't it? Two Hershes, both associated with fish."

Marge shrugged.

"You know," Decker said, "Jews name after their deceased relatives. Rina once told me she had a cousin Rina, both of them named after her maternal grandmother."

"Think Big Hersh is related to Psycho Hersh?"

"It's a possibility."

"Did Big Hersh mention anything to you about a cousin Hersh?"

"I didn't talk to Big Hersh directly. I talked to his wife and maybe she doesn't know he even has any relatives named Hersh." Decker thought a moment. "Think I'll give him a call."

"What do you hope to find?"

Decker said, "If Psycho Hersh is related to Big Hersh, he can give me a little more background about Psycho Hersh. Or maybe they have relatives out here . . . maybe that's why Hersh flew out here with Noam."

"They didn't hook up with anyone when they came into Los Angeles, Pete."

"Well, maybe it'll take them a little time to get their act together. Get all the raunchy stuff out of the way, all the forbidden fruit. I don't know, I'm just spouting off the top of my head." Decker looked at his watch. "It's one-thirty over there. It'll have to wait until morning."

Marge said, "You still hungry or did the doughnut do it for you?"

"I can always use another cup of coffee," Decker said.

Two Hershes, both connected with fish. And what also struck him as a coincidence was that the fish shop was in Williamsburg—where Psycho Hersh had lived—not Crown Heights, where Big Hersh was living.

He thought about it all the way to the coffee shop.

Crouched in the back alley stinking of garbage, Noam was sweating even though it was cold. He could tell the temperature by the gun in his hand. The metal was chilled—like the handlebars of his bike after it had been left out overnight. It must be the ski mask that was making him so hot. The ski mask and fear.

When Hersh first set him in the alley, he nearly gagged from the stench. He was also petrified to be left alone. But he was more afraid of Hersh's temper than he was of being attacked by a stranger. As the hours wore on, his fear had blossomed into terror. Shadows were people waiting to jump him, every

sound was magnified into an explosion. He felt like
the rock pulled back on a slingshot, everything tight
and ready to spring. Perspiration was preventing him
from getting a good grip. Twice he even dropped the
gun. Then he thought maybe he should just tell Hersh
he'd lost it.

But Hersh would get mad. Maybe even kick him
out. And it was just like he said. He had nowhere to
go at this time of night. Just the police. And he was
terrified of that.

What if the druggist reported him as the one
who stole those *things*? *Vey is mir*, what if they arrested him, put him in jail?

No, he couldn't go to the police.

They might even be looking for him now.

He felt his hands shake uncontrollably and told
himself to stop thinking about that. Just go through
the night one minute at a time.

Just let the night be over with. He prayed to
Hashem to give him guidance, but as always he found
no answer in *tephila*. Just empty words. Hashem never
answered him. But maybe he didn't pray right.

He was so confused.

At least Hersh hadn't made him load the gun.
The clip inside was only for show.

*You're gonna look like an idiot if you show someone
some steel and there ain't no clip in it. You're gonna look
real stupid.*

Hersh swore that the clip was empty. He showed
Noam that it was empty. But still Noam wished that
the clip wasn't there at all.

Maybe he should just pull it out.

But then Hersh would get mad at him.

Something warm and wet was leaking from his body. He must have gone to the bathroom twenty times, but there was still something in there. He felt his head swell up, throb with pain. He felt his knees knock together.

He began to hear himself drawing for breath.

Third time tonight he began to gasp for air. He knew what to do by now.

Deep breaths. Slow yourself down to deep breaths.

The tears started coming, blurring his vision. He wiped them away on his jacket.

He heard a sound and felt himself stiffen.

A second of silence.

Another hoot.

His hand gripped the gun, turning his knuckles white.

Then nothing.

No one.

The alley was deserted. So were the streets. This back way was in the better part of the city, not too far away from all the courthouses. Where they were staying . . . that area was full of weirdos and bums, most of them blacks or Puerto Ricans. (Did they have Puerto Ricans in California or was it Mexicans?) There were loads of drunken old guys talking to themselves, walking with limps, pulling on their hair. They all stank from liquor.

After waiting for Hersh in this alley, he probably stank too. Hersh promised to get him an Aerosmith T-shirt after this was over. Though Noam wanted the T-shirt, he wondered whether it was smart to spend on clothes when they needed money for food and a place to stay.

But Hersh became real mad when Noam told him his concerns.

Hersh was great to talk to as long as you were complaining about your parents, about the rabbis. When you complained about anything else, he pounced on you like a tiger.

Better not to speak unless spoken to.

Again the tears. How he wanted to *go home*, but he was so afraid. What if his parents wouldn't take him back? Course they had to by law, but . . . what if they wouldn't forgive him?

They'd have to forgive him if it was Yom Kippur. That's what Yom Kippur was for. If he didn't make it back by this Yom Kippur—which was in four days—he'd have to wait a whole other year.

What he really should do was drop the gun and run as fast as his legs could carry him. But where? He didn't have any money. And *chas vachalelah*— God forbid—he should bump into these crazy street people at this hour at night without a gun.

So confused.

Then he heard the noise—voices. People talking.

This time it was for real. The words garbled and echoing.

Getting closer and closer. Hersh's voice talking and laughing. A deep voice answering him. It also sounded happy.

Noam looked up, couldn't see a thing. Slowly he rose and flattened himself against a brick wall. He didn't move.

The deep voice was louder—he was slurring his words.

Who was this guy?

Noam inched his way to where the alley met the surface street and peeked around the corner. The two shapes took on recognizable forms. Hersh all dressed up in his Shabbos pants and coat, shiny boots on his feet. The big figure in a suit and tie.

A big guy.

Maybe six feet.

Hersh said the mark would be little.

The big guy was staggering as he walked.

Was he drunk?

Noam had never known any *real* drunks. Some of the rabbis got drunk on Purim, but they weren't *drunks*. Noam didn't know whether the big guy's drunkenness would make him easier to rob or if it would make him mean and eager to fight.

They approached, closer and closer.

No one on the streets except Hersh and the mark. Deserted. Alone.

They talked loudly. Hersh was talking with a half-German, half-Yiddish accent. He seemed like he was having a good time.

Sweat pouring into Noam's ski mask, turning it damp. The smell of wet wool. It made him nauseated. He pleaded to God to get this over with!

They were coming.

Closer and closer.

His heart was beating out loud, the gun quivering in his hands.

The salty smell of his sweat.

The blood rushing through his head.

Closer and closer.

A high-pitched ringing in his ears. Then it stopped and his head was filled with a *whoosh, whoosh, whoosh*.

His heart hammering against his chest.

Lub dud, lub dud, lub dud.

Whoosh, whoosh, whoosh.

Lub dud. Whoosh.

Faster, faster.

Now!

He leaped out and stuck the gun in the mark's back. Said his practiced lines.

But it didn't go as planned.

A large arm pivoting, turning.

A heavy thump across his head.

Losing balance.

Something warm and wet inside his mouth. Something hard floating in his saliva.

But the gun in his hand.

Move and I'll kill you! someone screamed.

Someone screaming in *his* voice. He spit out the hard thing as he screamed.

Blood pouring from his mouth.

An arm going around his throat, choking him.

Noam pushed the gun deep into a soft gut. Pulled the trigger.

Nothing.

Pulled harder and still nothing.

The arm choking harder, his head becoming light. Blood choking him.

Was he shot in the mouth?

God, he was going to die!

Coughing. Coughing. Coughing.

Going to die!

Say your last prayers.

Say kaddish!

Gasping for air. Coughing blood.

His body floating away.

Gasp.

Choke.

Floating away. Say kaddish quick. But the words . . .

And then the arm releasing him.

The body slumping down on the ground.

Hersh on top of the body, his hand plunging into the man's chest.

Something shiny in his hand.

Hersh screaming something.

But Noam could barely make out the words as he spit out blood.

Then he understood.

GODDAMN IT! CHECK HIS COAT POCKET!

Noam reached inside the man's suit.

Wet and warm.

The man was wet and warm.

On his chest shreds of fabric. A wet hole. A few bits of something that felt like chopped meat.

The man not moving.

HURRY, GODDAMN IT!

Noam searched the inside coat pocket. Pulled out a wallet and showed it to Hersh.

Hersh grabbed the wallet, then Noam's hand, and ran. One block, two, three, four.

Noam sucking for air, spitting out blood. Deep pain in his chest.

Then Hersh yelling at him to slow down.

They stopped a block later.

Quickly Hersh took off his coat and used it to wipe the knife. He threw it into a Dumpster and tucked the knife into his boot, peeled off Noam's ski mask and stuffed it in his pocket.

Hersh whispered, "Give me the wallet."

Noam did as told.

"You still got the gun?"

Noam nodded.

"At least you had the fuckin' sense not to drop the gun." Hersh rummaged through the wallet, fished out a thick fold of bills, fanned them out like playing cards.

"Man, we hit the mother lode." Hersh scanned the ID. "Fucker used a fake name with me. His driver's license says he's Thomas Stoner and he told me his name was Todd." He laughed and threw the wallet in the garbage. He eyed Noam. "You look like shit."

Noam started to speak, but held back because he felt his stomach contents begin to erupt.

"Dafuck he do?" Hersh said. "Knock out your tooth?" He spit on Noam's face and began to groom him like a monkey. "We gotta get outta here, but we gotta clean you up first." He spit into his hand again. "Not too bad. Let's go. And relax. He ain't gonna be yellin' for help."

Slowly, they walked back to their hotel room.

The man at the desk barely noticed them when he handed Hersh the key.

Once inside, Hersh bolted the door. Then he plopped down on the bed. Noam sat on the edge.

Hersh said, "You know if you woulda loaded the fuckin' gun, we coulda done it much cleaner. I mean the gun was a total waste. And you bein' there was a total waste. I spent more energy tryin' to keep you safe than I did takin' him out. Only thing you were good for was the element of surprise." Hersh paused a moment. "It coulda been worse."

Noam tried to stop shaking. "Is he . . ."

Hersh threw him a disgusted look. "Was he movin'?"

Noam shook his head.

"Then use your imagination, pal."

"Oh, God," Noam moaned. A deep moan from inside his soul. He ran to the bathroom. Bolted up his dinner in deep waves of grief.

Such an *aveyrah*, such a horrible sin. A sin against man, a sin against God. He was the lowest of the low. *Please God, be merciful and let me die.*

After vomiting, he washed his face. His head was hurting so bad, he thought someone must have shot it. His mouth was fuzzy, his lip split, swollen to twice its size. A piece of front tooth chipped off, scraping his tongue.

That man. Warm and wet.

The hole in his chest, oozing with warm blood.

Oh, God, let me die!

"Whatcha doin' in there?" Hersh shouted. "Get in here, we gotta talk."

"A minute," Noam managed to say. Again he washed his face. In a moment of self-loathing, a moment of fury, he balled up his hand and punched the mirror. The glass shattered, cutting his hand and wrist. Noam didn't care.

A pounding at the door. Hersh saying, "Dafuck you doin', Nick-O?"

"I'll be out in a minute," Noam heard himself say. Still shaking, he washed his hand and wrist. Then he saw it, a glittering piece of glass. Sharp . . . so sharp. He picked it up. Made a practice cut across his wrist. The line instantly bled.

But suicide was another *aveyrah*, another sin.

Two sins. Sin leads to sin. *Aveyrah gemat aveyrah*. Easier to get killed than to kill yourself.

Hersh would make him do it again. He knew it.

Let the *aveyrah* be on someone else. He bandaged his hand with the towel.

That was the only way.

He felt calmer, hitting upon a solution that would be good for everyone.

Him dead—no longer a burden to anyone.

But first he must make confession—*vidduy*—especially before Yom Kippur. To whom? To anyone who'd listen. Had to be tonight. Tomorrow might be too late.

Had to be tonight.

When he came out, Hersh was examining his knife.

"Musta broke the tip off inside the fucker. God, that makes me pissed." He stuck the knife inside a leather sheath and looked up at Noam.

"What happened to your hand?"

"I smashed the mirror in the medicine cabinet." Noam waited for Hersh to get mad. He didn't care anymore.

"Why'd ya do that?"

"'Cause I felt like it," Noam said.

Hersh smiled. That horrible lopsided smile.

"Pretty tough, kid. The hand, the face . . . looks like you just went ten rounds with someone heavy. The shit puts a little man into you."

"You killed him," Noam whispered.

Hersh said, "You think I'm a monster for doin' that?" He stood up and poked a finger in Noam's chest. "Let me tell you something, Nick-O. I heard you clickin' the Beretta. When you pulled the trigger, were you thinkin' if the gun was loaded or not?"

He poked him again.

"Huh? Were you?"

Noam shook his head no. No, he wasn't thinking about that. More *aveyrahs*. To get himself killed was the only solution. "No," he said. "You're right. I wasn't thinking about it."

"Hey, you think it's bad you pulled the trigger, I think it's *good*. That's why I helped you. I could see that you're a mover and shaker. I mean, you fucked up this time. But that was your first time at bat and hell, I can give you a little grace period. Next time we go with a loaded gun."

Next time, Noam thought. Confession tonight. Because next time would be the last time.

Hersh was staring at him. Trying to read him.

"I mean if there ever is a next time," Hersh said.

"We got a pretty good haul. And like I said, the dick-head's money should be comin' my way soon."

But all Noam heard was "next time." Next time, the last time.

"You'd better start packin'," Hersh said. "We gotta split."

"Where are we going?"

Hersh gave him a pat on the back. "Not to worry, Nick-O." He winked. "I got it all worked out."

23

The jarring ring of the telephone jolted Decker awake. Hand flailing out to pick up the receiver, he answered the call "Decker" from force of habit.

"Akiva?"

Akiva? Decker thought. Static on the line. The voice feminine and nervous. Someone from New York. The boys? Dear God, don't do this to me.

"Yes, this is he. Who am I talking to?"

"Who is it?" Rina asked.

Rina. He'd forgotten about her. Reminded himself to speak more softly.

The voice said, "This is Miriam Berkowitz. Noam's aunt?"

"Is everything okay?"

"No, it isn't."

"What is it, Peter?" Rina asked.

He waved her quiet. "Are you calling about Noam?"

"Yes, I—"

"Wait," Decker interrupted. "Then my boys are okay?"

Rina gasped. *"What?"*

"Your boys?" A momentary pause. "Oh, you mean Rina's . . . They're fine. Oh, my goodness, I must have frightened you. I'm so sorry."

"No problem," Decker said. "Give me a second to talk to Rina." He covered the mouthpiece. "It's Miriam Berkowitz. Noam's aunt. It's about Noam. The boys are fine."

"*Boruch Hashem*," Rina whispered. She covered her mouth and exhaled, tried to slow her breathing. "Don't worry about me. I'll just collapse."

Decker grabbed a pencil and a piece of paper and came back on the line. "What's going on?"

"I heard from Noam," Miriam said. "He was hysterical. Crying . . . sobbing. He was talking about something bad that he did. A terrible, terrible *aveyrah*. Something he did to a man he met in a bar. He was talking so fast, I don't think I got it all down. I didn't know who to call—"

"You did the right thing by calling me," Decker said. "Slow down a moment, Miriam."

"I'm sorry."

A male voice in the background said, "Did you tell him about the gun?"

Miriam said, "Not yet."

Decker said, "Wait. Slow down, Miriam, and listen carefully. I'm going to take you over the conversation step by step. Okay?"

"Okay," she said. "I'm sorry—"

"You don't need to apologize," Decker said. "You did the right thing. First, when did he call?"

"I just hung up with him."

"Okay," Decker said. "Did he say where he was?"

"I asked him," Miriam said. "First thing I said is 'Noam, where are you?' But he didn't answer. All he did is talk. More like rambling. He didn't make much sense. He was talking so fast, I could barely get a word in edgewise."

"Like he was talking on the run?" Decker asked.

"Exactly."

Sneaking away from Hersh to make a telephone call. The two of them must still be together. Damn, damn, damn. He should have had answering machines hooked up to all the relatives' phones. Most have recording devices. Press a button, the entire conversation would have been taped. A stupid slipup on his part.

Miriam said, "I guess I should have pressed him on his exact location. But you told us he had checked into a motel in Los Angeles, so I guess I assumed that's where he was. I was so shocked and he was talking so fast. It was five in the morning—*My goodness!* It must be two-thirty for you."

Two-thirty-six to be exact. Decker said, "At least we finally have proof that Noam's still alive. That's really good. Now sit back and relax, Miriam. I'm going to ask you a lot of questions. Okay?"

"Okay."

"First thing," Decker said. "The phone rings, you pick it up."

"Yes."

"What's the first thing Noam said?"

"Uh, something like 'Tante Miriam, it's me and I'm in terrible trouble.'"

"He didn't identify himself?"

"Uh, no," Miriam said. "No, he didn't. But I recognized his voice. He used to come over here a lot. He likes my cooking."

"He must also trust you to call you," Decker said. "Okay, Noam says he's in trouble and what do you say?"

"I asked him where he was."

"And he didn't answer."

"No."

"Then what did he say?"

"He said he was in big, big trouble. Worse trouble than I could imagine. He did something terrible—a big *aveyrah*, one that even Yom Kippur couldn't take care of. I asked him what the *aveyrah* was and he said that he did something terrible to . . . to some queer man he met—"

"Hold it," Decker said. "Noam said the words 'queer man'?"

"Uh, I believe so."

"Or did he just use the word 'queer'?" Decker said.

Miriam was hesitant. "Maybe he just said 'queer.'"

"As in homosexual?" Decker said.

"Maybe that was the meaning," Miriam said.

Decker said, "What were Noam's exact words, Miriam?"

"Uh, 'I did a terrible *aveyrah* to a queer I met in a bar.'"

"In a *bar*?"

"Yes," Miriam said. "In a bar. I thought that was very odd, too. I asked him *what* did he do, but he wouldn't tell me."

"Did Noam say, 'I can't tell you,' or did he just ignore the question?"

"He just ignored the question. All he said was that he did something terrible to this queer man he picked up in a bar downtown—"

"*Downtown?*" Decker asked. "Noam used the word 'downtown'?"

"Yes," Miriam said. "Yes, he did. He said he picked up a queer man in a bar downtown. Does that help you?"

"I don't know," Decker said.

Downtown Los Angeles was not a place to find gay bars. Downtown San Francisco was. Maybe the two of them hopped a plane north. Or it could be Noam was in West Hollywood—the primary bastion of the L.A. gay community. It had some tall buildings. Maybe it looked like downtown to Noam.

Miriam said, "He kept saying he did a terrible thing. My mind was racing so fast. What would Noam be doing with a . . . homosexual and how did he get into a bar? Then, he said he had this gun, but he didn't use it. But he still did a terrible *aveyrah*. Again, I asked him what did he do? But he didn't answer me."

"He said he had a gun?"

"Yes," Miriam said. "Then he said he really didn't use it. I don't know what he meant. I don't know if he tried to rob this poor man or . . . or force him to do something . . . or . . ."

Or even worse, Decker thought. He was writing as he spoke. "Go on."

"He asked for my forgiveness," she said. "Begged

for it. I said everything would be all right, he would be okay, but he *needed* to go to the police, *right now!* Whatever he did, he should go to the *police.* Then we could help him." She began to cry. "That was the wrong thing to say. He hung up. I should have told him I love him. I should have told him how much we miss him and how much his parents love him. I should have told him that no matter what, he was forgiven. I should have told him a dozen things . . . and now it's too late. I'm such an idiot—"

Decker said, "It took you by surprise. You did great."

"I didn't—"

"You did," Decker assured her. He heard her sniff over the line. "You did great."

"He was talking so fast," she said. "And I was so confused. . . ."

"Miriam, did Noam mention any names of people? Any streets, establishments, landmarks?"

"Just the bar."

"He told you *he* picked up the homosexual in a bar?"

"Yes."

"Did he tell you the name of the bar?"

"No."

Decker asked, "Did he call the bar just a bar? Or did he call it a queer bar or a gay bar? Or a lounge? Did he mention eating there?"

"He just called it a bar," Miriam said. "He was talking so fast. Just that he picked up a . . . queer . . . I hate that word. Why do the kids use it?"

Because kids can be little bastards, Decker

thought. He said, "How did he know the man was gay?"

"I don't know," Miriam said.

"Okay," Decker said. "When he called, did you hear any background noises?"

"Uh, maybe there were some," Miriam said. "I wasn't really paying attention to any other noises."

"That's normal," Decker said. "Let me ask you this. Could you hear his voice very clearly? As clear as my voice, for instance."

"Your voice is clearer," she said. "Maybe I'm more awake." She paused. "You know, he might have been calling from a phone booth. When I think about it, it sounded like a phone-booth line. There was traffic in the background. You know, the sound of cars passing by."

"A lot of traffic? A little?"

"Medium."

"Whooshing sort of sounds?"

"Exactly."

"Did you hear any sort of a siren?" Decker asked.

"No."

"The traffic sounds you heard," Decker said. "Any of the sounds rumble, seem to shake up the line?"

A long pause. "Yes," Miriam said.

She sounded impressed.

"Good," Decker said. "How many times, Miriam?"

"Um . . . maybe three or four times."

"And how long did you talk to Noam?"

"About two minutes."

Three to four rumbling sounds in two minutes. Trucks roaring by. And a medium amount of whooshing traffic noise at two-thirty A.M. A concentration of cars driving fast. It seemed logical that Noam had placed the call close to a freeway. There were no freeways in West Hollywood or in the heart of downtown San Francisco. No thoroughfares or highways in either location. But there were plenty of freeways in the downtown L.A. area.

"Noam said he had a gun," Decker repeated.

"Yes."

"But he didn't use it?"

"Exactly."

"Did he mention any shooting?"

"No . . . no shooting. Just that he had a gun and he didn't use it."

Decker stopped a moment. Sounded to him like Noam and Hersh had rolled a gay. Used a gun as a prop and robbed him. With any degree of luck, it was just a simple robbery. But Decker was dubious. Noam kept using the phrase "a terrible *aveyrah*"—a grievous sin. Would a kid like Noam consider simple robbery with no one getting hurt a grievous sin?

"Did he mention blood?"

"No, nothing like that. Just that he did a terrible *aveyrah*." Miriam stopped talking. Then she said, "I haven't called my brother yet. I called you first thing."

"You did right," Decker said. "I'm going to work on it right now."

"Should I phone my brother?"

Her voice was very hesitant. Decker said, "I'll make the call if you want. But Ezra's going to call you anyway. He'll want to talk to you directly."

"You're right," Miriam said. "I'll call him myself.

I dread it but I'll do it. Why didn't he call his parents?"

"He was probably too ashamed," Decker said.

"Why me?" Miriam was talking more to herself than to Decker. "Why *me*? Oh well. At least he called someone. If only I would have handled it right . . ."

"You did fine," Decker said. "Miriam, I want you and all your family to go out and buy a phone machine that can record conversations—"

"Oh, my goodness!" Miriam exclaimed. "We have that kind of machine! I didn't even think of it. How stupid!"

"Well, I forgot to tell you to use it," Decker said. "So I won't berate me if you don't berate yourself, okay?"

"Okay."

Decker then gave her very specific instructions on what to do if Noam called again. What to say, what to ask, what to listen for. How to calm him down. Then he told her to pass all the information on to the rest of the family. He also suggested that the family consider consulting with an attorney. Those words of advice were met with silence. Finally, Miriam agreed it was a good idea.

When Decker was done, she said, "Akiva, I can't tell you how much my family appreciates—"

"My pleasure," Decker said, cutting her off.

"No," Miriam said. "No, it isn't your pleasure. It isn't the way anyone should spend their honeymoon. Yesterday, Shimon said what you were doing was the highest form of *tzedakah* and all of us agreed with him. Real charity is not just giving money. It's not just giving an hour here or there for an organization. Real *tzedakah* is giving . . . is giving of *yourself.*" She started to cry again. "Thank you *so* much."

"It's okay—"

"It's not okay."

"Really, it is."

"Please thank Rina, too," she sobbed.

"I will."

"*Shana tova tikatevu ve teychatemu.*"

Decker thought about repeating the blessing back to her, but decided his mind wasn't functioning properly enough to get the Hebrew right. "Same to you and your family."

Family, he thought. The woman was his half sister. He'd never had a sister. Of course, he really didn't have one now. He wished her well, hung up the phone, and gave Rina a synopsis of what had happened as he dressed.

"I'll use the telephone in the dining room," he said. "You go back to sleep."

"I'm wide awake," she said. "Use the telephone here."

"Nah, I'll probably be going out shortly." Decker pulled up his trousers, slipped on a white shirt. "When it's quiet you'll get sleepy."

"I wish I could help you."

"You could help me by getting some sleep."

"I love you."

"Love you, too."

Rina stared at him a moment. He appeared asymmetrical. "Your shirt's cockeyed, Peter."

Decker looked down. His shirttail was two inches longer on the right. He'd missed a button.

"I'll fix you up," Rina said. She gave him a kiss on the neck.

"I love it when you dress me." Decker paused, then said, "I love it better when you undress me."

Smiling, Rina finished buttoning his shirt, then gave him a light pat on his rear. "You be careful out there."

It had been ages since anyone had said that to him. Ten, even fifteen years. Detective work wasn't dangerous. Still, he was touched that she had said it. It was nice to matter to someone.

So far the night had buried six bodies, four of the homicides the outcome of gang warfare in Southeast Division. There had also been a fatal stabbing at a bar in Hollenbeck—all parties accounted for—and an irate wife had shot her cheating husband in bed with his lover in the Devonshire district. Which meant that either Noam's victim had yet to be found or Noam's *aveyrah*, his grievous sin—was not murder.

The sin could have been assault or robbery. For such a religious boy, it could even have been anal intercourse with the man he supposedly picked up. *Supposedly.* Without hearing him directly, without talking to him, it was hard for Decker to assess the accuracy of the call.

He called West Hollywood Sheriff's Station and asked about the nightly activity. A Detective Jack Cleveland reported no murders. There had been assaults but all the suspects involved had been apprehended. The rest of the roster was taken up by burglaries and robberies—none of the details seemed to match the information Noam Levine had given his aunt. It was useless to go down and start questioning the patrons of local gay bars. Nothing public was open at this hour. He'd come back to it if necessary.

Next he phoned Central Substation. Downtown L.A. At last, he received some promising information. An ADW had gone down about four hours ago in an alley near the Hall of Records. The detective just assigned to the case was named Felipe Benderhoff. He reported that the victim—a six-one, two-hundred-pound, middle-aged WM named Thomas Stoner—was in serious but stable condition at Good Sam. Rather than get the details over the phone, Decker asked Benderhoff if he'd mind waiting for him to come down. It'd be easier to talk to him directly. Benderhoff said if Decker had some solid leads, he'd be happy to wait.

Decker hung up and tiptoed into the bedroom. Rina had conked out, her body entwined with the bedcovers. He smiled and imagined her leg draped around him instead of the quilt. He kept that picture in his mind as he rode the freeway to downtown.

Central Substation, on the corner of Wall and Sixth, was a block-long brick, windowless building fronted by an ornate mosaic of LAPD's finest at work. Catercorner to it was the Greyhound Bus Terminal, a haven for the homeless on a rainy night. The other two corners were occupied by parking lots. Upon first glance, they seemed empty. But Decker took a further look and before long all sorts of furtive, feral things started darting through the darkness. Central was deep inside the mean streets, the surrounding blocks taken up by mental cases cursing at the moon, by drunks and addicts huddled under doorposts, shivering in tatters. Then there were the dealers. There was a watch spot right on the roof of the stationhouse. Officers would watch the buy go down with a telescope and swoop in for the arrest. But it was like an eagle going after an anthill. Mess things up for a moment, but come back the next day, there's another anthill.

He parked the unmarked in the back lot, entered the reception area and was escorted to the detectives' squad room by a black plainclothes cop whose biceps were straining the sleeves of his shirt. The room was good-sized, much larger than Foothill, but it wasn't furnished any better. The desks were either metal or raw wood and none of the chairs matched. Decker did notice that they had computers at most desks and push-button speaker phones.

Crimes Against Persons—CAPS—was situated against the back wall next to the lockers. A dark-complexioned man—the only person in the squad room—was seated at one of the desks, poring over some forms. He looked up when Decker entered. He was in his mid-thirties and had a long face capped by thick black hair. His nose was flat, his cheeks stretched over pronounced cheekbones. His eyebrows were bushy and topped startling bright blue

eyes. He told Decker he was Benderhoff and motioned him over.

"Take a load off, Sergeant."

Decker swung the seat around and sat with his
chest leaning against the back of the chair. On top
of the detective's desk was a placard that read LIFE'S
A BITCH, THEN YOU MARRY ONE.

"I'm just finishing up the paperwork," Benderhoff
said. "Like I told you, victim was hit on Third and
Temple, multiple stab wounds to the chest. He placed
his own nine-one-one call at a pay phone. Held on
long enough to do what he had to do. Cruiser was
there forty-five seconds later. He was just about out."

"Was he assaulted in the phone booth?"

"Nope," Benderhoff said. "We followed the blood.
It led to a back alley about a block away. The victim
must have crawled to the booth."

"They do emergency surgery on him?"

"Yeah, but it wasn't a long one. Forty minutes or
so, mostly muscle damage but he lost blood. He's
in recovery, in stable condition. He managed to tell
the patrol officers his name and phone number before he went under the knife. His wife's with him
now. Needless to say, she's upset."

"He came out okay considering."

"Some people are lucky," Benderhoff said. "He
can talk, but for the most part, he's out of it. Best as I
could make out, he works downtown. He was walking to his car when a couple of guys jumped him.
Now there was no cars around where all the blood
was. But they could have dragged him out of the
public lot into the back alley."

"Awful lot of work for the perps," Decker said. "Stoner's a big guy."

"Yeah, something's not right," Benderhoff said. "His wife said he was supposed to be having a dinner meeting. But there are no real restaurants around where his car was parked. Now, maybe he was dropped off. But it would have made more sense for him to take his car to where he was going. Wanna know what I think? Guy was having a little nookie, his girl dropped him off a couple blocks from the office so no one he'd know would see him. He got jumped on the way home. The uniforms told me he was reeking of booze."

"He wasn't with anyone when he was attacked?"

"Nope. That fits in nicely with my dropoff theory."

Decker said, "Do you know if Stoner is gay?"

"Gay?" Benderhoff's eyes widened. "No indication. Why? What do you got for me?"

Decker showed him the pictures of Noam and Hersh, and, at length, explained the purpose of his visit. Benderhoff stared at the pictures as he listened, nodding at certain points. After Decker had finished, Benderhoff thought a moment, ran his fingers through his hair.

"You know," he said, "this is a little out of my field. But there are a couple of local places where . . . you know, if you're Mr. Businessman-in-the-closet-with-everything-to-lose, you can go somewhere for a little fun. Very posh. Very discreet. Far as I know, there's been no trouble with the law. All of the members are the law-and-order types. But you might want to try Vice on that. They'd know more than I would."

"The clubs would all be closed at this hour, wouldn't they?"

"I'm sure they would."

Decker said, "I think the easiest thing is to show Stoner a bunch of the pictures. We'll age-match them and I'll throw mine in with the stooges."

"Might be difficult with Mrs. Stoner there." Benderhoff let out a small laugh. "I could use my charm. Smile at her with my baby blues and she'd follow me anywhere."

"When were you planning to talk to Stoner?"

"I don't know," Benderhoff said. "Around seven, maybe eight. Something like that." He glanced at his watch. "It's four-thirty now. Good Sam's in the neighborhood. We can grab a couple hours' sleep upstairs, gulp down some coffee, and give it a whirl."

Decker said that sounded good.

Benderhoff paused, then said, "This kid a relative of yours?"

"No," Decker answered without pausing. "I'm doing a favor for my wife. She's friendly with the family."

"Must be some wife."

Decker pulled out a photo of Rina—a professional one she had taken right before they married. Decker had wanted something to put on his desk. And he wanted to see her with her hair flowing long and loose, knowing the tresses would be covered or braided after they married. At first, she hadn't wanted to do it—the time, the money, all the to-do with makeup and clothes. But he asked so little of her that she agreed without much of a fuss. All the proofs had turned out magnificently. The photographer had remarked that she could be a professional model and had wanted to put her portrait in the window. But Rina had asked him not to, clearly embarrassed by all the attention.

Benderhoff stared at the wallet-sized picture for a long time. Then he said, "Know what? If she was my wife, I'd do a favor for her, too."

Thomas Stoner's head lay on the pillow, as inert as marble. Tubes were in his nostrils, needles were in his arm. His hospital gown was open at the neck and curly gray hairs sprouted from his chest. His head hair was silver and thin, very damp with sweat. His eyes were sunken, his thick lips almost bloodless. Decker was on the right side of the bed, Benderhoff was on the left. They sat very close to the man, gave him a minute to adjust to their presence. At last, Stoner gave them the go-ahead by nodding.

Benderhoff took out half a dozen photographs, including pictures of Noam and Hersh. "I'm gonna show you some faces one by one, Mr. Stoner. Nod if you see someone familiar."

The first two snapshots produced no response. The third was a picture of Noam. That was also met with a blank stare. When Benderhoff showed Stoner Hersh's high school picture, the man's eyes widened several diameters.

"That's him," Stoner said.

"You're sure?" Benderhoff said.

"Positive," Stoner whispered. "Mother*fucker*." He coughed from the exertion, deep grunts that almost blew out his nasal tubes. Then he quieted, lay very still.

Benderhoff and Decker exchanged looks.

Decker said, "You said two men jumped you?"

"Yes," Stoner said.

"You can nod if it's easier," Decker said. "Okay, two men jumped you." He pointed to Hersh's picture. "One of them was this man?"

Stoner nodded. "The other . . . masked."

Decker paused for a moment, addressed the comment to Benderhoff. "Funny, one was masked, the other wasn't. Doesn't at all sound like a typical mugging."

Stoner's eyes widened again.

"Mr. Stoner," Decker said. "These guys are going to mug someone else. You were very lucky. Their next victim might not fare as well. I need to know exactly what happened, so I can find out how these two operate. Do you know what I'm driving at?"

Stoner's eyes closed.

Decker said, "We sent your wife out so we could all be honest."

Benderhoff said, "There's no need for anything you say to be repeated outside this room."

Stoner didn't respond verbally, but tears rolled from his closed eyes.

"Mr. Stoner?" Benderhoff said.

"Go . . . on," Stoner said. "I know . . . you know. But my wife . . . married thirty-two years. She . . . can't find . . . out."

"I understand," Benderhoff said.

"Go ahead," Stoner said.

"I'll make this as quick as possible," Decker said. "The clubs you go to . . . they're very exclusive. How did this man get in?"

"My guest," Stoner whispered.

"You knew him from before?" Benderhoff said.

Stoner shook his head. "He . . . was waiting . . . outside."

"You brought him in," Decker said. "He must have been dressed nicely."

Stoner nodded. "So . . . young . . . virile. Told me he'd . . . he'd lost his ID card. He . . . was furious because . . . not letting him in. I believed . . . Looked the part. Spoke in a foreign accent . . . the right manners. I invited him . . . as my guest. I was . . . a fool. Should . . . know better. A weird smile."

"Weird smile?" Decker said. "How?"

"Off-kilter." Stoner turned to Benderhoff. "If my wife . . . she finds out . . ." He started to cough—pitiful, hacking sounds that caused him a lot of pain.

Decker waited until he quieted, then said, "So you invited him into the club. Had a couple of drinks."

Stoner nodded. "Afterward, he suggested . . . we go . . . to his suite . . . at the Belle Maison."

"His *suite*?" Decker said.

"Told me he was a German count. Heinrich Stremmer." Stoner looked up. "I thought it was . . . bullshit. A hustler . . . lots of them . . . at the club. But he spoke . . . fluent German."

Decker's first thought was it might have been Yiddish. To the untrained ear, the languages sounded identical. Then again, Hersh could have known German, too.

Stoner said, "His suite . . . too public. Then he suggested my office. I had told him . . . worked around here. He said . . . if someone saw us, I . . . could say he was . . . a client."

Decker said, "You were attacked along the way."

Stoner nodded.

"He set you up," Decker said.

Stoner said, "I . . . a fool. Drunk . . ."

"He knew where you worked," Benderhoff said.

"Yes," Stoner whispered. "He must have."

"Which one stabbed you?" Benderhoff said. "Or did both of them do it?"

"Heinrich," Stoner whispered. "He stabbed . . . me. I was . . ." Tears rolled down his face. "So *betrayed*."

"What about the other one?" Benderhoff said.

"The other?" Stoner shook his head. "Didn't stab me. He tried to shoot me . . . but there were . . . no bullets."

Decker thought: Everything Miriam had said was making sense. "So you never saw the one that tried to shoot you."

Stoner shook his head.

"Only this one," Decker said, pointing to Hersh again. "This is Heinrich. The one who stabbed you."

"Yes," Stoner whispered.

Benderhoff said, "Did Heinrich say anything about himself? Where he lived?"

"He said," Stoner whispered, "he said . . . he lived in Germany. He spoke German."

"And he was staying at the Belle Maison?" Benderhoff asked.

Stoner nodded.

"We'll check it out," Benderhoff said.

"They took your wallet," Decker said.

"Yes," Stoner said.

"Your wife can provide us with all your credit-card numbers?" Benderhoff said.

"Yes."

"Your attackers may try to use them," Decker said. He stood. "They could be a valuable lead as to where they are."

Stoner nodded and closed his eyes again. Benderhoff knew he'd had enough. He stood and said, "Thank you for your time, Mr. Stoner."

Stoner said, "My secret . . . I have a wife . . . who I wouldn't hurt . . . my children as well."

Benderhoff told him they'd be discreet.

Stretched out in the passenger's seat of the unmarked, Benderhoff slurped coffee from a Styrofoam cup and said, "So what if it goes to the DA? Your little boy's gonna plea bargain for state's witness against Heinrich, who did the stabbing. All the gay stuff is gonna come out."

"You're assuming there's enough evidence against my little boy to prosecute," Decker said. He was driving south on Figueroa, heading back toward Central Substation.

"Yeah," Benderhoff said. "Good point. State don't got no witnesses, no physical evidence, state don't got diddly-squat on your boy. Just the word of Count Heinrich and that's worth shit. So maybe we can keep the old guy's secret a secret, huh?"

"I hope so," Decker said. He finished his coffee, bunched the Styrofoam into a ball and threw it in the backseat.

Benderhoff said, "Know something? The coffee's pretty good."

"It should be at two fifty a throw," Decker said.

"No one ever said the Belle Maison was cheap," Benderhoff said. "They really should have comped us."

Decker said, "At least no one can accuse us of taking graft."

Benderhoff laughed. "Well, Count Heinrich was never a paying guest there. You know this dude better than I do. Where do you think he is?"

Decker said, "I think my boy called his aunt using a booth near the freeway interchanges. I'm going to check out locations. We could also try the local dives in this area."

Benderhoff said, "I'll check out the downtown sewer holes. I know all the guys anyway."

"Sounds good," Decker said.

"Although if I were them, I wouldn't stick around too close to my dirty work," Benderhoff said.

"Yep," Decker said. "They've probably split. I've got about another four, maybe five days until I officially come back to work. I'll keep looking. I find anything, I'll call you first."

"Likewise," Benderhoff said. "Nice working with you."

"Same," Decker said. "Let me ask you something. How'd you get a name like Felipe Benderhoff?"

"A Peruvian mother and a German father," Benderhoff said. "Their marriage was shit from day one. My old man was twenty years older than my mother. If truth be told, I think he was an ex-Nazi. Anyway, my mother was hot-blooded, always going hysterical. My father had ice water in his veins. But something good did come out of it. My coloring. My baby blues and my thick black hair. Drives the women wild."

He paused, then said, "I'm colored like your wife."

Decker said, "She's fairer."

"Yeah, but I mean the hair and the eyes."

Decker said that was true.

"Maybe I'm her long-lost brother," Benderhoff quipped.

"Not a chance," Decker said.

❧ 24

There were four public booths near the 10-East, none situated near fleabag hotels. But Decker did notice that one of the booths was fifty yards from an overpass. Beneath it was a sheltered spot used by the homeless. At eleven in the morning, most of the transients were up. Men with matted hair were stuffing their respective belongings into torn plastic bags. They were of indeterminate age—any one of them could have been from twenty to fifty. Next to the pack rats, a grizzled old man with a gray beard was sucking on a bottle of Thunderbird. He was lying on his side, running his finger across moist dirt stubbled with weeds. Across from him, two other men were talking to themselves while eating a breakfast of dog food scooped out of cans with their fingers. They looked at Decker with fearful eyes, cradled their meager possessions as if they were babies.

Decker lit a cigarette, not because he wanted a smoke but to kill the stench. He puffed out a few clouds, then pulled out a fin and the snapshots of Hersh and Noam. Everyone eagerly nodded, said yes they were here, then held out their hands. Worthless information.

Decker flicked the bill between his fingers.

"Where did they go?" he asked.

Again, he got answers, but nothing that he believed to be true.

Then the grizzled man with the Thunderbird spoke up. He pointed a finger at Decker and said, "They were here."

His statement was followed by a drone of: "They were here! They were here!" Then out came the empty palms. Decker pushed the palsied hands aside. He bent down next to the old man until they were face-to-face. The coot reeked of alcohol, as if he'd been preserved in the stuff. On top of that, his teeth were so rotten, Decker could smell putrefaction on his breath. He took a very deep drag on his cigarette.

"What makes you so sure about it, old man?"

"'Cause one of 'em gave me sompin'," the coot said.

"What'd he give you?" Decker asked.

The coot shook his head. "Uh, uh, uh. You gonna take it from me, if I show you it."

Decker flashed the money in front of the old man's face. "You show it to me, and if I like it, I'll buy it from you."

The old man scrunched his eyebrows. He ran his tongue against his hollow cheeks. Then he continued sucking on his wine.

Decker showed him the pictures. "Both of these guys were here last night?"

The coot broke suction with the bottle. "For a coupla hours. This one"—he banged his hand against Hersh's picture—"he slept. But this one"—this time the hand went to Noam's picture—"he got up and came back later . . . and he wasn't 'apposed to do that. 'Cause the big one said . . . 'Don't go away.' But the little one . . . he wennaway anyhow."

Decker said, "Know where the little one went?"

The old man shook his head. "Just . . . away. But he came back. And he saw me lookin' at 'im. And he knew he wasn't 'apposed to go away. So he says to me . . . 'You can have this, but only if you don't say nothin'.' So I don't say nothin'."

"What did he give you?" Decker asked.

"You wanna buy it?"

"Maybe," Decker said. "I've got to see it first, old man."

"Well . . ." The coot reached under his hip and pulled out a ski mask. "Itsa good one." He examined it and offered it to Decker. "No holes."

Decker stuffed the five inside the old man's pocket and took the mask.

Rina started when she heard the car pull up into the driveway. She'd been reclining on the living-room sofa, reading, and without realizing it, had fallen asleep. The drapes were open, the afternoon sun shining through the picture window. Rina rubbed her eyes, glanced around the room. A warm, friendly place even though it was uniformly masculine: roughhewn beam ceiling, fir-planked floor topped by a Navajo rug, buckskin chairs framing the fireplace, driftwood coffee table in front of the sofa. All of the furniture made extra-large to accommodate her husband. She heard the front door open. Ginger started to bark.

"Peter?"

"Yeah, it's me."

His voice sounded tired.

A plastic bag fell next to her leg.

"What's this?" she asked.

"Don't open it," Decker said.

Ginger kept barking.

"Could you acknowledge your dog, please?" Rina asked.

Decker bent down and scratched the setter behind her ears. Then he sat beside Rina and ran his hands over his face. "In that bag is physical evidence that puts Noam Levine at the site of a very nasty assault."

"Oh, my God!"

"You said it." Decker looked up and broke into a smile. "Man, you're a sight for sore eyes. Give your old man a hug."

Rina embraced him tightly, kissed his chest. He stretched out on the couch and laid his head in her lap. She brushed hair off his forehead and said, "What are you going to do with it?"

Decker said, "I wish I knew Shakespeare. He must have a line that would fit this kind of moral dilemma." He sighed. "I'm not legally required to turn it in because I'm not working in any sort of official capacity. But I'm a cop, I saw what they did to the victim. No one should be allowed to walk away from that kind of thing."

"What did Noam actually do? Or shouldn't I ask?"

"Well, I'm not sure he actually *did* anything," Decker said. "But I think he was present when the assault took place. How much he participated . . ." He shrugged.

"You're very tired, aren't you?" Rina said. "And you smell of tobacco and alcohol. Where'd you find the evidence?"

"In a little shantytown beneath an overpass of the Ten-East. Apparently, Noam gave it to one of the transients."

"They spent the night there?"

"Part of the night," Decker said. "They're gone now. They're not in any of the downtown spots. Benderhoff checked them out."

"Should I know who Benderhoff is?"

Decker smiled. "No, you've never met him. He's from Central—a CAPS detective assigned to the case. Hersh and Noam aren't in any of the homeless spots in the downtown area, either. I checked those out personally. I haven't the foggiest idea where they went."

"If you think they might be hiding with the homeless, what about Santa Monica? Lots of them roam the Palisades just above Pacific Coast Highway. They're always there. Even in the wintertime. Venice, too."

"Actually, the beach is warmer than the valleys in the winter. Something about the ocean currents . . ." Decker turned onto his side, snuggled deeper in her lap and closed his eyes. Ginger stood on her hind paws and licked Decker's nose. "I planned on checking out the beach area. But first I need some sleep."

"Are you hungry?" Rina asked, stroking his hair.

"Too tired to be hungry." He petted Ginger's head. "Man come to feed the horses?"

"Yes, dear."

"Good."

"I'm making a big dinner," she said. "By the way, Cindy returned your phone call while you were gone. She asked me what we were doing back here so early. Rather than explain it all on the phone, I invited her to dinner."

"Is she coming?"

"She said yes."

Decker smiled. Whenever he thought about his daughter, he smiled. Then he thought about Frieda Levine and her family. Was it fair with his news to hold this knowledge from Cynthia? After all, she was a blood relative to these people. He had told her about his origins when she was eight, after she'd mentioned that nobody in Daddy's family looked like each other. It was hard, but he thought she was mature enough to deal with the truth. She'd understood it all very well. She also knew better than to pry deeply into Daddy's life and never again brought up the topic.

It wasn't from lack of curiosity. Cindy had been a very inquisitive child, interested in everything. But she respected Daddy's privacy, just as he respected hers. He loved her enthusiasm, loved to talk to her. He was delighted she was coming to dinner. Maybe he'd bring up the adoption tonight and see how she'd react.

No, he probably wouldn't.

Too much to assess on so little sleep. He'd think about it later. Rina was talking to him.

"What are you going to do about the evidence?"

Decker opened his eyes. "The evidence?"

Rina held up the bag.

"Oh, that," Decker said. "I've come to a decision—a semi-ethical compromise. When this thing is over— if it ever gets over—I'm going to evaluate Noam myself. If I think he's salvageable, I'll close my eyes to justice and throw the damn thing away. But if he's not . . . I throw *him* to the wolves, and damn the family consequences."

"I think that sounds very fair, Peter," Rina said.

"You're very supportive," Decker said. "Good night."

When he was deep asleep, Rina slithered out from under him. She debated for a moment whether she should write a note, then thought, the heck with it. He'd just have a fit and it wasn't worth that.

She went inside the kitchen and found Peter's spare key ring hanging on the wall. He must have twenty keys in his possession—probably a key to every men's bathroom at the station house. It looked like a janitor's ring. Among the lot were bound to be the keys to the Porsche.

She jingled the ring for a moment, then peered inside her purse. The gun was nestled at the bottom, tucked beneath loose tissues. She slung her bag over her shoulder and closed the door quietly behind her.

Hank brushed lint off English-worsted gray-flannel slacks, thinking: If the boys back home could see him now. Hundred and fifty bucks for the pants, seventy-seven for the shirt—Sea Island cotton. Then there was another fifty for the tie cause it was pure silk and imported from Wopland. Count Heinrich Stremmer would wear pure silk ties, natch.

Only trouble was that the duds ate up almost half the take. The rest was taken up by food—a real waste, you'd eat it, then shit it out—and cash shelled out for the roachtrap they had checked into. Then, there was Nick-O. As promised, Nick-O, or *Nicholas*, when Heinrich Stremmer was in his German mood, got his Aerosmith T-shirt and a new pair of black jeans. Hank thought Nick-O would be happy, but the kid just tossed the bag on the fleabag mattress and went back to sulking.

Hank had screamed, *I just spent a fuckin' hour pickin' that out for you and you toss it away like it was garbage?*

Nick-O had a strange expression on his face. All he had said was: *So return it.*

Strange reaction. Hank wasn't sure he liked it. Last night had changed Nick-O. He sulked, but he stopped whining. Which was good in a way 'cause the whining was really getting on Hank's nerves. But it was bad, 'cause Nick-O didn't seem as scared of him. Yeah, he still did what he was told to do, but it was the 'tude. A totally different 'tude. He wasn't freaked when Hank brought in the fish, when Hank started sharpening the knives. When he brought in the trout, Nick-O told him—yeah, *told* him, not *asked* him—to take it in the bathroom.

You tellin' me what to do?

I'm not telling you what to do, Nick-O had answered. *I'm just telling you to take it into the bathroom. I'm tired of smelling the fish. What is it with you and fish anyway?*

Hank would have backhanded the kid right there and then, but Nick-O was playing with the gun. And it was loaded this time. Hank didn't think it was smart to backhand a kid when he was holding a loaded Beretta.

Why are you so hung up on fish? Nick-O had pressed.

That little *fucker*. Questioning him again. And with no respect! Hank would have pounced on him, gun or no gun, but a little voice stopped him. And that same little voice had told him maybe it was good that Nick-O was a little tougher. Did he really want a wimp to protect him? Still, he had to keep Nick-O in line. But do it subtle like. Don't explode. Forget about the pounding in the head, the hot fire behind the eyes.

Teach him with class.

Slowly, Hank had sauntered over to the kid, twirling the knife between his fingers as if it were a baton. Measured steps, each one brought just a tiny bit of fear back into Nick-O's eyes.

Good, good.

With lightning-fast reflexes, he swatted the gun

out of Nick-O's hands, locked the boy's head in his arms, and held the knife under his nose. Then Hank had said,

I like fish, 'cause I like to practice gutting *things.*

Nick-O didn't answer. Not even after Hank had released him.

Very good.

Hank had noticed immediately that Nick-O's eyes weren't quite as cocky as they were a moment ago. But they weren't as scared as he would have liked, either. Then Hank had broken into a smile, feeling the right side of his lip curl higher than the left side.

But if it bothers you, Nick-O . . .

Slap on the shoulder.

Hey, if it bothers you, guy, I'll take it in the bathroom. Running water. Easier to clean up anyway. After I'm done, we'll get ourselves some duds.

Yeah, the clothes were great, but they couldn't possibly compare to *that* feeling. That first stab when you break skin and feel that wet stream roll over your fingers. And you dig a little deeper until you feel the guts of the fish. Then you uncoil it slowly, bit by bit, inch by inch. Stick your hands in the blood. Then you look up at the sucker's face and see it flail and squirm. But goddamn it, it knows it's trapped.

Squirm, squirm, squirm.

And the fish begins to fight for its life. Just like the dickhead would squirm for his life.

But the dickhead would know it was over. Over, man, it's *over.*

Now, you slice. A little nick here, a little nick there. The dickhead's beggin' you.

No mercy. No *rachmanos*.

Did the dickhead have *rachmanos* on you when he made you wear those smelly old clothes and all the kids made fun of you?

A deeper slice.

Or did the dickhead have mercy on you, when he made you sit alone in your room and spend hours tryin' to read shit you couldn't understand?

A sudden big stab.

Or when he punished you by not talkin' to you for days. Or when he laughed at your schoolwork. Or when he called you dumb. Or when he told you you were just like the old lady. Or when he left you alone with the old lady for weeks at a time 'cause he had to go away on business.

Sure, it was business. Pussy business.

Then you plunge the sucker in!

Harder!

Harder! Harder! Twisting! And turning! And mashing until the insides ain't nothin' but soup.

Tears streaming from his eyes. His zeyde telling him to stop. Screaming at him to stop.

Hershela, what's wrong, bubelah?

I was mad, Zeyde, he had answered back in Yiddish. *Mad at my tati.*

Zeyde shook his head sadly. Even he knew his son was for shit.

Everyone knew the dickhead was for shit.

*   *   *

The noise of a supercharged engine idling woke Decker. He stretched, wiped beads of sweat off his forehead. His brown suit was as wrinkled as a discarded paper sack and he smelled like a distillery. Ginger was barking. He quieted her, craned his head to see Rina walking through the door.

"Hi."

"Hello there," Rina said. "Did you have a nice nap?"

He stood up, feeling as ripe as a compost pile. "Don't come too close. I need a shower." He stretched. "What time is it? It's dark outside. Where were you?"

Rina said, "It's around six-thirty. And it's more dusky than dark. I was at Santa Monica sorting through the homeless—"

"What!"

"I didn't find Hersh or Noam," Rina answered. "I'm not sure what I would have done had I spotted them. Probably called you. I took the Porsche. Found your spare key ring. I hope you don't mind."

"I *do* mind," Decker shot back. "What on earth *possessed* you to go searching out there?"

"To help you out," Rina said. "You looked so tired—"

"I can't discuss anything with you, can I?" Decker peeled off his jacket and shirt and gathered them under his arm. "What are you trying to do, Rina? Play Batman and Robin? I don't want your help. You're not helping me when you do these kinds of things."

"All right, all right," Rina said. "Take a shower—"

"Stop dismissing me," Decker said. "Some of those

homeless are dangerous. And don't tell me not to worry because you had your gun."

"I did have my gun."

Decker said, "Rina, I've worked with these people. We've got a host of them in our area. They're junkies, they're psychos, they're cons and ex-cons. We are talking dregs of dregs—"

"I'm used to that, darling." She went inside the kitchen and took three cleaned game birds out of the refrigerator. "I've been living in New York."

Decker followed her into the kitchen. "Rina, I don't give a good goddamn—" He stopped abruptly. "New York!" He pointed his finger in the air. "I forgot about New York."

"Yeah, New York," Rina said. "The big city on the Atlantic Ocean." She shook her head. "How does Cornish hens sound? I'll make rice stuffing. I know Cindy likes rice. Is three enough? I know you can eat a whole bird by yourself."

"What time is it?" Decker asked.

"It's still around six-thirty," Rina said. "Why do I feel we're not communicating?"

"Around six-thirty." Decker scratched his head. "That would make it nine-thirty in New York. I've got to make a phone call."

"I've already called the boys this morning," Rina said. "I didn't know when you'd get home. You can call them again if you want. They'd love to hear from you."

The boys?

He'd forgotten to call the boys.

"I've got a *few* phone calls to make," Decker said.

"We'll discuss you and your pathological need to help later."

Rina smiled. "Okay, Peter."

"You're shining me on," Decker said. "I hate that." He looked at the clothes tucked under his arms.

"Would you like me to take those for you?" Rina asked.

"The jacket has to be dry-cleaned."

"I know that, Peter."

Decker saw her wrinkle her nose. "Don't worry, I'll shower before dinner."

Rina thought that was a very good idea.

25

"*Hersh Schaltz is* my first cousin." The deep voice paused a moment. "I haven't seen him in years. What did he do this time?"

Decker could have kissed the phone. Big Hersh, the fish vendor from Crown Heights, was indeed a link to Psycho Hersh's past. Even if the man couldn't provide information as to Psycho Hersh's whereabouts, perhaps he could shed some light upon his enigmatic cousin.

"How's he related to you," Decker asked. "I mean, are your mothers sisters or what?"

"You tell me you're a cop and a *frum yid*," Hersh said. "You tell me you're looking for Hershie Schaltz. Now you're asking me personal questions. *Vos macht?*"

Decker wasn't sure what he meant, but the fish vendor's tone of voice seemed to indicate he wanted to know what was going on. Decker spent the next ten minutes rehashing the last six days, explaining Hersh Schaltz's involvement in the affair. Afterward, there was a long pause on the other end of the line.

"I have no idea where Hershie is," Big Hersh said. "Like I said, I haven't seen him in years."

"You don't have any family connections in Los Angeles?" Decker asked.

"I have second cousins living in Beverly Woods," Big Hersh said.

"You mean Beverly Hills?" Decker said.

"No, Beverly Woods."

He meant Beverlywood—the gilded ghetto of L.A. Jewry. Beverlywood housed a lot of L.A.'s Orthodox professionals, many with parents who'd been camp survivors. Would Hersh try to make contact with distant relatives? It was worth looking into.

"Can you give me their names and addresses?" Decker said.

Another pause. Then Big Hersh said, "You sound honest. And my wife does remember talking to you. But I still feel funny about giving out my cousins' names over the phone."

Decker told him to hold on a moment and called Rina. He covered the receiver with his palm and said, "I've got Hersh Berger, the fish vendor from Crown Heights, on the line. He's first cousins with Hersh Schaltz. I'm trying to squeeze information from him, but he's reluctant to talk to me. Talk to him. Convince him I'm legitimate."

Rina stared at him, thinking: So now you want my help? Instead, she took the receiver and spoke to Big Hersh in Yiddish. They talked for five minutes, mentioning a lot of names Decker had never heard before. Then she handed him back the receiver and nodded.

Decker said, "Mr. Berger?"

"Okay," Big Hersh said. "I know friends of your wife's family. As a matter of fact, she knows my second cousins in Beverly Woods. But I'll give you their address anyway. You got a pencil?"

Decker said he had a pencil. He wrote down the names, address, and phone number.

Big Hersh said, "Anything else?"

"Can you give me a little background on your cousin?" Decker said. "What's he like? I don't have a good feel for him."

Big Hersh laughed. "You're not alone."

"Hersh was always a cipher?"

"A *meshugener*, you mean? Yes, he was always strange."

"Can you tell me a little bit about him?"

"You've got some time?"

Decker said he had all the time in the world.

"First thing you've got to realize," Big Hersh started out, "was that Hershie's father was a bought son-in-law, so you know there had to be major problems with the marriage."

"Bought son-in-law?" Decker said. "I'm not familiar with the term."

Hersh told him to ask Rina—she'd know exactly what he meant—but he explained it anyway. Bought sons-in-law were men purchased by rich couples to marry their daughters. They were all very similar. Had some education but were usually not professionals. They were handsome. They dressed well. Spent some time in a proper yeshiva but rarely did they go into the Torah education for their *parnassah*—their livelihood. Usually, they worked in the lucrative businesses of their fathers-in-law. The main purposes of these marriages-for-money were to give some physical presence to their Plain Jane brides and to sire good-looking children—grandchildren for the bride's parents.

Okay, so there was nothing wrong with a handsome dowry. But so many of these men were *gonifs*— scoundrels. They cheated in business; often they cheated on their wives as well. They were ostentatious, lived for the finer things in life—the fanciest home, the finest mink for their *shtreimel* hats, the best silk and wool for their suits. They demanded respect—*kavod*—and if they couldn't earn it, they'd buy it.

In short, Hersh Berger said, they represented everything wrong with society, sacrificing spiritualism for *gashmius*—crass materialism.

Today, the going rate for a good one with education was about a half-million. Grooms who didn't have heads for learning, but had looks and some business sense, could be had for a quarter-million. The precise financial arrangements were worked out between the individual parties before the wedding. The original prenuptial contract.

Hersh Schaltz's father had been bought for a half-million twenty years ago. Why so much? Peretz Schaltz had been very handsome—a big man, over six feet with powerful shoulders. He had also graduated from college with a degree in chemistry, but that wasn't important to Mr. Kornitski. Uncle Perry was very learned in Talmud. That *was* important to

Mr. Kornitski. Even so, Mr. Kornitski hadn't paid that much because Uncle Perry was learned. He paid that much because his daughter, Bracha, was crazy.

Everyone knew Bracha was crazy. She had periods where she could function—she even taught for a while in the local girls' school. But she was always very bizarre. Aunt Bracha used to dress in ten layers of clothes. Aunt Bracha used to shave her head and wear terrible wigs—long witchlike things, the black tendrils falling down to her waist. Aunt Bracha never threw anything away. Her house had been crammed with every shopping bag, every receipt, every box she'd ever taken home from a store. Her closets were stuffed with every article of clothing she had ever worn, every pair of shoes that had ever graced her feet. Aunt Bracha was also so fearful—crazy fearful. If a dog or a cat got within petting distance, she went *meshugenah*. She'd lock herself inside her room and wouldn't come out for days. Even the sight of a fly could throw her into a panic. She eventually lost her job because of that. You couldn't teach and go crazy every time a fly buzzed by.

Aunt Bracha and Uncle Perry lived in a big house in Kew Gardens because Uncle Perry didn't want to live where people knew Aunt Bracha's history. He used to keep the drapes drawn, the lights out, and the door locked and tell everybody in the neighborhood that his wife was very, very ill.

"Which was true," Big Hersh said. "She is sick."

"How were you related to them?" Decker asked.

"My mother and Peretz Schaltz were brother and

sister," Big Hersh said. "Bubbe and Zeyde Schaltz were the nicest people on earth. Simple people. Zeyde was a fish vendor. I took over the business after he died and I turned it into a business. Zeyde, *alav hashalom*, used the business for charity. Give this away, that away. And people took terrible advantage of him. If a lady said a price was too high, he'd lower it. If another said the fish wasn't fresh, he'd give her a refund even if the woman's husband ate the fish for dinner. And he never raised his voice in complaint. I think Zeyde was the only one of the bunch who really cared about Hersh. He used to drive over to Kew Gardens on Sundays and pick him up to work with him. He made like he needed Hersh in the business, but that also was charity. Zeyde felt sorry for Hersh. And he loved him. I think Hersh loved Zeyde. Zeyde was the only person Hershie was ever close to. But Zeyde was close to everyone. Everyone loved him—really *loved* him."

"Did Peretz love his father?" Decker asked.

Big Hersh let out a bitter laugh. "You got me on that one. Well, I was young but I couldn't see it. Uncle Perry was nothing like him. He had nothing but disdain for the fish business and it seemed like he had nothing but disdain for his parents, also. But he had grown up poor. My mother used to say they had nothing. So when Aunt Bracha came along, my mother said, Peretz jumped."

"How did your Uncle Perry relate to his son?" Decker asked.

"I couldn't see any . . . any bond," Big Hersh said. "But I wasn't with them a lot, so who am I to judge, *nu*? Most of his disgust seemed to be directed toward Bracha. He hated everything about her, but if he wanted the money, he had to stick with her. Bracha's parents didn't give him the money all at once. They doled it out, bit by bit. And my mother told me they had put all sorts of conditions on the money. Uncle Perry had to be a Satmar Chasid—which he was at the time. So that wouldn't present a real problem. Bubbe and Zeyde Schaltz were Satmar Chasidim, grew up in Williamsburg. But Uncle Perry hated that too, couldn't wait to get away from the whole thing. Then Bracha came along. I guess the money was too tempting. So Uncle Perry had to dress like a Satmar, speak Yiddish like a Satmar, raise his son to be a Satmar."

"So why'd they live in Kew Gardens?" Decker asked.

"Uncle Perry put his foot down on that," Big Hersh said. "He said he wouldn't marry her if they had to live in Williamsburg because she was a big embarrassment. So my mother told me they reached a compromise. They could live in Kew Gardens until Hersh was ten. Then Mr. Kornitski wanted his grandson to be part of the Satmar community. Uncle Perry agreed because he really wanted the money. And once he got it, he spent it as fast as they gave it to him."

Decker asked him what he spent the money on. Big Hersh answered on things—and on women. Everyone knew Uncle Perry ran around with women.

"Did his son know?" Decker asked.

"He found out as soon as Uncle Perry married a shiksa," Big Hersh said. "He divorced Aunt Bracha as soon as Mr. Kornitski died. The old man left him a little cash in his will, but the bulk of the money was left to Bracha's brother, who wouldn't loan Uncle Perry half a cent if his life depended on it. So Uncle Perry divorced his wife and married his *kourve*—the shiksa."

Big Hersh didn't speak for a moment.

"It's all very sad," he said. "It's easy to blame Uncle Perry, but he did live with the woman for twelve years. Gave her some sort of a life. And then he died so terribly. You know about that?"

Decker said he did. Then he asked if his cousin might have had something to do with it. Big Hersh said there was never any indication that he did. But everyone still wondered. It would probably be one of those things where no one would ever know.

"When did Hersh start acting out?" Decker asked.

"You mean acting crazy? For as long as I remember, he acted crazy. Even as a little kid working in the market, he was weird. Quiet. A loner. Then, after Zeyde died, he began acting even *more* crazy. He only came down to the market once or twice after the old man passed away. I'd taken it over by then. I was only nineteen, but I had enough experience. Hershie wasn't interested in the market, only in Zeyde."

He paused.

"Last time I saw Hershie was at the business. He asked if he could keep some of Zeyde's fish knives. I thought that was very strange. Why would he need the knives if he wasn't going to work in the market anymore? And I certainly needed the knives. But I told him to take what he wanted, figuring that

was what Zeyde would have wanted me to say. He
didn't deplete my stock, mind you. But he did take the
best gutting knives, a cleaver, a hammer, a butterfly
knife, and Zeyde's sharpening stone. Very odd."

Hersh hesitated again.

"While he was picking and choosing the stuff, I
remember thinking to myself, 'He's just like his
mother. Only a matter of time before he goes off the
deep end, too.' Even when Zeyde was still alive,
Hershie was strange. He had a weird smile, Sergeant.
It even made me a little nervous. I kept waiting for
him to go crazy. But he never quite did. Maybe
Zeyde's love kept him sane."

Sane—but only for a while. Decker thought about
all the fish that had been in Hersh's rooms. He
asked if Hersh—Hershie—had liked working in the
fish business.

"Hershie *hated* the business." Big Hersh hesitated,
then said, "I should say he *hated* the customers.
Never smiled. When he did, it was that weird smile
I told you about. I think he scared the customers so
Zeyde told him he could do the back work and leave
the counter to him and me. That seemed to be a
good arrangement. Hersh used to love gutting the
fish. Sometimes he'd do it while they were still alive.
I hated when he did that. *Tsaar baalei chayim*—you
know. Cruelty to animals is a terrible *aveyrah*. I used
to tell him to kill the fish first, just slit the gills. But
he wouldn't do that. Sometimes he'd step on their
heads or slice them off. It was strange."

"How'd you get along with him?"

"We were on speaking terms if that's what you

mean," Hersh said. "But we kept our distance just the same. He was a very weird kid. But not so hard to understand if you know about the family."

No, Decker said, not so hard to understand at all.

Big Hersh's cousins lived on Guthrie Drive—the poshest street in suburban Beverlywood. Decker spoke to a Dr. Sam Beiderman—a cardiologist—who knew about his cousin Hersh Schaltz from Brooklyn but had never met him and wouldn't know him if he looked him in the eye. Dr. Beiderman said he'd contact him immediately if Hersh called. Decker thanked him for his time, disappointed by the lack of progress but not surprised.

After the conversation with Big Hersh, Decker felt even dirtier than when he had been with the homeless. He took a long shower, then phoned the boys in New York. It felt wonderful to talk with them even though Sammy spent most of the time complaining. Then, in a burst of insight rare for a twelve-year-old, Sammy said he knew that Decker was working. That this wasn't the vacation he wanted either.

Decker said it wasn't a vacation, but he could understand the boy's frustration. He was frustrated, too. In less than a week, they'd all be together again. He promised to make up for lost time and asked the boys what they would like to do.

They both wanted to build a rocket with him. Decker said, first thing when they all came home, he'd take them to the hobby shop and they'd get the biggest, most complete rocket kit ever.

He finished the conversation just as the doorbell

rang. Rina answered, greeting his daughter as if she were her best friend. Cindy returned the salutation by giving Rina a hug and breaking into giggles. Decker could hear Cindy's laughter, hear her chatter coming from outside.

Decker peeked inside the living room. His daughter was now officially a young lady. Her lanky frame had softened into the gentle curves of womanhood. Her skin glowed with health, her hazel eyes sparked with youthful passion. She'd grown her hair out, the red locks grazing her shoulders. She looked down the hallway and when their eyes met, she broke into a radiant smile.

She cocked her hip and said, "Well, are you coming out or what?"

All Decker could do was grin. He felt all warm inside. Cindy's voice did that to him every time.

Stretched out on an unmade bed, Noam watched Hersh straighten his tie while looking in the bedroom mirror. It was old and cracked and the surface dull. Another dump, he thought, the room smelling as stale as a laundry hamper. At first, he welcomed the sloppiness. What a change from his mother's own fastidiousness. But now the dumps were just depressing—like everything else he and Hersh had done. All of it was hateful and depressing.

He knew it was only a matter of time before Hersh would want to hit the streets again. He just didn't expect it to come so quickly. He was calm: The driving need to take his own life had faded.

Hersh wanted to score again. Noam didn't want to

hurt any more people. Hashem knew he didn't want to do that. But he didn't want to die or go to jail. Whenever Hersh spoke, an awful nausea churned up Noam's stomach. His head began to throb.

"Yo, Nick-O," Hersh said. "We gotta get movin', ya know?"

Noam didn't respond.

"Cha' hear what I said, Bud?"

"Yeah, I heard you," Noam said.

"So, we gonna make some plans or what?" Hersh said.

Noam looked up. "I thought you said we scored enough so we don't have to do it for a while."

"Duds cost money," Hersh said.

Noam returned his eyes to his book, but he couldn't concentrate on the words. Think, he yelled to himself. Think! Think! He said, "Couldn't we use the guy's credit cards?"

"I threw them all away with the wallet," Hersh said. "Can't use stolen cards. They can be traced."

"Well, we could use them and then split—"

"Forget it," Hersh said. "Too messy."

"But killing someone is clean?"

Hersh pounced on the bed and slammed the book out of Noam's hands. He grabbed Noam by the shirt and pulled his face close to his nose. "You fucked up!" he whispered, spittle spraying the teenager's face. "If you wouldna fucked up, that guy would be walkin' today."

Noam felt his heart beating out of his chest, but he forced himself to remain rigid. Hersh held him close for a moment, then pushed him down on the bed.

Noam straightened his shirt and wiped his face. He was scared, but not as scared as he had been in the past. He had two choices: He could go along with Hersh or he could refuse. The look in Hersh's eyes told him he couldn't refuse right now without getting beat up. Better to go along with him now, decide what to do later. Figure out what's going on when Hersh wasn't around.

"So what do you want to do?" Noam whispered.

The lopsided smile appeared. "Now you're talkin'."

"Know what?" Noam suddenly blurted out.

"What?"

Noam paused. Shut up, he told himself. Don't say it; just shut up.

Hersh said, "What's on your mind, Nick-O?"

"Nothing."

"Go ahead," Hersh said. "I won't do nothin'."

Noam's words came out in a rush. "I think we need the money. But I also think that you like to hurt people."

The smile vanished. Noam braced himself for punishment, the sudden attack. Hard fists in his already bruised face. He balled up his body and tucked in his head. But whenever he expected the worst, he never got it.

That's what was so weird. Hersh was so unpredictable. Noam lifted his head. The lopsided smile had reappeared.

Hersh said, "So what's wrong with that?"

The setup was almost identical to the first one, except this time Hersh went to a queer bar full of queers who *admitted* they were queers. Queers, Hersh said, were the best victims 'cause they were like women. All they did was scream and prance around, but they never fought back.

A crock, Noam thought. The guy that Hersh had killed had fought like a tiger!

Noam felt his stomach buck. He let go with a series of dry heaves. He'd been vomiting off and on for an hour. He felt weak, but was afraid to say anything to Hersh.

One more time. This was it!

This time they were in western Hollywood, far, far away from Grauman's Chinese. Everything in this section of western Hollywood was fancy, fancy. Big health clubs, lots of shops, lots of restaurants. And lots of queers. All sorts of them. Some of them looked like women. Some even wore makeup. But some of them looked tough and wore leather and long hair and had earrings and mustaches and beards. They looked as tough as Axl Rose. It was weird to see tough guys holding hands with other tough guys.

He had so many stories he wanted to tell his brothers.

His brothers.

He'd always hated them. Now he missed them. Missed the tiny room they shared. When he lived at home, he could never get any privacy, never do anything. Now he had more freedom than he had ever had in his life and never had he felt so trapped.

Hersh had placed him in another alley. The area might be much better than downtown Los Angeles, but the garbage still smelled like garbage.

He thought it would be easier the second time around. Just the opposite. It was harder. He was vomiting more, sweating and shaking like he had the flu. Maybe he did have the flu. But he knew that wasn't it. He'd felt okay until Hersh said they had to score again. Nothing—*nothing* about it was easier the second time. If anything it was harder because Hersh insisted that the gun be loaded this time. To prevent what happened last time.

Noam was about to ask why they would need a gun at all if Hersh was so sure that queers didn't fight back. But the look in Hersh's eyes—the glare of a mad dog about to attack—told him to shut up and keep his thoughts to himself. Besides, right at that point, he had to make a sudden run for the bathroom.

So now the gun was in his hands again, as slippery as ever. But now Noam didn't dare drop it. It could misfire, blow off his leg.

God, why didn't he just run away right now?

Why?

Noam thought, well, why didn't he just do that?

Just pick up his legs and run away.

Do what Tanti Miriam told him to do.

Go to the police.

Even jail must be better than this.

Had to be.

But what about his parents?

They'd never forgive him if he went to jail.

They'd never speak to him again.

He shouldn't have called Tanti Miriam and let

her know he was in trouble. He should have waited it out and run away when he could.

Come home when he was safe, keep these terrible *aveyrahs* his secret. But now Tanti Miriam knew he was in trouble.

There would be questions.

But there would have been questions anyway.

Just run away.

Run now.

Do it!

DO IT!

He stood up from his crouch, his brain pounding against his temples. His legs felt as limp as noodles. Even though he felt as if he were about to faint, he knew he should run right now.

But it was too late.

He saw Hersh.

Saw the victim.

This one was tall, just like the first one.

This one was thick, just like the first one.

Hersh swore he'd get a smaller one. What was it? Did he have a wish to die?

Trapped.

One more time, Noam swore to himself.

This was it.

Take the guy's money and then this was it!

One more time.

That's it!

Noam jumped out, pushed the gun in the man's stomach, said his practiced lines.

But again it didn't go as planned.

Again there was a screwup.

The man didn't react like he was supposed to.

Whacked the gun out of his stomach, pushed Noam away. Noam fell on his rear.

The gun was hurled into the air.

The clunk of something falling.

Noam looked up. Hersh and the man were fighting, each one trying to get control of the other.

But Noam's own body free.

Free!

Grunts and moans came from the men.

What to do? Noam thought quickly.

Run. *Run!*

Noam felt sudden energy injected into his legs. He bolted ten feet and ducked behind a Dumpster stinking of rot. He peeked over the side.

The man and Hersh were still fighting. Blood over their faces. Hands moving so fast, like they were fighting in a cartoon.

The man was screaming something about a setup.

He had Hersh in a headlock.

Squeezing Hersh's neck.

Noam ran another ten feet, his breaths choppy and shallow.

Run!

Another few feet. Then he forced himself to look back.

Hersh's eyes bulging out. His cheeks like balloons. His lips as puffy as marshmallow. His nails digging into his attacker's arm. Drawing blood. But the man still had him trapped.

Trapped.

Run! Noam thought.

RUN!

Noam looked to his right, to his left. Behind him, in front of him.

No one.

RUN!

Harder, harder, the man squeezed. Hersh squeaking out sounds.

A glint of something metallic caught his eye.

The gun.

Noam had forgotten about the gun.

Hersh trying to free his neck—grunting, squealing. His nails carving deep, bloody lines in the man's muscle.

Run!

Hersh's legs buckling under.

Then he spoke.

His words.

Helf mir!

Help me!

Like a lost child.

Like himself, Noam thought. He remembered that horrible feeling when he was under attack. The man had tried to choke him. The feeling of going under. Noam remembered it very clearly. How he thought he was dead.

Hersh had *helped* him. Risked his *life*.

Run! Noam shouted to himself.

But then came the cry again.

Helf mir!

Noam ran toward the gun.

The man freeing Hersh. Coming toward him.

Both diving for the gun.

Hersh gasping.

Noam felt the full impact of the big man's weight. The big man jabbed an elbow into Noam's shoulder, clawed at him. But Noam managed to sink his fist into the big man's gut.

The big man doubled over, took in a deep breath. But was still blocking him from the gun.

Again, Noam punched the big man's stomach, his eyes shooting off sparks of pain each time his hand crunched against rock-hard muscle. He prayed Hersh was still around, wouldn't desert him.

Desert him like he was going to do to Hersh.

The gun.

Go for the gun!

Noam took a deep breath and shoved his way forward. The big man fell back only an inch. Noam's fingers spider-walked toward the gun, cool metal grazing the tips. Closer and closer until the butt was at his fingers, locked into his hand.

Out of the corner of his eye, Noam saw Hersh leaping on top of the man, pulling out his knife.

Noam's own finger curled around the trigger of the semi-automatic.

It was hard to tell which came first. The plunges of the blade or the muffled spitfire.

26

The phone rang three times before Rina became aware of its intrusion, before she realized that Peter was sleeping through it. She reached over him and picked up the receiver. The man on the other end asked for Sergeant Decker.

It was still dark. She shook Peter's shoulder and brought him to consciousness. He snapped open his eyes, took the phone and was all business.

"This is Sergeant Decker," he said.

"Yeah, I'm Jack Cleveland with the West Hollywood Sheriff's Station. I spoke to you last night. You wanted to know if there were any assaults or homicides that might have resulted from a gay pickup? I told you there weren't any."

"Yeah," Decker said. He was already out of bed.

"You were a day off," Cleveland said. "We've got a vicious . . . man, vicious ain't the word for it. It's a *monstrous* homicide—WM named Oliver Harrow, in his fifties, around six one or two, two hundred pounds. Sound like something you'd be interested in?"

"Yep." Decker slipped on his pants. "When was the call fielded?"

371

"About midnight," Cleveland said.

Decker looked at the clock. Quarter to two. He put on his shirt and said, "Any of the bars still open?"

"Not now," Cleveland said. "But they were open an hour ago, when I took a picture of the victim's face and told my men to circulate. The guy's body . . . you'll see for yourself." There was a sigh over the line. "We found someone. A bartender who knows the victim, has a vague recollection of the guy he left with. Bartender's with a police artist now. Then I remembered your call. I figured maybe you have something to offer me."

Decker said he'd be right down.

They're on a spree, Decker thought. *On a goddamn killing spree.*

At six feet four and two hundred forty all-muscle pounds, Jacques Antwine Cleveland had played high school football, basketball, and baseball. But a bad slide into home at the age of eighteen quashed his dreams of playing big time. Just bad luck. That's what they told him after bodycasting him from the waist down.

Bad was an understatement. It was downright shitty luck. Instead of raking in millions, here he was, at two-thirty in the morning, scanning the ground for pieces that had once been part of Oliver James Harrow.

He saw something and dropped to his knees. Another piece of gut. He hailed a tech, and the lab man dropped the coil of innards in an evidence bag. The scene was swarming with people—a doc from the

ME's office, print men, lab men, a photographer, and the uniforms who fielded the call, their faces colored like overcooked peas. From behind him, he heard someone call his name. He stood—turned around, surprised to find himself looking *squarely* into another man's eyes. The guy was as big as he was.

"Help you, sir?"

Decker introduced himself.

Cleveland shook Decker's hand and looked him over. Without thinking, he said, "You ever play for the pros, Pete?"

"No. Why? Did you?"

"No, but I wish I did. Matter-of-fact, I'd like to do anything except what I'm doing now." Cleveland caught the stunned expression on Decker's face. He wiped a band of sweat from his broad mocha-colored forehead. "This is not our usual killing. That's why we have so many people out."

"Man, this is just *horrible*," Decker said.

His eyes swept over the alley. A slaughterhouse. It *smelled* like a slaughterhouse. Thank God there was a cold breeze blowing, providing a bit of aeration.

Decker forced himself to look at the body. The photographer was snapping pictures. The corpse was on its back as if prepped for a grotesque operation. The face was intact, no knife marks, no gunshots. Harrow's eyes were still open, still electrified with shock. Brown eyes. Big round brown eyes. Harrow had had full cheeks and no upper teeth. His spine was straight, his arms had been placed neatly at his sides, his unbent legs had been pressed together.

Decker continued to study the corpse. The

throat had been slashed, the chest a gaping hole filled with brown clotted blood. His belly had been eviscerated—completely emptied. Decker could see the man's kidneys—perfectly intact kidneys. He jerked his head away.

The killing had occurred in the back alley of one of the most exclusive restaurants in West Hollywood— a trendy night spot known for movie-star patrons and a high-priced menu. While the good folk up front dined on salmon carpaccio and goat-cheese mousse, this poor man was out here being dissected by a friggin' psycho. The thought made him sick.

Decker wished to God he could turn around and go home. He was ten feet from the body, and even at this distance, there was a mammoth inkblot of blood spray. The monster must have sliced Harrow's aorta while he was still alive. Nothing else would make blood spurt so far.

Had Noam been an active partner in this gruesome killing? Decker just wouldn't let himself believe that. It was *Hersh* who liked to play with knives, *Hersh* who loved to gut fish while they were still *alive*. Noam just *couldn't* have been a willing participant in such savage butchery. What had Noam been thinking when Hersh did this thing to this unfortunate man? Decker felt a wave of fright, felt what he hoped had been the boy's terror.

Hersh had finally shown what he really was. Noam had to be in fear for his life.

If Noam still had a life.

Because psychos were solo creatures.

Decker swallowed back a wave of nausea, choosing to assume that Noam was still around to need help. He'd have to call the family, tell them to hire legal counsel immediately. He turned to Cleveland and said, "I've seen corpses in worse shape—victims exposed to the elements. They're hard to look at, but that's nature. Even though the face is whole, I'm having a lot of trouble with this one. I don't think I've ever seen a homicide this cold. Someone enjoyed the surgery."

"My thoughts to a T, Pete," Cleveland said. "From the distance of the arterial spatter, the victim was probably stabbed in the throat and chest first, then died from blood loss. Hit the carotid or the aorta, don't take more than a couple of minutes to bleed out. He was probably gutted afterward." He shook his head in disgust.

Decker said, "Where's the witness? The bartender?"

"In the patrol car," Cleveland said. "I'll take you to him."

Decker followed the black detective through the throng of technicians. The bartender was sitting on the backseat of a black and white sheriff's deputy patrol car. Even though the man was swathed in a blanket, he was shivering. His unsteady hand was holding a flashlight, illuminating a series of mouths spread out on the backseat by a female sketch artist who sat beside him. He had a mustache, gaunt cheeks, and a pointy chin. His eyes squinted with concentration as he stared at the mouths and shook his head.

"None of them are right," he said.

"Ritchie?" Cleveland said.

The blanketed man looked up.

Cleveland introduced, "Ritchie Parker, this is Detective Decker."

Parker stuck out his hand, Decker took it. It was wet and cold.

"Detective Decker wants to show you a few pictures, ask you a few questions," Cleveland said.

"Uh, excuse me," the sketch artist said. "Can't this wait until we're through?"

Decker said, "I might have a picture of the perp. It would make your job a lot easier."

"Go ahead," the artist said. She sat back and crossed her arms over her chest.

Decker ignored her anger, pushed aside the mouths, and spread a half-dozen photos over the backseat. Ritchie Parker jumped up, his head hitting the top of the car roof. His forefinger nearly speared the picture of Hersh.

"That's *him*!" he shouted.

Decker smiled at the police artist. "Have a nice evening, Officer. Get some sleep on me."

She let go with a reluctant smile, gathered her mouths, and got out of the car. Decker took her place at Parker's right; Cleveland sat at Parker's left. The thin man's eyes darted nervously between the two detectives.

Decker said, "You're sure you saw this guy"—he held up the picture of Hersh—"leaving with the victim."

"*Pos*itive," Parker said. "Mr. Harrow is a regular. A very big tipper and a big drinker. It's easy for me to keep tabs on him—no pun intended."

Cleveland asked how it was easy to keep tabs on him.

Ritchie said, "See, if he's having a good time, it's drinks for everyone. If not . . . he drinks to forget the rotten night he's having. When that man"—he stabbed Hersh's picture—"when he came in, I noticed him right away. He was dressed like he was on the hustle. But I knew he'd find someone because . . . well, because he was good-looking. In a tough sort of way. Except when he smiled. He had a weird smile."

Decker looked up from his note pad. "What was weird about it?"

"It was . . . I don't know," Parker said. "Lopsided, I guess you'd call it."

"Okay," Decker said. He wrote down the word: *Lopsided*. It would jibe nicely with Thomas Stoner's account of Hersh. Tie the two crimes together. "Go on."

"Where was I?" Parker said.

"He was tough-looking," Cleveland said.

"Yes, he was," Parker said. "Kinda hypermacho and he spoke with an accent—a German accent. A lot of the leather set get off on the German accent so that's nothing new. But this guy, he sounded like he really did speak German."

Decker wrote: *German accent?* He said, "He was dressed in a leather getup?"

"Oh, no," Parker said. "He was dressed very nicely. Sort of a casual but expensive look. Just that the leather set is into Teutonic things. I knew Mr. Harrow would go for him. He likes . . ."

Parker suddenly paled and held his head. "My God, that poor man . . . I feel sick."

Both Decker and Cleveland jumped out of the car. Parker stuck his head out and retched. After he was done vomiting, he wiped his mouth on the blanket and apologized.

Cleveland threw a beefy hand on Parker's thin bony shoulder. "You're doing all right. I'm not feelin' so good myself."

Decker pulled out a tube of VapoRub. "It's the smell. Coat your nose with this." He pushed out some VapoRub onto Parker's fingertips. "It blocks the smell."

"But it doesn't hide the memory . . . seeing him." Parker shuddered.

True enough, Decker thought. "What time did Mr. Harrow leave with the man in the picture?"

"Around eleven," Parker said.

"You're sure?" Cleveland asked.

"Looked at the clock myself." Parker sighed. "Without Mr. Harrow feeding the kitty, I knew it was going to be a long night."

Reaching into his coat pocket, Decker pulled out a flier with pictures of Hersh and Noam on it—a copy of the ones he and Marge had used when they'd canvassed Westwood. He pointed to Noam's picture. "Ever see this boy before?"

Parker studied Noam's picture, then shook his head.

"Any other patrons see Harrow leave with this guy?" Decker was pointing at Hersh again.

"They might have." Parker shrugged. "I don't

know. I don't know if they met others afterward, I don't know if he was . . . killed . . . right after he left."

Decker looked at Cleveland, cocked his head to the side. Cleveland called over one of the uniforms and said, "Mr. Parker, would you mind going with Deputy"—his eyes went to the name tag attached to a khaki-clad deputy with buck-teeth—"with Deputy Sanders and giving him a complete statement?"

"Not at all," Parker said. "I couldn't sleep right now if you gave me a thousand Seconals. It's that man's face." He pointed to the picture of Hersh. "It's going to haunt me for the rest of my life."

"Yeah," Cleveland said. "Try to calm down. Deputy Sanders, can you take him into the squad car?" He waved them both away, then looked at Decker.

"You want to tell me what's going on?"

Having told the story so many times, Decker had pared it down to its barest elements, recapping all the salient details in ten minutes. When he was done, Cleveland didn't respond.

"I'm not trying to horn in on your case," Decker said, "but I've got sixty, seventy of these fliers in my car. I think it might be a good idea for me to check out the local motels. If the murder took place at eleven, eleven-fifteen, the perps probably have taken off by now. But they couldn't have gone too far without a car."

"You're sure they don't have a car?" Cleveland asked.

"I'm not really sure of anything," Decker said. "As of eight tonight, they hadn't rented anything under their names or any of the known aliases. Now they could be using other names. Or they could have heisted a car. At least we should try to find out where they were."

"You want to check out the fuck pads in Hollywood proper, that's okay by me," Cleveland said. "It's LAPD's jurisdiction anyway. I'll have my men take care of West Hollywood."

"Perfect," Decker said.

"Course even if we find where they *were*," Cleveland said, "that don't mean shit as to where they *are now* . . . or where they're *gonna be*."

Decker said, "Well, *if* they stick around the city, I'll hunt them down. No doubt in my mind, I'll find those fuckers. I'm just wondering if they might be thinking about leaving town. I'm going to ask my partner to go down to Greyhound Bus Terminal. Just to make sure. She can pass out fliers while she's there anyway."

"Might try the train station, too," Cleveland said. "And the airport."

"Yup." Decker thought: Marge could probably manage the bus terminal and the train station—they were both downtown. The airport was another story. He couldn't poke around the Hollywood motels and check out the airport at the same time. He'd call Hollander. Tell Mike to run by the house and pick up the fliers of Hersh and Noam.

Decker said, "I'll send someone over to LAX."

Cleveland said, "You got a feel for these psychos?"

"Somewhat."

"If Butch and Sundance split, where would they go?"

Decker shrugged. "Maybe San Francisco. It's close, lots of gays."

"Yeah, this has all the earmarks of a gay killing," Cleveland said. "The blood, the violence, the anger. Psycho's definitely a latent."

"Hersh?" Decker shrugged. "He might be, but he might be heterosexual. I don't have any indications as to which way he swings."

"Both his victims were gay," Cleveland said.

Decker conceded the point but still felt that wasn't it at all. The age of the victims, the *size*. Every time Hersh rolled a big man, he took a chance. But Hersh *wanted* large, older men. What he wanted was to kill his *father*. He only went after gays because they were a hell of a lot easier to pick up. How else was he going to get a big man to follow him into the night?

Using the unmarked's radio, Decker was patched through to Marge. He updated her, explained what he needed. She was ready for action even before he finished. He asked her to call Hollander for him and Marge reminded him that Mike was on vacation as of yesterday.

"Damn, that's right," Decker said. "What about Fordebrand? He's good about favors."

"I think he's still in the field," Marge said. "A nasty bar killing just went down in our parts around an hour ago. I was called down because it was over a woman and someone mentioned rape. But the woman wasn't raped."

There was a long pause over the line.

Marge said, "I could ask MacPherson."

"You mind calling him?"

"No," Marge said.

"Thanks. Tell him to drop by my place, pick up the fliers from Rina. I'll call her so she'll have them all ready for him."

"You trust Paul alone with your wife?"

Decker laughed and said, "She has a gun."

Rina saw the car pull up in the driveway. She answered the door before MacPherson knocked. He stood, huddled under her doorstep, his head covered with a knitted ski cap. His eyes were sunken, his forehead was bathed in sweat.

"Hullo, Mrs. Decker," he said in a nasal voice. "The good sergeant said you have some fliers for me?"

"You can't go out like that, Detective," Rina said. She leaned over and felt his forehead. "You have a fever."

"I'm a little under the weather." He sneezed. "But don't worry—"

"Go home and go to bed right now," Rina said. "I'll pass out the leaflets."

"Mrs. Decker, I don't think that's what the sergeant had in mind."

"Was the sergeant aware of your physical condition?"

"I'm really all right."

"Absolutely not," Rina said. "You put yourself to bed right away. I'm perfectly capable of passing out fliers and talking to security. Besides, if anyone can recognize Noam, I will. Feeling the way you do, I'm not sure you could recognize your own mother."

Probably true, MacPherson thought. Still, he didn't feel good about letting her go out to LAX alone at this time of night. If anything were to happen to her, he'd catch deep shit. And he'd feel bad for her, too.

"I don't think so, Mrs. Decker." He sneezed again.

Rina said, "Detective MacPherson, I'm not going to give you those fliers and without the fliers you have no reason to go to the airport. Now get out of here and stop sneezing on me or we'll both be sick."

MacPherson sighed. He was too tired to argue. In all honesty, he was grateful for the reprieve, even if he felt funny about it. But if the lady wasn't going to give him the fliers, it really didn't make sense for him to go to the airport, did it? He couldn't force her to give them to him so the hell with it. Next time, Decker should speak to him directly if he wanted a favor.

"If you insist," he said.

"I insist," Rina said. "Now good night."

She smiled, then closed the door.

She knew Peter would be furious, but that was his problem. Paul was in no shape to work. And she was too jumpy to sleep.

Every time she pictured Noam's face, she thought of her own sons. How would she feel if they were in such imminent danger? And Noam was in terrible danger. Even Peter had seemed shaken when he summarized what had happened. She remembered his thoughts out loud.

It's only a matter of time before Hersh realizes he doesn't need Noam to kill. Then the boy becomes a liability rather than an asset.

She just couldn't hand such an important task over to a sick man who was just going through the motions. The job required someone who *cared*.

Peter would be mad, even angrier that she used the Porsche at this time of night. It was an attention grabber and that wasn't good. But that was a chance she'd have to take.

She tied a kerchief atop her head and slipped on her coat. The bags of fliers were heavy. If only she didn't need her purse. How did men travel without one? No matter, she'd manage. She took the spare key ring off the wall and hefted it. More weight. Maybe she should just take the Porsche keys and leave the rest of Peter's keys here.

No, best not to separate them. If anything got lost, Peter would be even more irate. She flung her purse over her shoulder and looped her hands around the plastic bags. Before she closed and locked the door, she checked for her gun.

Like an old reliable friend, it was where it was supposed to be.

❧27

It had been a long and silent bus ride—a blessing for Noam. He hated the sound of Hersh's voice, but hated his own voice even more. He hated, hated, hated everything about himself.

Hersh and he didn't talk on the bus. They didn't even sit together, choosing aisle seats opposite each other. At first glance, Hersh appeared to be dozing, but whenever Noam moved, even to scratch his nose, Hersh's eyes would pop open, tracking him like a wild animal.

They hadn't even talked much right after it happened. Both of them had been like robots, rushing into the motel room, throwing their meager clothes into the suitcases. He'd taken the gun, Hersh had taken his knives. A fair split—the gun was a more dangerous weapon, but Hersh was quicker with the knives.

Not that Noam really cared whether he lived or died. After what had happened (what had *gone down* as Hersh had put it) everything was over for him anyway.

What he had done.

Over and over, he racked his brain, trying to figure out what he *should* have done. But it all happened so fast. He couldn't think straight, not with Hersh's eyes bulging out of his forehead. Not with him crying out: *Helf mir!* The man was *strangling* Hersh, for God's sake; he couldn't just walk away. He just couldn't.

The tables turned so quickly. Now *they* were the attackers. A moment later came that haunting picture, that awful look on that poor man's face. A death mask.

Noam screwed up his eyes, shook his head fiercely, trying to throw the image out of his brain.

After it was over, Hersh went nuts with his knives. Noam knew he should have stopped him—what Hersh did was pure evil. Nobody normal did those things. But all Noam had done was cry, too afraid to make him stop.

That smell, that terrible smell. Like the back of a butcher shop. Noam gagged just thinking about it. He felt his breath begin to go choppy, his head begin to spin. He heard Hersh telling him—no, not telling, *ordering* him—to get a grip on himself.

Get a grip on yourself.

Noam kept that thought. It was the only thing that prevented him from going insane.

It helped to breathe into his hands. A few minutes later, Noam felt his head clear. He glanced over at Hersh, who was lying on his back, hands under his head, his eyes wide open.

Noam knew he was making plans.

Get a grip on yourself.

Hersh and his plans—his *evil* plans. Noam hated, just *hated* his plans. But back then, after what had happened, he hadn't been able to think up his own plans. All he'd been able to do was follow numbly. Somehow Hersh had managed to guide them to the right bus, no one inside giving them a second glance.

Everyone riding the bus had seemed like a lowlife, just like he was. People who carried their belongings in bags instead of valises. People who looked like they hadn't had a bath in a long time. There'd been a woman, her face covered with acne. She had scraggly red hair and wore newspapers on her feet. There'd been a fat guy that almost took up two full bus seats. There'd been two skinny black teenagers, their hair in matted curls. They'd had real mean eyes, and whispered to each other as soon as he and Hersh boarded the bus. But Hersh had easily stared them down. No one had meaner eyes than Hersh. A few seconds later, the black guys had slumped back into their seats, ignored them for the rest of the trip.

No, there hadn't been any chance to talk on the bus. But now they were *alone*, both of them camped outside for the rest of the evening, and still they weren't talking about it.

What was there to talk about?

Noam knew his hours were numbered. After what he had witnessed the last few days, after what he had just done, he knew he was beyond earthly salvation, beyond Yom Kippur.

The ground was hard, the chilled night air smelling like industrial fuel. The fumes made Noam's head throb, his eyes bursting with sharp pain every time his brain hammered against his skull. His body was enveloped with aches—sore ribs, a swollen lower lip, a bruised jaw, a stomach so thick with acid it could jump a battery. Though dressed warmly, wrapped in a woolen jacket, he shivered, the shakes sometimes so violent his knees knocked together. He propped himself up, leaning his back against a concrete pillar. Slipping his hands back into his pockets, he rolled himself up into a ball. Both of them awake, both refusing to sleep, fearing that the other might be *planning* something.

Nothing between them except deadly suspicion.

It was almost three in the morning. The watch Abba had given him for his bar mitzvah worked like a mule. Noam had been so mad at his father, angry that even for an occasion like his bar mitzvah, Abba had been too cheap to buy him the watch he really wanted. Now Noam clung to it as if it were the only tangible link to his past.

He no longer cared about his safety, knowing it was just a matter of time before something irreversible would happen. The only thing that gave him solace was *tshuvah*—repentance. Since the last ordeal, Noam had been silently praying, begging Hashem's forgiveness for all the evil he had done. He knew it was too late for him in this lifetime. Even if he should live to be reunited with his family, he couldn't do anything to undo the terrible, terrible things he had done. Nothing would ever, ever be good for him again. But that was the way it should be. He didn't deserve goodness.

But he hoped he would show himself to be worthy of Hashem's forgiveness. If his repentence was sincere, if his confessions to God—*vidduy*—were complete, maybe he could earn a tiny fraction of salvation in the world to come.

He must suffer. It was the only way to achieve forgiveness.

Pray, he told himself. Try to save your evil, worthless soul. Pray.

Thoughts of his family kept interfering. The only good thing about it was that the images of their faces made him suffer even more. Noam looked up, tears finally flooding his eyes. The sky was moonless, an eerie misty gray lightened by streetlights and clouds. It seemed to beckon him upward, seemed to have visible folded arms just waiting for him to fall asleep. Then they'd part and swoop down, yanking him into an empty void.

A lifetime ago, the thought would have terrified him. But now he couldn't have cared less. Hashem was merciful. Hashem would let him live long enough to do his *tshuvah*. The only thing that scared Noam now, was how *long* it would take him to repent. If he was sincere enough, he could do his *tshuvah* quickly and die. If he wasn't, he'd have to keep going, suffering for years, until it was done properly.

Every day, waking up to ask Hashem to forgive you. Every day, having to live with that horrible picture of that poor man burned in your brain, reminding yourself what you had done.

The pain was overwhelming, dwarfing any fear he once had of dying, any fear he once had of Hersh.

He would leave Hersh once they arrived in San Francisco. Just walk away from him on the open streets. If Hersh attacked him, killed him, so be it. But more than likely, Hersh would let him go.

He would never go back to his family—that would be too good for him. He would hide out somewhere, live on nothing. When he could pass for eighteen, he would find some weird *ba'al tshuvah* yeshiva that didn't ask questions. He would become a *nazir*—a man who drank no wine, refused to touch a razor to his head. He would spend his remaining days in learning and prayer and repentance.

Noam knew he had only a slim chance for redemption. Still, a slim chance was better than none. That was what was so wonderful about Hashem. He was always willing to give you a slim chance.

After the thirteenth ring, Decker slammed the phone down.

Where in the bloody hell was Rina?

It had been almost an hour since MacPherson was to have picked up the fliers. If he hadn't seen her, he would have radioed something back.

Calm down, Decker told himself. Taking a deep breath, he asked the radio operator to patch him through to MacPherson. The voice on the other end of the line was hoarse and thick with sleep.

Without introducing himself, Decker said, "Paul, were you sleeping?"

There was silence on the other end of the line. Then: "Pete, let me explain—"

"I can't get hold of Rina. Did she go to the airport in your place?"

"I think so—"

"You *think* so," Decker repeated quietly. "Buddy, I'm going to deal with you later. Now, I'm going to rush over to L.A. International and hope to God my wife is okay."

MacPherson said, "Pete, I'm sure she's—"

Decker hung up on him. He grabbed his keys, jumped into the unmarked, and gunned the engine. His gut was a mixture of fury and anxiety. He was mature enough to know that there were always a few trouble spots in a marriage, but he hadn't expected them to surface so soon. Rina was pushing him beyond the pale, as if she got a charge out of driving him crazy.

The honeymoon was definitely over.

For the seventh time tonight, Rina explained to a security officer the purpose of her visit. This time she was at TWA, the domestic terminal farthest from the entrance to the airport. The place was eerie in the wee hours of the morning, not deserted but lots of open space for very few travelers. Footsteps echoed, voices rang out even if you spoke at normal volume, so Rina began to whisper. People were scattered around the gates, some dozing in their seats, fingers tightly clutching the handles of their suitcases. Others were awake, scanning the room with glazed eyes that never quite focused on any single object.

The woman manning the security checkpoint was big-boned and black, agreeable but not really helpful. She took the flier, gave a quick glance at the printed faces, then asked if these guys were so bad, why hadn't she heard about it through official channels?

Rina had no answer. She hadn't any idea what the procedure was for this kind of thing. She wasn't even clear on the details about what had happened in Hollywood. But she couldn't tell the security lady that, so she mumbled something about things like this taking time.

Her lack of success and lack of sleep were dragging her spirits down. She should call Peter, tell him what she was up to. But she knew how he'd react and wasn't in the mood for his temper. Not that Peter was temperamental, but he could be very parental. Lecturing her all the time . . .

Well, what did she really expect when she married a man twelve years her senior? Wasn't that what she wanted after all these years of living alone? After having sole responsibility for her children, didn't she want someone to lean on?

Peter had been sent to her by Hashem, her special gift for surviving that *terrible* ordeal. From the beginning, Peter had been nurturing and reassuring, his physical presence so formidable she'd felt instantly safe whenever he was around. Over the last two years, he had rebuilt her sense of self, and now, thanks to him, she was strong and self-reliant.

She was fine, but *Peter* was having a hard time adjusting to her independence. What bothered her most was that he didn't trust her judgment.

Not that her judgment was so wonderful. Admittedly, she seemed to have a knack for putting herself in vulnerable positions. But she refused to be a hothouse flower. Noam was out there, kidnapped by a maniac. She wasn't about to try heroics, but if she could help by passing out fliers, why not? Even if that meant going down to the airport at three in the morning. Over and over she thought: What if it had been one of her sons . . . ?

She pumped herself up with renewed determination, tucking the remaining fliers back into her folder, preparing the speech for her next stop. As she walked, she heard heavy, rapid footsteps behind her and spun around.

The look in Peter's eyes. She felt her shoulders sag. She was about to explain her intentions, but he spoke first.

"At least you could have had the courtesy to leave me a message!" He dropped his voice a notch. "What the hell gets into you, huh?"

Rina didn't answer, but did manage to make eye contact. His face was filled with tension, but his body drooped with fatigue.

He started to speak again, but stopped himself. He ran his hands over his face, looked at her and said, "Why waste my breath? You don't listen anyway. Did you find out anything interesting?"

Rina felt ashamed. "I should have left you a message—"

"Forget it," Decker said. "Got any new information for me?"

"Nothing," she said quietly.

"You've done all the terminals on the left side of the airport?"

Rina nodded. "I'm sorry—"

"I said *forget* it! This is what we're going to do, Rina. We'll cover the other terminals *together.*" He walked away from her. She had to run to keep up with him.

"Can you stop for a moment?" she asked.

Decker halted so abruptly that Rina overshot him. She backed up and said, "I'm not making excuses. But I came here out of deep concern for Noam. Peter, every time I think of that child, I feel I have to do *something.* Paul MacPherson was as sick as a dog and I was worried he'd do a shoddy job. Besides, if Noam was here, I, more than anyone, could recognize him."

Decker said, "That's precisely what I was worried about. How do you think Hersh might have reacted had you confronted Noam? Think he would have said, 'Sure, little buddy, go on home and I'll just continue the murders on my own'? And what makes you so sure that Noam's an *innocent* victim? He might have reacted violently himself."

Rina didn't speak.

Decker said, "Rina, the body left behind had been *eviscerated.* Does that scare you? It scares me."

Rina remained silent.

"Then I find out you're out here all alone, like some friggin Pollyanna." Decker pulled out a cigarette and stuffed it into his mouth unlit. "Your little stunt scared the shit out of me."

"I understand—"

"No, you don't *understand* a whit. 'Cause if you did understand, you wouldn't be here!" He yanked the cigarette out and pointed it at her. "You want to stay married to me, you stay *out* of my business. We are *not* partners. You do *not* pick up my slack, because you don't *help* me when you do. You are *hindering* me. I get so goddamn nervous trying to *baby-sit* you, I can't do my friggin *job*."

"After this, no more."

"I've heard that before."

"I promise, Peter, no more. It's just that Noam is a special case."

"He's *my* special case, not *yours*. Rina, I *hate* talking to you like this, but I feel that unless I do, nothing's going to get through."

"It's okay, I'm not upset. See, I'm smiling." Rina smiled. "See, I'm happy."

The smile looked as if it was going to crack her cheeks. Decker had to laugh. He sighed and hugged her fiercely. "You're such a pain in the ass. But I love you."

"I love you, too." Rina hugged him back. "Sorry for worrying you. It was stupid, but all I could think about was Noam. And Paul looked so sick."

"You think he's sick now, wait until I'm done with him."

"Don't take it out on him," Rina said. "I wouldn't let him have the fliers."

"I don't expect him to be able to reason with you." Decker put the cigarette back in his pocket. "Lord knows I can't. But he should have told me what you were up to." He grimaced, then looped his arm around her shoulder. "C'mon, let's finish up and go home."

Rina said, "Peter, if Hersh is a suspect in such a horrible murder, why aren't there other people looking for him?"

"Because we really don't know where Noam and Hersh are. This is just a guess, a precaution. In case they decide to leave the city. Marge is checking out the bus terminal and the railroads. I did find the motel where they'd been staying. They checked out in a hurry. The clerk had no idea where they were headed."

He glanced around the gates. They were all closed, the next flight out an hour away. A male body was stretched out over a row of chairs, a newspaper over his head. From under the comics came deep grunts and snorts. A Hispanic janitor, dressed in navy-blue coveralls, was mopping the floor. Muzak was being piped through the loudspeakers.

They walked for a moment in silence. Though bone-weary, Decker found a current of energy in Rina's touch, her arm around his waist, her fingers tucked into his seat pocket. He hugged her shoulder as he walked, almost lifting her off her feet. Then he stopped abruptly.

"What is it?" Rina said.

"No big deal. I was so nervous about you, I left my beeper in the car."

"You want to go back for it?"

"Nah, I'll just call in. See if Marge has come up with anything."

He slipped his hands into his pocket, pulled out a handful of silver. The phone booths were at the back of the terminal. After getting through to Central Dispatch, he asked to be put through to Marge. A moment later, he heard her voice on the line.

"Finally," Marge said. "Where have you been?"

Decker said, "I'm at the airport. I don't have my beeper."

"That's obvious," Marge said. "An urgent call came through for you about ten, maybe fifteen minutes ago. A Frieda Levine from New York. She was so frazzled when the operator couldn't get hold of you, she didn't leave her number. I've tried Manhattan information, she isn't listed."

"She lives in Brooklyn," Decker said, "I'll call her. Thanks." He cut the line and called out to Rina. "You have Frieda Levine's phone number?"

"No," she said. "But they're listed. Her husband's name is Alter Levine, Brooklyn's area code is seven-one-eight."

Decker slammed the door shut and popped another quarter into the phone slot. After getting the number from information, he pulled out the phone card and gave the operator the Brooklyn exchange. Frieda picked it up on the first ring.

"It's Sergeant Decker, Mrs. Levine." He paused a second, realizing how cold that sounded, and softened his tone of voice. "What's up?"

"I heard from him," Frieda said. She was breathless. "Someone was with him . . . I could hear another voice. Noam didn't speak more than a minute. He was worried the line was tapped. He sounded . . ." She had to pause to find her voice. "He sounded hysterical, in terrible trouble. Is he, Sergeant?"

"Call me Akiva," Decker said. "Yes, I think Noam's in trouble. But first things first. I want to know exactly what was said during the conversation. I'm going to ask you a lot of questions, so just try and relax and we'll take it from the beginning."

"I can do better," Frieda said. "I set up a phone machine like you told us to do after he called Miriam. I have it on tape. I've played it back and it recorded. I've just got to rewind . . ."

Decker told her to take her time, thinking: Hallelujah! Someone *heeded* his advice. He said, "I'm going to pull out my notebook."

"Okay," Frieda said. "All right. I'll turn it on. If you can't hear, shout 'Louder.'"

"Gotcha," Decker said. He stuck his finger in his free ear and listened. He heard the click of the machine, realizing it had started recording in midsentence. Frieda had probably turned it on as soon as she heard Noam's voice. The woman was on top of it.

Frieda: . . . are you, Noam?

Noam: I can't tell you that. I can't see you again. I want to say good-bye.

A lot of static.

Frieda: (desperate): Noam, don't hang up, don't hang up. I love you. I want you to know that I love you.

Noam: (crying): I love you too, Bubbe.

Frieda: Noam, no matter what you've done, I don't care what you've done. I love you. We love you. We want you back here. We don't care . . . (crying) . . . we'll help you. No matter what you've done.

Background voice (low, guttural): Thirty more seconds.

Noam: (still crying): I can't talk much longer. In case the phone is tapped.

Frieda: It isn't tapped, I swear, Noam. I swear on the *Chumash*.

Background voice: Twenty.

Bad static.

Noam: . . . Abba and Eema, I love them too.

Frieda: Noam, come home to us. *Please*.

More static.

Noam (pause): I can't come home.

Frieda: (more crying): Yes, you can. I love you, darling. I don't care what . . . (crying) . . . just come *home*.

Noam: Don't cry, Bubbe. Please, don't cry.

Background voice: Ten.

A giant rumble, drowning out the voice. Then Decker heard Noam's voice but he couldn't make out the words.

Frieda: . . . come home. We all love you so much.

Background voice: Five.

Static.

Noam: I gotta go now. *Slachli*—Please forgive me. Please do that. Ask everyone to forgive me. I love you all.

The line went dead. Frieda came back on the phone, her voice so soft, Decker had to ask her to speak up. She cleared her throat and said, "I . . . I couldn't think of what to say other than I love you."

There was so much pain in her voice—in her

grandson's as well. Noam might be big for his age, but his voice was still tuned to a child's timbre. A soft, adolescent lament so full of despair. It was gut-wrenching to hear him speak.

Decker said, "You did what you could."

"You don't know where he is?"

"As of five hours ago, he was in Los Angeles," Decker said. "He may still be, I don't know."

"He's in bigger trouble than the last time?"

"Yes, he is." Decker sighed. "Mrs. Levine . . ."

Again, he paused. *Mrs. Levine?* Well, what else should he call her? Sure as hell she wasn't *Mom.* "Mrs. Levine, I want you to play me the tape again. I was listening to the conversation and there were some background noises I was tuning out. Now I'm going to tune them in."

"Certainly," Frieda said.

She rewound the tape and pushed the button. Again, Decker was struck by how young Noam sounded, how despondent he was. He wondered whether suicide was one of the boy's options and listened carefully, his ears trying to hear beyond the static.

The other voice was deep and spoke with a Brooklyn accent. More was *mo-ah.* In the background were the steady whooshes of cars going past. They must be near a freeway again. There was nothing else of interest until that one big rumble.

Unmistakable.

A low-flying airplane.

They were near an airport.

Only two major airports serviced the Los Angeles

area. L.A. International and the smaller domestic terminal—Hollywood-Burbank. Decker knew from experience that Hollywood-Burbank shut down around one, two in the morning. So did most of the charter airports.

Unless Hersh and Noam hightailed it over to Orange County and took off from John Wayne International, he was probably right on top of them.

When Frieda came back on the line, Decker asked her when she received the call.

"Six-eighteen," Frieda said. "I looked at my digital clock."

Three-eighteen our time, Decker thought. What was landing or taking off at three-eighteen? He asked her to hold on and checked the television monitors inside the TWA terminal. No activity here at 3:18. He checked his watch—3:47. "Mrs. Levine, I've got a lot of work to do. I'll call you back in an hour."

"Please keep me informed, Akiva," Frieda said. "It's not knowing that's so hard."

"I understand. In the meantime, if you haven't already done it, you must call up Ezra and Breina. Let them know you've heard from Noam . . . that he's alive."

"*Baruch Hashem*," Frieda whispered. "I haven't called yet because I wanted to keep the line open for you. I'll phone them right now."

"Good. I'll keep in touch." Decker hung up and came out of the booth. He gave Rina a rundown as they hurried down the escalator, jogged down the long corridor toward the baggage exit. "I'm going back to my car and contact all the remaining LAX terminals. I can do it faster with my radio than I can by phone."

Rina was running to keep up with him. "They're somewhere at the airport?"

Decker couldn't tell if Rina's breathlessness was excitement or overexertion. He slowed his pace. "I don't know if they're *in* the airport. I'm pretty sure Noam didn't make the call from inside a terminal. You can't hear freeway noises when you're inside those booths."

They walked outside the building. The night was cold and misty, the air around them humming with generator sounds. They stopped at the curbside. Decker listened a moment, then said, "Can you hear the freeway?"

"A little bit."

"Well, I heard it clearly," Decker said. "Heard it over the static of a long-distance call and a cheap phone system. And I didn't hear that drone in the background either. They didn't make the call from inside the airport. I'm positive about that."

"So they're not here," Rina said.

Decker said, "They weren't here as of a half hour ago. But they may have slipped in. Or they may be planning to come here later." He clapped his hands and rubbed them together. "I'm going to call Marge, have her cover the airport while I go hunting around the area."

"Want me to stay with Marge?" Rina asked. "I'd recognize Noam better than she would."

Decker stared at her. "You don't get involved. Remember?"

"I just thought—"

"*No.*"

"*Okay.*" She tucked in loose strands of hair under her kerchief. "What are you going to do?"

"Check out the local sleep-joints. They had to have gone somewhere."

They resumed walking.

The huge expanse of blacktop parking was by no means empty. He wondered what all the cars were doing in the lots if the terminals were nearly deserted. Then he thought of all the businessmen on overnights. They parked their cars in the lots and picked them up the next morning.

Not knowing exactly where Rina was, he had parked the car a quarter-mile away from TWA. As they walked, he thought: *If* Hersh and Noam were planning to leave the city, a case could be made for trying to nab them as they boarded the flight. It seemed insane for him to go running around the city, looking for two people who might show up soon anyway. Inglewood was spread out. They could be anywhere within a ten-mile radius.

But what if they *changed* their minds and decided not to leave the city? Then Decker would have missed a golden opportunity. Worse, what if *Hersh* changed his mind at the last minute and decided to do away with Noam—who was, thank God, alive as of a half hour ago. No, he couldn't wait, he couldn't take that chance.

Maybe they went back to Clint Willy's dive. Pigeons returning to roost. He'd check that one out first. Luckily, all the dumps were near each other—

He interrupted his train of thought.

Why was he assuming they were holed up in *any* motel? Having committed a horrible, *bloody* crime, clothes soaked with blood, faces possibly scratched up, maybe they thought it was wise to avoid any motels—just like they did after assault number one. If they didn't want to be noticed first time around—and that victim lived—they'd really want to lie low after what they had done.

He stopped walking. Rina asked what was wrong.

"You know, after they attacked their first victim, they didn't register at a motel. They camped out under an overpass." He paused. "I'm wondering if history might be repeating itself."

"Does Inglewood have hideout spots under its freeways?"

"Not around Century or La Tijera." Decker thought out loud. "And on Imperial Highway, there's nothing to speak of except aviation freight companies and Hughes Aircraft." He paused. "You know what's out there? The unfinished Century Freeway. It's next to LAX *and* to Four-oh-five freeway. That could account for the noises I heard. That stretch of land's deserted this time of night. Don't know if there are any phone booths around there, but I'm going to have me a look."

They arrived at the car. Decker pulled out his keys and said, "I'm going to update Marge. Then I'm going to drive you to your car. You're going home."

At first, Rina didn't reply. Then she said, "Fine. Take me to my car. I'll go home."

Decker didn't like it. She was agreeing way too easily. Was she sincere or was she planning to do something stupid? Return to the terminals or—worse—follow him.

Goddamn it, if only he could trust her.

He hated to admit it, but he couldn't. At least not with this case. It was probably better to have her near him so he could watch her. *Control* her. He despised his decision, but at the moment, he felt as if he had no choice.

He said, "This is what I'm going to do for you. You really want to come with me, come with me. Just don't get into any trouble, okay?"

"*Really?*"

He opened the passenger door. "Really."

"What's up your sleeve, Detective?"

"I like your company," Decker said. "Besides, if you're next to me, I don't have to worry about you, do I?"

"You're giving me mixed messages," Rina said.

Decker ignored the comment. "You can call in for backup if I need it." That part was true. "I figure you can't get hurt too bad locked in the unmarked with the keys." He smiled. "Hop in."

Rina smiled back, but knew something was amiss. Not that Peter's face was offering her any hint as to what was up. He could be unreadable when he wanted to be. Rina didn't believe him at all. But she kept her thoughts to herself.

❧28

After the phone call, Nick-O seemed better.

But it was too late.

Hank had made up his mind. The last time, man, it'd taken him too fuckin' long to react. Yeah, he did react, one of the reasons why Hank didn't do him on the spot, but in Hank's mind, Nick-O had blown it.

If Nick-O hadn't been there, Hank would have planned it all differently. First off, he would have had the gun. *He* would have shot the mother himself, not waited for Nick-O to finally snap out of it and *do* something.

No, Hank didn't like that at all. Nick-O was definitely more trouble than he was worth.

Still, Hank was glad that he had brought the kid along. The kid, without knowing it, helped him know what he *really* wanted. And the kid had done all the scut work. And he'd been someone to talk to in the beginning.

Too bad.

It could have worked out, if the kid had toughened up. Nick-O was a smart cookie, but he was too damn young. He was just too much responsibility.

And there was always the constant worry of the kid dropping a dime. Not that Hank thought he'd ever do that. Nick-O had been scared real bad, especially after what had happened.

You killed him, Nick-O. Make no mistake about that, buddy. I may have carved him up, but you killed him.

That's what really pissed Hank off more than anything, what had proved to him that Nick-O would have to go.

The kid went ahead and killed the faggot—finally! And then, he became unglued when Hank started having a little fun. Dafuck difference did it make? The dude was *dead*.

Hank trembled with excitement when he thought about it. The gunshots had ripped several holes in the faggot's stomach, but there was still plenty of skin left for that initial cut. He shivered when he thought of the knife slicing through warm flesh, the belly opening as easily as parting a pair of curtains. The metallic, sweet smell of freshly butchered meat: the oily, almost slimy feel of the innards, soothing blood washing over your fingers.

The one thing he regretted most in life—never having the pleasure of feeling the *dickhead's* intestines, his body bursting like a bloody balloon in the explosion.

A big regret. Had to make up for it. Besides, just like he said, the faggot was already dead. Why *not* have some fun?

Nick-O bawling like a baby. Kid could be so *stupid* sometimes. Like a dead person could feel?

He was already dead. For the millionth time, asshole. You killed him. Don't ever forget it.

Then they were quiet for a long, long time. Gave Hank the opportunity to think over what was really going down.

The decision was just so clear-cut. The kid had to go.

That's when Hank suggested that the kid could make a carefully supervised phone call if he wanted to. Nick-O nearly kissed his feet. Hank felt pretty good about that. Hey, let the kid go with some last words, you know.

The original plan was to do the kid just as soon as they returned from the phone call, then hop a plane out the next day. But it was too weird to think about spending the rest of the night with a corpse.

And besides, Hank wasn't so sure he wanted to leave L.A. just yet.

What was the hurry?

No one knew who they were, where they were. If there were any witnesses to the killings, cops would be looking for a duo. Soon, he'd be just an *uno*. No problem.

Still, he wanted to stay close to the airport just in case he felt like splitting. There was no real hurry to do Nick-O quick. And it would be more exciting to wait a little bit. After all, he'd just finished up with the faggot dude.

So let the kid have his phone call. He'd do him right before dawn, while it was still dark enough to get away with it, but there was enough light for him to see what he was doing.

Yeah, he had it all figured out. The kid couldn't keep awake too much longer. Hank would have fallen asleep much sooner if the faggot last night hadn't given him that magical cellophane envelope.

It had been up to Hank. Did he want coke or money for his services? Knowing he was going to get money anyway, Hank figured, why not take the coke? He had snorted the last of it around an hour ago.

Blastoff. Instant energy for the brain.

When the kid dropped off, he'd get the gun.

One quick blast.

If he had time and *if* he felt like it, he'd finish the kid off like he did the faggot. Like he should have done the dickhead.

If only he'd known better.

He looked over at Nick-O. Kid still wasn't asleep, he was praying again. Let's face it, the kid had to know his time was up. He didn't even seem to care.

It was almost like he was putting the kid out of his misery.

That was a good way to think about it, putting the kid out of his misery. A quick blast to the head and it would be over. Then he'd do the kid if he wanted to. Yeah, he'd probably do the kid, 'cause hell, the kid would be dead anyway. Thinking about it, he began to get excited.

But the kid would *definitely* be dead first. Hank was no monster, he'd never do the kid while he was alive. It was like Nick-O wasn't a bad sort.

Just too young.

Just too green.

Just not tough enough.

The next kid would have to do better.

One quick blast.

Why make him suffer?

Sitting like a postmodern Stonehenge, the unfinished Century Freeway coursed along a stretch of dirt that hugged Imperial Highway. Four-story concrete pillars supported disjointed slabs of to-be highway that abruptly ended in exposed grids of rusted-metal spikes, the gray mist softening sharp edges like hairspray on a camera lens.

Under the freeway sat two-story mountains of gravel and clusters of heavy construction machinery. Directly south of the highway, looking like a Hollywood movie backdrop, were groves of palm trees completely out of place in the industrial area. That was Los Angeles, Decker thought. Nothing matched. Beyond the groves was a housing development and a complex of yet-to-be-rented office buildings.

Decker drove parallel with the construction. No signs of life, but that was to be expected. If the boys were camping out, they'd be hidden. He told Rina to look for any phone booth. As they drove west, the embryonic freeway came to a sudden halt at Aviation Boulevard. Decker crossed the intersection, passing over railroad tracks, and continued in the same direction. The construction resumed on the north side of Imperial Highway, the south side taken up for blocks by Hughes Aircraft and office structures.

As he drove west, Decker was coming closer to the airport, but distancing himself from the 405 freeway—the only thoroughfare that hosted a number of motor vehicles at this time of night. Surface streets were deserted, blacktop reflecting converging lines of Christmas-colored traffic lights. Neither he nor Rina spotted any phone booths. He backtracked to Aviation. There were no through streets that paralleled the other side of the construction, so he was forced to detour through a working-class residential area, a neighborhood filled with trucks, vans, and decade-old American cars.

"What are you looking for?" Rina finally asked.

"Me and the chicken that crossed the road," Decker said. "We're trying to get to the other side."

His voice was tense.

"Aren't we near that outcall service place?" Rina asked.

"You've got a good sense of direction, honey."

He wove through streets lined by small stucco homes until he came to Tropical Island Biway. He swung left, passing the palm groves sprouting from an expanse of newly planted sod. In front was a waterfall gushing down a Mediterranean basin; above it black script letters scrolled on white tile identifying the development as the Tropical Island Business Park. A long driveway led to a group of white stone buildings striped with green windows.

The business park was within walking distance of the construction and across the street from the 405 freeway. But there didn't appear to be any phone booths near the offices. He continued on the Biway, slowing down the unmarked, hoping he'd see something.

As he approached 116th Street, he noticed a small unpaved service road that ran along the south side of Century Freeway.

He slowed, then stopped.

"What are we doing now?" Rina asked.

"I'm trying to decide whether I should park here or turn," Decker answered. "Tires on an unpaved road would make a lot of noise."

"I don't see a phone booth," Rina said.

Decker said, "I don't see one either, but it's dark. I don't think I should chance it. I'll stop here." He turned off the motor and looked at her. "You're going to stay put?"

"Of course," Rina said. "What do you think? I'm going to follow you?"

That's exactly what Decker thought. He explained to her how to use the radio. "Give me a half hour to look around. If you don't hear from me or I haven't returned, call for backup."

"Okay."

"I'm going to lock the doors and leave you keys to the car. Keep your eyes open. If anyone approaches, take off. Don't worry about me."

"Okay."

"Don't try to contact me on my radio. Your voice will echo and the noise might alert them if they're nearby."

"Okay."

"Remember, if I'm not back in a half hour, don't

start looking for me. Just call for backup and stay put."

"I understand."

Decker paused, gauging her responses. She seemed sincere, but as much as he hated to admit it, he didn't trust her judgment.

"What is it?" Rina asked.

"I'm sorry, Rina," Decker said. "I'm really sorry to do this, but it's for your own good."

Rina stiffened. "What are you talking about?"

Decker pulled out a set of cuffs and quickly encircled her left hand with a ring of metal. The other cuff was clamped to the steering wheel. Rina stared at him, aghast.

Keeping her voice in check, she said, "You take these off me now and I'll pretend this was a joke."

Decker said, "You can reach the car radio, you can reach the ignition key, you can reach the door lock." He picked up her purse and put it on her lap. "You can even reach your gun. The only thing you can't do is get out of the car and try to come after me—"

"Take these off me now!"

"Rina, I'm truly sorry, but I can't."

"This is extremely low, Peter," Rina said. "A civilized man would not do something this *low*!"

"I'm trying to protect you."

"I don't need *your* protection!" Rina fumed. "I will never forgive you for this, Peter. You're doing irreparable harm!"

"So be mad at me. You do reckless things and I want assurance that you're going to be out of the way."

"There's no marriage if there's no trust!"

"Have you given me reason to trust you?"

She didn't answer.

Decker opened the door, told her to slide into the driver's seat.

Rina didn't respond.

"Okay, be like that. It just shows me my judgment was right because you're acting like a baby."

Rina looked up at him, tears streaming down her face. Decker felt like an ogre who had kidnapped the princess. It was a despicable thing to do, but what was his alternative? He wanted her safe and *out* of the way. He took the car key off his ring and stuck it in the ignition. "I'm going to lock the door now, Rina. I'll check in with you in thirty minutes. Don't answer any of my calls unless I tell you to, all right?"

His words were met with silence.

Decker raised his voice. "All right?"

"I heard you."

Decker said, "You can be mad at me all you want later. But I have to be able to count on you. Can I?"

Rina wiped away tears with her free hand and gave him a stony look. "Yes."

Decker came out of the car, depressed the car lock and shut the door. Her face staring out of the glass. Her beautiful forlorn face: He had clipped the wings of an exotic bird. He went to the trunk, took out the flashlight, then gently closed it.

One last look at Rina. He tapped on the window; she looked up. He mouthed an "I love you."

Rina paused, then mouthed back a "Be careful,

Peter." Decker would have preferred an "I love you" but that was too much to ask for.

It was damp outside, the fog hovering over the barren stretch of land. The service road was almost indistinguishable from the construction site—both full of loose gravel and dirt. Decker tried to walk as quietly as he could, but his shoes stirred up plumes of dust, his soles scraped against loose pebbles.

Decker hooked the flashlight onto his belt. It was still dark, dawn at least two hours away, but there was enough light from streetlamps. One less thing to carry. Droplets nipped at his cheeks. He rolled up his collar, stuck his hands in his pockets. He walked slowly, scanning the area for anything significant.

Strolling, observing.

He looked down, then looked up.

If he hadn't looked up, he would have missed it.

A serpentine rise of black cable line connecting to the T-grid of a telephone pole. The line arced down, stopped at a wooden pole one hundred feet in front of him. Decker walked over. A black rotary phone was fastened to wood by metal rings.

Having worked construction in his teens, Decker had seen this kind of thing before. At major sites, the project owner often installed a temporary line for the foreman's outgoing calls. The line was disconnected as soon as the work was completed. But this one had no lock on the dial. Unusual. Maybe it had never had one, maybe someone had jimmied it off. Decker wrapped his jacket sleeve around the receiver and picked it up.

A dial tone.

He called Brooklyn information. As soon as the operator answered, he hung up. He had just wanted to see if the line was capable of connecting long-distance calls.

It was.

At the sound of footsteps. Noam jerked his head up, his dreams of his family dissipating instantly. He saw Hersh standing over him, his hand behind his back. Fully awake, Noam grabbed his bag, stood up, and stepped back.

Hersh moved a step forward and said, "Just going to check that we didn't forget anything. You can go back to sleep."

Noam didn't answer.

Hersh said, "Go back to sleep, Nick-O. Catch some Zs while you can."

Noam took another step backward, holding his bag against his stomach as if it were an armored vest. "Not tired."

"I want to check your baggage," Hersh said. "Make sure you packed everything."

"I did." Noam retreated. "Everything's okay."

"Gun loaded?" Hersh asked.

Noam shook his head and took another step backward. "You said, what would be the point of loading it? That we were packing it inside the valise and checking it through."

Hersh stepped forward and said, "Well, maybe it wouldn't hurt to load it anyway."

Noam retreated some more and said, "That

doesn't make any sense. It might go off accidentally; then we'd be in trouble for no reason."

Nobody spoke for a moment. Noam could tell that Hersh was mad. He was looking at the bag. He wanted it. He wanted the *gun*. Yet he wasn't making any moves toward it. Then Hersh gave him that weird smile and Noam saw why. Hersh was holding a gutting knife in his right hand. He wasn't exactly threatening him with it, but he was kind of waving it around.

"Give me the gun," Hersh said. His voice was steady. "Hey, I'll load it for you, Nick-O."

Noam's heart raced in his chest, his head banging like a gavel.

Like that book Hersh always read—*Marvin K. Mooney*.

The time had come.

This was it!

He was positive that Hersh was going to kill him. The thought of being butchered like those other men made him dizzy, made him sick. But he couldn't get sick now. Not with so much *tshuvah* left to do.

What to do?

Run?

Not a chance. Hersh was quicker.

Think, Noam told himself. He was so tired, so weak, nauseated from what had happened and no sleep.

Play dumb. Try to get a little more time.

Noam backed up, never taking his eyes off Hersh. Slowly, he unzipped his bag. He'd pretend he'd lost the gun. That was a good trick.

He reached inside, attempted to feel around. Yes, there was the gun. And to his surprise, it was *loaded*. At least it had a clip in it. Whether the clip was empty or not, he didn't know.

But Hersh didn't know either.

Noam pulled the gun out slowly, pointing the barrel at Hersh's feet. He forced himself to breathe in slowly. Then the words came gushing out.

"It's still loaded. With everything such a mess at the motel I must have forgotten to take the clip out. I thought I did, but I must have forgotten." Noam hugged the butt tightly and took a deep breath. God was still with him. "I think I'll hold it until right before we're ready to go. Just in case, you know?"

Noam watched as Hersh rocked forward, then rocked back into place. He could tell that Hersh was *really* mad. Really, really mad! Hersh wanted to kill him, cut him up. Hersh just *loved* cutting that poor man up. He was a monster from the other world, the *yetzer harah* in a man's body.

But Noam also realized that he had the power. He was the one with the gun in his hand. Hersh was stuck! Stuck, stuck, stuck!

Hersh shrugged. "Sure, whatever you want." He returned to his spot and sat down on the ground. "You can stand guard for the next hour. Then we'd better head out."

"You gonna sleep?" Noam asked.

Too much hope in the voice.

Hersh gave him another big, lopsided smile. Gently, he began to trace images in the ground with the point of the blade. "Nah, way too worked up to sleep. If you want to—"

"I don't."

"So we'll both stay awake."

"Okay," Noam said.

Hersh kept tracing designs. "We'll sleep on the plane."

"Okay."

"I got it all planned out." He was doing a neat pattern of concentric circles. "We'll go business class. We'll check into an A-one hotel, we'll do it all up first rate. We deserve a little fun, Nick-O. Hey, I didn't mean for it to go this messy, but sometimes that hap—" He flung his head upward.

"What is it?" Noam asked. His knuckles were white from clenching the gun.

"You hear that?" Hersh whispered.

"Hear what?"

"That noise?"

"What noise—"

"Shut up and listen," Hersh whispered.

Noam didn't hear anything. *Get a grip on yourself!* Hersh said, "Someone's out there."

"I can't hear—"

"Shut up!" Hersh whispered furiously. "It may be nothin', it may be somethin'. Give me the gun!"

"No," Noam said, backing away. "Leave me alone!"

Hersh whispered, "Lower your fuckin' voice!"

Noam felt his knees shake. "You're trying to *trick* me. You're planning to kill me. You're making all this up—"

"Shut up!"

"You're making all this up so you can kill me!" Noam screamed. "I'm not going to give you the gun! Ever! And if you come any closer, if you move, I'll shoot you! I'll shoot you *dead*!"

Hersh stared at him. "You're crazy, Nick-O! Flip city! Someone's gettin' close and you're gonna get us both killed!"

"You're lying!"

Hersh whispered desperately, "Don't you fuckin' *hear* it? Can't you *hear* footsteps? I don't believe . . ." He began to pace. "Well, you stick around, bud, but I'm callin' it a day!"

But then Noam leveled the gun at Hersh's eyes and Hersh halted in his tracks.

The noises became louder.

Instantly, Noam panicked. There *were* noises. His chest got tight and he began to wheeze. Hersh hadn't been lying. Someone *was* out there.

What to do? What to do?

Hersh read the fear in Noam's eyes and whispered quickly, "Put the gun away, Nick-O. If it's a cop, we'll pretend we're bums and he'll just send us on."

Noam lowered the gun. Was this another one of Hersh's tricks? If he put the gun away, Hersh might jump him. No, he couldn't put the gun away. Without the gun, he was dead.

"Put it away!" Hersh screamed in an angry whisper.

Noam was paralyzed with fear. *Get a grip on yourself!*

Then Hersh lunged at him.

* * *

Pointing the Beretta, Decker jumped out of the darkness and yelled, "Freeze, motherfucker!"

Hersh stopped almost in midair.

"Drop the knife, you motherfucker!" Decker shouted. "Drop it! Drop it! Drop it now! Drop it! Drop it! Drop it!"

Hersh let the knife fall to the ground and raised his hands in the air. "He was trying to shoot me—"

"Hit the ground," Decker screamed to Hersh. In the back of his mind, he knew Noam was holding the gun. But Hersh was his main concern. "Now! Hit it! Hit it! Hit it!" He moved forward, reaching behind his back for his cuffs. Then he *remembered* where they were.

He cursed his stupidity. Was that friggin poetic justice or what! Hersh was on his knees. Decker pushed him all the way down, kicked his legs into a spread-eagle position. Kneeling, he yanked Hersh's hands behind his back, then tried to undo his belt. As he fumbled with the buckle, he felt the presence of another body close to his. He looked up.

Noam pointing the gun at him.

Decker felt sweat pouring down his brow. "I was sent here by your family, Noam." He was trying to free his belt. "Sent here by your abba and eema. Put away the gun, son. All I want to do is just take you home, back to Boro Park. I spent *yom tov* at your bubbe's. Everyone was so worried about you—"

"Bullshit, Nick-O!" Hersh interrupted. "You know how they really feel—"

Decker jerked the arm upward. Hersh let out a yelp of pain.

Noam just staring, his eyes far away.

Decker said, "Noam, I'm Sammy . . . Shmuli and Yonkie's stepdad. I'm married to Rina Lazarus. You know Mrs. Lazarus, don't you? She knows you. She always said what a fine boy you were."

Hersh said, "Bullshit. They all hate you, Nick-O. You know that."

"He's lying," Decker said calmly. "They all love you very much." It had been about twenty minutes. If he ever got the sucker's hands tied, he'd call for backup.

Hersh said, "He's lying, Nick-O." He broke into laughter. "Guy's not a cop. Look at 'im, Nick-O. He don't even have handcuffs! This dude's probably a bounty hunter. He's getting bread to break our balls—"

Decker jerked Hersh's arm up again.

"Goddamn *sheygetz* Nazi!" Hersh grunted out.

Decker pushed Hersh's face into the dirt.

Noam blurted out, "Don't do that!" He was shaking hard now. The man on top of Hersh was definitely a *cop*. He knew that because Mrs. Lazarus *had* married a *sheygetz* cop from Los Angeles. Everybody knew it. Noam knew that this man was going to take them both to jail. Forever. That was what cops did. And this cop was acting like a Nazi. "You're hurting him. Stop hurting him."

"He's not hurt," Decker explained patiently. "If I wanted to hurt him badly, I could. But I don't want to do that. I'm not going to do that. Noam, put the gun down. Please! Think of your family who love you—"

"Bullshit!" laughed Hersh. "They think you're a piece of shit! You told me that!"

"He's lying, Noam," Decker persisted. "They love you. They haven't slept a moment since you've been gone. They're so worried about—"

"My bubbe must have called you," Noam interrupted.

"Your bubbe loves you very much."

"The call must have been traced," Noam said. "How else would you know I was here?"

"The call wasn't traced—"

"She lied to me," Noam said, tears streaming down from his eyes. "She swore on the *Chumash* that the call wasn't traced. But how else would you know I was here?"

"Because I'm a cop, Noam. I know these things."

At last, Decker had felt his belt come loose. One final yank and it was free. Then he saw his hand radio go flying into the air and crash-land ten feet away. He'd forgotten it was hooked on to his belt loop.

Swell.

He wondered if it was *on*, if the talk button was depressed. He yelled out to Rina to call for backup and hoped for the best. Then he began to wrap the belt around Hersh's wrists.

"Stop it," Noam screamed to Decker. He was pointing the gun and sobbing. "Stop it, stop it, stop it! Leave him alone!"

Decker stopped tying Hersh's hands. Goddamn psycho broke into a grin and Decker knew what he was thinking. Noam was going to be his savior. Well, fuck that noise.

"Noam, put away the gun. Every second you hold on to it, you're taking the chance of putting yourself in deep trouble. Put it down before something terrible happens."

"I'm not going to jail," Noam said.

Decker said, "Of course you're not. You're a victim. Nothing's going to happen to you."

Noam was gripping the gun, panting like a dog. "I don't believe you! You're lying! Just like my bubbe lied!"

"Noam, your bubbe didn't lie," Decker said, softly. "I figured it out on my own. Like I told you, I'm a cop. I'm a Los Angeles detective specializing in finding kids. Finding kids is what I've been trained to do, what I do for a living."

The boy quieted, appeared to be listening.

Hersh said, "He's full of shit, Nick-O—"

"I *hate* when you call me Nick-O, Hersh!" Noam shouted. "I hate it, hate it, hate it! I hate *you*!"

Decker looked at Noam, looked at the gun. The boy was still holding it tightly, but it was pointing at the ground.

"Noam, you've got to trust me. Show you how much *I trust you*, I'll do this. You've got a gun, I've got a gun. I'll put mine right here next to me." Decker gingerly placed his weapon at his heel far enough for show but close enough to be retrievable. "Now you do the same."

Noam didn't move.

"Noam, you're not going to shoot me. You're not going to shoot anyone. I know you wouldn't do that—"

"Dafuck do you know?" Hersh laughed out. "*He* shot the others."

"Liar!" Noam screamed, shaking out of control. "Liar, liar, liar, liar, liar!"

"You're goin' crazy, Nicky," Hersh screamed back. "Fuck-in' looneytunes! Do somethin' before this dude does somethin'—"

"Shut up!" Decker tightened his grip on Hersh. "Put the gun down, Noam. Put it down now!"

Hersh shouted, "Shoot him like you shot the others, Nick-O!"

"Liar!" Noam screamed. "Liar! You're my *yetzer harah*. I know it now. I hate you!"

"Drop the gun, Noam!" Decker said. "I'm going to take you back to your parents, but I can't help you unless you drop your gun!"

"I hate you, Hersh Schaltz!" Noam shrieked. "I hate you, I hate you, I hate you!" He gasped for breath. "I hate everybody! I hate *me*!"

In one swift motion, Noam brought the gun to his head.

"Noooooo," Decker screamed as he jumped him. The gun discharged, nicking the top of the boy's head. An instant red part oozed from his scalp. Noam brought his hand to his head and screamed that he was dying.

Decker knew it was only a graze. But Noam was the least of his problems. Out of the corner of his eye, he saw Hersh lunging for Noam's fallen Beretta, his fingers wrapping around the butt.

Decker charged him, protecting his own head. The two of them hit the ground, inhaling dirt and grit, trying to land punches. Decker had at least fifty pounds on Hersh, but being light, Hersh had the advantage of speed. Decker reached out, hugged him at the waist, but Hersh wriggled out of the grasp. They hit the ground again, but this time Hersh had positioned himself on top.

With the gun firmly planted in his hand, Hersh tried to aim, but Decker saw the move coming and made a play for the weapon. Hersh yanked the automatic aloft, out of Decker's reach. With both hands, Decker grabbed Hersh's wrist into a vise-lock and held the wiry outstretched arm, trying to point the barrel away from both of them.

Squeezing the wrist as hard as he could, hoping to pop the piece out of the fucker's fingers.

Hersh hanging on to the weapon.

Son of a bitch had iron clamps for fingers.

Decker kept squeezing, feeling Hersh squirming on top of him. A moment later, something hard was jammed into his solar plexus. Psycho had knee-dropped him. Decker was forced to loosen his grip, but he didn't let go.

Still, the sucker moved in. Decker saw his fate too clearly. The wrist flexing forward, the gun pointing at his face. The finger on the trigger.

The gun fired.

Instantaneously, Decker rolled to the side, saving his cheekbones from shattering, but the first slug ate through his left shoulder. He screamed.

The second bullet hit Decker's left arm.

Blood spurting onto his cheeks.

A muzzle aimed at his *face*, a crooked smile behind it.

Once again, Decker rolled to the side as the gun discharged, the bullet whizzing past his temple.

Noam flailed his arms and shrieked out, "Stop it, Hersh!" He began to pummel Hersh's back. "Stop it! Stop it! Stop it!"

Hersh was forced to push him away, giving Decker just enough time to move in. He kicked upward, made contact with Hersh's belly, causing him to double over. But Hersh still had Noam's gun in his hands.

Decker kicked him again, then scrambled for his own gun, just inches away. Blood had drenched his clothes; he felt himself growing weak. Inching over to his weapon, he knotted his fingers around the butt and fell onto his back just as Hersh had caught his breath. No time to aim. Decker picked up the gun and fired upward, pulling the trigger at the same time Hersh discharged his weapon.

Hersh's bullet ricocheting off the ground.

Decker fired again. And again.

Hersh staggering forward, two intersecting red holes between his eyes—scarlet Venn diagrams.

Decker kept shooting.

Noam let out a blood-curdling scream.

Hersh's forehead squirted fountains of blood. Then he fell, landing on Decker with a thud.

Decker pushed him off with his good arm and gripped the gunshot wound on his arm.

Noam's cries echoing in the still of the night.

Shut up, Decker thought. Shut the fuck up!

The air so damn cool. Blood pouring out of his body. At least, something in his body was warm.

He told himself: Gotta get up. You're going to bleed to death out here, you asshole. Get the fuck up!

Noam still screeching like a macaw.

Decker lay on his back, clasping his bloody arm with his fingers, his body soaked with cold sweat. "Get help, dammit!" he shouted to Noam.

But the boy remained immobile.

Then Decker heard a voice. He couldn't see who it was: It was dark and misty and his vision had blurred. A female voice crying out, "Oh, my God! Oh, my God!"

Sounded like Rina, Decker thought, as blood ran down his chest. But wasn't she cuffed to the wheel? He was disoriented. He was seeing things, hearing things.

Rina kneeling over him now, still crying out, "Oh, my God, oh, my God." Her gun was shaking in her hands. Decker thought: I could have really used that sucker a minute ago.

Rina put down the gun and ripped off her kerchief, wrapping it around his arm. Pressed the cloth hard against his wound. Deep-throbbing pain. But he could take it. What was bothering him most was Noam screaming. Rina must have read his thoughts. She yelled at the boy to shut up and his screams immediately quieted to tiny, sniveling gasps.

"That motherfucker shot me!" Decker grunted out. He was getting increasingly agitated. "I don't *fucking* believe it! That motherfucker actually *shot* me!"

Rina didn't answer. Decker took one look at her face and knew he was in bad shape. He was cold, he was numb, he was slipping. And Rina, poor kid, trying so hard to hide her hysteria . . .

"You gotta tie above the wound," Decker whispered. "Fucker hit my *artery*! I'm gonna *fucking* bleed out unless you *fucking* do something!"

Rina pulled off the bloody kerchief and tied it farther above the wound.

"Tie it tighter," Decker said. He was starting to tremble badly. Swell, he thought. I'm going into hypovolemic shock. All those bleeding bodies he had tended as a medic in Vietnam. What a way to *go*! "Arm's gotta feel numb for the bleeding to stop."

Ripping off the kerchief, Rina tried again. Peter was quaking violently. Oh, God, please don't let him die! She yanked the ends with all her might. It wasn't enough. Blood still leaked out.

"Get a stick," Decker said, chattering. "You gotta tie . . . the knot—"

"Yes, I know, I know," Rina said. "Don't talk, Peter." Lots of scrap on the ground. She found a metal spike and tied the ends of the kerchief around the middle of the spike. Rotating the spike around its center, she twisted the cloth tighter and tighter. Blood spurted, then spurted again, finally sputtering to a slow leak, then nothing.

But blood was still flowing copiously from his shoulder. Rina took her jacket, wrapped it around his shoulder, and, using all her weight, pressed down.

"Good . . ." Decker whispered. "That's . . . good."

Slowly, Rina eased the pressure. Blood came gushing out again. Once more she pressed down, desperately trying to stanch the flow. Counting to sixty, then one hundred twenty. Again she eased pressure.

The wound still oozed blood, but the red river had turned into a rivulet.

"You're starting to clot," Rina said. *Either that or shock was shutting down his system. Oh, God, don't You dare let this man die!*

"My arm's . . ." Decker bit his lips and tried to control the shakes. "Try . . . loosen the tourniquet."

Rina untwisted the knot a few turns.

"Better," Decker's entire body was caught in a frenzy of palsy. "How's . . . Noam?"

Rina glanced at the teenager, who was also shaking, and ordered him to lie down and put his knees up. He was in shock, but his condition was from fear rather than blood loss.

"He's okay, Peter." She took his hand and rubbed it hard. It was as if she was rubbing a dead lizard. "He's okay."

In the background, the wail of sirens.

"Help's coming, Peter. I called in as soon as you told me to. I heard you on the radio, honey, but I couldn't figure out how to answer you. I blew it. I was nervous. I wouldn't even have come except I heard the shots."

Decker didn't answer.

"I had your spare key ring, you know, the big, heavy

one . . ." Rina was babbling now. "It had all your keys on it, including a copy of your handcuff keys. That's how I got out. I know you told me not to." She tried unsuccessfully to blink back tears. "I'm sorry, Peter. Please don't be mad at me."

"I love you," he whispered.

"I love you, too." She wiped her cheek. "Help's coming, honey. You're going to be fine."

Decker continued to shiver.

"You're going to be fine, honey, just fine. The ambulance is getting closer, Peter. I've got to flag down the paramedics. They don't know where we are. You have a blanket in the car?"

"Trunk."

"I'll get it for you. Just hang in."

Rina ran to the unmarked.

Decker moaned, still trembling, his feet and legs as inert as logs. His vision was completely blurred, so he closed his eyes. He could feel his arm throbbing, his shoulder engulfed in pain, and welcomed the sensations. It was a sign that blood was flowing through all of his body, down to his fingertips. He prayed there was enough plasma in him to keep him alive, enough circulation in his arm to keep it from developing gangrene. Even with minimal blood flow, his arm should be okay.

The sirens shrieked, then stopped. How long had it been? Three minutes? Maybe less?

Thank God Rina had heard him.

Rina.

All he wanted was to hold her. Please God, let him be able to hold her.

He tried to breathe. It hurt. It hurt bad. At least he felt something. That was good. Goddamn, that was good.

His gun, Rina's gun. Both lay quietly at his side. He had emptied his Beretta but Rina's gun was still loaded.

With heroic effort, he gripped the butt of Rina's .38, lifted his head and faced left, knowing he had pushed Hersh's body in that direction. He raised his right arm. Even moving his good arm caused pain to sear through his body. He was seeing double, but that was good enough.

But the shakes. He was trembling so fiercely, he couldn't support his head. It fell back down.

He didn't give up. Like a mesmerized genie harkening to its master, he forced his hand upward. With all the strength he could amass, he aimed the gun a few inches from Hersh's head and fired. The force of impact at such close range caused the body to jerk.

Noam started screaming again.

Fuck 'im, Decker thought. Let him scream. He emptied the chamber into Hersh's head.

PART THREE

Tshuvah—Repentance

29

Initially, it was Peter's physical convalescence that worried Rina. But after it became clear he was out of mortal danger and on the road to recovery, she became increasingly concerned about his psychological welfare. Immediately after he was stabilized, Peter *seemed* to be functioning pretty well. He was in obvious pain, but his arm and shoulder had a good range of mobility.

On the emotional level, Rina *knew* he was keeping it all inside—refusing to discuss *any* details of the ordeal with her, with Marge or Mike, with the doctors or even with the psychologist sent out by the department. If anybody wanted to know anything, Peter had said, just look it up in his report.

The paperwork was mountainous, the questions by his superior officers repetitive and insistent, but Peter fielded them well, wrote reports until his fingers swelled, until Rina insisted he stop.

The bulk of his labors went to securing Noam's release—a necessary diversion. As long as Peter concentrated on Noam, he was able to forget about his own problems. And there was a slew of work to be done on that front.

Peter worked not only as a cop but as a lawyer, devising defensive strategies, then penning police reports that would support his conclusions. His contention was simple: Noam had been a victim, pure and simple. Though he might have left New York voluntarily with Hersh Schaltz, he had never intended to engage in criminal activity. Upon their arrival in Los Angeles, Hersh now felt comfortable enough to display his true sociopathological nature because Noam was at his mercy—a minor cut off from his family and without any means of support. Noam had completely relied on Hersh for all the basics—food, clothing, and shelter. Hersh used Noam's total dependency on him and combined it with the constant threat of death to hold the boy in a Svengalian trance. Noam had been forced to abet Hersh, acting out of fear for his own life.

There had been prior cases in the books to support the defense. But luck was with the boy and any legal defense turned out to be unnecessary. The higher-ups in the department felt the same way Peter had. Without witnesses or physical evidence to link Noam directly to the crimes, the DA felt the case was too weak to try. Charges were dropped—not even plea-bargained down. Simply dropped.

But the boy's problems were far from over. In fact, it seemed to Rina, they were just beginning. She had stolen away for an hour and visited him before his parents came into town. Noam had become a shell, regressed to something only vaguely definable as human. Physically, he sat curled in his jail cell, shoulders to his knees, head tucked into his chest. He was unresponsive to her words, to her touch. Nothing—except constant prayer—held any interest for him.

Acting as a go-between for Peter and the police, Rina made the arrangements for the family to pick Noam up. But as the hour neared, she knew she wouldn't come down and meet them at the station house. She told herself that it was Peter who needed her, not the Levines. And that was true. But she knew she couldn't bear to see the look on Breina's face once she had witnessed what her boy had become.

So Rina concentrated on Peter. On giving him pep talks, on making him as comfortable as possible. He didn't complain much. That was just Peter.

She expected him to be slow to open up and she wasn't surprised by his sudden, short-lived flare-ups of temper. When he refused pain medicine, she thought that he was just being stoic.

But she knew something was *terribly* wrong when Peter started acting *illogical*. Peter was the original rational being. If it made sense, you did it. If it didn't, you didn't.

Weakened by loss of plasma and dehydration, he had adamantly refused any blood from the bank, ranting about AIDS and other infectious diseases. It was his body and he'd do damn well what he pleased with it. If he was meant to die now, then just get it over with. Better that than a lingering death.

The doctors reluctantly went along with his demand, figuring a man of Peter's size would be able

to recover from the loss of two pints of blood. After
the primary trauma had passed, he appeared to be
settling down.

All illusion.

Having rested a meager two days, knowing that
Noam was back in the womb of his family, he suddenly checked himself out of the hospital AMA—
against medical advice—and booked a flight back to
New York.

That was insane, Rina had insisted. There was no
way she was going to sit by and let him kill himself.
He absolutely was *not* going anywhere.

But again Peter had shut her out. She had sat by
helplessly, watching him bite back pain and throw
clothes into a suitcase.

He was going to New York, he had announced.
Now that Noam was out of his hair, he felt strong
enough to deal with the family. Might as well get the
damn thing over with, say his good-byes and never
see Brooklyn or any Levines again as long as he lived.
Period! Discussion ended! And while he was back
east, he was going to stop by and visit his parents in
Florida. If she and the boys wanted to come along,
okay. If not, he'd go alone.

His entire chest had been bandaged, his wounded
arm wrapped in surgical gauze and stabilized by a
sling. Still, he had insisted on doing his "*own* packing,
thank you very much." His movements had been
slow and painful, every twist and turn making him
wince. His face was gaunt, his coloring ashen. Any
second, Rina had thought he'd keel over. But he had
plodded along, using stubbornness as a shield against

logic. No amount of pleading, crying, screaming, or reasoning had been able to sway his muleheaded decision.

Peter's pathological denial finally caught up with him in New York. While riding to Brooklyn from the airport, his radial artery abruptly opened, blood gushing from the bandage, drenching him and the backseat of the cab. He was rushed to the hospital in dire need of blood, which he still refused to take from a bank.

Rina knew Peter's blood type—B negative—was uncommon. Then she remembered that Cindy had arrived in town, a new freshman at Columbia. Rina called her and Cindy rushed over to the hospital only to discover that her blood was incompatible with Peter's.

Fortunately, there was a nearby donor with compatible blood. At first Peter refused. But Rina *persisted*, gaining a hard-fought victory. Finally, Peter relented and accepted a pint of blood from Frieda Levine.

He was dozing when he heard a knock on the door. He checked his watch, knew it wasn't time for Rina's visit.

Can't get any peace even in a friggin hospital. He'd transferred himself to a small, private place about an hour away from Brooklyn, having given Rina firm instructions that only she, Cindy, and the boys were permitted to visit. But he knew it was only a matter of time before *one* of the Levines would make overtures despite his request. Guess that was human nature.

And being a civilized person, he'd probably talk to whoever it was. But deep inside he wished they'd all disappear.

Might as well get it over with. Hadn't that been the reason for his rush to New York in the first place? And didn't Yom Kippur start tonight? They probably wanted to ask him for forgiveness.

There really wasn't anything to forgive. Wasn't their fault he'd been shot up by a maniac. Wasn't anyone's fault. Wasn't even God's fault. Bad things just happen sometimes.

And sometimes good things happen for no particular reason. Like how he met Rina, fielding a routine rape call.

Win some, lose some. No sense getting all bent out of shape. As soon as his body healed completely, as soon as the nightmares faded, he'd be just fine. So maybe there'd be a little twinge of pain now and then. He could live with that. Goddamn doctors trying to pump him up with pain-killers. What'd they think he was? A goddamn girl?

Again, the rapping at the door.

Persistent bugger.

He adjusted the tilt of his bed, trying to get himself comfortable. Truth be told, he felt as if he'd been flattened by a runaway John Deere. But hell, mending takes time. He told the caller to come in, his eyes widening when his brother opened the door and walked across the threshold.

Randy Decker was six one, his large frame pumped up to massive proportions by years of weight lifting. He was dark-complexioned, with black piercing eyes and shiny black hair, which he wore long and tied in a ponytail. His black and gray beard covered most of the keloid patch on the right side of his throat, the scar caused by a .38 slug through the neck. His left ear sported an iron-cross earring, his right forearm was tattooed with a naked lady. His universal sleaze-bag look—combined with his fluency in Spanish and Portuguese—allowed him to switch to any under-cover detail at a moment's notice. But his primary bailiwick was Narcotics.

Randy had dressed for the occasion. His jeans were whole and he wore sleeves—a camouflage T-shirt to be exact. On his feet were canvas loafers without socks.

"I specifically told Rina not to tell you," Decker said.

"She didn't tell me," Randy said. He had a throaty smoker's voice. He pulled up a chair next to the bed and sat, the seat drooping under his weight. "You think I'm a dumbfuck, Peter? Mom calls and tells me you broke your arm, you're coming for a visit." He shook his head. "That don't make no sense. You don't visit your parents when you just got married and had the good luck to break an arm. You stay at home and fuck the daylights out of your wife. You visit your parents when you've seen your life flashing before your eyes, know what I'm talking about?"

"I know what you're talking about."

"I ate it three different times and every single time I told you right away." Randy hit Decker on his right arm—his good one. "Whatchu keeping secrets from your brother, huh?"

"I didn't want to worry you."

"You didn't want to worry me, huh?" Randy hit him again. "What worried me is when Mom told me you were coming down. I didn't know where the fucker plugged you. When Rina told me it was only your arm and your shoulder, I was *relieved*. Hey, you got your three B's—your brain, your back, and your balls. You'll be fine."

"What a guy!"

"Yeah, well, I'm not making light of it or anything. I'm just saying it could have been a lot worse."

"You're right."

Randy bounced his leg up and down. "Guy's dead, huh."

"He's dead."

"That's good. Nice and clean. Otherwise, it eats you up, you know. You start thinking crazy. That don't help anyone."

Decker nodded.

"Where'd you plug him?" Randy said.

"Between the eyes."

"Where else?"

"What do you mean?"

"You musta emptied the chamber in him."

Decker raised his eyebrows. "A chamber and a clip."

Randy laughed. "See, I know the story. Get him in the balls, Peter?"

"No," Decker said. "I probably would have if I'd been able to aim."

"A chamber and clip, huh?" Randy said. "Turned

him into Swiss cheese. How'd you explain that to the department?"

"Department's been okay," Decker said.

Randy said, "That's good. Last thing you need is the department breathing down your neck. How you really doin'?"

"I'll be okay."

"Department set you up with a shrink?"

"I went through Nam," Decker said. "I don't need a shrink."

"Talk to the shrink, Peter. First of all, anything that you can stick to the department, you take. Second, lots of the shrinks are good-lookin' women. Not so bad to spend an hour talking about yourself to a good-lookin' woman, huh?"

"I'll see."

"Do *me* a favor, okay?" Randy said. "Do it for your *brother*."

"I'd do anything for my brother." Decker's voice cracked.

"Yeah, same here."

They embraced gently. Randy noticed Decker grimacing.

"You takin' anything for the pain?"

"It doesn't hurt too badly."

"You mean, it hurts like shit, but you're not complainin'."

"The pain's more of a nuisance than anything else. How's the family, Randy?"

"You mean Mom and Dad? They're okay. Roxanne's a pain in the ass. Same old shit. She spends it faster than I'm makin' it. Wondering why I'm not making as much as half my compadres. Never dawned on her that they might be on the take. All she sees is the cars, the swimming pools—" Randy knocked his head. "What am I goin' on about? I must still be nervous. Your call to Mom really had me worried. You really doing okay?"

"I'm really doing okay. You need money, Randy? Don't be shy."

Randy made a sour face. "I didn't come here to borrow money, Peter."

"I'm not saying you did. I just asked a simple question."

"I'm okay." But his voice was tight.

"I'll send you something," Decker said.

"Nah, don't do that. You got a family to support now, Sergeant Bro. Two little boys. You spend it on them."

"It's not a problem," Decker said. "What do you need? Couple hundred tide you over?"

Randy shrugged.

"You need more?"

"No," Randy said. "No, no, no. Couple hundred's fine." He smiled sheepishly. "I won't even bother to say I'll pay you back."

"Good."

Randy's eyes began to water. He took his brother's face in his hands. "I love you, Bro." Salty streaks ran down his cheeks and dissolved into his beard. "You take care of yourself. Don't fuckin' do anything like this again."

Decker took his brother's hands and clasped them firmly in his own. "I'm not planning on it."

Randy stood up, wiped his eyes. He pointed his finger at Decker and said, "That's real good. I'll see you at the house."

"See you," Decker said.

"When you coming down?"

"A major Jewish holiday starts tomorrow—"

"That the one where you eat the crackers?" Randy asked.

Decker smiled. "That's Passover. This is the one where you fast for twenty-four hours."

"But you don't have to do that in your condition, right?"

"Right."

"You're in no condition to fast."

"I don't intend to fast," Decker said. "But I'm going to do a lot of praying, I can tell you that much."

"Nothing like a bullet to make you a religious man."

"So what's your excuse?"

"Me?" Randy said. "I don't go to church, but I pray a lot. Every time a deal's about to go down, I'm praying like the Pope at Christmas Mass."

Decker laughed, then tightened with pain.

"So when you coming down to F-L-A?" Randy said. "In a week?"

"More like two, maybe three days."

"You need to rest," Randy said.

"I can rest at the house," Decker said. "Between Mom and Rina, I don't think I'll lift a finger."

"Especially after Mom sees your condition," Randy said. "She ain't no dummy, you know. She's really worried. That's why she called me."

"Tell her I'm fine."

"You ain't fine, you need rest. And I ain't helping any by keeping you up. But I had to see you for myself, you know." He stared at his brother, then sighed.

Decker said, "I look like shit, huh?"

"Sergeant Bro, you're alive and that looks beautiful to me."

Rina came into the hospital room, closed the door, and took a seat by his bedside. "How are you feeling?"

Decker smiled. She was wearing a soft pink sweater and a gray wool skirt. Her hair was pinned into a chignon, the knot covered by pink netting. Her eyes were pool-water clear, her cheeks held a soft blush, her lips had been glossed a deep rose. He held out his hand. She took it and kissed his fingers one by one.

"Feels good," Decker said. "Where are the boys?"

"They're going to phone you later." She brought his hand to her cheek and kissed it again. "You must have had a nice talk with Randy. You look better."

"I was happy to see him."

"I didn't tell him, you know," Rina said. "He just showed up at my in-laws' house aware that something was wrong. He scared the daylights out of Eema Sora. She saw him through the peephole and wouldn't answer the door. Luckily, I was there. She didn't understand why, *if* Randy was a policeman, he was dressed so sloppily. Clearly, the subtleties of undercover police work have eluded her."

Decker laughed, then winced.

"Since you weren't at the house when Randy showed up," Rina went on, "I *had* to tell him where you were and what really happened."

"It's okay, Rina," Decker said. "I'm glad he came." He hesitated a moment. "Really glad."

"If you can't count on family, who can you count on?" Rina said.

"True."

"It's always wonderful to have family to pull you through."

Decker looked at her. Something was on her mind. He asked her what it was. Rina sighed.

"Mrs. Levine is downstairs. It was her idea. Now, she'll go *right* home if you don't want to see her, she was *adamant* that she wanted to respect your wishes. But if you have the strength to see her . . ."

"It's okay," Decker said.

"If this is too much for you to handle—"

"It isn't. Send her in. It's okay."

And it was okay. After all, the woman had given him blood. And she had given him life. She wasn't his *real* mother, but he did owe her something.

Rina's eyes started to water. "You're very nice to see her after what you went through."

"What's the diff?"

"She's very nervous, Peter."

Decker smiled. "I'll be nice."

Rina kissed his nose and started to rise, but Decker held her wrist. "Couple of things first."

"Sure." Rina sat back down. "Anything you want."

Decker cleared his throat. "I'm sorry I cuffed you. It wasn't one of my more well-thought-out plans."

Rina smiled. "Lucky I had your keys."

"I wondered why your purse was so heavy," Decker said. "I thought it was the gun. You forgive me?"

"I forgive you. I know you had pure intentions. I'll stay out of your business, but you must learn to trust me."

"Agreed."

"Anything else?" Rina said.

"Yeah." Again, Decker cleared his throat. "Thanks for having the presence of mind to do what you did—"

"Peter, please—"

"No, let me get it out." He looked down, clasped his shaking hands. "You acted like the consummate pro, Rina. What else can I say? I owe you big, kiddo."

Rina took his face in her hands. How she loved him. May he never know what was really going through her head. One husband had already died in her arms, she wasn't about to lose another. God had heard her pleas. God had been with them. She held back tears and said, "You want to even the score, do this for me. When we get home, *promise* me you'll see somebody."

"A shrink?"

"Not a shrink—a *doctor*," Rina emphasized. "A psychiatrist or a psychologist trained to help people. Goodness, Peter, I'm going to see one just as soon as I get back. I have things I want to talk about. I need some help. So do you!"

"Want to go together?"

"No, Peter," Rina scolded. "We need *individual* attention. We're not talking about marital counseling, we're talking about horrendous stresses that need to be dealt with and—"

"All right, all right!" Decker sat up, sending a bolt of pain through his chest. "I had a good talk with my brother. He told me to see a shrink. Not that Randy's high on insight, but I think he saw one a couple of times and it helped him." He adjusted the bed until he was semi-comfortable. "So to please you and my brother, I'll see someone. Happy?"

Rina kissed him and said she was very happy.

🪝30

Frieda Levine raised her fist, about to knock, then abruptly retracted it to her bosom.

She had it all worked out in her head. Akiva was not the sentimental type, so histrionics were out of the question. She would act civilized, conducting herself with respect, and most of all, she would *listen* if he talked. No matter how painful his words might be, if he talked, she would listen.

If he preferred that she do the speaking, she would explain the purpose of her visit: to convey her family's deepest thanks and to ask for personal forgiveness.

At no time would she lose control of her emotions.

If he wanted more—*if* she were lucky enough for that to happen—then of course she'd welcome him into the family as she had welcomed him into her heart.

It was dangerous for her to hope too much. Resolution was far away, best to take it one step at a time.

She knocked, the door moving forward a few inches as soon as her hand contacted the wood. She waited for the door to swing open, and when it didn't, she peeked inside.

"Come in, Mrs. Levine," Decker said. "Close the door and come sit down."

He adjusted the bed upward, studying the woman who'd given him half his gene pool. She wore a gray tweed jacket, a red blouse, and a black wool pleated skirt. Her legs were encased in black stockings; on her feet were sensible flat shoes. Draped around her neck was a wool red and black knit scarf. Her wig was blunt cut, the artificial tresses salt-and-pepper-colored, her eyes hidden behind tortoiseshell glasses. A black bag was slung over her shoulder. The only makeup Decker could detect was a spot of rouge on each cheek.

She cut a handsome demeanor—very professorial.

Frieda sat, draping her scarf and bag over the back of the chair. "It was very nice of you to see me."

"I want to thank you for giving me blood," Decker said.

"It . . ." Her throat was clogged. No, this would never do. She cleared her throat. "Let me see. Where do I begin? My family . . ."

She stopped, aware that she was hoarse. She cleared her throat again.

"Would you like a glass of water?" Decker asked.

"No, thank you, Akiva," Frieda said. "I'm fine."

Decker waited for her to continue. She fumbled for her bag and pulled out a white envelope.

"This is from Ezra," she said, "and Breina of course. At some time later . . . when you're up to it, they would like to talk to you in person. Thank you personally . . ." She pulled out two more envelopes. "This one's from . . . let me see . . ." She turned the envelope over. "This is from Shimmy and this one's from Yonasan. Not only do we talk a lot, we write a lot."

She smiled weakly.

Decker said thank you and took the proffered envelopes. They were thick, at least four or five sheets. He put the letters on his nightstand.

Frieda said, "The girls . . . Miriam and Faygie . . . they say thank you." She felt her eyes well up, turned her head, and cleared her throat for the fourth time. "The girls wanted to bake you a cake."

Decker smiled.

Frieda laughed nervously. "I told them it was silly to bring you a cake before Yom Kippur. Afterward was better. So if you don't mind, I can send Rina with the cake tomorrow night."

"That's fine," Decker said.

"Or I can bring the cake if you want."

There was an awkward moment of silence.

Decker said, "How's Noam?"

Frieda bit her thumbnail, her lip beginning to tremble. What had happened to that chubby little baby who had bounced in his crib, a silly toothless grin on his face? Her beautiful grandson with those sweet, big eyes. Dear God, where had he gone? Nine days ago, an obstreperous teenager had disappeared. What had returned was a broken soul steeped in agony. A little boy drowning in a whirlpool of pain. Whatever he had done, he should not suffer so bitterly—not at such a young age.

The hardest part was Noam's constant refusal of comfort. He had hardened his ears to any words of solace, crying out that he deserved his terrible fate.

Everyone feeling so helpless, waiting for him to make a breakthrough. Only time would tell.

"He's doing very bad, Akiva," Frieda said. "Ezra's not one to admit there's a problem, but he was so shocked by Noam that he immediately asked Yonasan to find him a psychiatrist. Even Ezra could see the boy's deeply disturbed."

"Rina said he was troubled," Decker said. "I'm glad he's seeing someone."

Frieda shook her head. "Noam refuses to go. He also refuses to live at home, saying he doesn't deserve a family. At the present time, he lives in the basement Beis Midrash of the shul. It was a compromise. Ezra and Breina agreed to it because they didn't know what else to do. Noam wouldn't even come into the house. So the rabbis said he could live in the basement, if he acted as the *gaba*—the helper. At least in the Beis Midrash, we all feel he will be safe."

She sighed deeply.

"So he does a little work in the morning. A little sweeping, rearranges the prayer books. Breina visits him. Brings him food. But he won't talk to her. When he isn't working, he acts as if he's in mourning. He wears torn garments, sits on the floor in front of the Holy Ark and does *tshuvah*. He eats nothing, he drinks a little water made bitter by baking soda. He cries out, tells no one to feel sorry for him, he brought it on himself. He will not talk to his family or to the rabbis. It's heartbreaking."

"Maybe Noam feels that God is the only One capable of forgiving him," Decker said.

"His sins were that terrible?" Frieda asked.

Decker hesitated a moment. "I don't really know, Mrs. Levine."

But he had ideas. Maybe Noam had just been a witness, but it was equally likely that he'd been more. The first assault victim recalled the masked boy sticking a gun into his belly, pulling the trigger but no bullets coming out. The murder victim *had* two bullet-hole exit wounds in his back. They were not noticeable at first because of the evisceration, but they showed up at the autopsy. It was conceivable that Hersh shot the second victim, then carved him up. Decker wanted to believe that's what had happened. Past history. What was the difference anyway?

Except that Noam knew the truth. And now he was crying out that he deserved his fate, that he should suffer for his terrible crimes. In a way it might have been better had Noam been charged with something. Retribution was cleansing. But Noam had walked, nothing concrete to tie him to the crimes.

Nothing except a ski cap, now buried under tons of refuse in some L.A. city dump.

Still, Decker felt justified about his decision. He knew in his soul that Noam's repentance was sincere. No doubt in his mind, he'd never do anything like this again. If *God* forgave those who did true *tshuvah*, who was he to do less?

Frieda shook her head sadly. "Ezra always wanted Noam to be more religious . . . but not like this. Not because of a heavy heart, Akiva. It's so painful to us all, but there's nothing we can do. Tomorrow is Yom Kippur. Hashem gave us the Day of Atonement to repent for all our sins, the minor ones as well as the major ones. Perhaps he'll learn to forgive himself."

"Maybe."

"You don't think so," Frieda said.

"I wish him well, Mrs. Levine," Decker said. "I wish you and your entire family well. But some things . . ."

"You never get over them," Frieda said.

Decker didn't answer.

Frieda said, "I came here to ask your forgiveness. First for my family for putting you in terrible jeopardy. Then for me personally." Her eyes became briny pools. "I've come to ask you to forgive me personally."

"There's nothing to forgive," Decker said. "I took on the case willingly, I knew the risks. That's how I earn my living. That's why I carry a gun. I'm sorry I got shot, but it wasn't anyone's fault except Hersh Schaltz's and he's dead.

"As for you . . . I've thought about this for a long time, Mrs. Levine. Sitting in this room, I've had nothing but time to think about it. I think I've been overly preoccupied with the thought of *who* my biological parents really were. For years, I thought about them in the abstract, especially during my teens when I was angry at my parents. At that time, I felt that I didn't really belong in my family. Course when you're a teenager you don't feel you belong to anyone."

Frieda nodded.

"But I don't feel that way anymore," Decker said.

"You know, lots of things go through your head when you're being shot. My first thought was: Dear God, I'm going to die. Second thought: What's going to happen to Rina? Third thought: Dear Lord, my mother's going to be heartbroken. My mother down in Florida—"

"I understand."

"Do you? In the past, I'd always been worried that *if* I met you, and *if* everything went ideally, how would I cope with dual loyalty?" Decker hesitated a moment. "There isn't any dual-loyalty problem, Mrs. Levine. You're a very nice woman, but I only have *one* mother."

"I want it to be that way," Frieda said. Her voice was heavy with sadness, her eyes were moist. "But your having a mother doesn't mean we can't have some kind of relationship."

"We do have a relationship," Decker said. "Not a close one, but a relationship. And if it's all the same to you, I'd like to keep things just the way they are. I'm not that same soul-searching adolescent anymore, Mrs. Levine, but I'm not heartless. I have an untold amount of affection, even awe, for that fifteen-year-old girl who gave me up for adoption. That poor little girl who must have been so scared, who must have had to cope with furious parents, a painful labor and delivery, and a secret she could never admit to anyone because she lived in a very strict, religious community—"

"Please, no more!" Frieda covered her face and broke into pitiful sobs. She hadn't meant to react this way, but his words . . . oh, how could he have known what she'd been feeling all these years? She cried and cried until she thought there was nothing left inside her. But the tears wouldn't stop.

Eventually, she felt a hand on her shoulder. She reached up and grabbed him, needing to touch him, her baby—*her* precious little baby wrenched from her breast by a stern, unforgiving father and a passive, bewildered mother. Oh, how she held her baby's hand, squeezing it until she noticed he was grimacing in pain.

"Oh, my goodness, I'm so sorry." She released his hand immediately. "Did I hurt you?"

Decker said no.

"I'm so sorry—"

"I'm fine." He patted her hand. "Really, I'm fine. Are you all right?"

Frieda pulled out a tissue from her handbag and dried her cheeks. "Akiva, do you know why I married the man I did?"

Decker shook his head.

Frieda said, "There is a custom in our religion called a *pid'yon haben*—redemption of the firstborn. Are you familiar with it?"

Decker said he was. It was based upon the final plague inflicted on the Egyptians by God, the killing of the firstborn males. A plague of revenge wrought by God because the Egyptian Pharaoh had ordered every firstborn Jewish male to be drowned in the river Nile.

Firstborn Jewish males were considered to belong to God. A family redeemed its son in a ceremony called *pid'yon haben*. Not an elaborate rite. When the baby was thirty days old, the family gave a *kohen* a token gift and the *kohen*—acting as an agent of God— gave the son back to the family.

"So you know," Frieda said, "that Jewish families do this ceremony except for those families belonging to the tribe of Levi, which includes the *kohanim*, the priests. *Levi'im* are not required to redeem their sons, because the *Levi'im* were never slaves in Egypt."

Decker nodded.

Frieda said, "I never married your . . . biological father civilly, but we were considered married according to Jewish law. So when we parted, I was given a religious divorce. Divorced women cannot marry a *kohen*, a priest. But they can marry men from the tribe of Levi. My father *insisted* I marry a Levi so if my firstborn with my new husband happened to be a boy, I would not be required to do a *pid'yon haben* and defile the ceremony. Alter Levine was *not* my heartthrob, Akiva. But Alter was a gentle man who loved me very much. And Alter was a Levi. So I married him."

She shrugged.

No one spoke for a moment.

Finally, Decker said, "How did you explain away the divorce?"

"Oh, that wasn't hard," Frieda said. "I simply told him that I had been engaged before, had made *tenoiyim*—a marriage contract—with another boy before him. Then we broke off the engagement. According to Jewish law, if a couple makes *tenoiyim* and breaks up, they must be religiously divorced whether they marry or not. To this day, Alter still thinks he married an untouched woman. And I am too cowardly to correct his impression."

Decker said, "That's not cowardice at all, Mrs. Levine. That's *shalom bayis*—keeping peace in the house. What would be the point? I'm sure you've been a wonderful wife, you've raised a wonderful family together. What's the difference?"

"The difference is," Frieda said, "that it is still *deception*. And in the back of my mind, I always knew there was a piece of me missing because of my deception. If I had admitted the truth to him—to everyone—I would have been a much more complete person a long time ago."

Decker said, "Mrs. Levine, that being the case, why didn't you ever try to contact me? I was on the list from the American Adoptees Association. You could have reached me anytime you wanted. Why didn't you?"

"I was so afraid, Akiva," Frieda said. "Afraid of what people would think. So superficial a reason, but this was the case. And I was very afraid of your rejection."

There was a moment of silence.

"Do you forgive me, Akiva?" Frieda said. "Do you forgive my cowardice?"

"There's nothing to forgive—"

"Yes, there is something to forgive. Please forgive me."

"If you want me to forgive you, I forgive you."

"Akiva," Frieda said, "if you cannot accept me as family, will you accept me as a friend? If not for me, for my children. They deserve the privilege of your friendship."

Decker paused a long time. "I like your children very much. I really do. But . . ." He hesitated again. "Mrs. Levine, this is hard for me too. I'm sorry but I don't think I can have a normal friendship relationship with your children."

"They're your *blood*, Akiva. And your daughter . . . she's my blood, as well."

"But your children are *not* my brothers and sisters in the true sense. And they never can be because of the nature of the beast. This built-in *secret*. As far as *my* daughter goes . . . I don't know. Maybe . . . maybe one day. But not right now. And if I'm being selfish, so be it. Mrs. Levine, it would be best all around if we let sleeping dogs lie."

Frieda lowered her head. "What if I *told* my children? Not my husband, I couldn't do that, but my children . . . they could handle the truth."

"No, don't do that," Decker said. "Please, don't do that. I'm not ever coming back to Brooklyn, so why even start? What purpose would it serve? You're a religious woman. What would Ezra think? What would your daughters think? Why should they think badly of you? And then what would happen if your husband accidentally found out? Why deal with all this . . . this garbage at such a late date? You've made peace with me. Go make peace with God. And don't be so hard on yourself. You're a good woman who made a mistake. I, for one, am very glad you did."

Frieda swallowed back a lump in her throat. She took his hand and kissed it, holding it, feeling its warmth. Decker took her hand and kissed it as well, patting it, then returning it to her lap.

"Please take good care of yourself," he said. "Take care of your family. Take care of Noam. I wish you all well."

Frieda nodded and reluctantly, she let go of him. She rose and walked to the door. Before she left, she wished him a tearless *Shana tova. Gemar chatima tova.*

Happy New Year. May your fate be favorably sealed.

Ordinarily a calm flier, Rina was jittery. What if Peter's wound opened up while they were in the air? She pleaded with him to wait an extra day or two, but he was still beyond reason. Still acting like a mule.

I have to get out of here, he had told her.

Fine, Rina had responded. They'd go to a hotel in upstate New York. Give the children a chance to see some beautiful autumn landscape.

I hate the cold.

So we'll stay in a nice heated hotel. Or a charming little inn. You love the countryside.

Forget it.

Then at least can we drive to Florida? If, God forbid, you need some help, you won't be thirty thousand feet up in the air.

I won't need help and driving is exhausting. I am taking a plane to Florida. If you want to come with me, you and the boys will also take a plane.

At that point, Rina gave up.

Now, sitting in a terminal at Kennedy International, waiting for their flight to be called, Rina was trying to will herself calm. Mind over matter. It wasn't working.

Peter was in a bad mood and in a lot of pain. Not that he admitted he was in pain. He was fine, if you bothered to ask. But she knew differently. So did the boys. They were petrified that he was going to die at any moment.

She assured them he wasn't.

He assured them he wasn't.

But he looked as if he were in such terrible pain, the assurances rang hollow. Sammy and Jacob were clearly frightened. She knew that because usually before a flight, they were bugging her to death. Now they sat like statues.

Completely out of character.

Rina drew two ten-dollar bills out of her wallet and turned to them. "Why don't you guys go to the shops and get something fun for the flight?"

They looked at each other. Then Sammy turned to Peter and said, "Is that okay?"

"Why are you asking my permission?" Decker snapped. "If your mom said it's okay, it's okay."

Sammy shriveled from his stepfather's tone of voice.

Decker sighed. "Sammy, I'm fine—well, no, I'm not fine, I hurt a little now. But I'm going to be fine."

"I'll stay out of your hair, Peter," Sammy said.

"Me, too," Jake chimed in.

"No, I don't want you guys to stay out of my hair," Decker said. "I love you both and look forward to spending some time with you two, doing stuff I did as a kid. But right now, I'm a little grumpy. Do me a favor and overlook it."

The boys nodded.

Decker said, "We never did take in a baseball game this summer."

Sammy said, "It's okay. We got lots of years to do that."

"It was a boring season anyway," Jacob said.

Decker smiled. "I'll buy some Lakers tickets. I've got a contact. You like basketball, right?"

"Sure," Sammy said.

Jacob asked, "Does your father have horses like you?"

"My father doesn't live on a ranch," Decker said. "He lives in a plain old house with a few chickens in the back. My mother loves fresh eggs. My uncle's the one with the *real* ranch. Acres of land with lots of cattle and chickens and goats and pigs and horses. A real working ranch. We'll spend some time there. It's not too hot at this time of year. Uncle Wilbert's a little offbeat. He chews tobacco, spits and cusses a whole lot. You'll have to get used to him. He's not like anybody in your family."

Rina said, "I can believe that."

"He's a great guy," Decker said defensively.

"Take it easy, Peter," Rina said. "I'm sure he is. I'm looking forward to getting to know your family."

"Yeah, I bet."

Rina took his hand. "You think I'm an incredible snob. I'm not at all. I probably have a lot more in common with your mother than you think. We're both basically homebodies, you know. We'll start talking food, all the ice will melt. Stop worrying."

"I'm not worrying," Decker said. He smiled at the boys, pulled the visors of their baseball caps over their eyes. Rina had allowed them to wear caps instead of kipahs. They were dressed in long-sleeved flannel shirts and jeans. Except for the fringes hanging out of their shirts, they were indistinguishable from any other American kid.

Reaching into his wallet, he pulled out another set of tens and said, "Go buy yourself something real nice."

The boys' faces lit up. "Thanks!" they said in unison.

"How come when I give them money," Rina said, "they check with you. When you give them money, you get this rousing thanks."

Sammy kissed his mother's cheek. "Thanks."

Jacob said, "Yeah, thanks, Eema."

"No kiss, Yonkel?" Rina said.

Jacob smiled and kissed her.

Sammy hit his mother's arm and pointed. "Look!"

Rina's eyes traveled in the appointed direction and widened when they fell on the right spot.

All of them had come.

Jonathan was the first to spot Peter. He was also the first one Peter noticed.

"Come on, boys," Rina said. "I'll take you to the gift shop—"

"Rina, don't you dare leave me alone!" Decker ordered.

"They don't want to talk to me."

"I don't want to talk to them!"

"Well, you don't have any choice about it, do you?"

Rina stood. Decker yanked her back down.

"*Please*, don't do this to me!"

She kissed his nose. "You'll be fine, Peter. Learn to trust yourself. Then, maybe you can learn to trust me."

"I'll never forgive you for this!" Decker said, helplessly.

Rina laughed. "I've heard those words before. Come, boys."

"I'll stay with you, Peter," Jacob volunteered.

"Now!" Rina ordered. She pulled Jacob up. "Come *on*!"

"Rina!" Decker whispered furiously. But she ignored him and scurried off with her sons.

Swell! thought Decker. No friggin rest for the weary. He got up slowly, his heart doing the steeplechase. Goddamn it, least they could do was come to *him*. He was the one that was *incapacitated*. But it was clear they expected him to make the first move. After all, he was the *eldest* in the family.

He started walking toward them; they started walking toward him. Descending on him. They met halfway.

Decker just stared, gawked. All five of them, even the *women*.

What *were* they thinking?

They were dressed according to type. Ezra in a rumpled black suit and slouch hat, Shimon in a tailored black suit and a homburg. The sisters were wearing long-sleeved blouses and long skirts. One had her hair covered in a kerchief, the other wore a wig. Both were clutching oversized bags, nails digging into the supple leather. Jonathan was dressed in a long-sleeved polo shirt and a pair of gabardine slacks. He wore a kipah atop his head.

The seconds ticked away.

Decker adjusted his own kipah, bit his lip, tried to think of something to say but couldn't. He swallowed hard, then swallowed again.

Shimon went first. He smiled, shrugged, then reached out and embraced Decker, kissed his cheek and whispered in his ear the word *Achi*.

Achi—my brother.

A Hebrew song rang through Decker's ears.

Henei matovu manayim, shevet achim gam yachad.

How lovely it is when brothers sit together.

Ezra joined in, hugging him as Shimon held him. He kissed him on the cheek. The men let go and the sisters, one at a time, hugged him and kissed his cheek. They had to stand on their tiptoes to reach him.

Last was Jonathan. They were eye-level with one another, Decker staring straight into hazel-green eyes that were shiny and moist. Gingerly, Jonathan looped his hand around Decker's shoulder, then pulled him into an embrace.

He said, "You just bought yourself one crazy family."

Decker burst into laughter, then into tears.

Turn the page for a peek
at *New York Times* bestselling author
Faye Kellerman's newest, thrilling
Peter Decker/Rina Lazarus novel

HANGMAN

Available in hardcover from

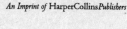

WILLIAM MORROW
An Imprint of HarperCollins*Publishers*

The pictures had photographed her swollen, battered, and bruised—a puffy lip, two black eyes, a bloated and bright face. Decker found it nearly impossible to reconcile those snapshots with the remarkable-looking woman who sat before him. Terry had changed in the fifteen years. She had morphed from a beautiful sixteen-year-old girl to an elegant, stunning woman. Age had turned her face softer and rounder with the fragile exquisiteness of a Victorian cameo. His eyes traveled from the picture to her face. He raised an eyebrow.

"Pretty bad, huh?" she said.

"Your husband certainly did a number on you." If Decker squinted hard enough at her face, he could see remnants of the thrashing—a greenish tinge in certain spots. "And these pictures are around six weeks old?"

"Around." She shifted her position on the sofa. "The body is a wondrous thing. I used to see it every day."

Being a doctor, Terry would know that information firsthand. How she managed to go through medical school and raise a kid while married to that maniac was a testament to her strength of character. It was hard to see her beaten down like this.

"Are you sure you want to go through with this? Meeting him here in L.A.?"

"I put it off about as long as I could," Terry said. "It really doesn't make sense to hide. If Chris wants to find me, he will. And it's not me that I'm worried about. It's Gabe. If he gets pissed off enough, he may take it out on him. I need to get him to adulthood, Lieutenant, before I make any decisions about myself."

"How old is Gabe?"

"Chronologically, he's about four months from fifteen. Psychologically, he's an old man."

Decker nodded. They were sitting in an elegantly furnished hotel suite in Bel Air, California. The color scheme was a soothing tone-on-tone beige. There was a stocked wet bar off the entry and a marble countertop for mixing drinks. Terry had curled up on the divan opposite a stone fireplace. He was sitting on her left in a wing chair with a view of the private patio lushly planted with ferns, palms, and flowers—an oasis for the wounded soul. "What makes you think that you'll last until Gabe turns eighteen?"

Terry gave the question some thought. "You know how cool and calculating my husband is. This was the first time that he ever laid a hand on me."

"So what happened?"

"A misunderstanding." She looked at the ceiling, avoiding Decker's eyes. "He found some medical papers and thought I had an abortion. After I finally got him to stop hitting me and listen, he realized that he had misread the name. The abortion had been for my half sister."

"He confused the name Melissa with Teresa."

"We have the same middle name. I'm Teresa Anne. She's Melissa Anne. It's stupid but my father is stupid. I still use McLaughlin, like my half sister, because it's on all my diplomas and licenses. He misread the names and he snapped. Not that he cares about children, but the thought of my destroying his progeny made him unglued. I'm just thankful there wasn't a gun within reach." She shrugged.

Decker said, "Why did you marry him, Terry?"

"He wanted it official. I could hardly tell him no since he was supporting us. I could have never finished medical school without his money." She paused. "Mostly he leaves Gabe and me alone. He buries himself in work or booze or drugs or other women. Gabe and I are adept at maneuvering around him. Our interactions are neutral and sometimes pleasant. He's generous and knows how to be charming when he wants something. I give him what he wants and all is well."

"Except when it isn't." Decker held up the photographs. "What exactly do you want me to do, Doctor?"

"I've agreed to see him, Lieutenant, not to go back to him. At least, not right away. I don't know how he'll take the news. Since I can't escape him, I want him to agree to a temporary separation. Not a marriage separation—that wouldn't settle well—just for him to agree to give me a little more time to be by myself."

"How much more time?"

"Thirty years, maybe." Terry smiled. "Actually, I'd like to move back to L.A. until Gabe finishes high school. I found a house to rent in Beverly Hills. I not only have to get Chris to agree to the separation, but I want him to pay for everything."

"How are you going to do that?"

"Watch me." She smiled. "He's trained me, but I've also trained him."

"And yet you feel the need for protection."

"You deal with a feral animal, anything can happen. It's good to take precautions."

"There are a lot of younger, stronger men than me, guys that would probably do a better job at guarding you."

"Oh please! Chris could take any of them down. He's more . . . careful around you. He respects you."

"He shot me."

"If he wanted to kill you, he would have."

"I know that," Decker said. "He wanted to prove who was boss." He blew out air. "More important, Chris likes shooting people. In plugging me, he got a two-for-one."

Terry looked down. "He's boasted that you've asked him for favors. Is that true?"

Decker grinned. "I ask him for information now and then. I'll use any sources I can to help me get a solve." He regarded her face—her milky complexion, hazel-gold eyes, and long chestnut-colored hair. There were a few strands of gray peeking through, the only sign that her life had been a pressure cooker. She was wearing a loose, sleeveless maxidress— something silky with geometric patterns in orange, green, and yellow. Her bare feet stuck out of the hemline. "When's he due in town?"

"I told him to come by the hotel on Sunday at noon. I figured that would be a good time for you."

"Where will your son be when all this goes down?"

"He's at UCLA in one of the practice rooms. Gabe has a cell. If he needs me, he'll call. He's very independent. He's had to be." Her eyes were faraway. "He's so good . . . the polar opposite of his father. Given his upbringing, he should have been in rehab at least a couple of times by now. Instead he's hypermature. It worries me. There's so much inside of him that's been left unsaid. He really does deserve better." She brought her hands to her mouth and blinked back tears. "Thanks so much for helping me out."

"Make sure I do something before you thank me." Decker checked his watch. He was due home a half hour ago. "Okay, Terry, I'll come on Sunday. But you've got to do it my way. I've got to think of a plan, how I want this meeting to take place. First and foremost, you have to wait in the bedroom until I've cleared him. Then you can come out."

"That's fine."

"Also, you have to tell Gabe not to come home until you've given him an all-clear signal okay. I don't want him popping in in the middle of a sticky situation."

"Sounds reasonable."

The room was silent for a few moments. Then Terry stood up. "Thanks so much, Lieutenant. I hope the payment is okay?"

"It's more than okay. It's very generous."

"One thing about Chris—he's very expansive. If I offered you anything less, he'd be insulted."

Decker said, "Look, if you don't want me to do it, I won't."

"Of course I don't want you to do it," Rina answered. "He shot you, for God's sake!"

"So I'll call her up and say no."

"A little late for that, don't you think." Rina got up from the dining-room table and began to clear the brunch dishes—two plates and two glasses. Hannah rarely ate with them anymore. She'd be starting college back east in the fall. With three months left of high school, she was as good as gone.

Decker followed his wife into the kitchen. "Tell me what you want." When Rina turned on the faucet, he said, "I'll wash."

"No, I'll wash."

"Better yet, why don't you use the dishwasher?"

"For two plates?"

Counting all the glasses, utensils, and pots and pans, it was a lot more than that, but he didn't argue. "I should have consulted you before I agreed. I'm sorry."

"I'm not looking for apologies. I'm concerned for your safety. He's a hit man, Peter."

"He's not going to kill me."

"Don't you always tell me that domestic are the

most dangerous situations because emotions get hot?"

"They do if you're not prepared."

"You don't think your presence will inflame the state of affairs?"

"It could. But if she doesn't have anyone around, it could be worse."

"So let her hire some other body. Why does it have to be you?"

"She thinks I have the best chance of defusing Chris's temper."

"'Defusing' is the right word," Rina said. "The man's a bomb!" She shook her head and turned on the tap. Silently, she handed Decker the first dish.

"Thanks for brunch. The salmon Benedict was a real treat."

"Every man deserves a last meal."

"That's not funny."

Rina gave him another dish. "If anything happens to you, I'll never forgive you."

"Understood."

"I don't care what happens to her. I'm sure she's a nice woman, but she got herself into this mess." Rina felt anger rising. "Why do you have to get her out of it? Her asking you for help is *chutzpadik*."

"It's like she's imprinted on me." Decker put the dish away and put his hands on her shoulders. The tips of her black hair brushed against her shoulders, giving her face a breezy look. Rina was anything but. Intense, focused, task-oriented . . . those were the appropriate adjectives. "I'll call her and tell her no."

"You can't do that *now*, Peter. He's due to show up

in a couple of hours. Plus if you backed out, you'd look like a wuss to Chris and that's the worst thing you can do. You're stuck." She stood on her tiptoes and kissed his nose. He was tall and big, but so was Donatti. "I think I should go with you."

"Not a chance. I'd rather back out."

"He likes me."

"Precisely why he'd be tempted to shoot me. He has a crush on you."

"He doesn't have a crush on me—"

"That's where you're wrong."

"Well, then at least let me ride over with you into the city. You can drop me off to visit my parents."

"I can do that." Decker looked at the kitchen clock. "Leave the mess. I'll get it when I come back."

"You're leaving now?"

"I want to set up the room before he arrives."

"Fine. I'll go get my purse. Call me when you're done and everything's okay."

"I will. I promise."

"Yeah, yeah." Rina brushed him off. "Isn't marriage about promising to love, honor, and obey?"

"Something like that," Decker told her. "And if I must brag, I'd say I've been pretty good with my vows."

"Pretty good at the first two," Rina admitted. "It's the third that seems to trip you up."

Straight out of a Diego Rivera painting, he showed up with an enormous bouquet of calla lilies that took up most of his upper body. Size for size, Decker matched every inch of Christopher Donatti's six-foot four-inch frame.

"You shouldn't have." Before Chris could register surprise, Decker took the flowers, tossed them on the marble counter near the door, and then turned him around, pushing him until he was flat against the wall. Decker's movements were hard and rapid. He pressed the nose of his Beretta into the base of the man's skull. "Sorry, Chris, but she just doesn't completely trust you right now."

Donatti said nothing as Decker patted him down. The man was packing good-quality pieces: the tools of his trade. He had an S&W automatic in his belt and a small .22-caliber Glock pistol in a hidden compartment in his boot. With his own standard-issue Beretta still at Donatti's neck, Decker picked his pocket, tossing his wallet on the counter. He told him to take off his shoes, his belt, and his watch.

"My watch?"

"You know how it is, Chris. Everything these days is micro-mini. Who knows what you're hiding inside?"

"It's a Breguet."

"I don't know what that is, but it sounds expensive." Decker relieved him of the gold timepiece. It was incredibly heavy. "I'm not stealing it. I'm just checking it out."

"It's a skeleton watch. Open up the back and you can see the movement."

"Hmm . . . it's not going to explode on me, is it?"

"It's a watch, not a weapon."

"In your hands, everything's a weapon."

Donatti didn't deny that. Decker told him to keep his hands up and his body against the wall. He slowly backed up a few inches to give himself some room. With an eye on his hands at all times, Decker began to remove the ammo from Donatti's guns.

"You can turn around but keep your hands up."

"You're the boss."

He rotated his body until they were face-to-face. Stripped of his weapons, Chris seemed impassive. There was flatness in his eyes; blue without any luminosity. It was impossible to tell if he was angry or amused.

One thing was certain. Chris had seen better days. His skin was patchy and wan and his forehead was a pebble garden of pimples. He'd grown out his hair from the crew cut he had sported a half-dozen years ago; the last time Decker had seen him in the flesh. It was brushed straight back, Count Dracula style, and trimmed to the bottom of his ears. He was still built lanky but with bigger arms than Decker had remembered. He had dressed up for the reunion, wearing a blue polo shirt, charcoal gabardine pants, and Croc boots.

"I'm starting to get a little pain in my arms."

"Lower them slowly."

He did. "Now what?"

"Take a seat. Move slowly. When you move slowly, I move slowly. If you rush me, I shoot first and ask questions later." When Donatti started to sit on the chair, Decker stopped him. "On the sofa, please."

Donatti cooperated and plopped down on the cushions. Decker tossed him his watch. He caught it one-handed and placed it back on his wrist. "Is she even here?"

"She's in the bedroom."

"That's a start. Is she coming out?"

"When I give her the okay, she'll come out."

"Where's Gabe?"

"He's not here," Decker said.

"That's probably better." Donatti dropped his head in his hands. He resurfaced a moment later. "I suppose your being here makes sense."

"Thanks for your approval."

"Look. I'm not going to do anything."

"Why the armory, then?"

"I always pack. Can I talk to my wife now?"

Decker stood at the marble countertop of the hotel bar, the Beretta still in his hands. "A couple of ground rules. Number one: you stay seated the entire time. Don't approach her in any way, shape, or form. And no sudden movements. It makes me jumpy."

"Agreed."

"Mind your mouth and your manners and I'm sure everything will go swimmingly."

"Yeah . . . sure." His voice was a whisper.

"You look a little pale. You want some water?" He opened the bar. "Something stronger?"

"Whatever."

"Macallan, Chivas, Glenfiddich—"

"Glenfiddich neat." A moment later, Decker handed him a crystal cut glass with a healthy dose of Scotch. Donatti took a delicate sip and then drank a finger's worth. "Thanks. This helps."

"You're welcome." Decker regarded the man. "Your color's coming back."

"I haven't had a drink all day."

"It's only twelve in the afternoon."

"It's almost happy hour New York time. I didn't want her to think I'm weak. But I am." Another sip. "She knows I'm weak. What the fuck!"

"Watch your mouth."

"If my mouth was my only problem, I'd be in good shape." He handed Decker his empty glass.

"Another?" When Donatti shook his head, Decker closed the cabinet. "What happened?"

"What happened is I'm an idiot."

"That's putting it mildly."

"I've always had reading comprehension problems."

"You're missing a crucial element here, Chris. You don't use your wife as a punching bag even if she did have an abortion."

"I didn't punch her, I hit her."

"That's not acceptable either."

Donatti rubbed his forehead. "I know that. I'm just correcting you because I knew I was using an open hand. If I would have punched her, she'd be dead."

"So you were aware that you were beating the shit out of her?"

"It's never happened before, it won't happen again."

"And she should believe you because . . ."

"I can count the number of times I've lost my temper on one hand. Look, I know she's scared, but she doesn't have to be. It was just . . ." As he started to get up from the couch, Decker waved the gun in his face. He sat back down. "Can I see my wife, please?"

"At least, this time you said please." Decker

stared at him. "Let me ask you a couple of theoretical questions. What if she doesn't want to talk to you?"

"She wouldn't have agreed to meet with me if she didn't want to talk to me."

"Maybe she just didn't want to tell you over the phone. That would give you time to plan something dangerous and probably stupid."

"Is that what she said?" Donatti looked up.

"How about if I ask the questions?"

"I'm not planning anything. I was an idiot. It won't happen again. Just let me see my wife, okay."

"What if she doesn't want to see you anymore? What if she asks for a divorce?"

"Don't know." Donatti kneaded his hands together. "I haven't thought about it."

"It would piss you off, right."

"Probably."

"What would you do?"

"Nothing with you around." His eyes finally sparked life. "Decker, she's not going to ask me for a divorce—at least not now—because, first and foremost, I've got enough money to engage her in a very expensive and protracted legal battle for Gabe. It would be easier for her just to wait me out until he's eighteen, and Terry is nothing if not practical. I've got another three and a half years before I have to confront this issue. I'd like to see Terry now."

He was panting. Decker said, "Another Scotch?"

"No." Donatti shook his head. "I'm fine." He took in a deep breath and let it out. "I'm ready when you are."

Decker gave him a hard look. "I'll be watching your every move."

"Fine. I won't move. My butt is glued to the chair. Can we get on with it?"

There was no sense putting off the inevitable. Decker called out her name. He had placed Terry's chair to the side so he had a clear path from the barrel of his gun to Donatti's brain. Not that he really expected a shoot-'em-up, but Decker was a Boy Scout and a cop and tried always to be prepared. Terry had curled her legs under her long dress, but her posture was erect and regal. Again, she was sleeveless, her long tanned arms adorned with several bangles. Her eyes were on Donatti's face even though he was the one who had trouble meeting her gaze.

"You look good," he told her.

"Thank you."

"How do you feel?"

"Okay."

"How's Gabe?"

"He's fine."

Donatti exhaled and looked up at the ceiling. Then he focused on her face. "What can I do for you?"

"Interesting question," she told him. "I'm still trying to figure that out."

He scratched his cheek. "I'll do anything."

"Can I quote you on that?" Before he could answer, she said, "I'm not ready to come back with you."

Donatti folded his hands in his lap. "Okay. Are you ever going to be ready?"

"Possibly . . . probably. Just not now."

"Okay." Chris glanced at Decker. "Could we get a little privacy, please?"

"Not gonna happen." Decker held up the flowers. "He brought you these."

Terry glanced at the lilies. "I'll call for a vase later." To Chris, she said, "They're lovely. Thank you."

Donatti fidgeted. "So . . . when do you think . . . I mean how much longer do you want to stay here?"

"In California or here in the hotel?"

"I was thinking away from me, but yeah, how much longer are you going to be here, too."

"I don't know."

"A month? Two months?"

"Longer than that." She licked her lips.

"That's getting a little on the expensive side. I mean, not that I'm begrudging you the money . . ."

"It is expensive," Terry said. "I want to rent a house. Technically you'd be renting it. I saw one that I'd like. I'm just waiting for you to write the check."

Decker was amazed at how confidently she spoke, daring him to deny her anything.

"Where?" Donatti asked.

"Beverly Hills. Where else?"

As she started to stand, Decker said, "What can I get for you?"

"I'm a little thirsty."

"You sit back down. What would you like?"

"Pellegrino, no ice."

"Not a problem. What about you, Chris?"

"Same."

"Give him a Scotch," Terry said.

"I'm fine, Terry."

"Did I say you weren't?" she snapped back. "Give him a Scotch."

Donatti threw up his hands. Decker said, "No problem just as long as both of you stay put."

"I'm not going anywhere," Donatti said testily. As soon as the Scotch reached his lips, he seemed to calm down. "So . . . tell me about this house that I'm renting."

"It's in an area called the Flats, which is prime real estate here. It's twelve thousand a month—about as minimal as it gets for that neighborhood. It needs a little work, but it's certainly live-in ready. The main reason I chose Beverly Hills was for the school district, which is a good one."

"No problem," Donatti said. "Whatever you want."

Judging by this conversation, it would seem that Terry was in control of the relationship. Maybe she was most of the time. Obviously most didn't equate to all.

Donatti said, "Do I get a key?"

"Of course you get a key. You're renting it."

"And how long do you intend to live out here . . . in the house that I'm renting?"

"Usually leases are for a year."

"That's a long time."

Terry leaned forward. "Chris, I'm not asking for a legal separation just a physical one. After what happened, that's the least you can do."

"I'm not arguing with you, Terry, I'm just trying to get an idea of how long. If you want a year, take a year. It's about you, not me."

She was silent. Then she said, "You'll know where I am, you'll have a key to the house. Come whenever you want. I'm not going anywhere. Fair enough?"

"More than fair." Donatti forced his lips upward. "It's not bad for me to have a hitching post on the West Coast anyway. It's probably a good idea."

"So I did you a favor."

"I wouldn't say that. Twelve thousand a month. How big is this sucker?"

Terry gave him a smile—a cross between humor and flirtatiousness. "It has four bedrooms, Chris. I think we can work something out."

Donatti's smile turned genuine. "Okay." He took a sip of his booze, then laughed. "Okay. If that's what you want . . . fine. Maybe you'll actually miss me when I'm gone."

"You can dream."

"Very funny."

"Are you hungry?" Terry's eyes ran up and down his body. "You lost weight."

"I've been a little anxious."

"How would you know what anxiety feels like?"

Donatti looked at Decker, his eyes unreadable. "The girl's a wit."

"Are you hungry, Chris?" Terry asked him.

"I could eat."

"They have a world-class restaurant." She glanced at a diamond wristwatch sitting among her gold bracelets. "It's open. I wouldn't mind something."

"Great." He started to stand, but then looked at Decker. "Can I get up without you shooting me?"

"Go down to the restaurant and get something for the two of you, Chris. Get a table next door for me. We'll catch up with you in a minute."

Donatti's expression turned sour. "We'll be in a public place, Decker. Nothing's going to happen. How about a little privacy?"

"I'll be sitting at another table," Decker said. "Whisper if you don't want me to hear. Go ahead. We'll meet you there."

Donatti rolled his eyes. "Do I get my steel back?"

"Eventually," Decker said.

"You can keep the ammo, just give me the pieces."

"Eventually."

"What do you think I'm going to do? Coldcock you?"

"I wasn't even thinking along those lines, but now that you mention it, you are unpredictable."

He turned to Terry. "Do you care if I pack?"

"It's up to him," Terry said.

"They're worthless without ammo." When Decker didn't reply, Chris said, "C'mon. It would show good faith. All I'm asking for is what's mine."

"I hear you, Chris." Decker opened the door. "But you can't always get what you want."

The two men faced off. Then Donatti shrugged. "Whatever." He swaggered through the door without looking back.

Decker shook his head. "That's one icy dude." He regarded Terry. "You handled him very well."

"I hope so. At the very least, it'll buy me some time to think."

Decker noticed she was shaking. "Are you all right, Terry?"

"Yeah, I'm okay. Just a little . . ." Perspiration dripped from her forehead. She wiped her face with a tissue. "You know what they say, Lieutenant." Nervous laughter. "Never let them see you sweat."